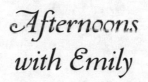

Afternoons
with Emily

Afternoons with Emily

A NOVEL

Rose MacMurray

LITTLE, BROWN AND COMPANY

NEW YORK   BOSTON   LONDON

Little, Brown and Company
Hachette Book Group USA
237 Park Avenue, New York, NY 10169
Visit our Web site at www.HachetteBookGroupUSA.com

First Edition: April 2007

While Emily Dickinson was a real person, Miranda Chase is fictitious, as are the conversations
and events surrounding their friendship in this book.

The excerpt on page 6 was taken from a longer obituary that appeared in the *Springfield
Republican* on May 18, 1886. This unsigned obituary was later attributed to Susan Dickinson.
Thomas Higginson's essay "Ought Women to Learn the Alphabet?" — a portion of which
appears on page 161 — was originally published by the *Atlantic Monthly* in February 1859 and
reprinted in Higginson's *Women and the Alphabet: A Series of Essays* (Houghton Mifflin, 1881).
The poem attributed to Maude W. on page 240 originally appeared in the *Springfield Republican*
on June 29, 1861. It was reprinted in Richard B. Sewall's *The Life of Emily Dickinson*
(Farrar, Straus and Giroux, 1974). The children's poem on page 260 was originally
published in *The New England Primer* in 1777.

Library of Congress Cataloging-in-Publication Data
MacMurray, Rose
    Afternoons with Emily : a novel / Rose MacMurray. — 1st ed.
        p. cm.
    ISBN 978-0-316-01760-2
    1. Dickinson, Emily, 1830–1886 — Fiction.   2. Women — Massachusetts — Amherst —
Fiction.   3. Female friendship — Fiction.   4. Amherst (Mass.) — Social life and customs —
Fiction.   5. Amherst (Mass.) — Intellectual life — 19th century — Fiction.   I. Title.
    PS3563.A318988A35 2007
    813'.54 — dc22   2006030581

10   9   8   7   6   5   4   3   2   1

Q-FF

Printed in the United States of America

All of the poems and letters attributed to Emily Dickinson in *After-noons with Emily* were written by Emily Dickinson, excluding the let ters that appear on pages 86, 95, 391, 450–451, and 467, which were written by Rose MacMurray.

Dickinson poems and letters from the following volumes are used by permission of the publisher and the Trustees of Amherst College: *The Poems of Emily Dickinson: Reading Edition*, Ralph W. Franklin, ed., Cambridge, Mass.: The Belknap Press of Harvard University Press, copyright © 1998 by the President and Fellows of Harvard College, and *The Letters of Emily Dickinson*, Thomas H. Johnson, ed., Cambridge, Mass.: The Belknap Press of Harvard University Press, copyright © 1958, 1986 by the President and Fellows of Harvard College; 1914, 1924, 1932, 1942 by Martha Dickinson Bianchi; 1952 by Alfred Leete Hampson; 1960 by Mary L. Hampson.

We met as Sparks — Diverging Flints
Sent various — scattered ways —
We parted as the Central Flint
Were cloven with an Adze —
Subsisting on the Light We bore
Before We felt the Dark —
A Flint unto this Day — perhaps —
But for that single Spark.

— EMILY DICKINSON

Prologue

&

AMHERST

MAY 19, 1886

Today is an Emily afternoon: the distilled essence of a New England spring. There is a chilly sun, high pale cirrus clouds like cobblestones, and delicate wind breathing. The maples wave tiny banners in her honor, perhaps making more show and display than she would have approved. An impulsive breeze carries an apple blossom spray—across the Dickinson meadow, past The Homestead, and into her open grave. Even my prairie springs have never been as beautiful.

Sue, Emily's sister-in-law, had told me about the explicit directions Emily had left for her burial, and I smile to see how carefully her sister and brother have followed them. Her wishes were precise, original, arbitrary, and inscrutable—like Emily herself. There was to be no church service, only a graveside ceremony. She had not attended a church service for nearly thirty years, and she loathed the lavish new building of the First Congregational Church. "God could never find his way in!" had been her comment.

The mourners gather at The Homestead in silence. The white coffin is open in the parlor, surrounded by a bank of violets and wild geraniums, but those of us who knew Emily best choose not to intrude on her long privacy.

Emily's younger sister, Miss Lavinia Dickinson, always the least serene of the three Dickinson children, trumpets to each new arrival, "I put that spray of hepatica in her hand, to take to Judge Lord when they reunite in Heaven." This was not in Emily's plan. She might have liked the remembrance of her last great "love," but she would have cringed at this delivery.

She had requested that the six strong Irishmen who had worked on the grounds and in the stable of The Homestead in years past should be her pallbearers. Now they hoist her casket and carry it along the circuitous, symbolic route she had designed.

A procession forms. We follow Emily out the back hall door—"my door," we called it, left always unlatched. I wonder now if she had continued to leave it open, waiting for my arrival, which never came in those later years. I walk with the others as we go into the great barn just behind the house—then through the hay-sweet afternoon and out into the vivid spring garden beyond. There the gay crowding tulips greet us—descendants of the bulbs Emily and I planted together, in all those lost autumns. How the lilies of the valley have spread under the oak! There would be enough for a dozen brides today!

At the Dickinson boundary we go cross lots to the cemetery, letting down fence bars as we go. I think of the last exquisite poem she sent me out of the blue, long after I had left Amherst, the very last:

> *Let down the Bars, Oh Death—*
> *The tired Flocks come in*

I study the procession of mourners as we walk. There are Dickinsons and Norcrosses, Sweetsers and Curriers—all family. There are college and village people too. I see childhood friends, relatives, and correspondents—but no current friends, since none exist. I am amazed to see the scandalous Mrs. Todd, Austin Dickinson's mistress, her body's lush geography fashionably draped in more mourning crepe than any of the grieving family members. In spite of the relationship, an open secret for four years, Mrs. Todd, like most of this group, has never laid eyes on Emily; but the funeral is another chance for this shrewd little arriviste to establish herself among the Dickinsons. She is on the arm of her husband, Professor David Todd, and I wonder how he withstands the gossip. Conventional Amherst can be unforgiving.

I search the group for Sue, Austin's wife, and see her standing beside her philandering husband. Her shoulders stoop; I have heard that it was she who prepared Emily's body. For today, the Austin Dickinsons fulfill their respectable and expected roles defined by family and social standing. Sue's grief must only be exacerbated by the public humiliation of Mrs. Todd's flamboyant presence. Emily's participation in her brother's sordid triangle had baffled and upset me when I had been informed of it. I never fully understood her stormy but enduring friendship with her brother's wife, Sue. Now they were all together in the same room, the forced meeting contrived by Emily's passing. I wonder if Emily would have enjoyed this layered drama, or would she have fretted at being upstaged?

Of course, it might be said that I never fully understood my own relationship with Emily. Perhaps that question, more than any other, is why I am here, once again pulled inexorably toward her. All of these people believe I am here as Emily's closest friend, that we'd been separated only by geography, and give me a deference I do not deserve.

I am surprised by the outsiders: important men of the world following the casket. While Emily lived, she annoyed and evaded them with her equivocal letters, those maddeningly opaque expressions of desire and distance. I know she had met only one or two of them face-to-face — yet her death appears to have been an imperious summons across New England. Personages have come to Amherst today, to walk bareheaded in the May wind. Their presence would have given Emily a delicious pleasure. The respected editor, Emily's "Preceptor," Colonel Higginson, gives me a knowing smile and a half salute. The other gentlemen ask him my name, and they bow gravely. I hope they are honoring me for my work on behalf of the nation's children and not for my uneven friendship with Emily.

We stand in a circle around the grave, and Colonel Higginson reads "Last Lines" by Emily Brontë. *"No coward soul is mine"* surely suits the English Emily, that stoic of the bleak Yorkshire moors. It hardly applies to our Amherst Emily, who loved the poem but kept her own soul snug and safe among the ancestral portraits, crackling hearths, needlepoint, and well-appointed rooms of The Homestead. Colonel Higginson adds nothing of himself, nothing personal, no fond remembrance or anecdote, since this is only the third time he has met Emily.

There is a prayer, a psalm, another prayer — and the circle breaks. I do not stay for talk after the burial, as I feel very strongly I am attending under false pretenses. Had Emily and I ever been true friends? Certainly ours was an unusual bond. Once our lives began to tangle into each other's, it was difficult to resist her pull, until the final inevitable break. Emily and I as friends existed in a hothouse of Emily's making, with little of the outside world allowed to creep in. All the steps I have taken to arrive where I stand today by necessity drew me away from the smaller and smaller space Emily allowed us to inhabit. Trying to fathom Emily was a hobby taken up by many. Perhaps, as it has been suggested, I was the one who had seen her most clearly. Yet I wonder how much she had concealed when deploying her stratagem of holding those who loved her *"near, but remote."*

I am rattled still by the obituary in yesterday's *Republican*. Although it was unsigned, I am fairly certain that it was Sue Dickinson who had penned the words:

As she passed on in life, her sensitive nature shrank from much personal contact with the world, and more and more turned to her own large wealth of individual resources for companionship.... Not disappointed with the world, not an invalid... not because she was insufficient of any mental work or social career—her endowments being so exceptional—but the "mesh of her soul"... was too rare, and the sacred quiet of her own home proved the fit atmosphere for her worth and work.... To her life was rich, and all aglow with God and immortality.... She walked this life with the gentleness and reverence of old saints, with the firm step of martyrs who sing while they suffer.

So already the mythmaking begins. Emily too fine for the world? That was not the Emily I knew, not the Emily with whom I battled both in her presence and in my own mind, forming the arguments I hoped she could not refute. Nor was it the Emily who entertained, who made me laugh.

I walk back to my house for the last time, through the village, through the drifting apple blossoms and memories. Tonight, I will sleep in my Amherst house one last time. Tomorrow, when I step on the train, I will be finally and forever relinquishing my ties here. The house will become the new home of the Frazar Stearns Center for Early Childhood Education and will pull me no more.

I should finish my packing, but my mind remains with Emily and the paradox of our long friendship. She held me too close, yet she made me test and explore. She was demanding and selfish, yet she was permissive and generous. She clung to me, yet she also pushed me away. And yet. And yet...

I will never again be what I was to Emily Dickinson, year after year—her neighbor and her friend, yet also her property and her creature. Once, I belonged to Emily; now, I belong to myself.

To explain all this, I must go back to years I never knew, to the time before I was born. I lean back on the sofa; I close my eyes and I begin to remember.

Book I

BOSTON
1843–1856

My story did not begin when I was born; no one's does. We are all the result of a thousand intersecting lives—when the chance action of some casual stranger sets Fate in motion. I exist only because a kindly teacher, on impulse, offered his book of classical myths to a serious little boy of seven. This small event of some ninety years ago eventually led to me, Miranda Chase—and to my sitting here tonight, recalling my life, tracing the path that led me to Amherst and to Emily, and then far beyond either.

I am a true New Englander, with ten or twelve generations of New England forebears on each side of my family. John Latham, my mother's ancestor, was one of the very first band of settlers that came to New England in 1620. The Chases, my father's family, arrived with the Dickinsons in 1630. Even the proud Dickinsons, Amherst's royalty, reached the stony shores of Massachusetts ten years after the Lathams. Emily knew this, but it always suited her to forget it.

My father, Josiah Bramhall Chase, was born in Springfield, a small prosperous iron-smelting city in western Massachusetts, in 1795. All his life, Father was proud that his birthday, December 15, was on the same date the Bill of Rights had been ratified by our new Congress in 1791.

My grandfather, Elliott Chase, was an engineer and chief metallurgist for the Springfield Foundry, which later manufactured most of the rifles for the northern armies of the Civil War. He was an imposing figure—influential, respected, and widely read. He patented four inventions that brought him a small regular income. He was admired for speaking fluent German and for entertaining metallurgists from abroad.

My grandmother, Jane Stafford Chase, conducted a "dame school" in her house for very young children. She and her sister taught a generation of four-year-olds and are still remembered fondly. I have seen some of her teaching notes and plans; they are spirited and charming, a world beyond the joyless Puritan methods then in use. Although she died twelve years before I was born, I have always sensed her influence on my own work.

My Chase forebears lived simply but comfortably. Their spacious white clapboard houses, set among splendid arching elms, were unadorned, not so much furnished as burnished. Whenever I visit the Chases or Staffords or Bramhalls around the valley, I am struck by how every plain surface—wood, metal, or glass—glows with care and pride.

These families were judges and farmers and shipbuilders on the Connecticut River. They prospered, yet there was none of the casual luxury—the hothouse fruit, the crystal and silver trinkets, the fine gold-tooled morocco leather bindings—that I remember in Boston on Mount Vernon Street and that I now recognize as the visible tips of the concealed fortunes of my mother's family. But my father and his younger sister, Helen, had one indulgence, one unlimited luxury.

"Our roof was supported by books!" Father once told me. He recalled that books were everywhere—overflowing from shelves onto windowsills and into corners. Defoe lay open on a table; Scott and Fielding were stacked in toppling piles at each bedside.

As soon as he began to read, Josiah Chase found the true passion of his life: a copy of Ovid, which his teacher had lent him, enthralled him with the myths of classical Greece. At eight, he began learning Greek after school. He stepped into Athens, sixth century BC, and never left it. At fourteen, he won a scholarship to Phillips Exeter Academy in New Hampshire, competing among the most brilliant boys of New England. The routine was spartan, the leisure scant, the study demanding—yet my father always spoke of his years at Exeter as the happiest of his life.

On his second day of school at Exeter in September 1810, Josiah Chase and another new student, Tom Bulfinch, met in Latin III and eyed each other warily.

"Which were best, Greeks or Romans?" Josiah asked Tom.

"Greeks, *of course!*" Tom answered Jos. Thus began an extraordinary friendship—one that lasted more than fifty years and made them both famous. Tom Bulfinch, with my father's encouragement and advice, wrote the seminal text *The Age of Fable,* while Tom served in the same capacity for my father's first compendium and analysis of the great classical plays.

Together the two young scholars worked side by side at the pace of a classical snail, never hurrying and never doubting their work would succeed someday. I can imagine the two leggy schoolboys, earnest and crack-voiced, building their shared dreams, piece by meticulous piece. I kept a few pages of Father's earliest notebook, written at Exeter and annotated by Tom when Father was fifteen. The notes are blotted and swollen from having fallen in the Swampscott River after a forbidden swim. I still smile as I recall them: "Check on Patroclus's shield. Look up 'laurel' (branch and leaf formation). Who was Phaëthon's sister?" And the endearing confession: "The rest of these pages used for the tail of our kite, May 9, 1811."

After Exeter, Tom and Jos went on to Harvard together. They studied their beloved classics and graduated with honors in 1814. Then they shared a tiny yellow house on Linnaean Street in Cambridge. Tom eventually clerked in a Boston bank, and Father instructed in Greek literature at Harvard. He once confided that before every lecture that first year, he fingered his lucky Greek coin for the courage to face all those eager students. He blossomed in that venue, growing expansive on the lecturer's stage. The devotion of his students long after they graduated was a testimony to the compassion and interest he demonstrated in his Harvard office. It was some time before that warming light shone on me, his daughter.

Mythology took up most of Josiah's and Tom's leisure, and the related travel used up all their money. As the years passed and their ambition and diligence never faltered, their friends gave them ironic classical nicknames. Father was "Hercules" (for his heroic labors) and Tom was "Sisyphus" (whose stone kept rolling back downhill forever).

Then it was 1840. Jos and Tom were middle-aged bachelors now, their great works still unfinished. Tom's father, Charles Bulfinch, had just returned to Boston as an elderly laureate, having completed the U.S. Capitol. He invited Tom and my father, whom he treated as another son, for sherry on Thanksgiving Day.

"You'd better bring that Greek coin of yours, Jos," Charles Bulfinch told Father. "I have a Greek surprise for you."

This proved to be Miss Marian Latham, a Bulfinch neighbor on Beacon Hill. She was a small, stunning beauty, a startling replica of the nymph Arethusa, whose profile graced my father's lucky gold coin.

"I have your head right here in my pocket," said my delighted father, taking out the coin to show her. There is no record of her reply to this startling and charming overture. I imagine she went on smiling, and my father went on staring. I cannot imagine them talking—that afternoon or ever. Actually, I have no memory of my parents in conversation.

The Marian Latham Chase I knew was an elegant figure, rarely seen, who spoke only platitudes and stared with lovely vacant eyes. My maternal grandmother, Eliza Cabot Latham, died in childbirth when my mother, Marian, was three. Many of my relatives remember the pretty, lonely child growing up motherless in the big house at number 32. Even then, the weakness to which she would later succumb had been present in the occasional gasping for air, the labored breathing as she slept, the flushed cheeks upon exertion. But this was rarely discussed and certainly never outside the immediate family.

Marian Latham finished her classes and lessons at eighteen. She was considered "accomplished"—that is, she wrote a pretty hand, sang a bit, and spoke flawless French. If she was remote, it was attributed to breeding, her stillness a quality to admire in a future wife. Furthermore, she was a noted beauty, an ornament to Boston society—and an heiress to a great fortune. Surely there must be a brilliant match waiting for such a belle! Yet at twenty-nine she was somehow still single. Her kindly relations had scoured Boston for years, collecting partners for Marian at their parties. But these introductions seemed to lead no further once the young eligibles learned that Marian's delicate eyes and complexion were but early symptoms of the inevitable declining health that lay ahead.

As a small child I wondered so often what she was thinking, what her secrets were. I soon learned that her secret was a terrible one: tuberculosis, the disease whose diagnosis was a virtual death sentence. This stalker of health spared no one. Even the rich and eminent—Chopin, Thoreau, Lanier, and Keats—were felled by it. Marian's father was a known consumptive, a semi-invalid who seldom left home. Marian herself was a "parlor case," with an early history of coughing blood but with intervals of better health and cautious activity. It is easy to see how my mother, already somewhat withdrawn by temperament and circumstances, would be further distanced from the world by knowledge of her fatal disease. It was there in the house already, eating at her father. Any morning it might turn and ravage her too. How could she ever be unguarded and carefree?

This was the situation in 1840 when my father, a stranger to Boston society, appeared with his proposal. What a sigh of relief must have emanated from the tired Lathams! I can almost hear them now, congratulating each other.

"A capital fellow!" the Howes and Lathams and Curtises assured one another.

"From somewhere in the Connecticut River Valley...a bit older, but that Marian needs a steady hand. Harvard '14, and on the faculty there now. Mark my words, Marian will be fine!"

My parents were engaged in a fortnight and married just after Easter 1841. There were reasons for this modish hurry; my Latham grandfather was seriously consumptive, and the engaged couple were not young. So the double parlors and the spiral stair at 32 Mount Vernon Street were hung with garlands of white lilac and crowded with relatives in silk and serge. The Chases, coming from Springfield, never guessed how few festivals had graced the handsome house.

The bridal pair spent a week in Newport, in a house lent by a pious Howe cousin whose rectitude had been enriched by a hundred years in the slave trade. Then they returned to Mount Vernon Street, and—after the round of family dinner parties to honor the newlyweds—my father unpacked his books and settled into his father-in-law's mansion.

If there were acquaintances who whispered that my father had sought to better himself by marrying up, they were mistaken. He loved comfort and convenience and beautiful things, but he was incapable of scheming to achieve them. He loved to travel and buy books and presents, but he had indulged himself in these ways when he was poor. Since he spent almost all his waking hours in the Athens of Pericles, it is quite possible that he never noticed the ease and elegance of his new setting. He slept on Beacon Hill, but by day he looked upon the agora from the acropolis.

Perhaps in my father, Marian had found the perfect partner. Wrapped up in his own world, he would never attempt to invade or intrude into hers. And she would not make demands of his time or attention, leaving him to visit with the ancients. Neither noticed or missed the daily interactions, the entanglement of lives that other marriages entailed.

My own story begins at 32 Mount Vernon Street, where I was born on September 16, 1843. I was installed on the fifth floor—the "nursery floor," up under the roof. My parents resumed their tranquil parallel lives, undisturbed. Father read and studied and taught. Mother supervised her father's servants; she dressed beautifully and skimmed French novels. Very occasionally, they dined out.

If my parents ever asked to "see the baby," then someone must have carried me in—all ribbons and shawls, like a squab on a garnished platter. The rest of the time I was cared for by Irish nursemaids. At three months, I was christened Arethusa, soon shortened to Ara by my grandfather, who I am told loved me dearly.

How I have searched my memory for the faintest trace of this gentleman! I retain only a huge, warm presence, a prickly kiss, a sense of being welcome and valuable. It is family lore that he would have me brought down at breakfast every day. He would hold me on his lap while he read the morning paper and tell me when to turn the page—and they say I never wriggled once. Father must have observed this often, to tell it so well when I would ask him.

My first actual clear-edged memory is of Grandfather's winter funeral—though the concept of death was meaningless to me. I remember the great snorting black horses, wearing curling black feathers and silver jewelry; they stamped and steamed in the cold. I remember the fresh, bright snow on the cobblestones and the quiet crowds of people in black. Their sharp shadows were blue on the snow, violet on the pink brick houses. This was in February 1846; I must have been two and a half.

When summer came that year, the big house was suddenly noisy with hammers and saws. Jolly red-faced men came and went, shouting and spitting in strange languages. I begged to see all this, and my bored nursemaid would take me downstairs to watch the carpenters working. They were changing my grandfather's old bedroom into a new room for my father's books.

When the loud carpenters disappeared, the house settled back into dense silence. My father vanished into that study, barely emerging. Sometimes I heard the heavy front door open and close; sometimes I heard the tall clock strike the hour calmly; but usually my big house kept its unbroken quiet.

My lively, sociable relatives all lived nearby, up and down Beacon Hill, in high, bay-windowed houses like mine. My mother seemed to me a whole other species than my brisk, busy, talkative cousins and great-aunts. I used to stand at the street windows of our famous double parlor on the second floor. From there, I would see my aunts and cousins passing in carriages or crossing to call on one another. They were always in twos and threes, talking earnestly. Sometimes they would look up and wave, but they did not often stop, I never expected them to. My grandfather's death, my mother's isolation, the frequent doctor visits, all spoke to one fact: we were dangerous. My family had a terrible disease, and the relatives did not want us very close.

I do not mean to suggest that my parents and I were complete outcasts in that family neighborhood. The relatives never abandoned Marian; instead, there was a distance. It was simply that Latham plans did not often include the Chases. "Marian wouldn't enjoy it," said the uncles. "Marian isn't well enough," said the aunts. "Arethusa probably shouldn't exert herself, just in case," said the cousins.

There was and is very little known about the course, treatment, and prevention of consumption. My grandfather had died of it, and after I was born, my mother's illness flared up; she went from being a "parlor case" to a near invalid.

The Lathams told one another that Dr. Jackson saw Marian every week and that he always listened to my chest too. They reassured themselves that we were being taken care of while firmly establishing among the connected families that I too either had or would soon come down with consumption like my mother.

Cousin Daisy Powell was the family's designated herald. Sixty or so, alert and stylish, she loved her duties of reporting news and carrying messages among the relations. She was unfailingly kind to me; she always expressed an official family sympathy and interest.

"We all want you to get better," she assured me. "What did Dr. Jackson say about your health this week?"

"Not much. He always asks if I have spat blood."

"And have you?"

"Not yet." And I would search her face for a clue as to whether this was the right or the wrong answer. There seemed to be an expectancy surrounding this question. I answered truthfully, and there did seem relief in my response, but the very routine nature of the questioning reinforced the idea that coughing up blood was inevitable. My difference, my unique unhealthy condition, was a fact, a given—like the Lowell cousins' freckles. Being "not well" was as much a part of me as my fair braids or the little hidden mole behind my left ear—or the secret that I did not really have a mother.

It was the task of one of the servants to take me for walks twice a day around the streets of Beacon Hill. Whenever I met relatives, they would always ask about my health. Again I was reminded that I was frail and sickly—and I accepted this, as children will. I had no basis of comparisons; I had never lived any other way.

Cousin Daisy was also the keeper of the web, the weaver of stray threads and loose people into the family tapestry. And in my case, she assumed many of the duties ordinarily handled by a mother. She took obvious pleasure in overseeing my wardrobe. Every fall and spring, she climbed to my nursery with little floppy books of cloth, accompanied by a sad, silent woman who measured me. Usually we copied the styles of dresses I already had, but I was allowed to choose the colors and materials. This selection was important to me; it was the only part of my life where I had any authority. I always looked for stripes, which delighted me; they still do.

Despite the family taint, we were always included in the great family occasions: weddings and funerals, Thanksgiving and Christmas. To do less would have been far more scandalous than the danger implied by the threat of consumption. I could also count on seeing all the Lathams collected every New Year's Day, when one of the linked families (never ours) took its turn giving a reception.

The loud, crowded house would be alight with candles and crystals, fragrant with evergreen decorations. One of the half-grown sons would stand importantly beside the candle-laden tree with a bucket of water at hand in case of fire. Every table carried silver bowls of eggnog and salvers of sliced fruitcake. Jolly strangers who all knew my name shook my hand and wished me better health in the New Year. They were always careful not to kiss me.

Mostly I would stand in my black velvet dress, watching the other children. I was amazed that my cousins seemed to know every detail of one another's daily lives. I wondered at their inscrutable jokes, their holiday events, their complicated interlocking plans. They seemed to me like one solid block of rosy energy and action.

"Did the sweater fit?" "She gave us all hymnals!" "O come, all ye faithful..." "We'll come sledding tomorrow after the service." "Jane got a pony!" "There's another ham in the dining room!"

I always noticed how a mother would straighten her daughter's ribbons; a father would smooth his excited son's unruly hair. They all seemed to touch one another easily and often. I was fascinated. My parents very rarely touched me; I don't recall seeing them ever touch each other.

Every year, going home with my parents, I took a piece of fruitcake in a little foil box, with the new date embossed on the cover. I always believed I had been part of the event. I never knew I should have been with my cousins for days beforehand, racing up and down the stairs, decorating the house, and wrapping the presents. I should have been asked to stay on for supper after the party, to finish the hams and the eggnog, and to sing our New Year's song one last time.

Still, I did not feel neglected. Since I had never had either companionship or parental concern, I did not know I was living without them. It was as if I had been born deaf and never missed music. I had a cramped, chilly nursery on the fifth floor, with three peaked dormer windows looking over the roofs and gardens and mews behind Mount Vernon Street. Here under the roof I had a scruffy parakeet and a jointed wooden doll named Lady Jane Grey—I forget why. Here were my paints and my scissors, my weaving and my beadwork. Above all else, here were a hundred books read to me by my nursemaids. What else could I possibly need? If a passing genie had offered to grant me three wishes, I would have asked him for a better lamp, a stove that didn't smoke—and a hundred more books.

Several of these nursemaids came and went; I have forgotten their names. One taught me a card game; another stole my clothes, one dress at a time. All of them took me for walks twice a day. Then when I was nearly five, I acquired a proper English governess: Miss Mabel Ellison. She was enormous, with hard red flesh and stiff black hair. She had a faint mustache and separate bristles coming out of round lumps on her jaw. Her huge arms and legs were hairy too, as were the backs of her thick hands. Her fingers were like stiff, strong sausages.

Whenever Miss Ellison handled me—a dress over my head, a hand on my shoulder crossing the street—she managed to make the contact rough and painful. I felt anger in the tips of her fingers, frustration on the callous palms of her hands. My dresses seemed to infuriate her—she'd yank them from the wardrobe, muttering, "Why should you have so much when my own darling suffers?" I would catch her glare, as if my existence were a blight, and if I misbehaved (and often I knew not the nature of my crime, just that I was being punished) the lecture included references to her perfect daughter back in England, whose childhood was one of deprivation.

On my fifth birthday, my father visited the nursery. When he entered, he found me crying. Miss Ellison was pulling my hair, completing the daily ordeal of my braids. She always told me this was extra difficult because my fair hair curled.

"Did Ara disobey you?" my father asked.

"No, Professor Chase, she carries on like this every blessed morning. She's just a great big crybaby about her braids."

"Is she indeed? Ara, please come with me to the library. I have a birthday present for you."

Something in his voice gave me hope that he would listen to me about Miss Ellison. If I could only tell him what she was like, then perhaps he would make her a little kinder. He might even send her away.

"Ara, talk to me about Miss Ellison. Why don't you like her?"

"Because she hates me."

"Why should she hate you? Are you rude or disobedient? Nobody likes a child like that."

"I'm not, I'm not! She hates me so she can hurt me. She likes hurting me." I was desperate to explain that Miss Ellison had a child of her own in England who was poor. She hated me because I was not that child. Squeezing and pinching and pushing me made her feel better. I knew all this was true, though it made no real sense to me. I did not have the right words that would make Father believe me.

"All English people are strict, you know," he told me. "You'll learn good manners that way. The English manners are still the best."

There went my chance; he had stopped listening. My father handed me my present, and I knew that the subject of Miss Ellison was now closed. There was no use talking about this to my mother; her burden of ill health was as much as she could bear. My jaw tightened as I fought back tears of frustration. Miss Ellison would stay.

I gripped the gift and realized my father was waiting for me to thank him. I stared at the leather sack in my hand. Curious, I opened it to discover hundreds of little ivory tablets, each with an alphabet letter. My father took a book from his shelf—I don't remember what it was—and showed me how to arrange the tablets to match words on the page, and then he read me the word. We played this game for a few minutes before he sent me back to Miss Ellison.

Then it was Christmas, then New Year's Day, and time to dress for another Latham eggnog party. I had some bronze kid slippers with a pearl button at the ankle; I had loved them when Cousin Daisy bought them for me the previous year. When Miss Ellison had trouble fastening them, I reminded her I had been saying they squeezed my feet.

"You wouldn't complain if they were the only shoes you owned," she snapped, yanking the buttonhook.

So I walked to Cedar Street with my parents, between the tall houses with their wreaths and candles, and then after the New Year's party I walked painfully home. By the next morning, my left heel was sore and red where the skin had rubbed off. I told Miss Ellison about this, because she was a grown-up and would know what to do. She was not interested.

"You just want new shoes, don't you?" she accused me. That ended the discussion.

There had been a heavy snow in the night, and the steep streets were difficult. We could not take our usual dreary walk, so I wore my soft knit slippers in the house for several days. I did not speak about my heel again.

Days later, my whole foot was red; it stopped hurting and began to beat like a little drum. There was a purple hole, with raised yellow edges, on the back of my heel. I wondered what would happen next.

I realized I had a secret, my first. I made excuses to take my bath alone; I managed not to limp in the nursery. Somehow I knew I was taking action against Miss Ellison; somehow my foot would be the end of her. I waited.

One morning, I couldn't get out of bed. Miss Ellison yanked off my covers and saw my foot, which seemed to have burst during the night. Her scream was all I could have hoped for. Dr. Jackson must have been in the house already, visiting my mother, for he was there at once—and my father too. Then everyone left the room, and I never saw Miss Ellison again.

When Dr. Jackson came back, he brought Teresa, a sweet, dark Italian girl who was learning to be a nurse in the big hospital near us. She spoke like someone singing. She was there all day and all night, the first person in my life who handled me gently.

Teresa had to soak my foot in scalding water a dozen times a day; she never minded when I cried out from the pain. She always touched me very lightly; sometimes she stroked my forehead with wonderful ice. One night because of my fever, she cut off most of my braids and never once pulled me about as she did so.

I believe Teresa stayed a long while, but the days and weeks ran together. I was never sure if it was day or night, for I slept in the daytime. Then the pain would wake me in the night, and whispering people would come in and out with lamps. I dimly recall Cousin Daisy Powell conferring quietly with Father. Teresa said my mother came twice. This stunned me. I must have been very ill indeed! It pleased and frightened me to have roused my mother from her room.

When I was well enough to sit up in bed, all the snow was gone. Teresa gave me my alphabet tablets, and I started arranging them on a tray. My father had brought me a fine new book on whaling, and I asked Teresa to read it to me—but she had a better idea.

"Let's copy the first line with your letters," she said—and we spelled out a dozen words on my tray.

"Now look at them as I read. 'The square-rigged *Nancy O.* was a whaler out of Nantucket.'" She ran her finger slowly along the tablets as she spoke. "What do you see, Ara?"

"Words. Sounds, I think. Oh, do it again!"

"'The square-rigged *Nancy O.* was a whaler out of Nantucket.' Now you read it to me."

I did, touching each letter as I said the sounds. I felt an entire world opening up—all those books that held my father's attention, I could find out what was in them. They would speak to me too!

"You're safe now, Ara," Dr. Jackson said one day. "You're not going to lose that foot." It was only then that I realized what I might have caused to happen.

Soon I was back in my nursery routine of books and dolls and meals on trays. I cried when dear Teresa had to go back to her hospital, but I was quite contented with my new nurse, elderly Nanny Drummond. She had been with several of the Latham families for many years and had raised their children till they were school-age; Cousin Daisy had arranged everything.

I found Nanny Drummond to be the exact opposite of Miss Ellison. She was kindly instead of hostile, slow instead of jerky, gentle instead of stern. She even felt different: slack and yielding and pillowy instead of hard as a cliff. Nothing in the world bothered her except when I called her "Scotch" instead of "Scottish"—so I never repeated my mistake.

Our meals came up from the basement kitchen on the creaking rope device called a dumbwaiter. After we ate, Nanny Drummond dozed in a rocking chair, and I began to slip downstairs to explore our beautiful silent house. I was quite familiar with the front parlor, having spent hours staring out the windows. But I wanted to see more. Soon I discovered no one seemed to care if I drifted about, looking and touching; only my mother's room was closed to me. I never would have had such daring with Miss Ellison about; when I was younger I suppose I had no interest, accepting my confinement under the eaves as another given of my life.

Starting at the bottom, I found there were pantries and kitchens and storerooms, clanging and steaming and busy. The servants there were always cheerful and welcoming. Mrs. Bullock, the round cook, ruled these quarters like an empress. I sensed the other servants were her inferiors, yet she was always warm and kind to me. I am sure now that my mother never once gave her orders; Mrs. Bullock wouldn't have taken them.

Sometimes she gave me bowls to scrape and lick. Often she made me a midmorning treat: a gingerbread man, with raisin eyes and a silly smile. Other days, Mrs. Bullock invited me to take my lunch in the stiff gold dining room on the floor above. Acting as my gracious hostess, she would make me a doll-size cheese soufflé. I reveled in the special attention: I knew I was being honored. She was not one to dole out false affections.

But once or twice I would overhear disconnected scraps of the servants' talk coming up from the kitchen. When they lowered their voices, I knew they were discussing my parents.

"There's a fine lot he doesn't see."

"He's a great one for *not* seeing, he is."

"That one sees only what suits him."

"There's a name for what ails that child, and it's not what the doctor calls it."

"Why doesn't she just pack her off to the orphanage and be done with it?"

"What would her grand high family be saying then, I ask you?"

I never really understood these snatches, but they made me feel uncomfortable and somehow guilty, and I would climb back up to the nursery before Nanny Drummond woke up and missed me. But always the next day I came back down again, wandering and looking, finding new alcoves, new rooms to explore.

In my steep tower of a house, above the basement kitchen came the elegant entrance hall. I liked the window resembling a lace fan above the tall front door. I admired the black-and-white marble, in huge cold squares. If I ever had a friend, I imagined we could play a giant's game of checkers here.

Then came the stair, and behind the stair the gold dining room, with its Chinese panels of beady-eyed birds perched among flowering branches. The birds seemed ill at ease, like me — though they spent more time there than I did.

From the entrance, the stairway rose in a graceful spiral, curving up to the second floor and the double parlors, the pride of the house. Each parlor had four windows, three in the bay and one beside it; these were hung in heavy white silk and looped with golden cords and tassels. Each room had a fireplace and a white marble mantel and an oval mirror in a precious golden wreath.

Though the walls were white, the beautiful rooms overflowed with brilliant color, exploding from rugs and velvets and brocades. And I was never quite alone. The Cabots and Curtises and Howes lived in the double parlors. They looked down on me from their arrogance and their gold-leaf frames, awaiting the guests who never came. The silent rooms gleamed for the portraits, the tireless clock, and me. I studied the paintings until they stopped frightening me, staring until their expressions struck me as funny on their imperious faces.

Above the parlors were two floors of bedrooms. My mother's door was always shut, though I knew her maid came and went, knocking and whispering her name — then the door would be opened and closed softly. Sometimes a stern minister called there too. Now and then I would hear my mother's silk skirt whispering on the stairs, and the front door opening and shutting heavily as she left the house. Her presence was an absence, even when I knew she was at home. I could feel her closed door all over the house. I never knew where my mother went or what she did. I had no idea whom she saw or when and what she ate—if she even ate at all. She was quite unlike anyone I had ever seen.

My father's library was on the same floor, at the front; he let me use it on weekdays, when he was away teaching. Once, I was sitting by his window with an enormous album of Greek gods in my lap, and it slipped out of my hands and landed with a loud thud. My mother must have heard and came to investigate. I was surprised; I had heard she was quite ill, and I had not seen her in weeks. She was dressed for the street in a blue velvet costume. She didn't look ill; she was very beautiful, as always.

"Ara, what are you doing with your father's books?"

"He lets me read them, if I put them back in the same place exactly," I replied. "We have a *treaty*."

"Really? That's rather surprising. You're only four, aren't you?" She went to the window and looked down at Mount Vernon Street, dulled by an autumn rain.

"I was five *ages* ago. And I know all about words. Shall I show you?" I opened the book to a page illustrated with an engraving of Apollo, and I began to read. "'Apollo, the sun god, was the brother of Artemis, the moon goddess.'"

Mother broke in. "That's fine, Ara. Now you'll be able to amuse yourself, won't you? Reading always helps to pass the time, I find..." Her voice faded; she rustled away, and I heard her door close.

Later, Nanny Drummond told me my mother had just come back from a month in South Carolina. I would have asked her about her trip, but I never knew she had gone away.

I was surprised that my mother thought I was still only four years old. But it did provide an explanation for a situation that had disturbed me. Ever since I turned five I had expected to begin lessons at home with a group of cousins—probably the freckled Lowells, who had a nice mademoiselle I had met on walks around Beacon Hill. I wanted to study properly, to spend time with other children. But no one said anything. Perhaps it was because my distracted parents continued to think I was still a baby of four that they had done nothing about it. I went to Father's library and asked him when I would be starting my lessons.

"Ara, we think you're still not well enough to be with the other children."

I frowned. Was he talking about my perfectly healed foot—or was the consumption that stalked this house still holding me prisoner, separating me from the cousins? Was it that I wasn't strong enough or was it that I was a danger? Somehow I knew not to ask these questions of my father.

"We'll have to find another way for you to learn." He rubbed his eyes as if my question had made him tired.

"I can read now. Perhaps I could teach myself," I offered, since he looked so sad.

He gave me a small smile. "That won't be necessary. Your uncle Thomas has a better idea, Ara. You know he's very fond of you."

I was glad to hear this. I had met Father's friend Thomas Bulfinch in Father's library, and we talked about the Greek myths he and Father were collecting. I had learned most of the stories from the engravings in Father's art books, and he told me new ones I had not heard.

"Is he to be my teacher?" I asked.

"No, Ara, his own teaching and research take up most of his time. But we will find you a tutor at Harvard. Meanwhile your uncle Tom thinks you should learn penmanship."

So twice a week Mr. Fisher came up to my nursery to teach me the strokes I use with pride today. He himself was of a formal Spenserian mode, stiff and correct. Then Mrs. Eaton, a friendly neighbor known to be poor and "artistic," was engaged to instruct me in paper dolls. Even at five, I sensed these accomplishments were not an education; I was consumed with curiosity and was eager to learn more about what lay beyond my nursery walls, our lonely house, even our beautiful street.

One afternoon in March 1849, when I was five and a half, I lay in bed, Nanny Drummond hovering over me due to my current sniffles and fatigue. The downstairs maid, Jenny, came to tell us that Father wanted to see me. My energy picked up because this was new and interesting. After a moment of worrying that I wasn't well enough to get out of bed, Nanny insisted on a clean pinafore, so I felt late when I hurried down to the library.

Father had a guest—a younger man, very tall and thin, with red hair and kind eyes. I curtsied, as Nanny Drummond had taught me, and tipped back my head to look at him. We must have seemed an odd pair—like a stork and a mouse, chatting. He sat down and motioned for me to come over to him.

"Hello, Ara," he said. "My name is Mr. Harnett. I have been your father's student at Harvard, and I am Mr. Tom Bulfinch's friend. I come from New York, and I have a sister five years older than you. I love her, and books, and the sea. What about you?"

"I never met the sea."

"But books, Ara?"

"Yes, I love to read. I read all the time."

"Which are your favorite books?"

"Stories and myths, I think." I went to the shelves and brought back Father's book of mythic engravings. "I like the stories in here."

"Tell me one of them."

So as best I could, I told Mr. Harnett about Apollo turning Daphne into a laurel tree. I had never had to talk in front of people; I think I must have sounded like a little bird in the big quiet room.

"You tell it very well, Ara." What a beautiful deep voice he had! And he was complimenting me. It made me want to talk more.

"I love reading about Greece," I told him. "The gods just run around in the sun, playing war and doing tricks. And I like the bright colors."

"Now tell me about Daphne." I felt the force of his concentration on me; he seemed interested in what I might have to say.

I studied the picture closely, although I had seen it hundreds of times before. I wanted to give this Mr. Harnett a worthy and considered answer. "She's not very old. Her face is scared. Do you see those little branches coming out of her arms? That would scare me."

"Me too." Mr. Harnett stood all the way up and shook my hand as if I were a grown-up. Then he turned to Father, smiling. "I'll come every morning at nine, starting tomorrow. It will be a privilege, Dr. Chase."

I had been feeling listless, with a lot of colds—or maybe it was the same one over and over again. Overnight, I was bounding with energy. When Mr. Harnett arrived the next morning, I was clean and braided and eager. My nursery table was entirely empty; nothing should intrude on whatever he was bringing to the first lesson.

"Good morning, Ara; it's a pleasure to be here."

I felt pleased to my toes. He genuinely seemed to be as happy as I was to begin this brand-new adventure, but he soon found I was very slow at figures. I could not connect them with my life, never having bought or measured or compared anything. Also I was puzzled by games, lacking the competitive spirit or any reason to compete. I was saved and made teachable, though, by that true scholar's gift: I was a born reader, effortless and insatiable. So all my history and geography came disguised as poetry or novels. My father, now a full professor at Harvard, gave us the freedom of his classical library. By the time I was seven, I must have known as much about Achilles as any Harvard freshman. I never noticed that my vocabulary was growing at a rapid rate or that my conversations with Mr. Harnett included topics in the newspaper. More important, my little attic became filled with colorful characters—first from this book, then from all the books that followed. From my dormer windows, I could look out and down over Beacon Hill and all the streets and roofs and rusty chimney pots.

Thanks to Mr. Harnett, I learned English history through *Beowulf* and Scott. I studied Norse legends and geography in the sagas. My class materials were sometimes very worldly. We soon discovered witty and wise Jane Austen. If it hadn't been for my family reputation of being consumptive, I would have never known my tutor and all his valuable unchildish teachings. I would have been taking traditional lessons with some cousin's governess or mademoiselle, but since this was not possible, Father accepted the need to educate me and did his duty brilliantly, if only by accident.

I recall one particular winter morning when I was eight. It had been snowing on and off for weeks, and the low, dark sky promised more. From my dormers, I could see the worn snow on Joy Street and Cedar Street and Pinckney Street, soiled from the passing carriage horses. Every chimney pot sat in its sooty circle on the snowy roofs. The view was a sad design of black and brown and gray. Inside, though Mr. Harnett had demanded a new nursery stove, I still wore mittens and a shawl. The lamp continued to smoke.

And in all this chill and gloom, I was more than content—I was eager and joyful! I had laid out our books and papers for the morning's work; we were deep into Viking studies. Mr. Harnett would sharpen our pencils when he came, using the little pocketknife I had asked my father to buy for him at Christmas. My tutor had given me some real English watercolors, in tiny tubes.

Our scale model of the Viking Tower at Newport was almost finished, and I had completed my assignment: a day in the life of Eric the Yellow, a cowardly Viking who sought every way to avoid fighting. Sometimes he lost his shield; often he fell overboard. Today, going for honey to make the mead, he had knocked over the beehive. Now his poor eyes were swollen shut from bee stings—he couldn't possibly fight!

I listened for the big clock on the landing. When it started striking nine, I began to recite aloud the Shakespeare sonnet I was learning. This week's was *"When to the sessions of sweet silent thought..."* And then Mr. Harnett's deep and expressive voice joined mine—*"I summon up remembrance of things past"*—as he climbed the stairs. We recited together to the end, with a final flourish at *"All losses are restored and sorrows end."* Then he said, "Good morning, Ara! Tell me what old Eric the Yellow has been up to!" and our class began.

That particular dark February morning was the precise moment when I realized that this companionship, this action and energy and laughter, were all gifts from Mr. Harnett. He had brought the world over the rooftops and into my cold nursery.

From 1849 to 1852, I marked time passing by the seasons—and whatever I was studying with Mr. Harnett. After the Vikings (who arrived here first, after all!) we spent about a year and a half on the Puritans and the Massachusetts Bay Colony.

"Here's your chance to learn all about your remarkable family," Mr. Harnett told me, smiling. "But we're not in the saint business; we'll have to talk about their faults too."

Thus I learned that my ancestors were brave and resolute but sometimes rigid and joyless. When we completed Boston and studied the other colonies, I decided Jefferson and Franklin were my true non-Puritan heroes—because they had humor and new ideas, and enjoyed living. And Jefferson loved the Greeks too, all his life.

One of these years, around 1850, I became aware of some Springfield relatives: Father's younger married sister, Aunt Helen Chase Sloan, and her family. Aunt Helen came to stay on Mount Vernon Street for a few days. I sensed a sympathy and a gentleness that my Latham relatives lacked. Nanny Drummond clearly adored her.

"I wish I could help your poor father more at this unhappy time," Aunt Helen mourned. She had a round face like a worn pansy.

"Why, Aunt Helen? He's fine. He loves being a professor."

"I'd like to be here to help him with your mother's illness—and to do things for you, Ara dear, since your mother can't be active. But I'm needed at home."

Aunt Helen had long private talks with Cousin Daisy and Dr. Jackson—and, I imagine, with Father. Afterward she sighed and hugged me—and sighed again.

"Someday we'll be closer, Ara," she promised. "Someday you'll know your cousin Kate. She's a bit older, but I know you'll be friends." This made me very curious about Springfield and Aunt Helen's life. But not for very long. My own life was now peopled by all the characters brought into my nursery by Mr. Harnett.

In geography, Mr. Harnett and I studied Captain Cook's adventurous voyages. One spring morning in 1852, we were down on our hands and knees, creating the Pacific Ocean. My tutor was sloshing blue paint on a sheet, and I was following him with a stiff brush, making wave ripples. Suddenly, Father appeared in the nursery, looking stern and remote.

"Ara, I want you to come with me to say good-bye to your mother."

"All right." I laid my brush down carefully. "Where is she going?"

"She has been gravely ill this month, and Dr. Jackson thinks she may leave us soon."

I knew this meant dying, and I was very interested. It did not concern me directly, for I had always considered "Mother" an honorary title in my life, but the closeness of death in the house intrigued me.

I glanced at Mr. Harnett's face; he nodded and I followed Father downstairs, where a serious nurse opened Mother's door. The room smelled of medicine and something new—death, perhaps. She was lying on her chaise longue in a beautiful creamy lace peignoir with knots of blue ribbon. She was turned toward the chestnut tree blooming at her window. She was wasted to a shadow. Her skin was almost ethereal in its transparency, and her breath was so imperceptible, a rose leaf might have slept undisturbed on her lips.

"I like to look at the chestnuts too," I said, trying to find something to say, something we might have in common. "I have one at my window. I can look all the way down inside it. It's like a little lace cave."

"I imagine it's very like this one," she said. "Chestnut trees are usually the same, I believe." Then she turned toward us. All the blood seemed to have run out of her flawless face. She could have been a marble statue.

There was a dainty piecrust table at her side, with her mirror and her medicines, and a pile of white cloths. I noticed the new *Atlantic Monthly* too, containing Father's article about Theseus in Minoan art.

"Did you like Father's article?" I asked.

"I haven't read it yet. Did you want something, Arethusa?"

I looked up at Father, uncertain, but his eyes gazed down at the floor.

"Father says I should say good-bye to you," I explained.

Mother nodded very slowly, as if understanding this statement came to her from a distant place. "That was very thoughtful of him. Good-bye, Arethusa. Thank you, Josiah." She turned her perfect head back to the window and reached for one of the cloths.

Father and I both knew we had been dismissed. He took my hand to lead me out of the room, gave me an odd questioning look, then sent me back to Mr. Harnett.

In the nursery, I was dismayed that Mr. Harnett had finished the Pacific without me. The thick paint dried very quickly; you had to work it while it was still wet. But Mr. Harnett offered me the challenge of doing the curving lettering as consolation, along with placing the islands with the haunting names. I felt his eyes on me as I faced the task with deep concentration, aiming for perfection and accuracy.

Two things happened that night: I woke up with croup, and my mother died. I was soon used to the steam kettle and the strange noises I made in the croup tent, which Mr. Harnett told me sounded like Maine seals calling back and forth. My mother's death was something more unusual, but my illness caused me to miss her funeral and interment.

My life in no way changed. As far as I could tell, neither did my father's. We had always operated in our separate spheres, one in which Mother was only a shadowy tangential fact, something one knew but not something one experienced.

Not too long after this, Nanny Drummond confided to Cousin Daisy that at the age of seventy-five she was now past raising children. I had made her last several years in the nursery as easy as I could, often not waking her until afternoon and carrying our trays from the dumb-waiter myself. Still, I knew she was right.

So the Latham family gave her a grand farewell tea at our house, in the double parlors. This was the biggest difference between before and after my mother's death: we hosted an event. The family gathered en masse at the house. How curious they must have been. Some had never been inside; some I knew only from seeing them at holiday gatherings elsewhere.

Nanny Drummond cried through most of the tea. Each of her "children" gave her a single rose—starting with Cousin Cabot Howe, who was nearly sixty, and ending with me. Then Cousin Daisy tied a ribbon around the bouquet with a rolled-up scroll in the bow. This was a copy of the family arrangement that would give Nanny a comfortable monthly income while she lived with her dear niece in Milton, and a handsome sum for the niece's farm when Nanny died. I could tell from the approving murmurs that this ceremony pleased all present.

With Nanny Drummond gone, I was mortally afraid of finding myself with another Miss Ellison as caretaker. I begged Mr. Harnett to speak to my father for me. It was arranged that Jenny, the downstairs maid, would sleep in Nanny's old room and help me with baths and dressing. As to my dreary walks, Cousin Daisy solved that too. A remote Lowell connection had a crooked spine and had to walk a mile a day in a special brace. She was a sour spinster who loathed children, and I was a sulky nuisance who would have preferred a book—but nevertheless, most afternoons found Cousin Jane and me walking up and down the Beacon Hill cobblestones for an unspeaking hour. The rest of the day was gloriously mine.

So for the next year or two, my life was shaped by Mr. Harnett and his lessons—our morning projects, our writing and Latin and French. When he went back to Harvard after lunch, I continued my related reading—although all books were joy. We decided to make a tremendous study of European history, starting with the Greeks and their colonies, because we agreed that everything good started in Greece.

Soon these afternoons were occupied by the occasional social interval. When my mother died, Cousin Daisy became newly active with my Latham connections—making sure the families who forbade my sharing lessons paid for this slight in other ways. Now at least once a month I had a birthday party, or an outing to the theater or the circus, or a concert to attend. There were many entertainments available for well-off Boston children at that time.

My studies with Mr. Harnett had made me better company and more confident in groups. Still, having been kept distant from my cousins for most of my life, I was awkward and stiff in social settings. My slight remoteness was matched by an uncertainty on the part of the others. Perhaps I was still tainted with the family secret, for despite my cousins' new willingness to include me, Mr. Harnett was still my only true friend.

We were just finishing Charlemagne on Good Friday 1853 when Jenny climbed the stairs to say that Father wanted to see us in the library right away, for an Easter surprise. Mr. Harnett and I stared at each other with raised eyebrows. This was mysterious.

We went down to the library and discovered an amazing sight: Father and Uncle Thomas were waltzing madly about the room and singing a loud Easter hymn:

> The strife is o'er, the battle done;
> The victory of life is won.
> The song of triumph has begun.
> Alleluia!

I could not believe any part of the fantastic scene, but Mr. Harnett gave a whoop of laughter and held out his arms to me. Had he guessed what had made them so astonishingly lively or was their extraordinary humor simply infectious? It didn't matter—as we waltzed, Mr. Harnett steered me very nicely. The four of us sang the lovely hymn and danced around the library, bumping often. Then Uncle Thomas stumbled over the book ladder on wheels. He sat down very hard on the bottom step. The ladder started up—and rolled him slowly along beside the shelves!

We laughed so hard at the stately way Uncle Thomas rode his chariot that my father started to cry. I stood gaping at him. Father? In tears?

"Ah, me." He gave a shaky sigh, small chuckles erupting as he crossed to the sideboard. He poured us four sloppy glasses of sherry, and finally the explanation for this extraordinary scene came: "My compendium of plays has found the ideal publisher!" Father declared. "And Tom has finished his masterpiece!"

"To our years of work, old friend!" Tom said, holding up his glass.

We toasted their good news, made even better by being shared. I held up my glass and took a sip. It tasted warm and nutty, but it burned as it slipped down my throat. I decided the cheerful toasting and clinking of glasses filled with amber liquid was the best part of sherry.

My proud father wanted to call out his news to all the neighbors on Mount Vernon Street, but Mr. Harnett could not seem to open the windows—so Father decided to take a little nap and try the windows himself later. We covered him on the daybed: he thanked us graciously. Next we put Uncle Thomas on the sofa with a blanket, clutching his completed manuscript to his chest like a crusader. Then Mr. Harnett and I went back up to our own floor and our own world, still laughing and singing, *"Alleluia!"*

"Don't forget this morning, my Ara," said Mr. Harnett. "I want you to start laughing more than you do."

So of course I tried hard to do this, as I attempted whatever he asked.

The rest of 1853 passed smoothly. Father told us that Uncle Charlie Sloan had died, and he was worried that the income left to Aunt Helen and my cousin Kate might not be enough. He went to Springfield once or twice, arranging that the Sloans receive a royalty from his book of plays, which was selling very well. We could afford the generosity; Mother's income had passed to him, leaving us with more than we would ever need.

My tutor and I studied the Dark Ages and the Crusades, and then we moved on to the Renaissance. We made a fine model of the Globe Theatre and staged scenes from Shakespeare. Mr. Harnett found us some all-purpose hand puppets that were easy to adapt to a particular role: a beard for Lear, a sword for Mercutio. Sometimes our productions turned into a rowdy roughhouse, but there was no one to hear our racket.

The years passed quickly and productively, and by March 1856, I was a serene twelve and a half. There was an infinity to learn, and dear Mr. Harnett was there to see that I learned it. I saw no reason for my life to change.

But he was a mysterious day or two late after Easter, and it worried me. When he reached the nursery, where I had made him a display of spring bulbs, he looked remote and distraught.

He motioned for me to sit at the table and then took his place opposite me, as he had for a thousand mornings. But this time he took my hand, which unsettled me badly. He had always insisted that a tutor and his pupil should never touch — except for a hard good-bye handshake and a birthday kiss. And of course that once when we waltzed in Father's library. His hand engulfed mine; it felt strong and warm, but I could sense an undercurrent I could not identify that frightened me.

"Ara, I have to talk to you." He began to speak, shook his head — then tried again. "My dear Ara, I must tell you... I'm moving back to New York."

I stared at him for a moment, trying to understand what he had just said to me. Then I cried out, "No, NO!" as if I had been stabbed through the heart like Mercutio. I pulled away from his grasp and covered my face with my hands. I wouldn't listen to him, to his good news of his new school, his chance to teach as he had taught me, to use the lessons we had invented together, that he was finding another tutor for me, that he was not leaving for another few weeks. The more details he offered, the more I felt the crushing fact of reality. I wanted to drown him out, repeating "no" over and over, almost as a chant. I covered my ears and ignored the tortured, worried look on his face.

He sat with me until I tired myself out. After making me wash my face, he began the lesson as if nothing had happened, as if nothing had changed. By the end of the day, I had almost forgotten Mr. Harnett's terrible news.

For several days, we operated in this pretend fashion. We worked together; I even occasionally laughed, as I knew it pleased my tutor. But underneath there was a dark sadness nagging at me.

One day, Mr. Harnett brought a young man with him.

"Ara, I'd like you to meet William Brooks," Mr. Harnett said. The short man nodded and smiled.

"Your tutor has told me a great deal about you, Ara," Mr. Brooks said. His voice had a soft accent; he sounded like he was speaking around a mouthful of velvet. "I am looking forward to our working together."

"Mr. Brooks will begin next month," Mr. Harnett explained.

My eyes widened as the implication of this statement chilled and stopped my blood. He was Mr. Harnett's replacement. The pretending was about to come to an end.

I began to cry wildly, helplessly, uncontrollably, with huge, regular shaking sobs that took over my whole body. I sobbed from my feet up.

Mr. Harnett asked Mr. Brooks to leave and then held me close, whispered a good-bye, and left; I believe he was crying too. I couldn't stop until evening, until midnight. Then Jenny told my father, who must have sent for Dr. Jackson. Suddenly the doctor was in my nursery, bringing me a bitter brown drink.

"Crying won't bring your friend back, Ara, so you'd better sleep. Drink this, and you can rest a little."

I tried to tell Dr. Jackson why I was crying—but as I drank, he went away in a spiral. When I woke up a day later, I accepted my loss as fact. Mr. Harnett was gone for good, and the worst of my terrible, desperate grieving was over. But now I was hollow and empty, like all the days and weeks that lay ahead.

At first, after Mr. Harnett left me, I would get up as usual and try to reenact my mornings with him. I would begin with our sonnet of incantation, although his voice never came to join mine. Then I used our old models and exercise books, trying to play both our roles. All the while I felt I was watching someone else do these things from a long, pale distance. So I stopped and I stayed in bed, reading our old texts but mostly sleeping.

One day Cousin Daisy stopped by for a visit. I could see her distress over my condition, but I didn't care. Mr. Harnett had gone away—that was all that mattered to me. I could overhear hushed discussions between her and Father outside my nursery door but couldn't muster enough interest to eavesdrop.

After Cousin Daisy left, Father came into the nursery. He seemed angry to find me dozing at two in the afternoon.

"I want you up and out of bed—starting right now. Take a bath and wash your hair; Jenny can help you. Then come to the library."

I was ashamed at his instructions, having never aroused his disapproval or disappointment in such a way before. I followed his orders and reached the library a good deal cleaner. He looked me over and handed me a big folder.

"Cousin Daisy feels it may be too soon to have you adjust to a new tutor," he said. "She seems to think you won't learn especially well in your current state. However, she...and I...both feel you need to have some activity. And perhaps a change of scenery might do you some good as well."

I nodded, not especially understanding but knowing some response was expected of me.

"Therefore," Father continued, "I want you to be my special secretary for children's letters. I have received several hundred about *The Great Plays,* and each child deserves a proper reply. You can work right here on this big table. Those are your materials," he added, nodding at the folder in my hands.

Then he gave me a small worn book. "And I think you're ready for the real classics now. Here is Chapman's translation of *The Iliad.* Please start it here with me, so I can help you on the meter. This is the one Keats liked. *'Much have I traveled in the realms of gold.'* It's my favorite too."

The children's letters were a good chance for practicing my penmanship—and *The Iliad* was a reunion of the complicated families of my nursery gods. It was unexpectedly vivid to me, as was my father's presence. Working daily in his study among his prized possessions, I felt him there too. I was often seated at the table when he arrived home from Harvard, and as he settled into his own work, we'd chat about the day and our discoveries in ancient times.

One day Father pulled down a large book of Athenian art, and he fingered the pages. His gaze went from a page in the book to me and back to the book. He studied me more carefully. He seemed to make a decision. "This has given me an idea," he said. "I will ask my barber to come and cut your hair this afternoon."

This was quite unexpected. My father had never taken an interest in my appearance before. And I had been rather vain about my braids, because Mr. Harnett called them the "Golden Fleece." Still, my braids seemed unimportant, and it would be a blessing not to have Jenny yanking at me every morning.

Later that day, Mr. Macrae, the barber, arrived. He wore a white smock; he had an accent like that of Young Lochinvar—or Nanny Drummond. First he chopped off each braid at my shoulders, making me look like a captured Gaul. Then he took out some thin pointed scissors and studied a page in one of Father's art books for a long time.

"Do you think you can do that for us?" Father asked him.

"Why not? The lassie's hair is as braw as heather."

As he snipped, I studied the illustration he was copying: a smiling boy, running carefree on a vase. His hair was cut like a wreath, more or less. I admired his tunic and trousers—they seemed to make running quite a bit easier for the boy in the picture. The boy looked happy.

"That's it! Sir, you're a true artist! That is exactly what we needed." My delighted father beamed at Mr. Macrae and at my shorn head in the mirror.

I could not think why either one of us needed short curls, but it did not matter much.

Not long after, a letter arrived: my first letter ever, with my name in Mr. Harnett's lovely spiked writing, like a row of tiny teeth.

April 19, 1856

My very dear Ara,

I could not bear to write you sooner, till our parting bled a little less. Soon we will not miss each other as much as we do now. In all my classes I have been using what you and I learned, and I will write you about the ways we are still working together.

Your father has made some wonderful plans you will hear soon. Do you remember when we learned how there can be a ship just below the horizon, still invisible—but heading for you, coming closer every day? Just such a ship is sailing your way. Your father is not a sentimental man, but he will always care for you and care about you.

Now I want you to read David Copperfield *and write a character sketch of Dora or Steerforth. Then make a play out of your favorite scene. Make a model of this. Be sure and show David very small to remind us how young he is. . . . But he ends up the strongest of anyone, and so will you.*

Remember that I am always going to be part of your life.

Your friend always,

Alan Harnett

I was quite curious about all that Mr. Harnett had hinted at — but I had another surprise in store. I was reading in Father's book of Greek art, the one that inspired my new hairstyle, when Father arrived with Madame Lauré, my mother's dressmaker. She used to make my New Year's velvet dresses and always called me *"La pauvre p'tite"* — so I could not tell her Mr. Harnett and I had been doing French for the last three or so years.

Madame Lauré had tiny black eyes like raisins and talked around a mouthful of pins. While she measured me and made strange chalk markings, Father told her, "I'm not sure what it is that we want, but we want something other than . . . this." He gestured to the dresses hanging in my wardrobe.

I must be about to gain an entirely new wardrobe, I realized, and Father himself is overseeing this procedure rather than Cousin Daisy. Surely this was somehow part of the plans Mr. Harnett had spoken of in his letter.

"M'sieur, please, one must be somewhat more definite in what one desires. I would hate to displease you."

"Something more . . . less . . ." Father seemed at a loss for words. This behavior I understood. It would have shocked me greatly if he had been able to discuss current women's fashion. It was somewhat reassuring that he wasn't a complete stranger to me!

"Father," I ventured, trying to stay as still as possible as Madame Lauré ran a tape from my ankle to my knee. "If I could have a new outfit, I would like it to be just like the one on the vase."

"Zee vase?" Madame Lauré looked perplexed.

I patted my shorn head. "The vase," I repeated.

A delighted recognition sparkled in my father's eyes. "Of course! Ara, it is a brilliant solution." I pointed to where the book lay on the table. He picked it up and showed it to Madame Lauré.

"Mais . . . mais . . ." she sputtered around her pins. "Zeese are trousers. Zee young lady—"

"A chiton will be quite suitable," Father declared, using the Greek name for the garment. He and I smiled at each other. We were united in sentiment and in shared controversy; it was our first true pact.

"It is decided," Father told Madame Lauré. "The Lathams are all coming for tea tomorrow," he then informed me. "They're all dying of polite curiosity to hear our plans."

I was curious to hear myself!

The next afternoon, I joined Father in the double parlors, full of spring flowers brought by Cousin Daisy. I curtsied twenty times, hearing a buzz of comment about my hair.

"So boyish," murmured the aunts.

"So...odd," rumbled the uncles. Then they folded their hands around their sherry glasses and waited to be informed.

"You were good to come this afternoon. I wanted you to hear some decisions I've made," said my father. This bold, confident voice must be his teaching manner. "From now on, my first responsibility must be to my daughter—her health and happiness."

This made me feel very proud. I had never heard him express much interest in my life, nor had I much evidence in the form of attention. But I knew my father was a truthful man, so this must be the case.

"I believe you've all been aware, over the years, that our medical adviser Dr. Jackson continues to watch Arethusa, fearing a tendency toward poor Marian's disease. He and I have decided I should take her to the Windward Islands for a year so that she may grow stronger in that climate."

There was one gasp, then many from the assembled Lathams. We surely had their attention now! I only wished that he had not stated this fear of my "tendency" quite so openly. But the gathered relatives seemed to be far more shocked by the mention of these islands than by the bold statement of my potential illness.

"I have a classmate in Barbados, a dear friend, Hugh James," Father continued smoothly. "I have visited him and his sister, Miss Adelaide James, several times."

I had not been aware of this; I had not been aware of most of my father's comings and goings. It did explain some of his absences.

"Their sugar plantation, York Stairs, is one of the handsomest on the island of Barbados. Hugh was a consumptive too, but he believes it was the clean, warm sea air that cured him. He is a physician and will care for Ara. He and Miss Adelaide expect us at York Stairs next month."

Astonishing! We were leaving Boston. We were going to live on a tropical island—straight out of Captain Cook's reports! I was truly about to have an adventure.

"So we are following Dr. Jackson's advice for Ara and seeking a warmer climate and an outdoor life. My arrangements are nearly complete, but I need your help on a family affair." He gave his audience a charming smile.

"I have rented number 32 to a colleague, but I find I will require a temporary home for the portraits. I hesitate to rent out your ancestors, even to a Harvard professor. Would any of you care to board them for a year or so?"

Father must have known this would be the perfect distraction from his startling news — and my short curls.

"I'll take the Copley: Eliza Cabot in yellow with the parakeet."

"But your chimney smokes! She'd be far safer in my dining room."

"I'll hang both Stuarts. They should stay together."

"But that's not fair! Marian would have wanted us to . . ."

No one noticed me leaving. The well-bred haggling followed me up the stairs. I went straight to my father's library and dragged his huge atlas over to the pale spring light. I turned to the index: BAC, BAL, BAR. I flipped to a page full of blue. From the moment of Father's announcement, I felt a flicker of returning interest. I was starting to be curious again. I found the island on the map, pressed my finger on it, and held it there a long time.

Madame Lauré returned the next day to fit me in the muslin model of the Greek costume. It was a loose sleeveless tunic with a pleat at each shoulder, ending just above the knee. There were very short, straight trousers underneath.

"A bit more in the pleats, please, Madame Lauré," said Father, looking me up and down. "She'll need plenty of room for running around."

I could not imagine myself "running around" — but if I was to become active, this would certainly be the costume for it. I was pleased with the feeling of freedom the clothing gave me. The boy on the vase seemed to be going somewhere; perhaps I was too.

My father seemed equally delighted by the Greek object I had become. "We'll need six of these, Madame Lauré, and six more in a size larger. Please use the toughest cotton you can find anywhere and the brightest colors — nothing dainty! And make us two in dark blue, with extra drawers — for the ocean. Ara will be swimming all day long!"

This seemed unlikely, but he knew Barbados better than I did. In all my life, I had never had so much attention and interest from my father. I would learn — gradually — that he would never fail me on the important things involving foresight and intention. He skimped only on the daily details of love.

"Now, Ara, show me your favorite dress," Father instructed.

This was a corded silk from last Christmas, for a cousin's wedding. I was meant to be the flower girl, but I had bronchitis instead. Cousin Daisy called the high waist and puffed sleeves "Empire." To my eyes it was straight out of *Vanity Fair;* I called it my Becky Sharp dress.

"Yes, that looks just right for Barbados," Father approved. "We'll need four like this, Madame Lauré—all in white, in different materials. Please find us something cool for the tropics."

"Zen I will make zee silk, zee mull, zee linen, and zee dimity. And I will make more décolleté, for zee heat."

"Splendid, Madame—splendid. And give her big hems, won't you? She'll be doing a lot of growing on the islands."

Preparing to leave in June was easy, since we were taking so little. Father packed his notes and references for the new book he had started. My chitons and new dresses arrived, looking like costumes for a play. I decided to leave my old doll and my playthings behind; I had never used them after Mr. Harnett came. Since Father said there were plenty of fine books at York Stairs, I took only my scissors and my watercolors. Jenny helped me with my trunk.

My father had arranged our passage on a packet through the Windwards, traveling among the islands and ending at Bridgetown in Barbados. Cousin Daisy was joining us for the sea voyage and then continuing on to visit an English friend in Saint Kitts. As ever, she was making a lively pattern out of other people's bits and pieces.

Uncle Thomas came to ride down to the wharves and see us off. As the carriage pulled away from number 32, my father looked back at Mount Vernon Street and the tall, curved pink houses.

"It's time we left Boston, Tom," he murmured.

Tonight, I wonder if he knew we would never sleep there again. Or that in Barbados I would finally begin to truly live.

Book II

BARBADOS
1856–1857

I had been deeply asleep. I woke slowly to a wonder of silence. There were no shouts and footsteps overhead, no creaking and flapping like a great bird's wing. There was a white mist around me and a solid white cloud underneath. I was no longer in and out of a world that slanted and heaved and twisted

I remembered our voyage and was bitterly ashamed. I had been a terrible sailor. My father and Captain Sisson had been patient and cheerful, promising that June was the best month at sea, that I would soon find my sea legs—but I went on retching. There were days and endless nights of sickness, with Cousin Daisy's worried face spinning somewhere over my bunk, and my empty stomach heaving up the tea she tried to feed me.

Twice Father had carried me up into the bright salty wind, and I winced at the sun. Once we saw some white plumes on the horizon; he told me they were whales. I was just barely able to say to him, "Thar she blows!"

I remembered last evening, when we landed at Bridgetown just after sunset. Cousin Daisy stood on the deck, waving good-bye. There was a harbor with stone jetties and a wooden wharf, and a town with lit streets—and torches with ragged flames repeated in smooth, dark water. It was unlike anything I had seen; it was hard to imagine it was real. Then came a long carriage ride through the night and an avenue with tall pointed trees.

Then there were more torches between white columns—and curving stairs, and strange voices in a sweet stirring darkness. Someone led me here, and someone else gave me cake and eggnog   did I actually eat?

I heard someone moving near me. I turned my head and saw a hazy figure approaching my bed and raising the netting with a delicate dark hand. She was young and slim, with a dainty figure and skin the color of brandy in a decanter. I had never seen anyone like her before. My eyes widened.

43

"Good day, Missy Ara!" She had a soft voice that rippled gently through the balmy air. "I am Lettie. I will be your companion. We will do many pleasant things together." Each of her words was as clear and edged as cut crystal.

"Mistress Adelaide is telling me you should be eating, so I bring you the eggnog you were liking last evening. Now, do you know banana?"

When I shook my head, she handed me first the drink and then a curved yellow fruit—or vegetable?

"First we peel it—see! Now, does it please you?" It was a big sweet pudding, complete in itself.

"It's wonderful! Please, might there be another?"

Lettie laughed as a dove might laugh—three charming notes.

"There is another and another. There are a hundred trees full of Barbados bananas! But first we must be settling you into York Stairs. We will arrange your pretty dresses in their new home." She knelt at my trunk, and I looked about the room.

This was white, all white, with a high ceiling pointed like the inside of a pyramid—a room as tall as the double parlors on Mount Vernon Street. It held my four-poster bed with its veil of netting; a cabinet with a pitcher and bowl; and several carved chairs. I saw a bookcase too, empty, and a chest of drawers holding a ceramic pitcher of blue and lavender flowers.

"Mistress Adelaide is welcoming you with her flowers. She is choosing the colors of our sea," Lettie informed me as she hung my clothes in a huge paneled wardrobe.

"These white dresses are most fashionable for a young mistress. These little suits I am not knowing. Is it the American mode?"

"They came from a picture," I explained.

Lettie nodded as if she understood, and she shut the wardrobe. "They will be doing very well for you here."

Lettie helped me wash, and we chose a violet chiton and trousers. She deplored my lack of sandals and promised to correct this very soon.

We left my room and went into a long vaulted hall with many shuttered doors. I was aware of sunlight through the louvers and air moving around me, even though we were indoors.

"These are the sleeping chambers for the family," Lettie told me. "They are below, to be cool when we lose the trades. The reception rooms are above, in the path of the good winds."

This all seemed very strange, but no stranger than dressing like a Greek runner, having a gracious golden friend who talked like a ballad, and walking through a house that was upside down.

We came to sunlight flooding through a tall archway. Everything at York Stairs soared; there were no oppressive low ceilings, no walls crowding in to squeeze me. I would no longer be living in a chilly attic under the eaves.

We climbed what felt like a stone stair, a lesser curve than Mount Vernon Street. I did not sense an actual wind, but I noticed the curls at my temples stirring as we walked forward a few steps in sweet lively air and reached what felt like a stone wall.

"Now, Missy Ara, here is your friend the sea, waiting for you."

Mr. Harnett had given me my watercolors; I reviewed the names on the little tubes, trying to find the right ones. Ultramarine, cerulean, Prussian — no single blue could approach the living, moving radiance before me.

Next I considered rainbows, which I knew quite well. I had seen a hundred from my window seat, arching unearthly over the drab roofs of Beacon Hill. But even a rainbow would have faded against this sea. The blues and greens and violets were the colors at the heart of flames. Luckily, there was a balustrade to protect us; it would have been so easy to fall into that space, into that beauty offered as simply as fruit on a plate.

"The good sea will be your friend, Missy Ara," Lettie told me, holding my shoulders lightly. "I will help to make you friends."

I leaned back against her, believing her promise, enjoying the multiple sensations: Lettie's warmth; the scents; the blue, blue water. When I could look away from the sea, I saw we were standing on a wide terrace, as long as the house itself. Half was covered by the roof, extended with plain columns; the other half was open to the stunning distance and the soft, steady wind. I held up my hand to feel it passing.

"Those are our fine trade winds," Lettie stated proudly. "Are you breathing the sugarcane?"

I realized I was: a deep, rich sweetness pulsing in the air, the very breath of Barbados.

Lettie took me from the terrace into the rest of the house, and we soon came to the library, where my father sat writing at a big table; large, curling pink shells held his papers down against the indoor wind. He seemed already to be entirely at home.

"Ara, good morning! Have you had breakfast? Lettie, please could you find Miss Adelaide for us? And on your way back, would you ask Naomi for another eggnog? We missed a good many meals coming down. We'll be on the gallery."

I followed Father onto the terrace. The view had changed. There were big loopy clouds over the sea now, making indigo shadows on the brilliant water.

"This is the best room at York Stairs, and I helped design it," Father announced proudly. "Hugh bought the plantation some twenty-five years back, when most of it had blown away. I suppose this style is mongrel classic. The columns are from a Greek stoa, and the stairs are pretentious enough to belong in one of Nero's villas. But in this heavenly climate, it all works well!"

"Of course it works! Don't confuse the child with all that history foolishness. You designed us a plain old Charleston gallery, just what we wanted!"

Here was a slim, graceful woman, with gray eyes in a delicate oval face. She wore her heavy silver hair in a low, soft knot. Her flowered lawn dress was more formal than a Boston lady's, and she carried a floppy straw hat. I thought of Father's big book of English portraits. Miss Adelaide James was a Gainsborough.

"Ara, good morning—welcome to York Stairs. I don't expect you to remember us from last night, but we feel we know you already. What a fine sleep you had on your first night with us. And here is the rest of your breakfast!" She handed me the eggnog in a little china tumbler.

I had never heard an accent like hers, soft and blurred and somehow intimate, a voice for telling private matters.

"Adelaide," said Father. "You and Ara must have a lot to talk about. You'll want to tell her . . . whatever it is she needs to know. I'll leave you to it . . ." His voice trailed away, and so did he.

His behavior did not surprise me. My father had just handed me over to Miss Adelaide; he was eager to get back to his writing.

Miss Adelaide laid a gentle arm across my shoulder. "Let's go and watch the sea together." She led me to the balustrade. "You'll notice the colors are never the same from one moment to the next. Each time you look, there's something different: the clouds, the wind, the light.

"Whenever one of us comes out on the gallery, we check to see what has changed. You're one of the family now; you'll find you do this too." Her smile and her voice spoke my welcome and my inclusion.

How kind she was! In just a few sentences, she had smoothed over Father's exit, reminded me of his past efforts for me, and guaranteed me a place in her family and its social life. And yet it was all effortless. I was curious what she saw or knew about me. I decided there was more to Miss Adelaide James than met the eye. She was like Elizabeth Bennet from Jane Austen's wonderful *Pride and Prejudice*, and I wondered if Mr. Darcy would appear too. I suddenly wondered why she was not married but knew that would be an impolite question to ask.

"Your father says no lessons for a while," Miss Adelaide continued. "He wants you to learn from the sea. Lettie will take you to the beach in the mornings with a picnic. Dr. Hugh says you must rest in the afternoon, but that will be a good chance for reading—and I've been collecting a secret cache of novels for us to share!"

"I love to read!" I exclaimed enthusiastically.

Miss Adelaide smiled. "Your father told me as much. Later we change for supper, which is at eight. We'll dine together, except for the nights when we have guests—and then we'll want you to come in and meet our friends."

Then Miss Adelaide looked at me seriously. "We will do all we can to make you happy at York Stairs, Ara, while you and your father get strong again. We are very quiet here, but we try to live purposefully and with grace and good manners always."

"The Greeks would agree with you, Miss Adelaide."

"There speaks your father's daughter!" A soft sadness colored her expression. "I'm afraid we're not very used to children here at York Stairs."

"That's quite all right," I assured her, not wanting to be the cause of any discomfort. "I'm not used to being a child either."

Father and Lettie must have arrived because I felt Lettie's light touch on my shoulder.

"Time to introduce you to the sea," Lettie said as she led me away.

"What did Ara mean by that?" I heard Miss Adelaide ask.

"Just what she said," my father replied. "Poor Marian was ill for ten years, and all her family..." He was still explaining when Lettie and I moved out of hearing and down the splendid staircase. It was so noble that I felt I was trailing robes of ermine.

We took a path of crushed white shells downhill and through a grove of the dark, scratchy trees we saw from the gallery; Lettie named them "cedar." There were other trees too: huge bending daisies called "palms" that swayed and rattled. Ahead on the path, between the ragged pillars of the cedar trunks, I saw glints of light gleaming and beckoning. We came out on a little bay, sheltered by two brackets of jagged gray rock. Clear green water rippled ashore onto sand that was—impossible!—the delicate tint of a tea rose.

"What is this place, Lettie?" I stared all around me, trying to absorb my splendid, overwhelming surroundings.

"It is Learner's Cove; it is the sea. Is there no sea in America, Missy Ara?"

"Not like this." I thought of the Atlantic at Nahant, near Boston, where I picnicked last year with my cousins. There was coarse sand and hostile waves, and dark heaving water. The afternoon I went to search for Barbados in Father's big atlas, I had been disappointed to find our island was in the Atlantic too. I recalled our voyage down and the deep indigo swells hissing past the ship. If these were all aspects of the same Atlantic Ocean, I decided, then this Learner's Cove version was the one I would use from now on.

"I'm going in," I announced. I sat down on the amazing sand and took off my Boston shoes. "I'm going into the sea right now."

The water invited me, and I accepted. I crossed the wet sand that reflected the sky in bright overlapping disks of rose and lavender. I walked past the ripples frilling like petticoats and ahead into the shallow water, where the green sea and the pink sand swirled together like the marbled endpapers of learned books. I stepped into the sea, into the morning, into Barbados, without a moment's hesitation.

Lettie must have been right behind me. She took my hand at the place where the waist-high water turned the pure crystal green of a broken icicle. I looked down and saw my toenails far away, all as small and clear as on a doll's foot. I grasped Lettie's hand, and I put my head under the glimmering surface.

I knew without teaching how to breathe and duck and wait, breathe and duck and wait. Soon I was floating facedown—and then faceup. We played in the clear supporting water till my fingers were wrinkled and my eyes were bleary—and still I begged for more. I knew I belonged here more than I ever did in Boston. I was safe; I was at home in the sea.

"Tomorrow, Missy Ara. The sea is not going away. Your new friend will be right here tomorrow and all the days to come," Lettie promised.

She had brought us chicken and cake and mango nectar in a little basket. We ate our picnic in the shade of the palms, for I was already hot and prickly from the morning's sun. As we picnicked, tiny transparent crabs scuttled off with our crumbs.

Back in my room, the cool linen sheets smelled of lavender. Miss Adelaide had put a new Dickens novel on my pillow. Did she know that Mr. Harnett used to do that for me? I started the first chapter of *Hard Times*. Then my room was brimming with amber dusk, Lettie was opening the shutters, and the sky was the color of evening. I stretched, feeling peaceful and boneless. In all my life, I had never felt so comfortable inside my own body.

"What a fine rest!" Lettie praised me. "The sea has given you its best gift. You will be telling Dr. Hugh. It is the medicine he is wanting for you."

We chose the white linen supper dress, and Lettie tied it in back, since I had no waist. Then she brushed my hair into a crown around her fingers.

"Your hair is happy in Barbados," she told me.

Then I — shy, stiff, standoffish Ara Chase — turned and hugged her very hard. I think I startled myself more than Lettie. I had never done that to anyone before. Proper Bostonians do not embrace; even Mr. Harnett and I did not until that last day, when we were both in tears.

"Ah, little one," Lettie said, patting my back. "This has been a fine day indeed."

The family met on the gallery in the bronze twilight; the clouds high over the eastern sea still held the last of the daylight. Dr. Hugh James was tall and thin and stooped like the blue heron we saw on the beach. He had smiling eyes like those of Uncle Thomas Bulfinch. His speech as he welcomed me was soft like Miss Adelaide's.

At table, the two men spoke the "big talk" of ideas, and I listened gratefully; there had been very little conversation in my life so far. I had never been included in family meals, we didn't have them. Father, Mother, and I had not functioned as a family.

"We never had the killings and the burnings they had on some of the other islands," Dr. Hugh asserted. They were discussing the former slavery on Barbados and the lives of the natives when they were still slaves, some twenty years ago. I was relieved to know that young Lettie had never been a slave.

A little sleepy from my big day, I looked around me. The large dining room was shadowed, lit only by candles in wall sconces and along the table. Each candle was protected from the constant wind by a crystal cylinder. But the centerpiece also shone: a silver bowl of enormous flowers, as creamy as a dessert. Miss Adelaide saw me studying them.

"Magnolias," she whispered, smiling. She was elegant in deep blue mull, like the shadows on the sea, with a little diamond constellation on one shoulder. After she had approved my dress and hair upon my arrival at the dinner table, she had settled into the role of an interested observer, allowing the men space to fill with their expansive talk. I didn't get the sense that she wasn't included—she occasionally slipped in a comment or directed a turn in the conversation, but she chose an active quiet. I imagined I could learn a great deal by following her lead.

After supper, we went out to the gallery, where there were lanterns, each with its cloud of clumsy bumbling moths. Some of these looked as big as my hand—but I soon saw they preferred the lights to me. We sat on woven straw chairs, hearing the sweet air moving in the palms and—far off—a low dull roar like a dragon breathing in his sleep.

"Do you hear that, Ara? That's the surf on the eastern coast," said Dr. Hugh. "We'll take you there after a storm. Our Barbados waves are famous! And we have another treat for you next month: a Shakespeare evening. Our neighbors come and read with us, and we'll want you to join us. We hear you're a fine reader."

"Oh, I love Shakespeare!" Mr. Harnett had already introduced me to two of the lighter plays, *A Midsummer Night's Dream* and *Much Ado About Nothing*. "I'd really like to read with your friends."

Lettie came to the gallery, and I curtsied my good nights. We went back down the grand stair, our oil lamp lighting our way through the arch and along the vaulted hall. Our shadows curved grotesquely on the ceiling. We came to my shutter door, my own beautiful, tall room—and I think I was asleep before Lettie had even untied my sash.

The next morning Lettie brought me my eggnog and my banana—and a letter from Mr. Harnett.

"Miss Adelaide is saving this greeting for you till after your first day at York Stairs," she told me.

So I began to read: "You and I worked for years together, preparing you for the new life you are starting now," Mr. Harnett wrote. "Now you will apply all the knowledge you have in order to gain more! Every part of this experience will be a pleasure and a profit to someone with your gifts—and to others later. Every question, every new thought, will lead to another— and I will be with you always, as you are with me."

"Your letter-writing friend must think you are very important indeed to be sure this message reached you on your arrival," Lettie said.

I nodded, her words warming me. "He was my teacher," I said. "He wants me to learn everything I can here."

"And so you will." She smiled. "You can answer him that you have new teachers now. Your Lettie, the sea, and Barbados—you will learn from all of us."

I picked up my sandals, grinning. "Then let's go to the sea, now! I want more lessons right away."

My second or third day at York Stairs, Dr. Hugh asked me to come to his hospital, a small outbuilding next to his office. This was his examining room, with glass cases full of his pills and powders and instruments. I liked the retorts, teardrop vials in stained-glass colors—and the high shelves all round the room, displaying hundreds of beautiful shells.

I met Ella, Dr. Hugh's nurse, tall and slender and formal in starched white. "I know you," she whispered. "You are my cousin Lettie's dear friend."

Dr. Hugh weighed and measured and tapped me, just as Dr. Jackson had always done.

"I like what I hear," he told me. "Our island air is working for you already! It cured me, you know. I was consumptive when we came here from Charleston. Barbados has been a favored sanatorium ever since General Washington brought his sick brother."

"Did Barbados cure him too?"

"No, he wasn't one of the lucky ones. But I was—and you will be too."

"Is that why you came here, Dr. Hugh?"

"One of the reasons. We arrived just after the big hurricane of '31, and this plantation was a ruin. Your father came to visit; he helped us design the great house. That double staircase was his idea, or should I say he was inspired by that Italian fellow Palladio?

"Anyway, it was so striking that we named the plantation for the staircase and for Yorkshire in England, where the Carolina Jameses came from. And after a while the trade winds blew my consumption away!"

This was exciting news to me—the possibility that this island could work its magic on me too. I vowed to inhale those trade winds very deeply!

"Now I want to hear about what you did in Boston, Ara," Dr. Hugh said. "Who were your friends, and what did you do together?"

"Well, I had my book friends, introduced to me by my tutor, Mr. Harnett." Dr. Hugh seemed very interested, so I told him a lot about our studies in the nursery. He had the same effect on me that Mr. Harnett had; I wanted to tell him anything he wanted to know and to tell it well. When I stopped for breath, Dr. Hugh smiled.

"I surely do wish I'd had a teacher like that! Now go on and swim with Lettie. Your lungs sound mighty fine to me."

The days and nights settled into a peaceful natural rhythm. Every morning, Lettie drew back my netting and handed me my eggnog and my banana. Often, she first had to take the book that I had been reading when I fell asleep the night before. Then we chose the chiton for the day. Sometimes we combined colors very boldly: a deep pink tunic and violet trousers! These were my favorite clothes ever, as comfortable and forgettable as my own skin. Now I had my Roman sandals, made for me by Lettie's uncle Gabriel.

We explored the beaches near the great house, and sometimes my father came to Learner's Cove; he was a fine swimmer. After a fortnight of learning with Lettie, I had become competent as well as fearless. Now Father showed me ways of moving in the water as a fish swims, without splashing. I hoped he would hold me, bending my arms for me or gripping my waist as Lettie did, but ever the teacher, he seemed to prefer demonstrating a position or stroke.

In my weekly letters to Mr. Harnett, I tried to describe the sea—since he knew only the North Atlantic. He loved my stories about York Stairs and the James family.

"You are having important experiences," Mr. Harnett wrote to me. "Ones that will last your lifetime. Everyone should know the sea, and everyone should meet at least one 'great lady.' It is a term one does not use lightly. Since Miss Adelaide James is evidently one, she can teach you things I never could. And your friend Lettie sounds delightful company."

One day Lettie and I went out to the reef. She had warned me that coral was sharp and poisonous, so I was careful when I lay down on my towel. We relaxed in the sun and looked back at the dark pointed cedars and our little beach.

"Lettie," I decided to ask, "am I your job?"

"You are both my work and my pleasure, Ara. Miss Adelaide employs me, but we Barbadians are free now. I would be your companion for your company, for no wage at all!"

I was happy Lettie dropped the "Missy" when we were by ourselves.

"Does Miss Adelaide pay you very much, Lettie?"

"Enough so I will be a wealthy bride."

"And who will you marry?"

"That will be Elijah, but he is not knowing it." She laughed and blew seawater, as merry as another child.

"And when will he know it?"

"When I am telling him!"

And she would say no more—so we swam back to shore and worked on our acropolis, which we were building beyond the high-tide mark. We had much to teach each other, it turned out. Lettie too had come to delight in the ancients, their feuds and infatuations. Her appetite for the Greek myths grew, the bloodier the better.

"That Hades, that foolish king of Hell," she fretted. "He should just be choosing a nice girl from his own village. Most girls would be happy to be a queen! I would marry Hades myself, except for Elijah."

In exchange for my myths, Lettie told me about her secret religion, and its drums and witch doctors and avenging ghosts. There were sacrifices too: bleating goats and flapping chickens. I teased her that my snobbish Olympians would never accept these barnyard offerings.

One morning, heading for the beach, we met Miss Adelaide in her shade hat. She had given up trying to make me wear one, and I was tanned an even café au lait. Miss Adelaide carried shears and a flat basket, so I knew she was about to make one of her flower arrangements. These were in every room of York Stairs. Some were brilliant and dominant; others were small and personal. No two were ever the same.

"I especially like the new one in the dining room," I told her. "I think you meant it to be a wave."

"You guessed!" She was delighted. "Now tell me, Ara—what is in the big copper vat on the gallery, the one from the sugar mill?"

"This week you used branches of cup of gold. Last week's was hibiscus and African daisies."

"How do you know the flower names?"

"I ask Lettie."

Miss Adelaide looked at me, head tipped, unhurried and grave—as if she were choosing or deciding something.

"Very well. That's settled. You may watch me work. I have never allowed anyone before now. Come here early on Tuesday and Friday mornings, right after you get up. It's a nice thing for a girl to learn, before she has her own house."

So on those mornings, I met Miss Adelaide at her big worktable outside the cookhouse. She rose before me, for the day's flowers had to be cut before the dew dried. She laid sheaves of color, fragrant and moist, by the containers she had chosen: an antique bowl, a conch shell, or a Chinese dish. She completed four arrangements a morning.

Watching, I sensed her working without a definite plan, following the flowers' intentions. When I was allowed to ask, at the end of each arrangement, Miss Adelaide was vague. She offered no rules or maxims when I questioned her.

"After a while, you'll know when it's right," she promised me. "The flowers will tell you, if you listen."

So I observed quietly and tried to guess what she would do next. One morning, I watched her making a golden sunburst (lemon lilies, coreopsis, and allamanda). Naomi, the cook, came out with a question about dinner, and Miss Adelaide was briefly distracted. She went back to her massed yellow flowers and picked up a crimson rose.

"Oh, no!" I cried out by mistake—our unspoken agreement was that I would learn through observation and would not distract Miss Adelaide from her task with questions or comments.

She laid the rose aside, saying nothing, and went on working with a smile. I could tell she was thinking something, but I wasn't sure what it might be. I found out the next day at the clinic. When Dr. Hugh had finished listening to my chest, and I was pulling my yellow chiton back over my head, I heard him say, "Miss Adelaide tells me you're a keen student. I was wondering if you'd like me for a shell teacher."

"Oh, yes!" I struggled to get my arms into their sleeves quickly so that I could burst my head through the neckline. "Will we go to the beach together?"

"No, I have a better idea: you'll bring the beach to me. We'll have a shell school — on the gallery, with Miss Adelaide's permission."

"Tools for learning have their own beauty, like kitchen tools," said Miss Adelaide when I asked her permission. "You may use the south corner of the back gallery."

Every morning, returning from the beach, I delivered my specimens — and every evening, just before the cloud show, Dr. Hugh and I sorted them. We laid out the shell classes (Cephalopoda) and the species (nautilus) within each class. He called this process of classification "taxonomy." I called it a fine new game.

What a variety of shell shapes! The elegant angel wings, the sturdy lion's paw, the secret inscriptions of the tellin. The shell names were beautiful in themselves: spirula, rosy harp, trophon, and my favorite, argonaut. I repeated them like poetry. And while I collected shells, I collected Dr. Hugh's bits and pieces of shell lore: that the cowrie is money on Captain Cook's islands...that the Egyptians made the first papyrus ink from the murex...that Michelangelo used the king scallop in his architecture. Dr. Hugh was very learned — and I took pleasure in learning from him.

Every week or so, after my reading rest, Miss Adelaide took me calling. Lettie brushed my hair, now streaked various shades from the sun. Jonah, Dr. Hugh's barber, cut it regularly, maintaining my short Greek curls. Miss Adelaide tied the sash of one of my supper dresses and each time gave it and me an unnecessary pat. I recognized the affection in these extra touches, and although I couldn't quite return the gestures, I could receive them as they were given: fondly.

Aaron the coachman handed me into the buggy as grandly as he did Miss Adelaide, making quite a fuss. He was Lettie's uncle but was much darker and thicker. The buggy was painted wicker and called a "governess cart." Aaron promised to teach me to drive it.

We called at Sudbury and Drax Hall or Villa Nova or Rosedown, the plantations nearby. Most of the great houses were in the upside-down Barbados design I was used to now, but none had a sea spectacle like York Stairs. We sat in the high, shaded drawing rooms, often shuttered in the afternoons, or on the galleries. We chatted and drank China tea, and ate little slices of dark spiced cake.

The plantation ladies were all English; some had titles in front of their names. Many of their families had been in Barbados more than two hundred years. Everything and everyone was polished and leisurely. If it were not for the dark, silent servants and the steady creaking of the windmills, one would believe this a world without work.

There was no one my age. The planters' children were sent "home" to England for boarding school from ages eight to sixteen. How they must long for the sun, I thought, just as I longed for youthful companionship. Would I never cease to be an oddity? Sometimes there was talk about my joining some older girls for lessons, but Miss Adelaide evaded this neatly with vague murmurs of "till she is stronger." And for a moment bright Barbados grew darker for me with the reminder of the old taint, stalking me even here. The clouds parted swiftly, however; there was far too much to see, to do, to discover.

Often, as we left, the plantation masters rode in from the fields. The men's sunburned faces lit up; they were reluctant to let Miss Adelaide go. I wondered, as before, why she was unmarried. I knew she helped Dr. Hugh with the sick children in his hospital and calmed the frightened parents. She did so much, was so vital to the people around her and to the smoothly functioning York Stairs world, yet she was careful to conceal it. It seemed she thought that the mark of a lady was to accomplish without visible effort. One day, I said timidly, "Miss Adelaide, why did you and Dr. Hugh come here?"

"Ara, one day I will tell you," she said. This sounded very mysterious to me, but I knew Miss Adelaide would keep her promise.

Every few weeks, after supper, neighbors came to York Stairs, and we read a Shakespeare play aloud. I was told this was a James tradition in Charleston; it had clearly become their particular way of entertaining here in Barbados. Back in my nursery, when Mr. Harnett and I used to read our scenes, we had only our two voices for all the parts. At York Stairs, with a dozen readers, each play became a vivid world in itself where interesting people told their feelings in noble language. I was enchanted. The Globe Theatre was here in Barbados, and I was on the stage!

The first evening, the group read *Love's Labour's Lost,* and I was a court lady. The next play was to be *The Tempest,* and Miss Adelaide asked me one day as we walked in the rose gardens behind the house if I would like to read the role of Miranda.

"Oh, I'd be so honored!" I exclaimed. "I will practice over and over."

"Don't try too hard, Ara," Miss Adelaide instructed with a smile. "Don't lose Miranda's sense of wonder."

As I rehearsed the part, I felt I recognized Barbados as the setting for the play—though Dr. Hugh assured me Shakespeare was writing about Bermuda, which had been discovered about a hundred years earlier. But I felt that I already knew the isle *"full of noises, / Sounds and sweet airs, that give delight and hurt not."*

I practiced my part for Lettie on the beach. And on the Shakespeare evening, I read it as though I lived it. I felt I was playing myself. From the moment I came to Barbados, I too began to *"suffer a sea change / Into something rich and strange."*

From that night on, to my great joy, everyone continued to call me "Miranda." I had a new life in a new place; it was right that I take a new name too. Even Father agreed I had outgrown "Ara" along with my Boston buckle shoes. From that day forward, I was to be Miranda Chase.

As I spent more and more time on and in the sea, I grew daily more curious about the sea creatures besides myself. Looking out to the violet shadows of the reef and then the indigo of the deepest water, I often saw gleaming curves of life breaking the surface, rhythmically appearing and disappearing. Sometimes black teardrop silhouettes leapt and fell in towers of diamond spray. I sensed enormous power and energy in these creatures.

"That is Dolphin," Lettie told me, using the noun as a proper name.

"They are warm-blooded and air-breathing, like us," Dr. Hugh elaborated at dinner. "Think of them as people in the sea—the nicest and smartest people you'll ever meet."

"There are dolphins in many of the Greek myths," Father contributed. "The gods were always fighting over them. Athena claimed them for their intelligence, and Apollo for their love of music. Poseidon wanted them for his attendants and messengers."

"Does Dolphin ever come close?" I asked Lettie as she saw me to bed.

"He will if he knows you, my Miranda. First we must go to meet Dolphin where he is living and make him a friend." She said this as she brushed a wisp of hair from my face with her fingertips.

So the next morning, a flower day, Lettie arranged with Miss Adelaide that Abel, Lettie's brother, would take us out in his fishing skiff. There was a slight delay, until Aaron could bring us a life preserver from Bridgetown at Miss Adelaide's insistence.

"Do not worry, Mistress Adelaide," Lettie teased. "If there is trouble in the water, it is Miranda who will be saving Dolphin!"

Abel was slim and honey colored, a little lighter than Lettie. His skiff was silvery unpainted wood, named for his daughter Granada. We glided with a low rustle in the glassy green water, looking back at the wooded island. I saw York Stairs on its hill, with its avenue of cedars. I saw the fields of cane bending in the trade winds, and—very faintly—I heard the windmills working. The beaches were invisible, but the waves made shining fans of spray against the rocks. Soon Abel began to blow a reed flute with a plaintive voice.

"Dolphin is a curious fellow," he promised me. "He will be wanting to know our business here today."

The smooth glistening creatures began to approach us, coming in twos and threes—swift dark shadows in the luminous water. They came on steadily; a dozen or more, arching up to smile and breathe, then arching down to speed nearer. Up close, they were shiny storm-sky gray, half as long as our boat.

I studied them. I discovered they had no angles, no sections, no additions except for their smooth fins; they were a single solid curve of beauty and power—in constant effortless motion all around us. They used the sea as I did, for purest pleasure; they projected ease and joy. I felt they were greeting and welcoming me.

"Lettie, Dolphin likes me!" I exclaimed.

"Dolphin is knowing his kin," she answered gravely.

As they played around our skiff, I reached to touch their warm skin, their taut muscled bodies. I felt the solid column of their breath, rising from the neat nostril in their foreheads. As they circled us, they chirped and chattered to one another like shrill, excited birds. I sensed their intelligent goodwill coming directly at me like a beam of light.

When they decided to leave us, they turned together, all at one time. Each dolphin rose in the water to give me a long, deliberate, memorizing look. Then they departed in a green swirl of grace and power.

As fluid as the waves around us was the passage of time in Barbados. I slipped through the hours as trackless as a dolphin's path. I knew we had arrived in late summer, but as the days and weeks passed, the winds and the colors around me were unchanging. Only my shell collection recorded time passing. Now that I had one of almost every Caribbean species, I was trying to replace imperfect or beach-worn shells with finer specimens, or collect examples in every color. So far I had eleven different shades of my new favorite, king scallop.

The sugarcane itself—the focus and center of our island, the reason white men lived and worked on Barbados—deceived us concerning time. The planters staggered their plantings in order to arrange a continuous harvest, so one cane field was being harvested as its neighbor was being tilled.

I often saw a stand of rustling emerald green cane, the tall stalks fully grown. On one side, there were feathery silver new shoots—and on the other, dry tawny stalks ready for the mill and rattling like newspaper. Just beyond were fields blackened by the burnover and others tilled for a new planting.

And always the great windmills turned and flapped, creaked and flapped, in the steady trade winds. When they died, when the air was slack and still, it seemed louder than the wind. Then Lettie told me the verse I would hear so often in the hurricane season:

> *June, too soon.*
> *July, stand by.*
> *August, come it must.*
> *September, remember.*
> *October, all over.*

"Now we prepare for Hurricane," Lettie announced. "He will come and he will go. There is no need to be fearing him."

"Will it be today? What time?" I was eager and excited.

"Miranda, my brave one, we cannot hurry him. Keep watch. You will know Hurricane when you meet him."

Without our trade winds, it was unpleasantly hot. The motionless cloud towers drooped and sagged above the ocean. The pale sky glared; the sea was dull and flat, and sticky when I swam.

At York Stairs, the marble tables sweated; Miss Adelaide's flower arrangements faded in a day. The unshielded candles burned straight up at dinner. When I woke at night, in wet clinging sheets, I heard clouds of mosquitoes circling and whining outside my netting. Something was going to happen.

The first two events were merely exaggerated storms, with high moaning wind and sheets of horizontal rain. We closed the shutters securely and read in the living room by unsteady lamps. I peered through the louvers and could see the cedars whipping about. A giant was shaking his paintbrushes! The gallery furniture skidded past in a hurry.

The next morning the sky was a delicate, innocent blue, as if to say, "Who, me?"

Lettie was right; when the big blow came, I recognized it. The sky was first gray, then brown, then swirling black. Single frantic birds darted here and there in panic. Then the wind changed from the familiar sorrowful keening to a sinister new sound, a howling. I heard this ominous shift in tone just as Dr. Hugh gave the order to take shelter.

"Time for the cellar, Adelaide." So we picked up the lamps and books and shawls we had prepared and headed for the huge storm cellar under the cookhouse. The house servants and the field hands and all their families were already there.

I saw several hundred torchlit faces massed in the limestone cavern. There was a banjo player and singing. Naomi had kettles of spicy fish stew and ginger beer for everyone. Rum was not permitted. It all seemed like my idea of a church picnic—a York Stairs plantation party, gala and friendly. The little children stayed close to their mothers; the older boys and girls made their own groups.

We four from the great house settled in the southwest corner, with a low symbolic wall for mutual privacy.

"We must be here but not here," Dr. Hugh explained to me. "Seeing us reassures the people, but they don't want us underfoot either."

I leaned comfortably back, watching. No one was bored; no one was frightened. I took my cue from the others and calmed my quickly beating heart. They had all experienced Hurricane before and were not quaking with fear; I would follow their example. The young people giggled and whispered, the babies slept untroubled in their mothers' laps. This event would provide fine material for my next letter to Mr. Harnett. I started to compose it in my mind.

Lettie appeared out of the twilight. "Miranda, will you come with me to hear Hurricane speaking?"

"Oh, yes, please!" I was eager to experience this powerful force closer at hand. We picked our way among the huddled families to the cellar entrance. Here the solid torrent of wind raged past us, screaming higher and higher yet, beyond control or reason. Lettie held my shoulders, reminding me with her light touch that I was safe, and we stood together—unseeing witnesses to the despairing madness of the hurricane.

At midmorning, we collected our belongings and trailed back to the great house. There were palm trees down, attached to huge balls of rooted earth. The grounds were carpeted with layers of leaves and twigs, pressed flat into a mosaic. We found limbs all over the gallery and a few shutters blown off their hinges. The gray sea looked dirty and stirred.

We had a cold lunch and exchanged damage reports. Dr. Hugh announced two windmills wrecked and innumerable chickens blown out to sea. Miss Adelaide showed us a grotesque rose from her picking garden, where the cruel wind turned her flowers inside out. I felt tired and let down now that the danger was over. Father must have sensed this.

"Would you like to help me with my manuscript, Miranda?"

I sat bolt upright. Father had employed me to answer his letters, but he had never before asked me into the tight circle he'd drawn around his private and privileged world of work. I was honored, and to my amazement I found that when we got down to work, I was actually useful. As I proofread his cool, precise prose, I twice suggested another word, and he took my advice.

"I'm promoting you to editor!" Father stated. "I always need someone as literate as you seem to be."

Of course, this was the sort of game Mr. Harnett and I had played for years. He would write a theme as badly as he could, and I would correct his absurd mistakes. I was pleased that this nursery experience was helpful to Father now.

With all the wonderful surprises being offered to me on regular days, I eagerly anticipated what would await me on my upcoming birthday. On the morning of September 16, Lettie came to me with my morning eggnog and banana.

"What are we going to do today?" I asked with a small smile. I imagined an extravagant outing.

Lettie selected a maroon chiton and paired it with pale pink trousers. "Is there something special the missy would like to be doing today?" Her open face carried no hint, no secret.

I decided to wait to see what had been planned. But as the day wore on and there were no acknowledgments of the day from Father, Miss Adelaide, or Dr. Hugh, I realized the unhappy truth: my birthday had been forgotten.

Father had never failed to remember it before—but this year he was entirely engrossed in his book about Pericles. And, of course, the Barbados weather of perpetual May offered him no reminders of autumn's arrival, I told myself. Perhaps he believed it was now Miss Adelaide's responsibility to arrange, as she did so much else. That would have necessitated informing her when my birthday was, however. Clearly that hadn't happened.

I should not have told Lettie, but I did want to hear "Happy birthday!" from someone and to feel thirteen—though I already did feel that, with all the new hard muscles in my arms and legs. Then Lettie must have told Miss Adelaide, who must have spoken to Dr. Hugh, who may have scolded Father. At any rate, dinner was quite late that evening. But there was a beautiful mango trifle with thirteen candles, and grown-up toasts with wine.

The carriage must have gone into Bridgetown late that afternoon. I was given a handsome album from Father, for recording my growing shell collection. Dr. Hugh presented me with two finely bound shell books from England; the endpapers had overlapping pectins, as at the water's edge in Learner's Cove. Miss Adelaide's present was the best of all: a tiny bar pin of aquamarines set in gold.

"I wanted you to have something that was mine." She smiled and touched my hand. "I wore that when I was your age, before I ever knew there was a true sea that color. In Charleston, the water is more like coffee."

"Or gumbo soup!" Father teased. We were all very festive, and the bad feeling about my delayed birthday was over. All was restored to its usual happy state. Then Dr. Hugh frightened me with his next words.

"Miranda, even though you're thirteen now, would you say good night? Adelaide, I need to talk to you and Josiah on the gallery." His request that I leave them alone, his unsmiling face, his calling Father "Josiah," all spoke trouble.

Back in my room, I paced and worried. Thoughts about my health were always in my mind, bobbing just below the surface. Dr. Hugh's examinations and his constant questions seemed ominous now. Only yesterday, he had weighed and measured me again. I must be sick, sicker than anyone will tell me.

Ladies and gentlemen said "consumption," but I had heard doctors in Boston call it "TB" or "tuberculosis." Will I have to stay in bed? I came to Barbados to get well—and instead I may be sick. I may be dying. I flung myself onto my bed and crossed my arms over my chest. Well, if I must die, it is a lot better to die here than up in the nursery at number 32.

I couldn't lie still. I got up and paced again. I knew that eavesdropping was vulgar and dishonest. (I must have read that in Jane Austen.) I had never been tempted before; what conversation was there to overhear in Boston? But this was not mere casual eavesdropping for gossip purposes; this was mortal. This was my life!

Honesty and good taste would have to wait. I opened my tall window and stepped out into the night. I was directly below the gallery and could hear every word of the conversation there.

"...Miranda's health, past, present, and future," Dr. Hugh was saying. "I will speak as her doctor, not as your friend. You won't like it."

"Please do, Hugh." That was my father's voice. "I count on you to tell me the truth. How do you find her lungs?"

"Perfectly sound. Miranda does not have tuberculosis; she never did. Her lungs were as clear as a bell the day she came to York Stairs."

I leaned against the wall and shut my eyes to concentrate. I was having trouble taking in what I was hearing.

"Hugh, what are you saying? Dr. Jackson is the finest lung specialist in Boston. He warned us to be careful and watchful always."

"Dr. Jackson was simply indulging Marian—and Marian was using her own illness to keep the poor child out of sight. Jackson and I have corresponded about this. He truly regrets not being more frank with you. It's hard to tell a man his wife is an inadequate mother."

"But what could poor Marian have done from a sickbed?"

"A great deal, Josiah." Dr. Hugh sounded exasperated. "She could have bought Miranda a pony, arranged music and skating lessons, found her a walking group, taken a summer beach cottage. But above all, she should have gotten a decent, educated nurse for Miranda. The child doesn't know it, but she was as neglected as any tenement orphan. She was on her own!"

"But Jackson was always asking me if she was coughing blood," Father protested. "She was pale and listless all the time. We expected the worst. She was always so tired—"

"She was tired of her life—of having no life at all." I heard Dr. Hugh getting louder. "She didn't need a doctor, she needed action and challenge and other children. Have you looked at Miranda lately? She's two inches taller and ten pounds heavier than when she came in June. She's on the move from morning till night! This must be the only normal life she's ever had."

"Hugh, with all respect, you've never been a parent—"

"And neither have you!" Dr. Hugh was actually shouting now. "You kept Miranda like a pet, like a goddamned canary! You call yourself a father? Did you know she had only one friend ever—and it was an adult hired to tutor her? Did you know she was brave and witty? Did you know her governess was abusing her? She says she tried to tell you."

"Hugh, let me speak." Miss Adelaide's gentle voice broke in. I could easily picture her laying her hand lightly on her brother's arm, the soft concern on her face.

"Josiah, we know you love Miranda. It is not a question of that."

"Yes," said Father softly.

"I think I can explain what Hugh means," Miss Adelaide continued. "I love my flowers; everyone knows that. But love is not enough—I must weed and water them too. And if there was a gardener who was supposed to help me, and then he didn't—then I would have to work twice as hard! You see, Josiah, I would remember it was I who started the garden. I planted the flowers in the first place."

There was a long silence.

"I hear you," my father said at last. "You are good friends; you have helped us both. I will remember what you have said and try to do better as a parent."

"Do give yourself a little credit, Jos," Miss Adelaide encouraged him. "You obviously found her a remarkable teacher."

"And you brought her here to us," added Dr. Hugh. "That is no small thing."

"Yes, I did, didn't I? Well, I thank you for your thoughts. I'd better go and sleep on all this. Good night, Adelaide; good night, Hugh."

I heard Father's departing footsteps.

"Hugh, do you think he heard a word of what we tried to tell him?" I believed Miss Adelaide was crying.

"I reckon it's too soon to say." Dr. Hugh still sounded upset. "As long as I live, I won't rightly understand how he just stood by with his hands in his pockets. He let Marian turn that lovely child into a puny invalid for her own selfish convenience."

"You were rather forceful, Hugh. I know he'll try to be a better father now."

Kind Miss Adelaide may have expected changes after tonight, but I did not. My father and I were fixed in our pattern of amiable parallel lives. He might make fine plans for our futures, but he would delegate my daily care to someone else—as I imagined most fathers did.

But none of that mattered in this moment. I took a deep, shaky sigh of easement and relief. I was no longer shadowed by an invisible disease and its silent inroads— and death. Now I could live like anyone else. Now I could grow up—and I intended to!

I learned tonight, from my shameful eavesdropping, that my lonely years up in the nursery were my mother's doing. Perhaps she had truly believed I was dangerous and was trying to protect her relatives from our illness. More likely, she simply did not know how to arrange a better life for me and had no friend to advise her. Maybe she was simply too selfish to bother and my father too self-involved to notice. But this seemed unimportant next to the shining new fact that I was healthy—actually, truly, entirely, and forever! Ara under the eaves, with her doll and her books and her dormer windows, tonight seemed as remote as a tiny landscape inside a china Easter egg—long, long ago.

Tomorrow I would wear my yellow chiton; Miss Adelaide said it matched my hair. Tomorrow I would eat the last of my mango birthday cake. Tomorrow I wanted to find more shells and see more dolphins, and learn to dive. This birthday began as a disappointment; it ended as the beginning of my brand-new life.

As the rhyme promised, "October, all over." The flowers recovered, the trade winds returned, the repaired windmills creaked again. November and then December were like a sunny April in New England.

With garlands of red and pink hibiscus twining the columns and the traditional swim on Christmas Day, we had a fine un-Bostonian holiday.

We received all the York Stairs families on the gallery on Christmas Eve. We exchanged presents of rum and sugarloaves, and Dr. Hugh gave each married adult a silver pound. Miss Adelaide and I had a toy for each child; we chose them in Bridgetown. Then we set off a fine dazzle of gold and silver rockets, and everybody cheered.

Father gave me a true young lady's present: a gold locket, heart shaped, on a blue enamel chain.

"Don't hurry to fill it up with a sweetheart!" he told me. "Wear it empty for a while."

I blushed at the idea while reveling in the knowledge that he was beginning to see the changes Barbados had wrought in me. I was growing up, and Father was finally noticing.

I bought Lettie an oil lamp with a pretty painted shade, and she made me a braided bracelet of tiny scallop shells in every tone of pink and orange. I put it on and wore it all evening.

I was overcome by my present from the James family. Miss Adelaide designed a small cedar chest of drawers for my shell collection, and Dr. Hugh arranged that Julius, the York Stairs carpenter, build it in his shop. There were many little drawers and cupboards, all lined in blue velvet. MIRANDA CHASE was carved on the top, inside a garland of pectin shells. I had never before had presents that were planned and made only for me. We sang Christmas carols until dusk, standing on the gallery in a warm wind flavored with sugarcane. Lettie, usually so well informed, asked me shyly about Good King Wenceslas and his snow, "deep and crisp and even." I sensed she did not really believe my answer.

Then it was 1857, and the winter sky was usually a deep, unclouded lapis lazuli. We sat out on the gallery after dinner, and Dr. Hugh taught me about the stars. First I told him the right myth (he always pretended he did not know it!), and then we located the constellation. This served to confirm my belief that the myths were truly part of the natural world.

After my astronomy lesson, I lay in the rope hammock beyond the lantern light. I had discovered that if I didn't talk and didn't swing, the grown-ups forgot I was there. I became as much a part of the darkness as the sweet wind or the swarm of moths at each lantern. I learned a great deal that way. This wasn't eavesdropping, I assured myself. I wasn't hiding—I was in plain sight, if any chose to see me.

"But Jefferson started that classical craze," my father was saying. "The best thing that came out of it is the Greek Revival architecture. Do you know it?"

"They were putting up those temples all over the South when we came here," Dr. Hugh recalled. "I remember you told us York Stairs was an island version of Greek Revival."

"Tom Bulfinch's father did a few beauties in New England. They are houses for gentlemen—unpretentious and livable. I'd like a Greek Revival house for myself someday."

"And where will that be, Jos?" Miss Adelaide asked Father.

"My letters have just gone off, Addy, so we will wait and see. It will be good for Miranda and me to be on our own, with a new start, away from Boston and all those Lathams looking down their Puritan noses at us."

I clutched the ropes of the hammock. This was news.

"On your own, then...away from Hugh and me...?" Miss Adelaide teased.

"We will always consider ourselves indebted to you. You have healed us in body and spirit. We need to think of *you* now, to take our leave and allow you to return to your old routines. We have been a handful, I should think!" With this, Father began to chuckle.

"Nonsense, Jos, we—"

Father raised his hand. "No, Addy. It is time for me to get back to work and to take Miranda home. To see she gets her chances. We want our own house, probably in a small town, preferably somewhere near my sister, Helen."

I longed to hear where this was leading, but Lettie arrived to remind me about bedtime. As we went down the sweeping stairs, I was very thoughtful. Until this evening, I had never imagined beyond Barbados. Everything that had happened to me in the past seemed to be in preparation for coming here. Now I saw that York Stairs too was a passage in time, leading on, leading elsewhere. I wondered when they would tell me what would come next.

Spring in Barbados was a bouquet. There were new flowers budding, old flowers returning; there were blossoming bushes, blooming trees. The delighted eye drifted like a butterfly, flitting from one pleasure to another, hardly knowing where to light.

One March morning, working with Miss Adelaide, I arranged some gardenias in an antique gilt tureen and wove the stiff glossy leaves into a garland around the container. Miss Adelaide made my arrangement the centerpiece on the dining table. Just as she promised me, I knew when it was finished; I knew when it was right. The flowers told me. For the first time in my life, I experienced the satisfaction of a successful creation. No one else in the world could have made exactly this; it was entirely my doing.

A few days later, I returned from a morning walk on the beach to find that everyone seemed to be waiting for me on the gallery. Though it was only noon, there was a mysterious excitement: a silver tray with champagne flutes, and smiles all about.

"Here she is!" Father cried. "Miranda, take your glass. We're toasting the future!"

"Whose future?" I inquired. I was given a glass of prickly golden wine and a kiss from everyone.

"Yours and mine, Miranda—yours and mine!" Father exulted.

I turned to Dr. Hugh, who was smiling broadly. "Please, will someone just tell me what has happened?"

"You know your father has been busy for months, choosing a college where he would like to teach and you both would like to live."

My pulse began to race. There was now actual shape and substance to Father's "plan."

"The excellent news is that two colleges wanted me." Father picked up the narrative here. "Both in small New England country towns—and both close to your aunt Helen Sloan.

"Then Dr. Hugh was inspired! He said we should write Mr. Harnett and ask about schools for you—and we just heard from him today." He waved the letter. "Mr. Harnett has written that one of the best schools in the whole country is right there in the village. How about that?"

"But where, Father? What village? Where are we going to live?"

"Why, Miranda"—he laughed and drained his glass—"I'm going to be head of classics at Amherst College, right near where I grew up. You and I are going to live in Amherst, Massachusetts! Now I'd better write and tell them so."

Father waved and went inside, as joyful as I'd ever seen him.

So now my future had a name and a setting, and I began to dread it. Boston was easy because nothing whatsoever was asked of me. Barbados was easy because I knew all that was required, and I enjoyed every aspect of my life there. Also, several people loved me, and I loved them back, which was most important.

But Amherst, Massachusetts? What will they want of me there? What about school? This was a great mystery. I had never actually been to school. I had had only four friends in my life: Mr. Harnett and Lettie, Miss Adelaide and Dr. Hugh, all grown-ups. I wasn't sure how to behave with other children. I remembered my awkwardness with my own cousins. Would I ever have a young friend who would forgive my being different and perhaps even value my bookish nature?

But I liked the idea of Amherst the village. Father told me a great deal about the place. I could picture myself walking about, along leafy streets and past painted wooden houses. I would know the names of all the families. I could even imagine having a friend in one of those houses. She might have read a lot; she would want to talk about books. She might think I was an addition to her life; she might have been lonely too.

As the days passed, I became more confident. I could see ahead to our last weeks here, to packing up and saying good-bye—and I went on imagining the friend who might be waiting for me in Amherst. Perhaps she'll have a garden behind her house, and I will show her how to arrange flowers. I will tell her about York Stairs, and then we'll lend each other books.

Father had decided to complete our full year in Barbados. He preferred to finish his book on Pericles in the peace of York Stairs, without the distraction of a new house and a new position. Since I did not yet belong to any school, there was no concern about my falling behind in my schoolwork. So we would stay until June, when passage would be easiest.

Miss Adelaide never once entreated us to stay on at York Stairs. This was an open invitation, unspoken but understood. But I realized that Barbados, however delightful, was a very small and limited world. All my reading had given me intimations of a larger one.

"You're right to go back," Miss Adelaide assured me as we sat on the gallery one April afternoon. "You're an American, you belong in the United States. Barbados is England, really—England with dolphins."

When we sat like this in the afternoon, we often played the *Hamlet* game: finding images and faces in the cloud shapes over the sea. I did this now to change the subject.

"Look, Miss Adelaide, to the left of the last cedar—a turtle dancing!" And then together we said the proper *Hamlet* response: "'*Very like a whale!*'"

In a strange way, Lettie left me before I could leave her. She was present during our time together, but her mind was elsewhere. She stopped going into the water with me and instead waited on the beach. She stopped my diving lessons too and never even touched our picnics. She lost interest in my myth people.

Lettie refused my earnest assurance of our return in two years and ignored my promise that Miss Adelaide would read her all my letters. Her lovely delicate face turned puffy, and she had a new sharp laugh. We were not in harmony. For the first time, I felt her hours with me were bought and paid for.

"This is a bad time for Lettie," Miss Adelaide explained when I consulted her. "She never meant to become so attached to you. You were just a job at first. Losing you is terrible for her, and her sweetheart, Elijah, has found another interest. I'm afraid, though, that it's already too late for Lettie." This was unclear, but I chose not to ask any further.

Suddenly our York Stairs life had a boundary; we heard ourselves saying, "Before I leave," and "After you've gone." The mail came and went like flights of paper gulls. Father's publisher accepted *Pericles,* and Amherst Academy accepted me. Mr. Harnett enthused over this school, "a beacon of learning."

Uncle Thomas Bulfinch reserved some hotel rooms in Boston for the week after our return. Cousin Ellen Curtis had been designated to help me buy clothes, as Cousin Daisy was abroad. Then Aunt Helen Sloan invited Father and me to Springfield for the rest of the summer, and my cousin Kate Sloan wrote me a shy welcome. I was impressed with Father's planning.

When we packed my trunk, it was almost empty; all my chitons and supper dresses were too small now. Lettie would use them for her niece Granada, who was the size I used to be.

"You're just like a little snake, Miranda! You've outgrown your old Barbados skin," Miss Adelaide told me. So we went to Bridgetown together and found me a dark traveling dress. It felt hard and strange; I had not worn sleeves and petticoats and buttons for a year.

Sad Lettie helped me wrap my shell collection and its precious cabinet. Dr. Hugh gave me his very best shell book—the French one with tissue paper over each delicate engraving.

"You can study these to know what to look for when you come back to York Stairs," he told me. "I don't want you to lose that sharp sheller's eye!"

When we sailed the first day of June, it was a festival. There were all our neighbor friends from the Shakespeare evenings, with books and little gifts for traveling. There was a wagonful of excited people from York Stairs with flowers and cakes, calling and waving.

"A lot of folks seem to like you," Captain Childrey remarked. Poseidon did too: we glided north with our own private trade wind. I was never seasick, not for an hour. I read on deck and watched for whales and remembered York Stairs. The smiling dolphins rode our bow wave. Day by day, the sea changed from beloved Barbados ultramarine to New England slate blue, where the last dolphins left us.

Book III

AMHERST

1857

I was dizzy from changes. Every day was a jack-in-the-box; new places and new people came leaping up at me. In a month, I had gone from Barbados to Boston to Springfield, poised between the past of Mount Vernon Street and the future in Amherst.

In Boston, we stayed in a very grand hotel with chandeliers as tall and glittering as ocean waves. Here Cousin Ellen Curtis met us — now Cousin Ellen Curtis Lyall, a lovely laughing bride. She always seemed to me the gayest of the Lathams. Mr. Harnett, who met her once, said she had joie de vivre.

She and I went shopping for wonderful dresses in styles and colors I never would have chosen. She said everything I wore must suit my eyes, my best feature, so dark green and brown were wrong; gray, azure, dark blue, and violet were right. As Cousin Daisy was still abroad, Cousin Ellen had picked up her mantle and was now the only Latham relative who seemed to truly like my short curls. I wondered what they would have thought of my radical Greek chitons. Though I tried, it was hard to warm to those relations whose tastes and inclinations were so conventional.

We went from Boston to Springfield on a train, which was loud and dirty and thrilling. (One called this "taking the cars.") There the Sloans, my aunt Helen and my cousin Kate, met us. Aunt Helen was as kind as I remembered. She radiated good sense and goodwill; there was no malice in her. I felt she and Miss Adelaide were kindred spirits.

And Kate Chase Sloan — however did I manage so long without her? She was three years older than I; she was calm and gentle and witty. She either didn't know or didn't care that she was a beauty-in-waiting, but I could hardly look away from her. Kate was slender, long-boned, and graceful, with pale olive skin that flushed apricot over her cheekbones. Her face was shaped like a valentine heart. Her hair was cloudy and dark, pulled back with a ribbon. Her eyes were hazel, green and gold like an iridescent hummingbird—but none of her beauty mattered compared to her generosity, her concern for others.

She had such a soft voice that I had to lean in to hear her—but whatever she was saying, it was sure to be wise and funny. I felt as if I had known her and loved her always. Like me, Kate was happiest with a book. She had not been able to do as much reading as I had, though, because she sang—oh, how she sang! When my father heard her on our first evening in Springfield, he was beyond social compliments. He became deeply serious.

"Why, Helen, I had no idea. You're really going to have to think about this, aren't you? We'll have to make some plans, I think."

So Kate's voice, as much as anything, led to combining our families and households in Amherst. Aunt Helen would rent her Springfield house and run Father's Amherst home for him. Kate would attend Amherst Academy with me and take voice lessons at the college. I would have the use of a mother and a sister, and Father, the paterfamilias-come-lately, was going to happily pay the bills for us all. Each one of us was delighted with Father's decisions and with the shape of our new family.

Once this was settled, Father moved to the village inn, and began his house hunt. There was not much selection in a town of less than three thousand, but he was fortunate to find a small house on Amity Street that could be extended into the Greek Revival design of his dreams.

We took the cars back and forth between Springfield and Amherst. Springfield was a small manufacturing city, and Amherst was a village in the woods. The two towns, and a dozen others, had grown up along the banks of the great, slow Connecticut River. This valley was like a medieval tapestry of woods and farms and settlements, with interlocking roads and now railways. It was a self-contained little kingdom, river-centered, hill-enclosed—very beautiful, and entirely unlike Boston.

When September came, we moved from Springfield to Amherst. We rented a German professor's house while the additions were being made to our own. Our temporary home was crowded and dark, with three or four sets of curtains at each window and heavy bowlegged furniture. So different from light and airy York Stairs! There were huge, aggressive ferns in every corner, so we called our house the "plush jungle."

We found few books, but we were given permission to use the college library.

As I walked about, I liked the tidy look of Amherst Village. There was a central block of brick stores and offices with brick sidewalks; this was called "downtown." A hardware store, a dry goods', a printer, and a post office were all on the main street. The doctors' and lawyers' offices were over them, on the second story. There was a fine bookstore, which the college required; Father said I might choose and send a book for Miss Adelaide every month. For she wrote to me:

I will always think of you as my daughter. No mother could miss her child more than I do you — or hold more tender hopes for the years ahead. I want you to tell me all your days, your triumphs and disappointments. Everything about your life is my dear concern. Your words will reach me in less than a fortnight!

There were two large, handsome brick residences that dominated the town. President Stearns of the college lived in one; the other belonged to the Dickinsons, the leading family of Amherst. The Dickinsons were founders of the college, builders of the community. Their rooflines and chimneys rose above the trees; all the other houses were smaller or built lower. Looking down from the nearby Pelham Hills, I found that the village itself was almost invisible. The forest appeared undisturbed.

I liked to walk along the village streets, looking into autumn gardens, imagining the lives of the families. I thought I could fit into a society on this scale. Already some people greeted me, and a few girls my age smiled shyly—suggesting that my oddities did not stand out yet.

Nevertheless, the night before the academy opened, I was full of apprehension and stage fright. I dreaded the crowds of strangers, already friends with one another. I feared my own mistakes and ignorance. I had no idea what to say and do tomorrow morning. I confessed all this to Kate; I even managed to make a funny story about my terrors. Kate laughed till she was weak.

"Stop, Miranda, stop! It won't be as bad as you think," she reassured me kindly. "You needn't worry about the boys, they're always nice to new pretty girls. Just smile and pretend they're smarter than you are."

I stared at her in amazement. I was going to be one of the pretty girls? Even stranger—I was expected to pretend to be less than I was. What a curious society to navigate. My nervousness escalated.

Kate hugged me, smiling. "It will all be fine. The other thing to remember is that the girls will like you if you don't chase the boys."

Following that advice would be easy!

That night, the first frost took vivid scarlet bites out of the tawny maples. On my fourteenth birthday, we walked to school under the brilliant trees. We went along the green and up the hill to the academy, a plain building of painted brick. Its three stories were starkly unadorned, stating that education within was serious and spiritual. "All frivolity abandon, ye who enter here!" I whispered to Kate, who laughed.

Entering, I was caught up in a swirl of noise and energy, and swept along in a stream of excited children pressing forward. Far from avoiding or criticizing me, none of the other students paid me the slightest notice. I was not conspicuous, not different; I was blessedly one of the crowd.

Somehow I found myself in the right rooms, with teachers who expected me and handed me books. Labels and names and directions poured over me, my ears rang, my eyes were dazzled—but all I received was the same hurried kindness as everyone else. I had expected so much worse on my first day. So far no one had guessed that I was a creature out of my element.

One of my teachers was Miss Lowe, a grave young woman with dark eyes and a level gaze. When recess came, she asked me to stay. I was relieved; I had not wanted to attempt jumping rope with my skillful classmates. I intended to ask Kate to teach me how when we got home.

"Miranda, tell me about the list of books you read this summer." She held the handwritten list I turned in this morning, as was asked of each pupil. She seemed worried. "Did you read all these with understanding?"

"Yes, Miss Lowe, I did." I wondered what it was about my list that concerned her.

"I see. Tell me, which was your favorite?"

"It was a tie—either *Emma* or *Henry Esmond.*" I thought a moment. "Definitely *Emma.* Jane Austen captures her characters so vividly, don't you think?"

Miss Lowe gazed at me appraisingly. "Yes, I do. How would you feel about being with an older class for literature?"

"I wouldn't mind at all, if they didn't."

"We often mix up ages; it makes for a more interesting discussion. Now tell me—do you like Longfellow?"

"I loved 'The Skeleton in Armor.' I even memorized it! But I think 'Hiawatha' was—well, childish." I hoped I hadn't spoken too freely. I looked at Miss Lowe for her response.

Miss Lowe smiled for the first time. "That will be our secret, between the two of us. And here's another: I don't like Sir Walter Scott!"

We grinned at each other. I knew Miss Lowe and I would have many book conversations in the future.

"That wasn't bad at all," I told Kate as we walked home with our armfuls of new books. "Miss Lowe is a little like Mr. Harnett."

"That is the best school I ever attended," Kate affirmed. "I can tell already."

"What good news from everyone!" Father beamed at dinner. "Nobody bit Miranda, and nobody eloped with Kate!" We all laughed, and I marveled at the change that had come over Father. He was more outgoing and open, even engaging in frivolities and jokes. And he and Aunt Helen were as happy as Kate and I about the school situation.

"Your academy was started by the same gang of Unitarian church-goers who founded the college some years later," Father informed us. "The two institutions are still very close and still hell-bent on saving souls. We won't tell anyone how corrupt and worldly you girls really are!"

I was delighted by Father's banter and our inauguration as a family. In Barbados, as much as I loved it, I was a welcome guest; here I felt completely at home.

The Pelham Hills blazed beside the river; we walked under the maple torches and oak beacons that were all along the village streets. Fires of leaves raked up into stubby pyramids smoldered along the lanes; violet smoke rose in twisted columns. Amherst in autumn was a stunning surprise of clear blue weather—but the colors deepened as the nights chilled, and the wind had a steel edge.

Kate and I were beginning to feel quite at ease at the academy. Half the girls in her class were only going through the motions of study until they could close their books for good and move into their prescribed roles as wives. Meanwhile the awkward boys, pimpled and bony and honking like geese, were handy to practice on until appropriate suitors came along.

The other girls were the scholars, the readers; they moved deep in projects, laden with books, eager for learning. Kate fit effortlessly among them. Because Kate literally did not see boys, the girls forgave her her hair, her complexion, her striking beauty.

I turned out to be a little hard to place in the academy, since I was ahead of my age in some subjects and behind in others. The teachers were all kind and uncritical; after a week of switching me about, they devised a patchwork schedule. I was with the fifteen-year-olds for history and literature, and (oh, shame!) with the ten-year-olds in mathematics. I had botany, geography, and French with my own age. I considered taking recorder lessons as some of the girls did.

Gradually I learned protective coloration, as if I were a small animal in the woods. I could skip rope at recess; it was simpler than it looked that first day. I learned jacks, which was a friendly and flexible game played in silence. I practiced jacks at home on our porch. I did not have real friends yet, but no one snubbed me.

In class, I tried not to raise my hand. If I was called on, I learned that no one minded my knowing the answer — if I produced it uncertainly. I never mentioned books except those that had been assigned. (Jane Eyre, forgive me!) I discovered that Barbados, so remote and exotic, made a fine excuse for my social naïveté — so I enlarged my time there and put my years in Boston far in the past.

All this fitting in was very tiring — but I had Kate every evening to hear my trials, to listen and laugh and encourage me. She accepted me as I was; I had nothing to conceal — and I was never lonely. One night I even told Kate that I thought Lolly Wheeler, the social center of the fourteen-year-old set, was starting to like me.

Every afternoon after school, Kate and I walked up Amity Street to watch the day's progress on our new house. There was to be a two-story wing to the west for Father, with a study downstairs and two bedrooms over it. One day, we met my father and Ethan Howland, our handsome young architect, frowning and pacing up and down the site. Ethan Howland came from Springfield for half the week to supervise the additions to our house. The work was going rapidly, but the large one-story addition behind the main house — my father called it the "temple" — had met trouble: immovable bedrock.

Mr. Howland and Father had been most congenial until this business of the rock, which loomed in the space where we had intended to build our large drawing room.

"Jos, you have to give in on something," Mr. Howland was pleading. "Follow the Parthenon ratio, but make the whole room smaller. We can build right up to the rock. That's thirty feet."

"I won't have it!" Father's rejection was explosive. "I won't have a skimpy temple that looks as if it had shrunk in the wash!"

"Then we'll have to build over the rock," said Mr. Howland. "You'll just have to lower the ceiling."

"Never!" Father glared and blew like a whale. It was a shame to see him so upset, when until now the progress on the house had given him so much pleasure.

I wandered off to study the rock, now our acknowledged enemy. There was no way to guess how deep it went, since what was visible was no more than the horn of a huge hidden mass. I returned to the building for a yardstick and measured the projection. Somewhere in my mind there was an idea moving and taking shape, as a deep-water dolphin glimmers its way up to visibility. I rejoined the men, who were still arguing.

"Father, I believe there is a way." I was very calm and confident, just as I was for my first geography test last week. I knew the answer; I only had to produce it. Both men stared at me.

"Do you remember our Shakespeare evenings in Barbados? And how we said we'd do them ourselves in Amherst?"

"Of course I remember. That's one of the reasons we must have a big room. You can't do Shakespeare in a stingy ten-by-ten parlor."

I saw Mr. Howland swallow a smile. Our parlor was actually a generous twenty-two by twenty.

"Well, couldn't we use a stage for our readings? The rock is twelve feet wide and only two feet high. So we could just build over the rock — and then drop down for the rest of the room. That way you could keep your temple measurements, and we'd have a stage too. What do you think?"

There was a long silence while Mr. Howland scribbled and smiled and waited for Father to speak.

"Miranda, what did Alexander cut?" Father said at last.

"The Gordian knot!" I laughed with delight at having been helpful. "And he got Asia in return!"

"Well, Alexandra, you've just cut our knot—but I'll give you a stage instead of Asia. Ethan, why didn't we think of that by ourselves? By God, we're going to build Kate a hall for her first concert!"

We all congratulated ourselves and one another, glowing like the brilliant leaves falling around us. I pointed at them, naming them for the colors of autumn from my paint box.

"Scarlet lake, vermilion, rose madder," I called.

"And burnt sienna and alizarin," Mr. Howland added.

"All the colors of happiness," said Kate, coming from behind and startling us all.

When we lived in Boston, we attended the Unitarian church near us. We went a few times a year and forgot God in between. In Barbados, on Sunday, we used to read prayers on the gallery for the house servants and their families. I suppose I was really very ignorant in religious matters. But I did love the Christmas story, and anything about angels, and the few hymns I knew. Also I was curious about the Holy Ghost when I happened to think about it.

All this casual religion changed when we came to Amherst. God was everywhere, all week long. We attended the First Congregational Church every single Sunday, all four of us. Father pointed out the important Dickinsons: an older man with a fierce, vain face; a younger couple, quite stylish; and another youngish woman. The church itself was pale yellow Greek Revival, a grave and dignified building. The music was the best part.

But religion didn't stop there! Aunt Helen attended the church sewing circle, which seemed to have enormous authority and influence. Father joined a Bible study group and went off Tuesday evenings muttering darkly, "When in Rome..." Kate had a Christian youth group whose purpose was unclear, other than social. I went to Sabbath school, as did most of my class at the academy. I soon learned that Ruth and Naomi were pretty tame, after Europa and the bull—but I knew not to say so. I decided Job would have made a fine myth.

And God went to the academy with me too, every weekday. I was reminded that my school was founded by ministers who then went on to start the college to train young clerics. Almost forty years later, the college itself was less religious—but God still loomed over the academy, influencing each class. In geography, when we studied the Red Sea, we were told that Moses parted it. In botany, when we studied stamens and corollas, we were reminded Who created them.

One day at recess, Lolly and two other girls pulled me aside urgently. They giggled, and I practiced giggling too. "Miranda, tell us—have you professed?"

"I don't understand. My father's the professor, not me."

"Have you converted? Have you affirmed? Are you saved?" For some reason, I felt they were waiting for me to say the wrong thing.

"I don't know. I'll ask Father tonight."

When I did, not surprisingly, he handed the problem over to Aunt Helen. He gave her a look, and she sighed, but not very deeply. With the big house, and the hired girl to help her, and Kate's splendid education, doing Father's work for him occasionally was well worth it to Aunt Helen.

"Miranda, you're asking about conversion," she told me. "To experience conversion, you must truly believe in the Almighty."

"Well, I do—I think. What else?"

"Then you must confess all your sins and wickedness."

"What wickedness?" I was instantly indignant. "I haven't ever hurt anyone, not ever!"

Now my father was quietly amused. "You know, Helen, I think she's right."

"Jos, this is serious. I won't have you *mocking* conversion! You don't know the first thing about it," said Aunt Helen.

"Well then, let's do this properly," Father soothed her. "We should, you know. I believe Marian was considering conversion, right at the end. I'll have Philip Meeker, the college chaplain, come and talk to Miranda. He's the one to answer her questions." Ever the scholar, my father chose to consult the experts.

A few evenings later, Mr. Meeker called on us. He was well named; I could not imagine anyone meeker than this little rosy man. He was an unbroken pink all over, including his hair and his tiny hands, and he had a nervous stammer. The college students must have seemed like ravening wolves to Mr. Meeker.

Father and I led Mr. Meeker into the study, where Aunt Helen waited with tea. She gestured for Mr. Meeker to take a seat.

As he did, he beamed. "Professor Chase, such a p-p-privilege!" His eyes came to me; the crinkles around them deepened as he smiled even broader. "And how may I assist the young lady?"

I had spent the afternoon listing questions for him, so I was all prepared.

"Please, what are 'profession' and 'conversion'?"

Mr. Meeker's head bobbed as he nodded quickly; these were questions he had clearly answered before. He was prepared too.

"They represent the experience of recognizing the Lord and submitting to His will for you."

I considered this; it sounded like a ceremony. "Where do you do it?"

"You profess in a church."

"Like a wedding?"

"Not really; it's more solemn. The whole congregation is witness to your act of submission."

"I wouldn't want strangers; I'd sooner have just my friends and family."

My strong opinion on this matter stopped his nodding. "We are all God's family," Mr. Meeker assured me, turning a deeper pink. We appraised each other like duelists; then he tried a new approach.

"Your father tells me you are concerned about sin," he offered.

"I'm certainly *not!*" I replied hotly. "I told him I was sure I hadn't sinned yet. I know all those commandments from Sabbath school. I know perfectly well I haven't killed, or coveted, or committed whatever it is."

"Sometimes, in a very young person, we accept the possibility of future sins, for present contrition." We seemed to reach a truce here, so he went elsewhere. "Tell me, Miss Chase, do you accept our belief in Lord Jesus as the one true religion?"

This shocked me. "I couldn't ever do that! There are other religions every bit as good."

Now it was his turn to be shocked; Father and Aunt Helen were merely surprised.

"Then am I to understand that you, Miranda Chase, believe in gods other than our Lord and Christ His Son?"

I dug in my heels; no one was going to take Poseidon and Artemis away from me. "Yes, I certainly do."

"How many, may I ask?"

I tried to count up the population of Mount Olympus, and then there were all the heroes and the demigods. "About a hundred, more or less" was my rough estimate.

Mr. Meeker turned to Father for help, but he was wearing his aloof onlooker smile — so Mr. Meeker stammered manfully on.

"And have you ever t-t-taken part in the worship of these gods?"

I thought carefully. So far I had told the truth — but the truth had made him so absurd that I would never accept him as a religious tutor. I decided to tell a half-lie and end the interview.

"Yes, I have — often," I said sincerely, remembering the beautiful altar to Poseidon that Lettie and I had built at Learner's Cove. We decorated it with shells and seaweed, and brought tiny crabs and lizards as offerings.

Here endeth the lesson. Father patted and soothed and steered Mr. Meeker out the door. When he returned to the parlor, I expected a scolding, though I wasn't sure for what — except perhaps for having been a bully. However, I was merely sent up to bed. From the stairs, I heard bits and pieces of Father's conversation with Aunt Helen.

"Always so truthful...Barbados. Her nurse there...outgrow it.... Wait a year or two."

This was ridiculous; I was scornful that Father could make such a mistake. Of course, I knew all about voodoo; Lettie and I often talked about the ghosts and the goats and the little wax figures. But I had not meant that at all. I was standing up for my right to the Greek gods and goddesses, who were my pleasure and my property. More important, I was standing up for myself. Therein lay a discovery that no teacher, neither Mr. Harnett nor even Mr. Meeker, could condemn. Or a parent.

Then it struck me: I took a position and refused to budge — and I won! Just a year or two ago, little white mouse Ara would have turned tail and scuttled back up to her attic.

I ran in to tell Kate all about it, and she laughed herself breathless over my version of Mr. Meeker. Then I showed her a victory paean that Mr. Harnett taught me, and then we laughed some more.

The next day at recess, it was easy to tell Lolly and her group that my family had decided to defer my profession for a while.

"We're just going to think about it this winter," I reported gravely.

The girls approved this prudent approach.

"Goodness, it took me a whole year to make up my mind," Lolly assured me. "What's the rush? God can wait!"

The others gasped at her daring. I knew they would all be saying it by evening.

"Anyway, this isn't a good year for a conversion. Wait until a revival year, when everyone's doing it!" advised a red-haired girl.

It seemed agreed that I was behaving properly. Then we began to plan which afternoon they would come to my house. They wanted to watch Mr. Stokes, the barber, cut my hair.

This was the closest I had come to being revealed as an impostor—a changeling, masquerading as a New England fourteen-year-old. Apparently I did right in pretending a hesitation over the conversion. What if I had told my classmates the truth—that I preferred the Greek gods to Christianity? Every day, I learned more about hiding just how different I was.

Two days later, I came home from school and went into the kitchen for the cookies and milk Aunt Helen always had ready. On the table beside my mug, I saw a small envelope with my name on it. Inside I found a note written in a delicate script like a garland:

> *My dear Miss Chase,*
> *A rumor flew and lit at my window. Do you too refuse Salvation? Let us then consider Perdition together—here on Monday, at four o'clock.*
> *Your unprofessed friend,*
>
> *Emily E. Dickinson*

Aunt Helen found me munching cookies and puzzling over this.

I gave her the note. "I don't know what she means," I complained. "I wish she'd just come out and say what she wants."

"She must have heard about your encounter with poor Mr. Meeker, Miranda." She laid the note back down on the table.

"But how could she? She doesn't even know me."

"The small-town telegraph is speedier than Mr. Morse's. You'll see.... Even our thoughts are circulated, I vow."

At supper that night, Father was pleased and curious. It occurred to me that leaving Boston and his in-laws had made him very sociable. Perhaps he always had been on Mount Vernon Street too, and Mother didn't join him.

"Think of it as an honor," said Father. "I hear she's very particular and choosy. She never goes out and only sees a handful of people. The Dickinsons run Amherst and the college, you know."

I was still reluctant. "Isn't she very old?"

"About thirteen years older than you, I'd guess—but you always like older people, Miranda. Perhaps she'll lend you some books."

I really wished Father would say, "Don't go unless you want to." He should protect me! My school days were hard enough, trying to pass as a proper fourteen-year-old. Why did I have to go and meet some snobbish old maid?

Monday afternoon, I brought my atlas and my watercolors home from school. I started a map of the Mediterranean in geography and had come to the best part: the dark wavy band along the coastline. Should this be a Prussian blue or a daring viridian? I would much rather stay and work on my map than call on a stranger-lady who wrote so oddly.

But Aunt Helen repeated the Eleventh Commandment—"An engagement is an engagement"—and buttoned me into my Sunday dress, my favorite violet challis. It had stripes of tiny roses, pink and crimson, and flat velvet bows at the neck and wrists.

"You look more like Beacon Hill than Amherst," my aunt grumbled. She was openly opposed to this invitation. Her reaction made me more apprehensive but also more curious; what was there to disapprove of? When pressed, however, Aunt Helen just shook her head and murmured, "I suppose it will be all right."

Going cross lots through people's gardens, it took less than ten minutes from our house to the Dickinsons'. As I approached, I could see the scalloped white cupola and the four brick chimneys above the maples, which were almost bare after last night's windstorm. I came closer, and the big house itself appeared, as solid as the rock under our stage. I sensed that it too was rooted deep underground.

I had heard that the Dickinson family called their house "The Homestead," and it surely made a statement of ownership and permanence. The brick walls were painted custard yellow. There were many large square windows, with Hooker's green shutters and plain white tieback curtains. The front door had a small portico with four square columns. Someone was standing at an upstairs window, watching me.

I was prickly with unease as I went up to pull the bell. The black door was opened promptly by a smiling no-age lady with massed dark hair, like that of an Indian. I had seen her in church on Sundays.

"Come right in, we're expecting you," she declared. She gave my hand a firm grip, nearly tugging me inside. "You're really quite famous!"

I stood awkwardly in the spacious square hall, wishing I were less famous and back in my own house. Was this woman my hostess?

"Just go right up," the woman directed, waving to the stairs. "She has your tea all ready."

That answered one question—the woman beside me was not Emily Dickinson. Before I could introduce myself or say another word, I heard a door open, and I looked up to the landing. A small, slight figure—a woman? a child?—stood in a doorway against the light. Then there came a voice that I imagined I would remember as long as I lived: a voice like an alto recorder. It spoke softly, intimately, as if confiding in me only.

"Is that the damned soul who comes calling?"

I froze on the stair, stopped by this shocking statement. A flash of indignation flooded my body, turning my cheeks a hot red. If she believed me to be "damned," why had she invited me into her home? Could she be joking?

"Mr. Meeker would certainly call me that," I agreed, starting to climb the stairs again.

"I hear he exited MEEKER than he had entered," the voice answered, and I broke into delighted laughter as I stepped onto the second-story landing. Yes, I was laughing at the very moment I met Emily Dickinson.

She was about my height but much more delicately built. When she shook my hand, I felt tiny bird bones, as frail as Lettie's. She had thick hair—the color of autumn oak leaves—looped over her ears, and a lively, plain round face. She wore a simple white dress with a full pleated skirt and a glorious scarlet shawl.

She stepped backward into her room, and I followed. "Come to the window where I can see you, Miranda Chase." She smiled with faint apology. "My eyes are not on duty today."

It was hard to follow her particular mode of speech. Anyone else would have said, "I have poor sight," or "My eyes are bothering me." With her, the eyes became soldiers not doing their jobs. Is it some kind of code? I wondered. I was not sure I could learn to read it.

"It was autumn until you came," she told me cryptically. What could she mean now? This message was a little harder to decipher. Perhaps she referred to my dress?

"These are called Christmas roses," I told her. "My aunt Helen has promised to change the bows to red velvet at Christmas."

"What a fine thought! Did you know some birds change for Christmas too? They put on a regular pageant for me." She pointed to a window, where I saw a birdhouse with a feeding tray in the nearest maple.

"Now I want you to meet my room," Miss Dickinson said, spreading her arms out wide in an all-inclusive gesture.

I looked about, admiring the spaciousness, the three large windows (two facing south, one west). I liked the dainty little stove murmuring on the hearth, though the autumn afternoon was warm.

"A corner room, facing south—the best in the house," said my hostess proudly. "All my family insisted that I have it when we moved here two years ago."

This did not feel like the kind of house that anyone had acquired recently, but I let it pass. It might have been another coded signal I had missed.

"May I look at your books?" I asked. This should be safe.

"They would be very hurt if you didn't."

I smiled at the idea of the books having feelings and crossed to the shelves. I saw a few Shakespeare plays, and the sonnets; there was some Thackeray, and some poets I didn't know.

"Please, who is John Ruskin?"

"An observer, like you." She smiled like a cat with a secret and arranged our tea on a small side table. She watched me too. Now I knew who was at the upstairs window when I arrived.

"This is Father's favorite molasses loaf," she said, cutting a slice of the spicy cake. "I make it just for him."

"I think that you use the hymnal and the dictionary the most," I told Miss Dickinson, coming to join her. "They look the most lived-in."

She was charmed by this phrase of Aunt Helen's. "Let's be 'lived-in' friends, you and I," she suggested, handing me a cup of tea. "We already have a common bond: we're both unconverted sinners."

This recalled Mr. Meeker, who had brought me to this room and this meeting and this odd, oblique conversation.

"Did Mr. Meeker want you to profess too?" I asked.

A cunning look crossed her face. She gave a wry, pleased smile and leaned close to me. "Many better men than Mr. Meeker have tried to persuade me—men who were much closer to God than he is." She sat back up and sighed. "And friends I dearly loved—even my own brother. They were all after me like a pack of hounds. Yes, they hounded me."

I could see she liked the analogy. I did too. "And what did you do?"

"For years I would say 'perhaps' or 'soon.' I hid in thickets and underbrush, and doubled back on my tracks. But you were braver; you turned to face them and bared your teeth, didn't you?"

"But you really can't call Mr. Meeker a pack of slobbering hounds," I offered. "He's more like a puppy nipping at the heels."

To my delight, Miss Dickinson gave a bright, full-throated laugh—and at a joke of mine.

"That is certainly true," she replied, still laughing. "Not just a puppy. The runt of an albino litter."

We shared a wicked laugh together at poor Mr. Meeker's expense.

"Enough of our close escapes," Miss Dickinson said. "Now I would like to hear about your name. Miranda. Inspired by Bermuda and the bard?"

I was enchanted that she knew the private Shakespeare origin of the name Miranda. How had she guessed? By the time I had told her about our Shakespeare evenings in Barbados, and why I was there, and the James family, and the dolphins—by then, Miss Dickinson knew a good deal about me. She listened quietly, her head tipped, her hands clasped. She asked very few questions, but her alert, intent eyes compelled me to keep speaking.

"You are a regular Sinbad, a Gulliver," she said at the end. "Parts of that were very interesting."

I ducked my head in embarrassment. I deserved that; I had talked too much.

If she noticed my discomfort, Miss Dickinson made no mention. "Now, about next Monday afternoon — you will tell me every word you said to Mr. Meeker," she stated.

I was pleased — a repeat invitation meant I had neither bored my hostess nor behaved impolitely. And to think I had tried to find excuses not to come today! What a chance for interesting and amusing conversation I would have missed.

"That will be fine," I responded eagerly, "since Lolly and I have our recorder lesson on Tuesday."

This seemed a good time to leave, since I had made her laugh — and I had learned to talk less.

"Thank you for the lovely visit, Miss Dickinson," I said at the door to her room. I waited a moment, expecting her to walk me out, but she sat in her chair and never moved.

"I think you have always called me Emily," she replied very gravely. Then she turned her head to gaze out the window, and I left.

At supper that evening, everyone wanted to hear about my visit to the Dickinson house, The Homestead. I felt like a returning Marco Polo.

"Did you actually see the two sisters together?" Father asked. "They say Miss Emily never leaves her room."

"The lady who opened the front door must have been the sister," I replied. "But she sent me straight upstairs to meet Emily. She never told me her name."

"And what did you find to talk about, besides salvation?" Father asked. He smiled. "Or your lack of it?"

"Lots of things." Father's patronizing annoyed me, since he was the one who had pushed my acceptance of the invitation. "She didn't profess either, though everyone tried to make her. She told me she turned it down, over and over."

"Why did she want to see you?" Kate asked, trying to steer our talk elsewhere. Religion was not a subject for the table.

"I think she's lonely. She needs someone to speak her language."

"Doesn't she speak English?" Aunt Helen was intrigued.

"Not really. It all comes out *sideways.* She likes to pretend things have feelings, as though they're people. Sometimes she talks as if she were a thing, and sometimes as if things were people. And she accents the *oddest* words in a sentence — not the ones I would choose."

"Excellent, Miranda!" Father liked my description. "Miss Dickinson has been good for your conversation, anyway."

"Can you really understand this language of hers?" Kate asked later, when we were alone upstairs. I knew Kate would want to know more than the brief account given at the dinner table.

"Most of the time." I cocked my head, thinking back to the precarious balancing act of the afternoon's conversation. "I think...it's a game," I said finally, "and it's fun, when you know how to play."

"Do you really want to go again?" I could see Kate was concerned for me. "You know you don't have to," she continued. "Uncle Jos just wanted us to be on calling terms with the Dickinsons, and now we are. You've done that for him once, and that's plenty."

"I think I do want to go again." I tried to define my mixed feelings, and not just for Kate's benefit. "Miss Dickinson seems to read a lot of books; I like that. And she knew all about *The Tempest,* and Miranda!"

I saw Kate suppress a smile. "Well, then, of course you must return," she said. "She knows *Shakespeare!*"

We laughed together. It was a bit silly for me to put such store in Emily's knowledge of Shakespeare; most educated adult women would also have read the great writer.

"Emily's very...*different,*" I tried to explain. "And I am too. We have that in common. And that is an even deeper connection than a mutual admiration of Shakespeare."

Kate looked perplexed. "Why do you say that? You are no different than I am."

Dear Kate. She was so openhearted that she accepted me without noticing the accommodating she had been doing to include me. She saw only the Miranda she loved, not the Miranda who struggled to fit into the Amherst world.

"Besides," I continued, "I think she likes me."

"Why shouldn't she?" My loyal Kate flared up. "You're funny and fun and very kind. You'd make a wonderful friend for anyone. You're my best friend ever."

Smiling, blushing, listening to all this, I could almost believe her.

The next Monday afternoon, I made the same journey through the gardens of frostbitten chrysanthemums. I went up the walk at four o'clock, imagining I felt Emily's gaze on me from the upstairs window. I resisted looking up to check, fearing it would make me appear childish or self-conscious.

I presented myself at the front door. As before, the smiling lady—whom I now knew was probably her sister—answered.

"I am Miranda Chase," I announced. "Miss Emily Dickinson has invited me to call."

"Bless your heart, child!" she exclaimed. "You have better manners than I do! I'm Miss Lavinia, Emily's sister. Emily has told me all about how you will be visiting every Monday."

I tried not to show my surprise that these visits were now assumed to be a fact in my regular schedule. I let it go as Lavinia continued talking in a bustling, slightly giddy manner. She seemed excited by the prospect of Emily having a regular visitor; suddenly the thought of spending weekly afternoons with Emily excited me as well.

"You'll use the back door. That will be easiest." She pointed to a door in the back wall of the high square hall. "I'll leave it unlocked for you. Emily prefers the house to be locked if we go out. You will stay for two hours and then leave by the same back door."

She stepped to a side table and picked up a tea tray. "I will leave a tea tray at the bottom of the stair." She handed me the tray. "Take this up. I made you Emily's favorite honey cake."

I nodded, trying to remember all my instructions. As I went upstairs, I wondered why Miss Lavinia managed the arrangements for my visits, as if Emily and I were both ten years old. But Emily, waiting and smiling at the door of her room, was gleeful that her sister had handled this.

"Lavinia does all the plans for Mother and me," she confided. "Vinnie's plans are the sturdy kind—they stay made. Mine UNRAVEL."

I noticed Emily said her important words in capitals. I would have to try this myself. It gave her conversation such urgency.

"Now, what have you there?" she asked, nodding her head at the book tucked under my arm. "Is that a present?"

Father had inscribed one of the "presentation" morocco-bound copies of *The Great Plays,* his compendium of classical plays, for me to give to her.

"'To my daughter Miranda's friend, Miss Emily Dickinson, with high regard,'" she read. "What a treasure chest you bring! I have entertained only a few of the lesser gods till now, and I have always wanted to enlarge my Olympian acquaintance. May I take a moment from your visit to thank him?"

"Of course," I said. I stood, uncertain what to do while her attention was elsewhere.

Perhaps she noticed my discomfort; she handed me a small book. "Why don't you talk to Keats, Miranda, while I'm busy?" Emily smoothed her skirts and sat down at a little writing table between the two windows.

I smiled at the lovely idea that reading was a form of conversation with the author. This unique perspective of Emily's was exactly why I loved to read, but I could never have expressed this so well.

I opened the book and discovered it was a collection of poems, new to me. There was a spray of violets pressed at "Ode on a Grecian Urn," so I started there. The poem was so packed with language and jammed with girls and garlands and flutes and oxen that I forgot Emily and myself. When I returned to awareness, my little enamel watch, the Jameses' good-bye present, told me my time was up.

Emily sat at her desk, paper littering the floor surrounding her small feet. She must have felt my eyes on her, for she looked up from the paper she scrutinized and glanced at me. Consulting a small clock on her table, she cried, "Oh, Miranda, what have I done with our time?" She smiled then, and I knew she felt her own time had been well spent. "A lady must always thank a gentleman promptly," she said. "Of course I needed DIAMOND-CUT language for your father. All this"—she poked the papered floor with a disdainful slipper—"is merely GLASS, unfit for him."

She ignored the cold tea and cut a big slice of honey cake as I stood to leave. She handed me the letter she had written to Father.

"I know you had better company than me with Keats," she said. "But let's not invite him next week, Miranda. It will be we two ONLY."

After all that, her note to Father turned out to be only a line or two, in her fine flowering script.

My Dear Dr. Chase,
    What Company I keep these days! First you send me Miranda, and then her Olympian Cousins do your bidding. The view from my Window is far beyond Amherst now.
    Your very indebted,

                                   Emily E. Dickinson

At supper, Father skimmed this and handed it back. He seemed amused.

"She likes to keep a fellow on his toes, doesn't she? But I do appreciate a woman who doesn't gush and spew when she thanks you."

I decided not to tell him that she had used up two hours and a dozen sheets of paper on this little note.

Next week, as directed, I entered The Homestead by the stair hall door and started upstairs — but Emily was already there on the landing.

"I thought I would introduce you to the rest of my house," she explained. "It's a good afternoon; EVERYONE is out." She made it sound as if she lived with a jostling crowd of housemates, even though I knew it was only the two sisters and their mother at home. Emily's father traveled often, and Austin, her older brother, lived nearby. But this was all I knew.

I expected a sort of tour with stories, the kind Miss Adelaide gave to visitors at York Stairs, but Emily led me straight to the kitchen. This was square and sunny, with two windows on each side facing each other, like a ship's hull. There were cupboards, a marbled pastry table, hanging platters, and big pots of herbs. I had the sense of the place as a happy workroom.

"Here is my other refuge and domain," Emily told me proudly. "This is where I create, and this is where I get angry. I'm very good at BOTH."

It surprised me that she should proclaim her anger as if it were a badge of honor. "What makes you angry, Emily?" I asked, expecting to hear about the frustrations of cooking, a skill I had not mastered.

"Usually stupid people," she replied. As my father had observed, Emily was someone to keep one on one's toes.

"Sometimes people's cruelty angers me as well. Never events or things. I come here when I have anger to USE UP. Most women weep or turn on those nearby—the innocent bystanders. But I make PASTRY instead!" She stroked the marble tabletop lovingly. It was well used. She must get angry fairly often, I thought. Her solution seemed far more productive than pouting or crying or shouting.

She moved to a corner of the kitchen. "The next best thing for anger is churning butter," she said, gripping the thick wooden handle and demonstrating. "If I find myself CHURNING in the middle of the night, I make butter!" Laughing, she replaced the butter paddle. "I'm told you can hear me thumping away at midnight from the street, but I don't mind. This way I'm famous for my pastry and my butter, instead of my anger."

I liked this approach. Perhaps when I was frustrated by something Lolly had said, or was bothered by upsetting events, I could use the feelings in this way, rather than pretending they weren't there.

Emily led me down the hall, passing several rooms. "I won't bother to show you the dining room and the parlors," she explained. "I don't use them anymore." We stepped into a library that looked out onto Main Street. "This is the only other room I consider even partly mine," she declared.

If she felt any glimmer of ownership, she didn't display it. Emily stood in the center of the cold, standoffish room, where all the books were behind glass. She gazed about as if she were a guest or a stranger.

She eyed the books vaguely, curiously. "You know, I used to read all these once. Perhaps there are still great minds here." She turned and crossed to the piano. "And I used to play the piano to please Father—and then he would tell me what books to read. Actually he still does. He's here in this room right now." She shivered.

It seemed best not to argue this; besides, I could also feel a presence—no, that was not precisely accurate. What I felt was an absence, the lack of warmth, the lack of conviviality and engagement. Perhaps that lack is what Emily felt as her father. I could understand absence as presence—it defined my childhood. My mother's ghostly place in my life; my father's distracted, erratic participation. It occurred to me that Emily and I had more in common than books.

But I didn't feel I could discuss any of this with her. Not now. Not yet. I knew enough to take my cues from her as to how to proceed; this was the same caution and strategy that allowed me to present the appearance of fitting in here in Amherst.

I peered at the titles of the dark, uninviting volumes. I loved books, but behind glass they seemed more like objects to be looked at rather than enjoyed—no "conversations" with these authors!

I turned away from the case and looked out the window. Two cloaked and bonneted women were coming in the gate. Did my hostess expect them?

"Emily, I think you have guests," I said.

She turned so pale that I saw her whole round face was covered with tiny freckles, like a sprinkling of cinnamon on a custard. She grabbed my hand so suddenly and so hard that I cried out in surprise. We rushed up the stairs and fell inside her bedroom together.

Her panic was infectious—who could those women be? What was so frightening? "Emily—"

"Hush!" She locked the door and leaned against it, trembling and listening. I stood silent, my wide eyes upon her, wondering what sort of danger we might be in. I could hear voices downstairs. Worried, I waited for Emily's reaction.

"Thank goodness, it's just Mother and Vinnie!" Her color returned. "My, what a narrow escape! It could have been ANYONE, anyone at all." The crisis was over as suddenly as it had begun; she poured me a glass of cider and gestured for me to sit. I lowered myself to the chair, slowly regaining my equilibrium.

"As you can see," she said with complete composure, as if she hadn't dashed up the stairs moments ago in fear, "my house is really very SMALL."

Small indeed, I thought as I nibbled diamond-shaped molasses cookies. They were very thin; Emily must have been particularly angry yesterday. We discussed John Keats, his sad, narrow life, his wasted love for the unworthy Fanny Brawne.

"If Keats had only had a sweetheart like you or ME…" said Emily.

I giggled at the thought. Then I wondered—did Emily have any sweethearts? She was a grown-up lady; certainly there had been—or may currently be—some suitor. Emily might be a good source of information on the subject of courting, being older than Kate and Lolly but not as motherly as Aunt Helen. But the conversation wound back around to writing, to poetry, and then my time was up.

When I walked from Northampton Street to Main Street, coming east, I always passed a large unfinished gray-green house next to Emily's. It was somewhat foreign in style, with elaborate parapets and a big square watchtower; the rest was hidden by scaffolding. It was evidently so new and stylish, so exotic, so deliberately different from its plain Puritan neighbors, that I could not resist asking Emily about it. She must know her next-door neighbors, I thought. I had to pick and choose my questions carefully; after several of our visits, I had observed that Emily evaded direct questions whenever possible. I could usually be successful with only one or two at most per visit.

As was often the case, Emily's answer produced more questions. "That is Austin and Sue's Borgia palace," she informed me. I knew that Austin was Emily's older brother; Sue must be his wife. "They are building their home for strangers and COURTIERS. That is where Sue will hatch her plots and do her poisonings."

Whatever could Emily mean? She spoke as if her sister-in-law were planning to murder people! She made it sound as if they were all partaking in one of the history plays from Shakespeare, complete with intrigues and royalty. But I dared not ask any more, and once again the talk turned to books and words.

The Mondays continued, a punctuation of my week. I looked forward to them, even as they perplexed me. I was never relaxed with Emily as I was with Kate, and as I was beginning to feel with Lolly and my schoolmates. But the tension I felt as I approached The Homestead wasn't an uncomfortable tension—it put me in a heightened state and made me want to perform well. I wanted to try out new words and hear Emily's slantwise perspective on things, which somehow turned out to be precisely right, despite the unusual juxtapositions in her speech. As with my dear tutor Mr. Harnett, I wanted to soak up what knowledge Emily had to offer and prove a worthy student. I still didn't quite understand why she wanted to include me in her small world but was flattered beyond measure to have been brought into it.

Another Monday, when I returned our tea tray to the kitchen, I met someone new in the hall: a striking woman with Roman features and complicated terraced hair. She wore jet and braid and rustling taffeta like a city person. She smiled and put a finger to her lips—and she carried an envelope in Emily's writing. This must be Sue, she of the Borgia palace, collecting one of the many notes addressed to her that I had seen waiting on the card tray. She placed an envelope of her own on the tray and then vanished out the door, her dress whispering as she walked.

Why had she not made her presence known to Emily? And why would Emily write so often if she felt her sister-in-law was one of the dreadful and dangerous Borgias? When I asked Aunt Helen to explain all these mysteries, she was entirely informed!

"Let me try to explain the Dickinsons for you, Miranda dear. Mr. Edward Dickinson, the father, is a lawyer. He has also served as the treasurer of the church and the college, and is the wealthiest man in Amherst. He is Amherst's leading citizen."

I imagined this was why Father had encouraged my encounter with Emily. He was eager to fit in too!

"There are three grown children," Aunt Helen continued. "First there is Austin, the son, whom the village calls 'Mr. Austin' to distinguish him from his father. He is a lawyer too; he works in his father's office. He recently married Susan Gilbert, an old school friend of Miss Emily's. You have seen them in church."

I nodded. Of course, that was where I had seen the woman before. Emily never attended but most of her other family did.

"The young couple were going to move to Michigan after the wedding, but Mr. Dickinson promised to build them a showplace mansion if they'd only stay here." Aunt Helen delivered a Unitarian sniff. "I call that vulgar house more *eyesore* than showplace!"

"Is there anyone else in the family?" I asked. Despite Emily's description of her world as being small, The Homestead could certainly accommodate many relatives.

"Well, there are the two unmarried sisters, Emily and Lavinia. Then there's their mother, Mrs. Dickinson, who's very..." Aunt Helen paused, searching for the right word. "Who's very sad, I would say. Miss Lavinia takes care of her."

"She does? But I thought she took care of Emily."

Aunt Helen sighed again. "She tends to them both. It's such a familiar sad story, the spinster sister who helps everyone and never has her own life. Miss Lavinia was engaged a few years back, but nothing came of it. Then her beau married another girl. We'll never see her wedding."

I was astounded, as always, by Aunt Helen's boundless store of facts about people she had never met. "How do you know all this?"

She put down the scalloped pink shawl she was crocheting for Kate and concentrated on her answer.

"Let me tell you about how gossip works in a small town like Amherst, Miranda. We women have to live very closely and help each other out on short notice. We have to know what to watch out for and what to expect—so we can be ready when someone needs us."

I puzzled over this. It sounded like a wonderful way to be, yet I wasn't sure how I felt knowing that there were people in Amherst who knew about my family in the way that Aunt Helen knew about the Dickinsons.

Aunt Helen must have sensed my deliberations. She weighed in with her own judgment. "Just remember, Miranda, the only bad gossip is the kind you make up."

"And does everyone always get to hear about everything?"

"Sooner or later, Miranda. Sooner or later, they do." She picked up Kate's shawl and went on working, smiling to herself. For a moment she made me think of Miss Adelaide. How they would enjoy each other! How happy I was to have them both in my life.

Fall hurried toward winter, and I hurried too. The week could barely contain all the people and events that came rushing toward me, those late autumn days. When I packed my schoolbag in the morning, crowding in my recorder, my atlas, my paints, my pencils and pens, my lunch, my loathed math workbook, my textbooks, and a clean pinafore if I was going on to tea—when I did this, I could not quite believe how smoothly my life had flowed into this new channel and its several branches.

By now I had worked out a strategy for life at the academy. I stressed my similarities with my classmates and concealed as well as I could my differences. I had grown quite fond of pretty, dark Lolly, with her tipped nose and her lively wit. I didn't mind taking her orders; they helped me to know what to do. I was becoming very skilled at producing the right Miranda.

For one thing, I discovered that mentioning visits to The Homestead had a complicated double response; it made me stand out in a way I had been trying to avoid, so I decided to imply, if asked, that they were a duty imposed on me by Father and Aunt Helen for some vague adult reason and that they were even a little distasteful. The ruse seemed to work, and I received looks of sympathy rather than resentment if I had to turn down a Monday invitation.

I loved writing Miss Adelaide about my new life, and reading her comments. She was enthusiastic about my new family, my school, my teachers—but less so about Emily:

> *I hope you will use your friend Miss Dickinson as a literary companion only, without letting her overinfluence your life. Her habits suggest an unhappy person who avoids reality. You are entirely without artifice and therefore defenseless against the purposes of devious people.*

I could not conceive of any motive or purpose Emily might have for our visits other than companionable literary talk, so I simply answered Miss Adelaide that I would indeed take care not to be overinfluenced, and then I changed the subject to Halloween. I had been disappointed by this, for I had always heard stories about my Boston cousins' costumes and gala parties. But my father explained that the Amherst Unitarians, the strict Congregational elders who had founded the academy and the college, and a group that included Edward Dickinson, believed every holiday should be a sacred festival only.

"Those sour old Puritans are simply opposed to fun," he grumbled. "At least they permit us some beauty, which was more than their ancestors did. Have you ever seen a lovelier church?"

Of course I never had, and I shared his enthusiasm; our columned First Congregational Church was Greek Revival at its purest and finest. When Mr. Howland completed our two wings and added the portico, our new house would look like the First Congregational Church's younger brother.

Our young architect came to Thanksgiving dinner with us and asked that we call him "Ethan." For the first time, I met a group of my father's students and found them easy and amiable. They enjoyed the riddles and limericks I had collected at school—but not as much as they enjoyed singing harvest hymns with Kate. She wore a new dress of deep rose velvet with a hoop and looked like a Christmas rose herself. Her cloud of dark hair was drawn back with a black velvet bow, and her sculpted oval face was flushed from the songs. She was quiet as ever, except when she sang; she was unaware that none of us could take our eyes off her.

Before the party, Aunt Helen and Kate gave me the easiest jobs for preparing our feast—like peeling and mashing—and I learned by observing them as we went along. As I watched them turn out the orange-spiced yam pudding and cranberry relish for the next day's dinner, I told them about my work with flowers and Miss Adelaide. They insisted that I create a harvest centerpiece. So I took out my shears and twine and made a long S of pine boughs and laurel, and placed dark Winesap apples along the curve, and to this added little scarlet crab apples, pinecones, and nuts. Aunt Helen and Kate praised my decoration, so I made a small wreath for Emily from the same materials. I brought it to her the moment I was done.

She gave me no thanks for this. "Miranda, you have put me down right in the middle of a QUANDARY! If I put your wreath on my door, it would be a lie. I do not ever intend 'Welcome.' For me, the key that seals my door opens the one to FREEDOM. And I can't hang it in my room either, for there I welcome no one but you."

Suddenly, and for the first time, I was tired of the whole business.

"I'll just put it at the foot of the oak tree on the east corner," I told Emily, gathering up my things. "The squirrels come there for acorns. They'll like the nuts for a Thanksgiving treat."

I walked briskly home. Tears stung my eyes, though I was fairly certain their source was the vicious wind. If emotion was the culprit, it would be anger, not disappointment or hurt feelings.

Emily needed only to have kept the wreath up for an hour, I thought. Just until I went home. What harm would it have done to be gracious, to tell a courteous lie to spare someone's feelings? I realized Emily was unaccountably rigid in her sense of integrity, in her unwillingness to compromise even the tiniest bit to perform an act of social nicety. I couldn't decide if her behavior was to be admired or admonished; I did know I felt my own gesture unappreciated.

This Thanksgiving wreath began a season of messages sent through style. As Christmas neared, each house displayed its family's position in decoration. I had worried that Puritan severity would limit our celebrations, then I discovered that only ribbon was never used by the most strict of families. Thus the degree of worldliness in a household was clearly stated by the wreath on the door.

The Dickinson mansion wore a spray of pine, with a discreet cluster of pinecones and no ribbon at all. However, The Evergreens, Mr. Austin Dickinson's showy Italianate villa next door, flaunted a huge circle of crimson velvet bows and streamers, with scattered glitters in between.

These last were not clearly seen from the street. When I described The Evergreens' wreath to Emily, she begged me to get a closer look. On my way home in the dusk, I went up Mrs. Austin's front walk, and I found that the trinkets were bulging silver cherubs, hoisting golden trumpets. When I described them to Emily, she was enchanted.

"They sound like that vulgar German blown glass to me," she gloated. Despite her condemnation of the ornaments as vulgar, there was delight in her tone. "You know, I really ADMIRE Sue. When she wants to say something, she makes herself HEARD!"

This was how I learned that Emily loved the small revelation, the telling detail. She had plenty of gossip from her sister and brother, from the hired girl and the stableman, but she was a natural collector of trivia and symbols, and hungered for the harvest of a keen eye. I began to gather them for her as I once gathered shells on the beach. These scraps, sprinkled in my letters, amused Miss Adelaide too, and I found that by seeking out these items to share, I was more fully aware in my own present. I had the opportunity to live my life twice—once in the moment and again in my retelling.

The snow came on casually, an inch here or there. We could still get about town easily. The days were clear and windless. I enjoyed the clean brilliance, the untrampled snow, unstained by the soot I remembered in Boston. Every day, I knew more faces to greet in the village or the classroom.

Lolly Wheeler and I had learned some carols on our recorders. Father suggested that Kate practice them with us; the sound was glorious. When I mentioned this to Emily, she asked if we would come to The Homestead and present our Christmas music.

"My good friends often come to play and sing for me," she assured me. "I can hear everything from the landing."

The others were willing after a proper invitation arrived. This was partly to see The Homestead, which aroused such speculation, and partly because it would please me to please my new friend.

Lolly came to Northampton Street at six. By chance, we all owned long velvet dresses; Kate and I had deep pink, and Lolly's was gold.

Of course Kate outshone us, with her young lady's figure and that arresting face. Father escorted us all. The houses we passed had candles in their windows, making halos on the snow. Aunt Helen and I competed to choose the most austere Puritan tree. Some had tinsel and stars and carvings; others had popcorn and cranberries only. I tucked this detail away for Emily.

Miss Lavinia came to the door and greeted me like an old friend. She put our cloaks on the sea chest in the hall. The Austin Dickinsons invited us into the parlor; Mr. Edward Dickinson was grave and steely eyed. He examined us carefully, as if looking for flaws in merchandise. There was no visible Mrs. Dickinson Sr., and we were given no explanation for her absence. Is it poor health or poor manners that keeps her in her room? I wondered. The parlor, I noticed, was barely festive, with greens over the doors and mantel but—as I had expected—no ribbons and no tree.

Sue Dickinson showed us a place to stand. I tried not to be nervous; after all, I had performed for far more people in our Shakespeare evenings in Barbados. There was something about the austerity of the place that made me feel so formal. But Lolly was excited—she always enjoyed being the center of attention—and Kate was serene as usual, simply enjoying an opportunity to sing among those she loved.

We did "The First Noel" and "Hark! The Herald Angels Sing." Then, to please Father, we presented *"Adeste Fidelis."* Kate sang "The Holly and the Ivy" alone; "What Child Is This" was her encore. We made not a single mistake, and everyone clapped. I could tell from Father's face and Aunt Helen's warm smile that we had made them proud. We drank Madeira like the grown-ups and ate Emily's fruitcake, which was heavily laced with brandy. Success!

I slipped out to the hall and looked up to see Emily, comfortable in a chair at the banister. She beckoned me closer, as conspiratorial as a spy.

"Tell your cousin I once heard Jenny Lind in Northampton," she whispered. "I judge your Kate to be far SUPERIOR to the Swedish Nightingale."

I was twice surprised: that Emily should have ever ventured so far and that she had such praise for Kate.

Back in the parlor, I found Mrs. Austin waving her fan and her eyelashes at Father. I sensed a strong will, a character to be reckoned with. She could make a mincemeat pie of the Dickinson sisters and eat it for Christmas dinner. Perhaps Emily was right to be wary.

"How you honor our little college in the woods, dear Professor Chase!" Sue Dickinson trilled. "Do you think we could lure Mr. Bulfinch here some evening to address our students?"

My father bowed; he was enjoying this. "He will come at your summons, madam; you have my word."

She tipped her fan. It was as entertaining as watching a play—how could Emily *bear* to miss this? Kate came to stand by Father, and Mrs. Austin ran a light hand along her cheek. "Andrea del Sarto," she murmured. Then Mrs. Austin turned brisk and businesslike.

"Professor Chase, my husband and I are having a small housewarming Christmas night. Could I persuade you and Mrs. Sloan and the young ladies to attend? Our guests would love to hear their charming music. President Stearns and other faculty friends are coming. So are representatives of Amherst's oldest families. This program would give them all so much pleasure!"

Father was smoothly elusive. "My sister and I will have to confer. Our girls are very young, you know."

We rounded up Lolly, who had been enjoying a second slice of cake (or was that a third?), and told her about the invitation. Walking back to Amity Street, Kate, Lolly, and I pleaded for Father's approval of the invitation. This would be our family's first party in Amherst.

When Father and Aunt Helen "conferred," she disapproved. Mrs. Austin announced her social ambitions too nakedly for my aunt's taste.

"They're not our sort, Jos. Why expose our girls to that rackety fast set?"

"Helen, I may not want to see this crowd as a regular thing, but I'm going to look them over. I want a foot in a lot of doors!"

"Perhaps the Wheelers won't approve either."

"Helen, that's ridiculous. Leslie Wheeler is in the Math Department. He's not going to insult Edward Dickinson's daughter-in-law. I mean this: I'm taking the girls."

So on Christmas night—without Aunt Helen—we crossed the village green and saw the constellation of lights that marked The Evergreens. Father laughed quietly at the rococo wreath of cherubs. Mrs. Austin opened the door, wearing décolleté black velvet with an enormous hoop.

"Winterhalter should be here tonight to paint your portrait," Father complimented our hostess.

"The empress won't let him out of Paris," she bantered back.

Mrs. Austin had made us three charming holly wreaths with pink and red ribbon streamers. She tied more ribbons on our recorders. The wreaths pricked a bit but probably less than a crown of thorns! I knew her abundant use of ribbon was a statement that I would again tuck away for Emily to decipher.

Our hostess led us through a noisy, glittering parlor or two. We came to a music room, crowded with smiling, formally dressed strangers. We reached a bay window with green velvet hangings. Mrs. Austin introduced us clearly and graciously, each by her full name—and we started the first carol. Luckily, we began before I had a chance to get nervous!

After our program there was real applause, as in a theater, and a buzz of compliments. I was puzzled that Mrs. Austin got as much praise for inviting us as we did for performing. Then Father escorted us to the dining room, blazing with red candles in elaborate candelabra.

The Yuletide feast featured a golden goose and oyster chowder, and bowls of steamed gingerbread pudding with creamy vanilla sauce. There were hot buttered cider and citrus-spiced tea, and more tarts, cakes, and jellied candies than I had ever seen in one place before. Kate rolled her eyes at me and at the extravagance of this non-Unitarian feast.

I tried to remember everything, to tell Emily, but the food was deceptive. Everything was decorated and molded into geometric shapes, and concealed in aspic or whipped cream. At home and at York Stairs, you could always tell what you were eating.

Father introduced me to President Stearns, who looked kindly and devout, and wore spectacles shaped like teardrops.

"Are you Ethan Howland's particular friend?" he asked me.

"He is our architect," I replied, confused. I liked Mr. Howland, but I wouldn't describe him as my "particular friend." "Do you mean Kate?" I asked.

"Ah, the beauty." President Stearns nodded. "Then you must be the clever person who got rid of the rock in the drawing room."

"Without once using gunpowder!" Father was delightful—relaxed and festive. He must have been happy to have new friends too.

It was glorious to be teased and included. It was pleasant to walk home under high, flickering stars, warm inside with eggnog and compliments. I had been to a Christmas party and was already invited to next year's. I had a family; I had friends and a school. Soon we would have our own house. As we began 1858, we were joining the circle that was Amherst.

Book IV

AMHERST
1858

Eighteen fifty-eight came down like a wolf on the fold. January attacked and stunned us. It was winter in its purest form, of an intensity new to me. In Boston there were very few places I needed to be, and haunted by the specter of consumption, we simply stayed indoors. The city seemed drab but manageable. Here in Amherst, winter was an invader, an occupying army. Every sunless day, the dark sky threatened or dropped snow. The defeated evergreens were burdened and bowed. All sound was muffled; even sleigh bells rang hollow and distant.

School was closed. I missed Miss Lowe, my classmates, the hum and shuffle in the halls. When Father rented a sleigh on Monday to go to his college office, he agreed to drop me off at Emily's. Because of the weather, it had been a few weeks since our last meeting. I was astonished at her delight in seeing me. Perhaps I was a more significant event in her schedule than I knew.

"How did you manage to leave your igloo?" Emily cried. "Oh, Miranda, I need you for my snowdrop—my reminder there is LIFE under all this! January has always been my nadir."

"I've been lonely too," I responded, removing my coat. I stomped my feet to knock off more snow. "I miss Lolly, though we try to walk back and forth when we can. And I've missed you, Emily." The moment I said it I realized it was true. Emily's company was like none other that I enjoyed. I loved Aunt Helen and Kate, and I enjoyed the fun of Lolly and the girls at school. But my visits with Emily were different. She was a singular experience, an arena in which to test words and concepts, a companion in the way characters in my favorite books were.

"I never said I was lonely," Emily corrected me. "I've spent years learning to be a solitary, you know. But January in Amherst is very like a tomb, a white TOMB—and there will be no snowdrops calling in there."

Her image amused me; it seemed so overly dramatic. "I know what you mean, Emily. I don't like it when it's too quiet either." I suppressed a smile. "But it doesn't make me think about *death*."

"Sometimes that's all I think about." Emily sighed and looked out at the hedge, sagging under its weight of snow. "Death has always been close by. I've known it almost as long as I have known myself."

This surprised me—from what I knew of the family, all were living. There were no lost siblings in this household as there were in so many other families.

"When I was a very small girl, not yet three, I spent a spring in Monson with my aunt, Mother's sister," Emily explained. "That was truly a HOUSE OF DEATH, Miranda.

"My uncle had just died of consumption. His wife, my aunt, was dying too, and one of their little children had it. And my own dear cousin, who was like a sister to me, was infected too. She died while we were still at school together."

I sat riveted, no longer feeling the cold in my feet. This could be my own story. This was an experience Emily and I shared.

"Everyone was more or less dying," Emily continued. "In that house, Death had always just left the room—but he hadn't gone far. And there was a custom in those days that no dying person should ever be left alone. We called it 'keeping watch.' So I often sat up at night with some-one who was dying, and once that person was a CORPSE by morning. I was four years old."

"How terrible for a young child!" I exclaimed, a bit more passion-ately than I intended.

Emily gave me a soft smile. "January always reminds me of that death-in-life time."

I was moved by her story, but for some reason I chose not to confide that consumption stalked my house too. Something held me back. Perhaps it was the relish with which Emily seemed to regard death's hovering presence.

Emily studied me a moment longer. "I am not very old—did you know I am twenty-seven? But I have already lost three beloveds from my dearest CIRCLE. These three are with me every day. I see them more clearly than those who remain."

Then I looked so downcast that she called me "a regular catafalque" and was pleased when I did not know the word.

"Now wouldn't that be a fine name for a *cat,* I ask you!" She took both my hands in hers—a rare physical gesture. Her hands were small but strong. "I must cheer you! And myself. We are not to succumb to the wintry solemnity. How can I spark this winter day?"

She stood and bustled about her room as if seeking inspiration. "If there must be winter, let us find in it some beauty! Or entertainment." She clapped her hands together as if she were a little child. "I have just the thing."

Her excitement was contagious, as so much was with Emily. When she felt sad, I felt sad; if she felt gay, suddenly my spirits lifted.

"What brightens the doldrums of winter?" she asked in a teasing voice. "Valentines! This is the true reason for the holiday being celebrated in stark February. To bring us some color."

She went to her bureau and brought out a big flowered box of old valentines. She sat at the desk chair, holding the box on her lap.

"They're so pretty," I said, carefully lifting a few delicate paper hearts from the box. As I examined the intricate paper cutting, Emily rummaged through the collection, seeming to search for a particular example.

"Here we are!" she said triumphantly.

I gently laid the hearts on the side table. Emily handed me a small newspaper bearing the college seal. "This is the *Indicator,*" she explained. "It used to be the college student publication. Look on page two, at the top."

There was a box, bordered with hearts and flowers, and a witty parody of a valentine.

Sir, I desire an interview; meet me at sunrise, or sunset, or the new moon — the place is immaterial. In gold, or in purple, or sackcloth — I look not upon the raiment. With sword, or with pen, or with plough — the weapons are less than the wielder. In coach, or in wagon, or walking, the equipage far from the man. With soul, or spirit, or body, they are all alike to me. With host or alone, in sunshine or storm, in heaven or earth, some how or no how — I propose, sir, to see you.

And not to see merely, but a chat, sir, or a tete-a-tete, a confab, a mingling of opposite minds is what I propose to have. I feel sir that we shall agree. We will be David and Jonathan, or Damon and Pythias, or what is better than either, the United States of America. We will talk over what we have learned in our geographies, and listened to from the pulpit, the press and the Sabbath School.

The delightful letter frothed and bubbled on, full of literary and political jokes and veiled flirtation. It ended:

> *But the world is sleeping in ignorance and error, sir, and we must be crowing cocks, and singing larks, and a rising sun to awake her; or else we'll pull society up to the roots, and plant it in a different place.... We will blow out the sun, and the moon, and encourage invention. Alpha shall kiss Omega—we will ride up the hill of glory—Hallelujah, all hail!*

"What a perfectly charming girl!" I exclaimed. I wished I had the talent to have written the piece.

"The editor agreed with you," Emily said. "Read just above the valentine border."

Sure enough, the smitten young man had stated longingly:

> *I wish I knew who the author is. I think she must have some spell, by which she quickens the imagination, and causes the high blood to "run frolic through the veins."*

"She certainly knew how to keep him interested!" I let out a romantic sigh. "What a wonderful way to meet and to fall in love. Oh please, tell me that they did!"

"Yes and no." Emily enjoyed teasing me, and in this instance, the game was one we could both enjoy. This wasn't always so. "That is, they met many times, but he never knew she had written that valentine letter to the *Indicator.* He thought she was just his classmate's sister. Actually, he came to the house often in those days."

My eyes widened with the realization of the author's identity. "Emily, you wrote it! You wrote that valentine!"

"Of course." She smiled an impenetrable smile. I couldn't interpret it at all. Was she pleased that she had tricked the boy? Or was she pleased that she had shown me some of her writing and I enjoyed it? More likely, it was her tantalizing storytelling that pleased her—my eagerness to learn more.

"Why didn't you tell him? There he was, madly desiring to meet you and all set to fall in love with you." I crossed my arms and gave her a look of grave certainty. "I can tell."

Emily turned to her window and looked out on the silent white village, its web of secret lives hidden in the deep snow.

"I had many reasons, Miranda. I knew my conversation, face-to-face, could not live up to my writing. I was sure he would prefer the lively flirt he imagined to the girl he already knew—the plain, *freckled* Miss Dickinson."

"Oh, that wouldn't have been true," I protested. "He would have adored you." I held out the newspaper as if the printed words would verify my opinion. "His response makes that clear."

"You are young, Miranda."

I took a step back and placed the newspaper on the table with the other valentines. Emily had never held up my age as a barrier to my understanding before. Then, we rarely discussed beaux—and in that area, I certainly *was* young. She could teach me, perhaps, but I was uncertain if I wanted those lessons to come from Emily.

"I was no recluse in those days," Emily reminded me. "I was quite the BELLE of Amherst! There were young people in and out of our house all day and all night. I played the piano for polkas and reels, and I wrote all the songs and charades.

"But I soon saw I didn't have the particular thing that DRAWS men. I used to study those other girls—the beauties, the ones people fell in love with. They had more than charm; they had an intense FATAL quality, a way of promising everything to a man. You must know what I mean. They say your cousin has it."

Emily was right; Kate did. And I knew I was learning something valuable from Emily, even if I couldn't define what it was.

"Well, for me—this was impossible. I could not REVEAL myself. I could not let anyone come close. I can't stand people CROWDING me. So I became everyone's confidante and adviser and go-between. I even wrote several ardent proposals!" She grinned; she could read the disbelief on my face.

"Anyway, I was safer this way." She shivered slightly and left the window. "Without the clutter of romance, I have more ROOM for true friendships in my life."

This puzzled me. As far as I knew, she saw no one. But I could be mistaken. Did I dare ask another question? She had never talked this freely about her personal relations. This side of her was new to me; I pressed on. "Do you have many men friends, Emily?"

"Indeed I do, a whole tapestry of them — and of a finer weave than schoolboy homespun." She was very smug now. "My friends tell me their PERSONAL hopes and aspirations. They do not waste our time together talking about DOILIES."

She spat out the word, scorning the trivialities these men doubtless discussed with any woman but Emily.

I could barely contain my curiosity. Was Emily-the-recluse merely a pose? "Do you meet these men often?"

"Whenever they choose to write to me. We are in constant touch."

She must have misunderstood me. "Do they ever come to The Homestead, I mean."

Now her eyes widened as if my question were surprising. "They're sorry if they do. I see no one; you know that. If we met tête-à-tête, I might fall into 'doily' talk myself — and our friendships would never recover. I keep my men friends by keeping them AWAY."

So that was her strategy: men as friends through their letters only! I could have talked all afternoon, making these giant strides in knowing Emily, but I heard a sleigh jingling outside. I crossed to the window and saw Father driving up the Main Street hill in the dusk with enormous dash and skill; I hoped Lolly looked out and saw his fine style.

Emily gave me a farewell touch — the second moment of physical contact in this meeting. These were rare; they underscored the intimacy of the territory we trod today. Usually she permitted only the least possible contact, rarely more than a pat on the shoulder. This was so unlike the embraces of my schoolmates. Lolly and I walked arm in arm; we hugged when we shared news. Kate and I lay side by side on a bed, holding hands and discussing our dreams, our lives. Despite Emily's objection to winter, her personal style was more like that of a restrained winter garden than that of the lushness of spring.

Placing her hand on my shoulder, Emily said, "If you can leave the North Pole next week, I'll try to find another surprise for you. But remember, these things are between the two of us ONLY!"

I felt flattered by her trust and promised her my total discretion. She counted on me, she confided in me — we were equals. I felt mature in her orbit.

Riding home in the sleigh, carpet tucked up under my chin against the cold, I pondered this talk of men friends and valentines. Lolly had begun lately to whisper about boys in our class, and I had noticed a distracted quality to Kate. I wondered if our architect, Ethan, had something to do with that. I had noticed that he had been staying more often for dinner and that Kate had been taking extra care with her appearance.

Would there be someone for me to send a valentine to this coming holiday? I stamped a path to my door. No likely prospects leapt to mind. This was something to discuss with Lolly—what was the proper behavior? I would have to observe the customs very closely to produce the correct Miranda now!

There was one more wild blizzard, and then our winter was tamed. All the footpaths were kept open by our squeaking, trudging boots, and the streets and lanes were packed down by ringing sleighs. We swept the farm ponds clear, and I learned to skate well enough—but sledding was my true joy. I could not get enough of the slow, portentous start, the gathering speed, and then the headlong downhill flight I discovered that sledding was intensely social; it changed us all.

The boys from the academy, so childish and clumsy in class, were suddenly mature and competent in the snow. Their vivid scarves and sweaters set off their clear, rosy skin; their bright hair was encrusted with snow crystals. They were protective on the runs, gallant as they towed our sleds back uphill. They behaved like courteous men. I felt I had never met a single one of them before.

"You shouldn't hide your hair," said Caleb Sweetser, pulling off my stocking cap. At school, he barely noticed me—so I must have seemed different too. Perhaps valentines would be in order after all.

The boys made us big snapping fires at the top of the hill. We brought stone bottles of hot cocoa from home and leaned them by the fire. We stood about between runs, blowing clouds of steam at one another as the drinks warmed us. Caleb was St. George, I was the dragon, and he chased me, laughing, around the flames.

The older single crowd sledded at the college, and the babies had their little safe hill in another place entirely, so we had our own noisy, mittened world all to ourselves. Above us a company of crows cast elliptical shadows on the snow, their cawing piercing the cold air in exultation. This was our kingdom, our domain; this was ours.

When I described all this in my letters to Miss Adelaide, she wrote me: "This is the life I wanted for you! You have so much to offer, dear Miranda—and this young society will make you see how attractive and engaging you are."

Kate came with me to Prospect Hill once or twice, and each time she disappeared. The second time this occurred, I confronted her in her room as she prepared for bed.

"Kate, where do you go? Are you sledding with Ethan?"

Her face told me the answer to that was yes. "Tell me!" I implored her, pouncing onto her bed. "What is going on?"

"I can't, Miranda. I don't know myself!" She sank onto the bed beside me. "It's so strange. I think about Ethan most of the time I'm awake. I just go over and over the same thoughts. You'd think I'd wear them out!"

"But what are they?"

She lay down and gazed at the ceiling. "Oh, I think about the place where his hair grows in a little whirlpool at the back of his neck—and I think about his back. It's warm and hard when I hold him on the sled, and I can feel his heart beating right through his sweater." She turned to face me. "It's true, Miranda. Our attachment is real. More than air to breathe or food or drink, I crave the sight of him."

I rolled onto my stomach and straightened her long hair on the pillow. I nodded, understanding yet not quite understanding her feelings.

Kate sighed. "If you have guessed, others shall as well."

I mentioned President Stearns's remark about Ethan's "particular friend" at the Christmas party.

A frown creased her high forehead. "Now that we are found out, I will have to talk to Uncle Jos. Do you think he will mind?"

"That his architect has found a form more perfect than the house he's designed?" I shook my head and smiled. "He won't notice—or if he does, he won't care. He's done his duty. Now Aunt Helen can do the worrying!"

I didn't discover what, if anything, Father or Aunt Helen had to say about the special friendship between Ethan and Kate. I noticed that Ethan's frequent visits were greeted with a small, secret smile on Aunt Helen's part and a vague, interrogative stare from my father. That was all.

We mourned that our merry month of February was ending, and after much consultation with both Lolly and Kate, I decided to send no valentines. I received three: one from Kate, one from Miss Adelaide, and one from Emily.

There was no good sledding in March, and to compensate I told Emily about the pleasures of Prospect Hill, as if in the telling I could relive the fine adventures. Emily became nostalgic about her own girl-hood in Amherst.

"It was the Goodnows' hill in those days," she said. "The whole month of February was a GALA for me and my friends. We had our parties and hayrides and charades all year, but February was the SOCIAL time. What a lively crowd we were!"

"Tell me about them, Emily." I was always interested in hearing about Emily's life before I had known her. I was curious about why she had retreated so far from the world and who she had been before she had.

"I had two particular friends, Miranda: Abby Root and Mary Warner. We were INSEPARABLE. People called us the 'Heavenly Triplets'!"

"What happened to Abby and Mary?"

"Abby married a minister, a missionary. They are off in some Arabian NIGHTMARE, converting the heathen."

She made such a funny, horrified face that I burst out laughing. "And what about Mary?" I asked as I gulped for breath.

"She's still in Amherst, they say. I think I heard she was engaged to a Mr. Crowell at the college."

"Mr. Edward Crowell? Why, he's in Father's Classics Department." This pleased me. "So you do have one 'Triplet' friend still!"

She shook her head sadly. "Not really, Miranda. I have found the marriage of a friend to be the death of a friendship. People change; time changes them. I have written Mary sometimes, but I do not see her anymore."

"Well, I can tell you that when Lolly and I grow up, if we are both still living here, we'll see each other just the way we do now."

Emily rose and went to the south window, where frenetic sparrows were rocking the bird feeder.

"Come and see something, Miranda."

I crossed to stand beside her, looking out into the twilight. Did she want me to watch the birds?

"I still do see my friends," Emily said softly. "Here we are now, the three of us, coming back from the academy with our books on a sled. We are going to Mary's to make a snowlady with a calico apron!"

"Do you like our new stocking caps? We all got matching red ones from Mr. Cutler's—but I've already lost the tassel on mine."

As Emily spoke, I shared her vision. I could see the three little girls there below us, laughing and pulling a ghostly sled along Main Street—in the faint blue dusk of a winter long ago. I was deeply struck by the power of words to capture the scene; by Emily's ability to transport me to her own childhood; and by the vivid presence of Emily's past in Emily's present.

Since the Monday afternoon when Emily described her friendships with men—and I learned that they were entirely on paper—I found my mind kept returning to her solitude. I thought of the correspondents she named for me proudly: all successful and worldly men. I saw that these editors, ministers, and authors were the company Emily chose to keep. This was where she saw herself, rather than in the limited society of Amherst.

No one could deny that the Dickinsons were the leading family in the village. Emily was frank about her superior standing. Once, when I admired the elevation of her house and the views from her windows, she said with emphasis, "My grandfather built ABOVE the town," as if by rights that was precisely where her family belonged.

That was one sort of family superiority—by patrician birth and breeding. But Emily went further than that. She also believed she was superior in intellect and in moral fiber. She was openly contemptuous of the occupations and preoccupations of Amherst women—especially their religion. "There is no God in it, just His housekeeping and His ACCOUNTS," she once said. She laughed at Aunt Helen's sewing circle and their "dimity convictions." These ladies certainly had few thoughts beyond doilies, according to Emily.

Her relationship with her sister-in-law, Susan Dickinson, was more perplexing. She often spoke of the wonderful times they had before Sue got married and her delight that her brother, Austin, had brought such a cherished friend into the family. Yet she also spoke disdainfully about Sue's way of life. She respected Sue—sometimes. She doted on Sue—sometimes. She certainly corresponded with Sue—all the time. Despite their proximity, the two women exchanged notes and letters on a very regular basis. From what I could see, Susan Dickinson had created at The Evergreens the circle of acquaintances that existed only in letters for Emily. Was some of her criticism of Sue motivated by jealousy? I didn't like to think that of Emily. She certainly didn't seem envious.

There were times after a Monday that I would return home and view my own family through Emily's eyes. I'd watch Kate and Aunt Helen in the kitchen or sit in on one of the sewing circle meetings, and I couldn't deny that much of the time among women was spent on the trivial — the day-to-day running of a household and a life.

But one day I realized something that eluded Emily. There was value in the seasonal round of teas, suppers, and shopping that bound neighbors together — the gatherings for no purpose other than female congeniality. These were the bonds that enhanced a life, that allowed information to be exchanged, intimacy to be experienced. Emily ignored the ladies' practical charity for the poor families nearby. She missed the good that women did one another through their active interest and participation. This secure and defined world of women had a dignified integrity just as noble as her personal pursuit of scholarship and letters.

I didn't know whether to be angry at Emily for her blindness, sensing it to be willful, or to feel sorry for her for missing such an important component of life.

"Does she criticize her own family too?" asked Kate, when I confided that this arrogance of Emily's offended me. We were tidying the linen closet as we talked.

"She surely does. According to Emily, her brother, Austin, is a weak husband, and her sister-in-law is a social climber and a shrew. Yet she still counts Susan as one of her best friends! She says poor Mrs. Dickinson is tiresome in her litany of symptoms, and Miss Lavinia spends too much time housekeeping to be very stimulating company. She wants a different life than all that. She wants to attend to her own thoughts, and all else is trivial."

"It's not so trivial if no one does the cooking!" Kate grumbled.

What a privilege to be responsible to only oneself, to one's thoughts, to one's desire, I thought. Emily continued to fascinate me.

One late winter Monday, I came upon Emily writing at her table, with the customary surround of paper strewn on the floor around her chair.

"You go through more paper than a publisher," I remarked.

"Don't look so disapproving! I have to have fresh paper for every new idea. If it's good enough, it goes in there." She pointed to her little chest of drawers. "It doesn't have to be finished; often I save just a WORD or two. But the FAILURES go in the stove."

"Are you separating the sheep from the goats, Emily?"

"No, I'm dividing the souls bound for Heaven from those tagged for Hell. Those words on the floor are fit only for burning, but those I save are for IMMORTALITY, sooner or later." She repeated this, rolling the words on her tongue like wine. "SOONER or LATER…"

"Can you tell me what you are writing about?"

"Circumference."

I gave her a coy look. "A geometry text?"

She was very amused; her lovely burnt sienna eyes gleamed and danced at the joke. "Hardly that. But my BUSINESS is circumference—just as Lavinia's is dusting the stairs."

Emily sensed this judgment displeased me and spoke seriously to explain. "Miranda, just listen to me. You know I am a fine cook. Father won't eat any bread but mine! I'm a specialist, a true expert. But there was one spring not so long ago—Mother was very ill, and Lavinia was away at school, and I became everybody's sustainer and retainer. Cooking and cooking again was all I did, all day long—and not fine baking either. Cooking CABBAGE! And in between I would dust and polish till it was time to cook another meal. The chores bled into one another; there were no boundaries. They call it 'household' because it holds you IN and holds you BACK," Emily concluded. "So it is my duty to MYSELF to draw a circle within which I can work. Now, shall we get on with our Battle of the Brownings?"

I allowed her to change the subject. We had a playful argument from week to week, with Emily advancing Elizabeth and me passionately defending Robert.

"Let's do 'My Last Duchess' again," said Emily, to please me. "I can just see Sue in brocade, there among the Borgias!" I gave her a slightly guilty smile—so could I!

In Amherst, March meant winter was over, but spring delayed. The eaves and the evergreens dripped, the ground was a sponge; the mud traveled everywhere through the damp houses. For the first time, I found Amherst dour and confining. I longed for the sun, for Barbados—for any other place.

"You never told me you had your own conservatory!" I gasped.

Emily was pleased by my obvious admiration. "It is my jewel box and hardly larger." She smiled. "You can't share something this size! And I write here too. You have to be alone for that. But my flowers visit around in the house; they enjoy the EXPERIENCE."

"Was it always here, Emily?" Light feathered the room. I went from shelf to shelf, naming the blooms. Breathing the rich, sweet air made me think of York Stairs. I was enchanted.

"No, Father built it for me when we moved back to The Homestead."

I found this very touching, coming from the formidable gentleman I met at Christmas. "You must be very dear to him, Emily."

"Zeus can't love mortals," she corrected me. "He OWNS us; he does not love us — and we don't PRESUME to love him either."

If only Emily could recognize her father's gift for what it was — an unspoken declaration of devotion. I thought about my own father's demonstrations of affection. They were obscure or indirect, but they were heartfelt, nevertheless. And I was much happier once I had decoded his system, allowing his gestures to speak as loudly as any words. But for Emily, words were paramount.

The days slowly became less cold, and the ongoing work on our house — which Father called "Grecophilization" — was now moving ahead and would be completed in midsummer. But we had reached an impasse almost as dismaying as the rock under the temple. How should Ethan connect the new temple wing to the old house?

Ethan had designed a small corridor between the buildings, ten feet wide and sixteen long — with a ten-foot ceiling to prepare one for the soaring temple. This passageway needed to have character, an identity. When I described Emily's glittering crystal chamber, Ethan's eyes lit up. He wanted to see it for himself.

"He may come to my house but not as *my* guest." Emily was adamant when I made the request the following week. "I do not RECEIVE anymore, and if I make an exception on his behalf, the whole town will expect invitations. He may come as the flowers' guest, or as yours. I will not see him."

"But you'd like him, Emily," I protested. "He never talks about doilies either."

"My dear Miranda, surely you understand by now that 'like' and 'don't like' are unimportant to me. I cannot spare him ROOM in my mind. I do not plant new acquaintances, for I am too occupied WEEDING OUT old ones."

I flushed very slightly from the pleasure of realizing that I had been accorded a privilege by being welcomed into her circumscribed sphere. This was made all the more sweet because Emily had not intended to flatter; she was merely stating the facts of her life. Emboldened by the knowledge that my visits were counted among Emily's accepted practice, I decided to tease her a little.

"He might attract you, Emily. He might turn out to be another letter-writing beau."

She chose not to be teased. "I think not. His work does not interest me. He is an architect and I am a poet."

So Emily stayed upstairs when I brought Ethan, who sketched and measured and hummed. I sat nearby, doing homework. I enjoyed seeing a man at work in his profession. Someday, I mused, I should like to be a woman who could share work with a man. I laid the book on my lap. Would I have such a chance? What work could I do that could be shared? This was indeed an important topic to discuss with Emily.

The professions open to women — what were they? Teaching, of course. Writing, like the Brontës and Jane Austen. But these were solitary pursuits. Surely there were more choices! Miss Adelaide's work was her home, and Aunt Helen's work was charitable.

Before I could follow this enticing train of thought any further, I heard Emily's door close upstairs. Some petals from an ailing arrangement on the front hall table shuddered and like soft rain fell silently to the floor. She had been listening. Ethan, absorbed in his work, didn't notice.

When we went home, Ethan persuaded Father to build the passageway as a conservatory too — an indoor pot garden, unheated, following the seasons outdoors.

"I love a pot garden," said Kate. "You see the dirt, but you know there's a bulb waiting inside. Almost like a baby."

"I collected another idea at The Homestead," Ethan told us. "Miss Dickinson has an Italian tile floor. I think that's what you want in the temple, Josiah."

"Big uneven squares of terra-cotta. Yes, I can see that. What a fruitful visit, Ethan! And then we should get some smokeless charcoal braziers from Italy too. They would be much more Greek than stoves." The men beamed at each other.

"I must write Uncle Thomas tonight," Father said. "I need him to choose the color of the house." He turned to me. "Would you and he like to do that together? You've really earned yourself a reward, Miranda. Just don't decide on a peppermint pink house."

Uncle Thomas's new book was *The Age of Chivalry*. He had used almost the same material as that of Sir Thomas Malory: the early British epic heroes and the medieval romances. He had told the Arthurian myths in lively prose and made them as historically accurate as possible. Uncle Thomas asked me to correct his publisher's proofs, a big honor for someone not yet fifteen.

Emily was very interested in Uncle Thomas's correspondence with Tennyson. With all her vaunted Independence, Emily was as impressed as anyone else by fame. Furthermore, she had confessed that she herself longed and worked to be famous someday as a poet.

"Shall I bring Uncle Thomas to meet you?" I teased her. I was feeling bold that day. Besides, she had allowed Ethan over her threshold; perhaps she was edging toward opening her doors. "Then he could tell you all about his new friend Alfred, Lord Tennyson!"

She ignored me. "Shall we go down to the kitchen?" Emily must have been feeling bold herself; we rarely spent time in the more public areas of the house. "I can make you some prune muffins as we talk—and today we must do some REAL talking."

I followed her to the kitchen, worried about possible prune stains on her spotless white dress. Emily wore various materials according to the season—dimity or challis or merino—but the cut was always the same: high-necked, with sometimes a pointed collar; long-sleeved and cuffed; pleated and full-skirted, worn without crinolines. Her shawls varied, and sometimes she wore a cameo brooch or a child's coral necklace, but her dresses were always pure white.

I was relieved when she covered up in a bibbed canvas apron and went efficiently to work. She had the rough slapdash confidence of an experienced baker.

I, on the other hand, simply hovered. "Is there anything I should do?" I asked.

"Stay clear of flying flour," she said, waggling her whitened fingers at me. I leaned against the counter, wondering what it was she wanted to talk about.

"Miranda, I have reached a decision," she announced. "I plan to ask you an important FAVOR, and you are more apt to oblige me if you understand why I am asking. So I have decided to tell you things about myself that no one else has ever heard. People guess and WONDER, but only you will know the truth!"

I was transfixed.

"Actually, some do know PARTS of this story, but no one has heard it ENTIRE. When you do, you will understand why I have made my world so NARROW. The wider world showed me its FEROCITY very early."

I hoped I was nodding in a mature and compassionate way. I worked to conceal my intense anticipation.

"Do you remember when I told you about my dear cousin Emily, who died before she ever lived? A part of me died with her; we were buried together."

I nodded. Of course I remembered.

"Soon after, I had a second *mortal* wound. I had a brilliant young Master who taught and trained me for a long, sweet time. He was my Preceptor, teaching what to read, what authors to admire, what was most grand or beautiful in Nature. And through his instruction, I learned that sublime lesson — a faith in things unseen. Mr. Newton believed in my own POWER, Miranda. He saw my future, and it was GOLDEN."

Emily worked at the pastry marble, brisk and skillful. She was untroubled by the tear that trickled down her cheek; her small hands were too floury to wipe her face.

Aching with compassion, desperate to be useful, I could think of nothing more than "Emily, shall I blot you?"

"Don't bother. I'll just weep again. This means that the muffins will be extra tasty. All my best baking is salted with tears, Miranda."

She gave me a brave smile. I returned it with a sad, encouraging one.

"Well, I can't stop my story now. My young Master was another DOOMED victim. Consumption, AGAIN. He forsook me in 1853, just before he was thirty." This time, she blotted her own cheek with her apron.

"Emily!" I was deeply shaken, thinking about my own precious mentor, Mr. Harnett. Our parting had been painful enough; to have lost him so finally would have been a blow impossible to withstand. "However did you bear it?"

"You bear what you must, I have learned. But I have more to tell. Did you know that my father once served a term in Congress? Lavinia and I went down to Washington too, for several weeks. That was in the spring, three years ago."

The picture startled me. "Did you live in a hotel? How did you like it?"

"Amherst is very much LIVELIER. I disliked the crowds pushing against me and the noise on the streets. I vow the whole town stayed up all night! And I never once heard a bird sing in Washington. But I do remember some good talk, though I never joined it. I was still looking for a way to be among STRANGERS in those days."

"And did you find one?"

"I might have, but..."

I heard the heavy front door open. Emily dropped her wooden muffin spoon and bolted for the stairs. As I followed her, I had a fleeting image of Emily as a ringmaster. She cracked her whip, and I performed. I pushed the unworthy thought from my mind. She had suffered, as had I; I should be able to be compassionate. But I was feeling overwhelmed by her autobiography, as if the weight of her losses were tangling themselves in my skirts, sinking me down.

"Where was I?" she said, once we were safely settled in her room. "After our stay in Washington, Lavinia and I stopped for a few days in Philadelphia, visiting our cousins. There, my life was forever changed. There, I met my FATE."

"What happened?" I wished I had lines to read. I had never played a confidante; I didn't know how.

"A rare INTIMACY. Not what the world would acknowledge, but OUR OWN. He will be my shepherd, guiding and guarding me always—even though we may not meet again. He will be my MASTER forever."

This was romantic and thrilling—but what exactly was Emily telling me? That she has a lover? Or once had a lover? That he died? That he was married, or imprisoned? And what of the dead Mentor, Newton? Had his attachment to her deepened to that of a lover's before death cruelly claimed him?

Whatever it was, I recognized the singular honor of her confidences. I would certainly not reveal my unworldliness by asking a lot of childish questions—so I waited.

"So now you know my INNERMOST secrets, Miranda, and now you CANNOT refuse my favor. My happiness depends on it—and on you."

"Of course I'll help you, Emily."

"Now that I have confined my bodily self, I need my spiritual freedom to SURVIVE. I need to voyage freely beyond my boundaries, toward greater minds than my own. I need your help—to reach and touch my FRIENDS."

Of course, she meant her correspondence. In a sense, her letters—from the authors and ministers and editors—were like my nursery visits from Mr. Harnett. Emily and I had both been marooned, each in our way, with this single vital link to the world outside. But my isolation had been involuntary, while hers was chosen, devised and perfected by Emily herself.

When I did not answer her, Emily became a pitiful Dickens waif, wringing her hands—still dusted with flour. My hard heart melted. I obeyed the crack of the whip; I leapt to my perch in the ring.

"All right, Emily. I'll mail your letters."

She nodded with a satisfied smile, then stood and paced the room. "I knew you would see this was NECESSARY. I have never liked to ask Lavinia, who PRIES—and the hired girls really can't be expected to know the VALUE of a letter. I will have them ready for you every Monday. Many personages in high places will be obliged to you, Miranda."

Astonishing. She went from waif to empress in under a minute.

Spring washed across Amherst like a Barbados breeze. The delicate blown petals moved in the wind like spray. Uncle Thomas, used to May in Boston, was lost in admiration and prolonged his visit. He and Father and I often walked in the afternoon, following the progress on our house.

"The workmen say we'll be in by midsummer," Father told us. "But Ethan predicts September."

"I should go home next week," said Uncle Thomas. "I'll come back when you've moved in. I'll help you with your library."

"You must stay over graduation, Tom," Father insisted. "I know you'll get a card to the Edward Dickinson reception. It's the high point of the week. He entertains all the nabobs under a tent in The Homestead garden, and I hear he spreads himself for once."

I wondered if Emily would make an appearance at her father's party. It was difficult to imagine her there yet even more unlikely that her father would allow her to be absent.

"Is that the handsome yellow Federal on the hill?" Uncle Thomas asked. "How my father would have loved that 'solid citizen' appearance."

"The Dickinsons are certainly 'solid citizens'—when they aren't paupers!" Father laughed.

This caught my attention: the lofty Dickinsons living in poverty? "What do you mean, Father?" I asked.

"Yes, Jos," Uncle Thomas seconded. "I sense a story here."

"Oh, there is one indeed," Father replied. "Samuel Dickinson, the old patriarch, built The Homestead around 1813. He also founded Amherst College and poured several fortunes into it. Finally he went bankrupt for its sake. He left the east and died as a horseback preacher somewhere in Ohio.

"His son Edward, the present squire, was stuck with his father's debts. He had to sell The Homestead and move his family into rented lodgings. It must have been a painful comedown, for such a proud man."

This was all news to me but explained many of Emily's cryptic remarks. Emily kept her secrets with the same calculation as she doled out her confessions. And what about Father? I gave him a sidelong glance. I would have to reconsider my notion that he was simply a befuddled professor. His nose may have been mostly in a book, but his ears had become sails that caught every passing wind. If I stayed quiet, I could learn much, I realized. Emily had taught me to listen.

Uncle Thomas was perplexed. "But, Jos—I thought you just said that he had sold the house."

"He did—and for years he ate humble pie, and not much else! He was a lawyer and was very political—always with a seat in the legislature, making deals. He's a very able man. Then in the early '50s, he brought the railroad and the telegraph to Amherst, and his money came rolling back. He repurchased The Homestead and added cupolas and conservatories and other costly modern trimmings—just to remind the village the royal family was back in residence! Squire Dickinson runs the First Congregational Church, the college, and the town — it's all his domain."

"What an American story!" Uncle Thomas was delighted. "Riches to rags to riches again. I love it."

"The Dickinsons have been here in Amherst as 'solid citizens' for two hundred years. It's old money restored and the old name repolished."

"What is the present Squire Dickinson like these days?"

Father smiled at Uncle Thomas and me. "One senses a certain satisfaction in what Squire Edward has accomplished, working with his partner, God."

I laughed out loud. "Father, that's exactly the sort of thing Emily says!"

Father gave me a grin. "Does she? Well, pride is often hard on the bystanders."

That evening, I related all my new Dickinson knowledge to Kate, who had been as puzzled as I over the Dickinson mythology. I found I was a little less critical of my friend's ways, now that I knew her family history. All that instability — no wonder she kept her life so closely contained within that hard-won homestead.

At first, I believed my new position as Emily's letter carrier was something she and I would never discuss — an unspoken understanding. She had, after all, entrusted me to the task because she feared "prying eyes." I discovered instead that Emily liked to be asked about the letters I mailed and the distinguished men she wrote to. She enjoyed recounting her social life, limited though it was to paper.

There was always a stack waiting for me; Emily must have spent hours each week writing to a wide-ranging audience. Knowing her exacting nature, I knew this meant she sacrificed reams of paper on a near daily basis.

"Samuel Bowles, Esquire," I read as I picked up a thick cream-colored envelope from the silver letter tray. "Who is he?"

"He is my INTIMATE friend," she said. "He is said to be the most brilliant young editor in the country. He has made the *Springfield Republican* famous."

I knew the newspaper; Father read it at home.

"We are studying Emerson and Thoreau together. I myself meet him in the PARLOR!"

She seemed to expect congratulations for this, that she actually met with someone face-to-face, and a gentleman at that! I wasn't quite sure I believed her. "Do you really receive him, Emily?"

"Oh, never alone. I do not want to cause trouble in his marriage. His wife is unstable and—POSSESSIVE. One hears she resents his admiring even a FRIEND."

I held up another envelope. "And Dr. and Mrs. Holland? I see they're in Springfield too."

"My dearest and closest friends! He's a journalist too. His wife, Elizabeth, is very WISE. She knows I would take her advice, so she does not give it."

With Emily's copious output, I wondered if she was also a recipient. "Do all your correspondents write back?"

"Most do. I am the gadfly they have to SWAT!"

There were often thick envelopes for Reverend Charles Wadsworth, Arch Street Presbyterian Church, Philadelphia. Emily's only Philadelphia addressee. I assumed this was her other Master, and accordingly alive. As she had never spoken of him again, I did not ask.

One May Monday, as I left Emily, she slipped a note in the pocket of my pinafore. I glanced at her, startled by the close touch as well as the secretive gesture.

"I want you to have this," she whispered. "But we won't discuss it." She stepped back and gave me a smile. "See you next week."

Curious, I couldn't wait to examine the note, wondering what Emily could write but couldn't say. I unfolded the crisp paper on my walk home. The sun shone brightly, and I had to squint a bit to read.

> *I never lost as much but twice,*
> *And that was in the sod.*
> *Twice have I stood a beggar*
> *Before the door of God!*

Angels — twice descending
Reimbursed my store —
Burglar! Banker — Father!
I am poor once more!

It was a poem, I supposed, but a far cry from Keats or Browning. It seemed plain and simple at first, but a second reading revealed an assault of furious invective toward God and Mr. Dickinson — who seemed to be the same person.

I was thankful Emily had forbidden discussion of this. What could I say to her? I slipped it back into my pocket and hurried home.

My end-of-school ceremony, and Kate's graduation, took place on a glorious day in May. After the convocation, Kate sang Mozart's *Ave Verum.* I was lost in awe and wonder after hearing that voice from another world. Where did Kate get such faith, such inspiration? She was just my own dear cousin, a merry, absentminded New England girl who lost her watch and burned the fudge. But her voice! When she sang the angels stopped to listen.

"Oh!" I let out a little exclamation. Lolly had poked me! I turned to her, puzzled.

"It's you," she hissed. "Stand up."

"What?" Then I understood! The headmaster had called my name for the history prize. When I went up to the rostrum to collect it, he awarded me two more: the medal for Latin and the one for English literature.

I gave Father a wide smile, which I hoped masked my surprise. I would have much to write Miss Adelaide and Mr. Harnett that evening! The history prize was a collection of medieval ballads, which Emily and I could read aloud. The other two were medals, with my name engraved. They would make handsome paperweights, for I always had several projects going at once.

As I watched the finishing students receiving their diplomas, I considered the vastly different prospects of the boys and the girls. Every single boy was going on to college — some to Yale or Williams or Wesleyan, most to Amherst. However, only one girl — Kate, who would continue with her music — had plans for enlarging her interests and her future. Kate's friends, half developed and half educated, were simply stopped short. No matter how intelligent and studious they might have been, whatever they had learned so far would have to last them a lifetime. They would not be going on.

"Go on looking and thinking," Miss Adelaide wrote me when I described these unsettling ideas. "I hope that writing to me will help clarify your thoughts."

"I'm glad you're putting your good mind to use over a girl's future," Mr. Harnett commented reassuringly, encouragingly. "There's no need for your education to end with the academy, you know."

During my next Monday visit with Emily, I brought up just this subject. We talked about a woman's few opportunities, compared to a man's freedom of choice.

"When I left the academy," Emily recalled, "all my friends took up the poor through the sewing circle at church. What virtuous ENERGY they had! All the poor were enriched, the cold warmed, the warm cooled, the hungry fed, the thirsty sated. I never went, not once, and my hard-heartedness drew me many prayers. I was never ever forgiven!"

"So what did you do instead?" I seized this mood of recollection. Emily would talk abstractions all day, but she seldom offered details of her actual growing up.

"I went to boarding school in Mount Holyoke, for a very BRIEF year. That was where they tried to save my soul. I had to fight them off! Everyone but me SURRENDERED to the evangelists. That was why I had to meet you when I heard you too had ESCAPED!"

"Did you like the boarding school?"

"The studies were the finest, but the rules were a cross between a convent and an ORPHANAGE! I liked the work, of course—but not that unnatural life. We had to make public APOLOGIES all day long!"

This would never have suited Emily. "So what did you do after that?"

"Then there came an EPIDEMIC of weddings, but I never seemed to catch the disease. Sue was the last of our crowd to marry. Did you know she taught school in Baltimore before she married Austin?"

"No, I hadn't heard that. Would you have liked teaching, Emily?"

"I wouldn't have lasted a week!" She was honest and rueful. "I cannot bear to be HANDLED, even by little hands. And I care only for children who love fine books and fine language—so who would teach all the OTHERS? Still, you might say I have been training myself to be a teacher of sorts," Emily said.

She went to the south window and looked out over a dazzling June Amherst. The sky was a pure cerulean dome, and there were two vermilion cardinals at the bird feeder. Emily had taught me awareness of the natural patterns around us.

"I am working for POWER, in and through my poetry, you know. I intend to gain DOMINION through ideas. That has always been my aim. When my skills are sufficient, then I will have INFLUENCE and POWER! You are the only person who has seen me refining my talent. Now I am telling you WHY. I want to teach through poetry."

I thought of the poems in my cedar box, known only to me and influencing no one. "Then you must publish, Emily. You must be *known!* You can't have power over people's minds unless your poems are read."

"They'll be read," she assured me serenely. "Don't worry, people will be reading my poetry a CENTURY from now. There's no hurry."

A day later, a note arrived for me from The Evergreens. Mrs. Austin Dickinson was inviting me for "lemonade and congratulations on a splendid academic showing."

"What do you hear from Versailles?" inquired my Puritan aunt, offended by the heavy parchment envelope and its crested seal.

"She has asked to receive me. It's very nice of her." I was always confused by the disparity between Mrs. Austin's mannered ways and the warm friendship I sensed underneath her elegance.

When I went to The Evergreens, I was intrigued by the fleshy red plants growing at the front entrance—more like meat than flowers. Mrs. Austin opened the door herself, modish in beige lawn and Battenberg lace. Her hair was *à la Eugénie*—a chignon of curls that Kate and I had tried in vain to re-create. She wore diamond earrings that would probably be considered unsuitable for the daytime, but I would not pass this particular tidbit on to Emily. It would be cruel to mock my hostess, who had dressed with such care to receive me.

I felt a bit nervous, wondering what we would talk about, until I remembered Emily's references to Mrs. Austin's literary interests and insights. We could talk about books!

"Miranda dear, you should be wearing your victor's crown," Mrs. Austin greeted me. "In Athens, the winners wore wreaths of violets. That would be nice with your eyes."

I followed her into the library. She had put away some satin swags and velvet dadoes for the summer, but she had added a few busts in marble and bronze, lest the room should be less suffocating.

"We'll have claret lemonade and pound cake," she declared. We settled on the tufted settee. I took a cautious sip; I'd never had claret.

"It's delicious," I said. I carefully placed the glass on the side table, nervous I might break it. It was covered in a fine gold filigree. Was she using her best to receive me or was this extravagance an everyday occurrence?

"For our scholar," she said with a smile. She handed me a present, Emerson's *Collected Poems*.

"Both Emily and I admire Emerson," I told Mrs. Austin. "I have learned 'The Mountain and the Squirrel' by heart. I thank you most kindly."

"Why, that is one of my favorites, I vow!" she exclaimed. "The next time Mr. Emerson comes to The Evergreens, I will ask him to inscribe your book. He *adores* young people."

Then she took up her embroidery hoop. "You and Emily discuss books, do you?" she asked.

"Oh, yes. We talk about poetry and novels and Shakespeare. We don't always agree and sometimes get into great debates over single words!"

Mrs. Austin smiled a knowing smile and nodded. "That sounds like Emily." She gave me a sidelong look from under her lashes. "Do you discuss other things as well?"

I cut a piece of my pound cake carefully with the side of my fork. I didn't want to get crumbs on my dress or the settee. "Oh, yes, we do," I said.

"Like what?" Her voice sounded casual, but her expression was unreadable. I could tell I was being led, but I was not sure where.

"We talk about our friendships." This was the truth and also vague enough to feel neutral.

"Ah." Mrs. Austin put aside her sewing and gave me a direct gaze. "Now, Miranda, you and I must talk."

I set down my pound cake. My heart fluttered a bit; I had no idea how to prepare for what might be coming next.

"My dear Miranda, we would never ask anything dishonorable of you. But Austin and I have excellent reason for our concern just now."

What could she possibly ask of me? "You know I would help you if I could," I assured her. "Though I can't think of how I could be of use."

She rose and began to circle the room, the lovely skirt floating gently after her. "I must have your promise that what I am about to share with you will be treated with the strictest confidence."

"Of course," I said, then wished immediately I had not. I had no idea what she'd be telling me; what if I needed help in understanding what to do? Grown-ups should not confide in people my age.

Mrs. Austin sighed and returned to her chair. She refilled our glasses before she spoke again. "We have a famous friend in Springfield, very much in the public eye. He is a true gallant; every woman he meets counts him as a conquest. His wife is quite used to his foolishness and doesn't really mind it. What she does mind is Emily believing his nonsense. Encouraging it. Exploiting it."

Mrs. Austin tapped the arm of the settee with some impatience. Emily's behavior seemed to bother her as much as it did the gentleman's wife. "Emily treats this gentleman like a beau, indeed, like a declared *suitor!* She is actually *possessive* about him, Miranda."

Then I realized Mrs. Austin was talking about Mr. and Mrs. Samuel Bowles, but I remained silent. I could keep confidences too.

"I know that Emily writes him often, although this didn't used to worry me," Mrs. Austin continued.

So the letters I carried were not strictly secret. Perhaps Emily discussed them with Mrs. Austin; perhaps, once, Sue mailed them for Emily herself. That could explain why I was now necessary — Mrs. Austin may have tried to discourage Emily from writing so often.

"They worry you now?" I asked.

She didn't respond directly to my question and instead circled around it. This was a trait she and Emily shared.

"Some time ago, when Emily was visiting in Philadelphia, she went to church and heard a sermon, a very fine one, I gather. From her pew, then and there, Emily fell in love with the minister! Emily is always so *excessive.*"

The back of my neck tingled. I had sent envelopes to Philadelphia, undoubtedly to this very person. But what did any of this have to do with Samuel Bowles?

Mrs. Austin must have sensed my bewilderment. "For you to feel the full force of my concern about Emily's...*excesses*...I need to go back a bit. Miranda, these extraordinary reactions are part of Emily's nature. It is a pattern. Some years ago, a young cousin died of consumption. She and Emily had been friendly but no more than that. Yet after her death, Emily went into a morbid decline. She mourned for an unseemly long time, months and months. Has Emily spoken of her and this tragic loss?"

"If you mean her cousin Emily, then yes, she has."

"Most of that friendship occurred in our Emily's mind after the cousin was buried! She has these violent, inappropriate emotions all prepared, ready and waiting—and she just *decants* them onto whoever or whatever the situation presents." She shook her head, then gave me a searching look. "Has she told you about young Ben Newton dying?"

"Yes," I whispered reluctantly.

"That is another example of Emily exaggerating things." She stood again and paced, as if this topic agitated her. I wished I could join her in her fevered perambulation, my own feelings were so stirred. But instead I sat, trapped on the settee.

"Ben was a perfectly charming young lawyer in Mr. Dickinson's office some years ago. He paid Emily compliments, gave her books, told her how talented she was. After all, she was the boss's daughter! They had a flirtatious good time together, but he was *never* her Mentor, nor were they *ever* sweethearts."

I had to protest. "How can you be sure of that, Mrs. Austin?"

"Because Ben married Sarah Rugg, that's how I'm sure! Did Emily tell you that?" Mrs. Austin paused for a heartbeat. "I daresay she did not. Ben died two years later, and from the way Emily emoted, you would have thought *she* had been widowed. It was, well, embarrassing. There was *talk* in the village."

My head spun over these revelations of Emily's distortions, but Mrs. Austin was not done with me yet.

"Just a bit more, Miranda. Now we come to the present day. My friend in Springfield —the wife whom Emily offends with her dangerous make-believe romancing—has a friend in Philadelphia. This Philadelphia woman says that Emily is now writing to a minister, the very same one whose sermon she heard there. Emily's letters to this man, I gather, are very emotional, very *unsuitable*. The actual word she used was *'scandalous.'*

"Unless Emily stops her imaginary flirtation with Mr. Bowles, Mrs. Bowles will tell Mr. Dickinson about the letters to that Philadelphia minister. And then we'll all be in serious trouble."

Intrigue upon intrigue. These adults were all behaving in such a complicated fashion. I wondered what kind of trouble Mrs. Austin was referring to and wondered as well what harm there was in letters. Emily never saw anyone—she must be the safest rival a wife could ever have.

Then I remembered—Samuel Bowles was one of the few gentlemen Emily did see in person. And scandal of any type could be ruinous for the Dickinson family.

"I do mail letters to Philadelphia," I conceded. "Of course, I don't know what they say."

"Does Emily say this man was her lover?"

I shifted a little on the settee. This was not a conversation I wanted to continue. I didn't want to betray Emily's trust, yet Mrs. Austin seemed genuinely concerned. This was not idle, mean-spirited gossip—this was a family member trying to determine the nature of a family problem. "She uses different words." There. Perhaps that would be sufficient.

"But does she say they are somehow close, linked in a relationship?"

"I think so," I told her. "But I'm not sure from the way she talks."

"Do I not!" She laughed sharply. "Miranda, Austin and I believe she barely met the minister, has hardly even *spoken* to him. He is a perfect stranger to Emily!"

"You mean she has invented the whole thing?" I was appalled. I knew Emily had flights of romantic fancy, but outright *inventions* were a different and serious matter.

"Oh, she probably shook the minister's hand leaving the church, but that's all it was."

"But why do the letters matter so much?" I asked. "Emily writes many people, Mrs. Austin. She must write four or five letters a day. Anyone who knows her realizes that!"

"They matter because I hear the letters to Philadelphia concern a very intimate and *personal* relationship. She writes about his teaching and guiding her, about him as *'Master'* and she as his disciple."

I winced at these familiar phrases. "Th-that's just how she puts things," I said. I was still trying to diminish her fears about Emily's erratic behavior. After all, I saw her every week; I would know if she was truly mad. "It's harmless." There. That sounded like a grown-up way to dismiss a child's foolish fancy. "Things sound more exciting when Emily writes that way."

My hostess looked at me intently and sighed deeply, shaking her head. She rose in a swirl of crinolines and crossed the room to fetch me a little carved ebony chest.

"I had hoped this would not be necessary," she told me. "I see that I must show you some extremely confidential letters — to convince you that there are tremendous stakes here. That what she writes *does* matter. Read one or two, and you'll see what I mean."

She opened the box and handed me one folded letter from among many — all in Emily's unique script, like a spray of buds and leaves.

Oh my darling one, how long you wander from me, how weary I grow of waiting and looking, and calling for you; sometimes I shut my eyes, and shut my heart towards you, and try hard to forget you because you grieve me so....

I was deeply embarrassed for us both and tried to return the box.

Mrs. Austin was ruthless. "Read another." She handed me a second piece of paper. I allowed my eyes to take in another paragraph:

...sometimes the time seems short, and the thought of you as warm as if you had gone but yesterday, and again if years and years had trod their silent pathway, the time would seem less long. And now how soon I shall have you, shall hold you in my arms....

I wanted no more of this. I slammed the top of the pretty casket in anger and disgust and held it out to her.

"You have no business reading Emily's love letters. You shouldn't *pry*. Even I know better than that."

"Miranda, try to understand." Mrs. Austin looked into my eyes and spoke so gravely that I could not doubt her. "These are *my* letters. Emily wrote these letters to *me*."

I couldn't help it—my mouth fell open in shock. Could she be saying what I thought she was saying? This couldn't be true.

Mrs. Austin opened the box and handed me another letter, selected at random. Sure enough, this one named her:

Susie, forgive me Darling, for every word I say—my heart is full of you, none other than you in my thoughts, yet when I seek to say to you something not for the world, words fail me. If you were here—and Oh that you were, my Susie, we need not talk at all, our eyes would whisper for us, and your hand fast in mine, we would not ask for language....

I was young and unworldly, but I had enough vague facts and hints to recoil from this as from a spitting adder. Horrified, I turned to Mrs. Austin for explanation. "Do you mean...was she in *love* with you?"

"No, my dear. Though certainly when Austin and I were engaged, she was crushed. She carried on as if we both had *jilted* her. No, I think hers was an unresolvable grief—one that comes from feeling unwanted, unloved, and left behind."

She took the box back from me and slowly closed the cover. "Now you see Emily's style in letters. That is the way Emily writes to people. She could have written these same letters to *anyone*—word for word. She would always use this same passionate and *possessive* manner when she wrote to Austin, her own brother. It was even more shocking that she would address *him* this way."

"What is it you want with me?" I was numb from crossing and recrossing these unsteady bridges of worry. I wanted only to crawl away from this confusion, this sadness.

"Well, I believe these old letters to me are *exactly* the sorts of letters she is sending to the minister in Philadelphia right now. Mrs. Bowles intends that Mr. Dickinson should know it."

"Mrs. Austin, this is...serious." I put my head in my hands, feeling sick and faint. I could only imagine how Emily's stern, patrician father would react.

"My poor child, of course it is. You can help Emily, if you will."

I looked up at her. Her face was drawn with concern, and I suspected some of that worry was on my behalf. She understood that I was too young for this but that she had no one else to turn to as an ally.

"You understand that Emily's letters to Philadelphia can ruin her. That is why we need you to be watchful. We should not interrupt the steady stream of letters, of course; perhaps the correspondence will exhaust itself. We can be vigilant by making sure this infatuation advances no further. If she begins to speak to you of plans—or promises—from a beloved or intended, if she speaks of running away to Philadelphia to be married, you must come to me at once."

"But Emily sees no one," I said, feeling a flicker of hope. "She would never do that."

Mrs. Austin gave me a sad smile. "It is never easy to predict what Emily would and would not do. Her fancy can take her many places—if only on paper." She gazed down at the box in her hands. "And as we have seen, words can have consequences."

"What would Mr. Dickinson do if he found out about the letters?" I asked.

"Miranda, he would stop at *nothing!* First of all, he would cut off all her mail—and you and I know that is her entire social life. Then perhaps he'd find a sort of attendant, a guard for Emily."

"No," I murmured. I thought of poor mad Mrs. Rochester and her cruel keeper—and I shuddered for my friend. I found I had decided.

"Mrs. Austin, you can count on me. I promise I will help you to help Emily!"

On the way home, I felt my knees failing me. My head seemed loose from my neck, floating as I used to float in the kind waters of Learner's Cove. I tried to think sensibly about Mrs. Austin's revelations, which had to be true. Those ardent letters from Emily to "my Susie" and the fat envelopes I mailed to Philadelphia were past argument—but at that moment I was sure of only one thing: I wanted to go home.

I entered silently into our kitchen, where Aunt Helen was making a pudding. She dropped the spoon and ran to hold me.

"Miranda, you look—why, child, you're burning up!"

She settled me on the parlor couch, where the plush prickled, and brought me some cider. When I cried out in pain from the acid drink, we both remembered there were cases of mumps at the academy just before it closed.

Because I was fourteen, I was much sicker than I would have been had I been a small child. I spent a swollen-faced, feverish fortnight, too dizzy to read much. I tried to think about Emily, and Monday afternoons, and Mrs. Austin's terrible letters—but it was all as elusive and amorphous as algebra.

I slept at odd times. I lay remembering the dolphins, who always looked so cool and tidy. At some point, I heard a steady *thumpery*, *thumpery* from the back porch; Kate was freezing coffee ice cream for me. When she brought it, the fever and my throbbing chipmunk face made it taste even colder and sweeter.

By the third week in July, I was pronounced cured of mumps but was suffering from a severe case of convalescence. I was weak and wavering and indifferent to everything, especially myself. Even Mr. Harnett's letters lay on my desk; I was too listless to respond.

I felt like a balloon that someone had let loose, floating above a world that didn't concern me. Not even the predicament of Emily's letters could muster my attention for longer than a few disturbed moments.

Then Aunt Helen announced, "Reveille for sleeping beauties!" She and Kate, with my father's blessing, had planned a fortnight at the sea. They had even arranged for chitons for us from Madame Lauré. I was happy to join these plans without the effort of making them. I felt a twinge of guilt—I had just promised Mrs. Austin I would keep an eye on Emily. But there was nothing to do about this. I allowed myself to be consoled by the idea that at the age of fourteen, the decision to leave Amherst was simply not up to me. Grown-ups had arranged these things.

We took the cars to Westerly, Rhode Island, and stayed in a gray farmhouse with stony pastures above a little tan beach. After my first swim—in clear water colder than that of Barbados, with slow unthreatening waves—I felt my energy flooding back. I was home again inside my body.

I attacked the simple farm dinner, pleasing our landlady, and challenged Kate to a jacks tournament after supper. At bedtime, I gave Aunt Helen an extra kiss. She turned her pansy face up from her book, calm and loving. She was the very embodiment of a concerned parent;

Kate and I had her interest and attention always. In a rush of feeling, I knew that I wanted to be this kind of mother.

She tugged a strand of my hair. "You've had a very trying year, Miranda, whether you know it or not. You need a little time to catch up with yourself."

At the end of the two weeks we had planned, Kate and I begged to stay on at the sea while Aunt Helen moved Father and some of the Beacon Hill furniture into the new house in Amherst. Our aunt seemed relieved that we were old enough and arranged that our landlady would act as our chaperone, keeping all our imaginary beaux from seducing us!

The interlude that followed was pure gold. I had the strangest sense that we were unattached to our pasts, not yet involved in our futures—simply living each blue and amber hour as it came toward us, as the waves crested and broke and fell on the beach.

We were brown and salty and laughing, stuffed with corn and lobster, murderous in our jacks contests, voracious in our romance reading. Then at night we talked in bed in the dark till one of us dropped off midsentence. Nothing was kept back; we had no secrets. I learned a great deal in those whispered confidences.

"Miranda, sometimes I worry about you and Miss Dickinson," Kate told me one midnight when we were half asleep. "She asks so much of you. Is she jealous of your other friends?"

"Emily, jealous?" I giggled at the idea. "Heavens, no—she thinks everyone else is too far beneath her!"

"She's so demanding, so *intense.* Is it worth it, trying to please her?"

Kate was right—Emily was both these and more. Especially in light of Mrs. Austin's revelations, which so complicated matters. But in spite of this new information, I was not willing to give up my friendship with Emily. I wanted Kate to understand it. "You don't see what she does for me," I explained. "Not just her wit and our literary games. She's taught me to speak and write and read better, and this is important for when I'm older. She is so clever and critical that it's like taking a course in style! And I like her very much. I really do."

"Do you trust her?"

"I know she can be unkind and untruthful—but she'd never hurt me, never."

"I wouldn't let her. I'll be watching." Kate let out a sleepy yawn and rolled onto her side, away from me.

I smiled in the dark at Kate's loyalty. I knew Kate would defend me in any altercation, real or imagined.

We never spoke of it, but we were fully aware that this seaside holiday idyll would not be repeated in our friendship. Kate was a young lady, finished with school, already in love; I was ending my childhood. Our real lives were waiting for us back in Amherst. But we still had another week of beach. We still had three more days. There was one day left.

Then it was time to pack.

Returning to Amherst, we found everything had changed, a little or a lot. It was summer while we were frolicking in the sea. Now it was autumn, and the first maple was frostbit into scarlet on my fifteenth birthday. Last year, we were tentative newcomers; now we were truly a part of Amherst. And the greatest change of all was that we had left the German professor's ferns and plush, and now lived in our own house—with our own furniture, our own books and treasures.

Uncle Thomas and I had spent spring days choosing the color for the outside. He had one inflexible rule: our choice must be part of the natural landscape all year long. I insisted that the shade be dark enough to set off the "Grecophilization": the white portico and columns and pilasters that Ethan had designed for us.

Between us, we eliminated all but the neutral colors. Finally we chose a pale Vandyke brown to match the trunks of our elms and maples.

"Tree trunks don't change, thank God," said Uncle Thomas. "We won't be sorry."

From Amity Street, you could see the original house, with the new portico and its four Doric columns. The front door and the shutters on the six tall windows were black. We had a front parlor with a fireplace, a center hall, a dining room with a stove, and a square, sunny kitchen. We added a washroom and a kitchen entrance with pantry shelves.

Upstairs, we had three big bedrooms and a storage and linen closet. Kate and I looked out on Amity Street, and Aunt Helen looked east over the garden. All of us were shaded by the "wineglass" elms arching over the house. There were maples along the little brook at the end of the property.

"Your mother's mahogany shouldn't have to compete with patterns," Father had stated, insisting on plain white plaster downstairs. But we ladies were allowed wallpaper in our bedrooms.

Our choices, made from an enormous album last spring, delighted the three of us. Aunt Helen had a tiny allover dot, like muslin. Kate's walls were delicate stripes of wildflowers. Mine were a miraculous design straight from Learner's Cove: tiny white shells scattered on a pale, rosy beach. I had not believed my eyes when I turned the page in the sample book and found this pattern waiting.

Like Emily, I had a corner room facing south and east. On the long wall between the windows, Ethan designed bookshelves for me, and little closed cupboards too. There was a high, tipped shelf all around the room, like a frieze; this was for my shell collection, with an invisible molding to hold it safe. All the woodwork was a rosy beige, like Barbados sand at the water's edge. My curtains at the three windows were white dotted swiss.

I wrote Miss Adelaide an exact inventory of my room. But though I could list its contents, I could never, ever describe how deeply my room satisfied me. It reflected me and my tastes, my interests, and my hopes. It was my image, my emerging self. In this room, *my* room, I had an identity; I existed as a valid person.

My father's new wing was to the left and repeated the windows and rooflines of the main house. It had a handsome library, with three walls of bookshelves and a fireplace using the same chimney as the parlor. The familiar mahogany ladder from Mount Vernon Street was back in use. There were two bedrooms up a little curving stair—one for Father, one for guests—with a round skylight in the stairwell like a ship's porthole. There was no access from the parlor to the library; my father came and went by his own outside entrance. He explained that his students preferred this.

The wing at the back—the temple—was the glory of the house. It was invisible from the street; you could not guess at its existence. From the parlor, you stepped into our crystal connecting passage. Father called this the "punch bowl"; Aunt Helen called it the "conservatory"; Uncle Thomas called it the "atrium." This led to the temple itself. Here, one's spirit soared to the sixteen-foot ceiling. There were three tall windows on each side, facing east and west, and a glowing floor of Italian terra-cotta in varied tones of burnt sienna. Otherwise, the great room was empty; the braziers had not yet arrived from Italy, and we were still deciding how to furnish so much inviting space. Kate and I had already tested the sound from the stage, doing our favorite scenes from *The Tempest*.

By the time we had completed the finishing touches—put away the linen and china, hung the small paintings, and arranged the books—it was the first day of school. Lolly Wheeler stopped by for me, and we walked up the hill, chattering. I barely remembered my last year's fear and shyness as I walked arm in arm with Lolly and waved at our converging friends.

The academy opened in the usual whirlwind of greetings and confusion. I found I had moved up one class in math, though I was still with embarrassingly younger children. I was now one year ahead of Lolly in Latin, and two in history and English. I did botany and natural science with Lolly and her friends; they accepted me cheerfully. The school year was a fine predictable vista: our recorder lessons, and Halloween, and then Thanksgiving, and Christmas.

When I came home to Amity Street on that first day of school, Emily had sent word she was expecting me for tea in a return to our former schedule. I was eager to tell Aunt Helen about my classes and show her my book bag full of new textbooks—stiff and squeaking and smelling of glue—but instead I hurried upstairs to wash and put on a clean pinafore. I tied the sash of my blue striped one, Emily's favorite. Aunt Helen had let it down as far as she could—along with all my other dresses. I had grown a waistline too.

Emily wrote me once in Rhode Island, hoping I was well again and *"inhabiting"* the sea. Except for that one amusing letter, I had not heard from her, and during my long stay at the beach, I had tucked her away to a corner of my life. Part of me wished that she not reenter center stage. This would be an easy time to stop the Monday afternoon visits—but did I really want to? More important, did I have a choice?

I walked from Amity Street to Main Street cross lots, enjoying our new neighbors' fiery marigolds and chrysanthemums. Mrs. Barton and Mr. Miles greeted me and praised the changes to our house. At The Homestead, I found the back door open. The big house was still and waiting; the hall clock ticked. I knew Emily was in her room at the head of the stairs, waiting. Only I had changed—I and my odd new reluctance.

Emily stood at her door, smiling. She had become at least four inches shorter than I.

"Oh, my Miranda, how long it's been! Without you, it was a CAGED summer."

"You wouldn't have seen me very often, Emily," I pointed out, wanting to keep her to the reality of things. "Even if I'd been here in Amherst. I come only on Mondays."

"That's true—FACTUALLY true. But I count on you as my window on Amherst. You're my SCOUT in enemy country! Having you nearby makes me feel CONNECTED."

Every word she said today had a charge to it; I was keeping an eye out for symptoms, for evidence, for exaggeration. I didn't enjoy scrutinizing every word and gesture, but I couldn't stop myself. Mrs. Austin had revealed too much for me to be with Emily without questions.

"Now let me look at you." Emily took my hands and held them out as she studied me. "You're STATELY!" she told me.

I smiled. A person of fifteen much preferred this to "How you've grown!" Emily chose the perfect phrase.

"How fortunate you are, to turn gold leaf in the sun," she said. "I become a single walking FRECKLE when I go outdoors."

Then she suggested we have tea. "I have devised a new lemon-peel cookie for us, and I packed a basket for Kate to try them too. Won't you please sit down, Miranda?"

Then—only then—I discovered what had been added to her room: a tiny red armchair, perched like a fat robin.

"It's yours, even though it must live here." She smiled. "You won't mind if I borrow it on winter nights, to be CLOSE to my fire?"

When Emily put her mind to it, she could be downright irresistible!

While we had tea, I brought Emily up to date: the mumps, the beach, our new house. I had learned over time that she became impatient and restless during casual, careless conversation. I was expected to tell a story, exact and brief, and illustrate it with a few revealing images. These must express my moods and feelings; they must justify the narrative.

At first it seemed pointless and difficult to talk this way, but Emily made it into a game. ("Can you say that in one sentence, Miranda?" or "Make me see that more clearly.") So today, instead of telling her all about our weeks at the beach, I described a single evening in late August, just before we came home.

The sea was *"wine dark,"* like Homer's Aegean—neither indigo nor purple. The air was so clear that you could see the tiny houses on Block Island—even the miniature lighthouse. As Kate and I picnicked, the sun sank lower and lower inland behind us, and the crests of the slow, smooth waves turned ragged gold. The same pure western light, coming straight from the horizon, gilded Kate's skin and her brilliant scarlet shawl. We stayed till dark; we could not bear to leave so much beauty.

Then I told about our new house on Amity Street—and my room in particular. When I was done, I made an impulsive attempt to share my joy.

"Would you come and see it? We'd send a carriage, and I promise there'd be nobody else there."

Emily sighed regretfully. "I cannot, I truly cannot. I have struggled to limit my horizons and my acquaintance. Now I have reached the point where I am no longer ENDANGERED by new people and new places."

"How could my house be dangerous?" I struggled to understand, struggled not to feel insulted.

"It would be—for me. I don't CONTROL it; anything could happen if I went there. I might act foolishly or say what I did not intend to say. I have my boundaries of SAFETY, and I have learned to stay inside them."

"But don't you get tired of being all alone?" I asked.

"But I'm not alone, Miranda, and I travel a great deal." She smiled at my perplexity. "I have conversations with some of the most brilliant men in the country—and I go everywhere!"

I knew she meant her letters and her books—all *secondhand* experiences. Thinking of Barbados and Westerly, and the living miracle of the ocean, I pushed her a little bit. "Emily, have you ever seen the *real* sea?"

"No, I have never seen the Atlantic AS SUCH." She was serene and untroubled; once removed was close enough for Emily. "But I can CONCEIVE the sea." So that was settled, on her terms—as usual.

We trilled and chirped a little bird-feeder news, and then she announced "a plan to uplift us—you and me and our Monday afternoons.

"I wrote a few letters this summer, asking advice on this attempt to improve our INFERIOR female intellects. At first this plan was vague as a cloud, but now it has a shape and an edge."

"Emily, tell me!" I was intrigued; Emily's plans could be exciting.

"I was looking for something we could study together, two companions, learning for pleasure only. I consulted your father—did he tell you?—and also Mr. Crowell, who has married my old friend Mary Warner. So we have some fine classical scholars helping us!"

Emily, so shy in person, had not hesitated to approach two professors she had never met, asking a favor. She could be brave when necessary. And Father—he had never said a word! Had he wanted to allow Emily to surprise me or, more likely, had he thought no more of Emily's questions once they were asked and answered?

"Both gentlemen agreed that you and I should study the Greek plays, the true LINEAGE of Shakespeare. They told me to begin with Aeschylus, he being the first playwright. Here is the translation they advised. Shall we start today?"

Thus, without discussion, I was swept along by Emily's will to her intention, and of course she chose right. *Agamemnon* was thrilling to read aloud, and I loved meeting all my old *Iliad* friends again. As she planned, it was both an uplifting and a sociable time. Even if I had been consulted, I could not have chosen better material for our afternoon.

"See you next Monday," I called as I left.

As I walked home from the post office to Amity Street, I prepared myself for Aunt Helen's questions. I would have to defend my decision to continue my visits with Emily. Aunt Helen would quiz me; my father would not care either way.

"Tell me why," said Aunt Helen, once I returned home.

"For fun, for one thing. Emily's very amusing. I think she talks better than anyone I know. And you have to speak really well for her. She keeps you on your toes, as Father said."

"What do you do together, Miranda?"

"We've just started a Greek play about all the same families as in the myths! She has a fine voice; I wish you could hear her read."

"Do you feel comfortable there? It's such an unbending house!"

"It is, but we use only her room and the kitchen. Those are both happy rooms. If I felt boxed in, you know I wouldn't go."

"I was afraid perhaps you were just being kind, because she is lonely."

"She's not the *least bit* lonely!" I made one last effort to explain. "I need her more than she needs me, Aunt Helen. She treats me like an *equal*. Sometimes I feel I'm much too old for Lolly Wheeler and the girls in my class."

This seemed to end the questions.

Up in my room, I felt guilty about what I had left out. The most important reason of all, the reason I had to continue my Mondays with Emily—the one I could not tell Aunt Helen: I had promised to watch Emily for Mrs. Austin. I must notice if she edges further from reality. I would try to protect her from incurring Mr. Dickinson's rage. It was a terrible responsibility for someone of fifteen—but from my knowledge of her small circle, I believed there was no one else to do the job. I felt that if it came to living with a guard or a keeper and being forbidden her correspondence, Emily would die. I believed I faced a terrible fact: I was responsible for Emily's welfare.

Book V

AMHERST
1858–1859

One October day in 1858, strolling from downtown, I turned onto Amity Street — and suddenly I saw that our house had settled in and joined the village landscape. It no longer perched on the surface; it had become part of the whole that was Amherst. I remembered how in the spring we had plowed and seeded the earth around the temple and put some pretty flagstones down in the shaded parts as a terrace. From there, we had a fine view of the Pelham Hills. Then we added some beds for annuals to the south, under my window; this would be my picking garden. In the summer, we added nandinas and hydrangeas in groups of three, softening the lines of foundation and cellar. In the autumn, we transplanted laurel and holly from the woods. Now I could see how that hard work had lost its newness — our house and our landscaping looked as if it had been part of Amherst for years.

When we came here, we were unsettled and unattached. We were newcomers; we did not belong. Gradually we put out tentative roots, joined the existing groups and patterns. Now we had made our place, and the town had closed around us. We were the distinguished professor; his nice sister from Springfield; his beautiful niece, who sang; and his tall daughter, who won prizes at the academy.

During my Monday afternoons with Emily, I watched her carefully for aberrations, as I had promised Mrs. Austin I would. When it weighed too heavily that I might be thought of as spying on my friend, I remembered what was at stake. Emily, however, never noticed my scrutiny; in fact she may have relished my even more attentive presence. She behaved as she usually did, including continuing to correspond with Mrs. Austin on a near daily basis.

Things took a different turn after Thanksgiving. Miniature snowflakes were falling in the early dusk as I told Emily about our musical plans for Christmas.

"We'll do our program here again," I promised. "Kate's voice teacher has found us a medieval Twelfth Night song. It's beautiful—very earthy and unreligious!" I knew that would appeal to Emily, reminding us both of our first meeting as cheerful unrepentants. "And Mrs. Austin has invited us to her party again."

"I may have to miss your music," Emily warned me. "I may not be here. I might have to go out of town."

This could have meant anything or nothing, so I proceeded carefully.

"Where will you be?" I tried to betray no concern, no suspicion.

"In Philadelphia. My Master has written; he needs me URGENTLY. I must go to him." Silently she handed me a letter; silently I read it.

My Dear Miss Dickenson

I am distressed beyond measure at your note, received this moment,—I can only imagine the affliction which has befallen, or is now befalling you.

Believe me, be what it may, you have all my sympathy, and my constant, earnest prayers.

I am very, very anxious to learn more definitely of your trial—and though I have no right to intrude upon your sorrow yet I beg you to write me, though it be but a word.

In great haste
Sincerely and most
Affectionately Yours—

C. W.

"You can see he is quite beside himself," said Emily, with evident satisfaction. "It is clearly my DUTY to go to him and comfort him."

What had she told him that would produce this disturbed letter in reply? I approached this with the utmost care—tiptoeing on eggshells. One misstep and all could have been lost.

"Emily, I believe he was upset because you told him *you* were," I said evenly. "Why don't you just write and tell him that whatever happened is over—that you feel better now?"

"And leave him in such TORMENT?" She was superior and scornful. "I owe him more than that. I must put his mind at rest NOW!"

"What will you do?" This was the information I needed the most—what were Emily's plans? And how could they be stopped?

"It will be a very long day on the cars, with two changes—but I have no CHOICE. I will be making my arrangements."

As she spoke, I could envision the whole appalling drama, and I shuddered: the train, the confidences to strangers on the way, the hansom from the Philadelphia station. Then the church, perhaps a confrontation at the altar in midservice. This must not be allowed to transpire!

I was so distressed that I cut my visit short and ran along the path to The Evergreens. Emily's room was at the front of The Homestead; she would not see where I was headed.

The hired girl let me in. Mrs. Austin was in her music room, seated at the piano, practicing Stephen Foster's "Hard Times." How apt!

The moment she saw my face, she knew that Emily's fantasies had outgrown her miniature garden and threatened to spill into the world at large—and with grave consequences. I related all I knew, panting and shivering, and Mrs. Austin pounded a fierce dissonance of angry notes.

"I knew it, I knew it," she muttered. She rose and paced about the sparkling, tinkling room, her purple velvet skirts swaying around her. She was like a great tropical bird.

"Miranda, we must stop this. I must find a way."

"I do have one idea," I told her. "It came to me as I ran here. Emily respects Dr. and Mrs. Holland. She has often said what wise advice they give her."

Mrs. Austin stopped pacing and turned toward me. I could see her thinking, mulling over the idea, her eyes never leaving mine. "Miranda, I do believe you're right! They are the only old friends she still sees, actually *sees*. And Dr. Holland is very sophisticated, very worldly; Emily admires that. He could tell her a *man's* point of view in an affair like this, and she'd listen to him." She nodded decisively. "Yes. Austin will be on the milk train to Springfield in the morning."

She crossed to me and took my hand in hers. Then she pulled me into a warm embrace, squeezing my shoulders as she spoke. "How can we thank you, you dear, sensible child?"

I had never liked her as much as I did that afternoon. I knew she was protecting the whole Dickinson family from scandal, but she was genuinely concerned for Emily too. She feared a "keeper" for Emily as much as I did.

"How old are you now, Miranda?" Mrs. Austin asked as she walked me to the door.

"I was fifteen in September," I replied.

"Fifteen — and yet our whole family depends on you! You really are a true friend to Emily. The Dickinsons won't forget this."

The rest of the week I had trouble sleeping, difficulty concentrating in school. What if my idea didn't work? The following Monday, Emily mentioned a delightful surprise visit from friends in Springfield who had made the journey solely to see her. I went on mailing her letters and noticed none to Philadelphia. Talk of travel had evaporated from her conversation. That was all I knew. On the rare occasions I saw Mrs. Austin — at church, leaving Emily's as I entered, in her garden — we never spoke of what had nearly happened, but we exchanged a complicated look: concern, gratitude, and promise. I did not intend to fail either woman.

Since that very first undiscussed poem, Emily had been giving me poems, one or two a month. She simply handed them to me or put them in my pocket; she rarely discussed them. I was sorry for this, as I needed her help to understand them.

Some of her poems were fresh and open and accessible. In them she had a clear, personal vision that made me see a bird or a snake or a thunderstorm as if I'd never noticed one before. But others were mysterious, oblique, deliberately confusing — as if she were hiding inside, sending out hints and waiting for the reader to discover her.

I put all her poems together in a sweet-smelling cedar box from Barbados as she gave them to me. Some were arranged properly on the page; others were written almost as rhyming prose, with little curling dashes as the only punctuation. I must have had nearly a dozen of them.

"Did you mean that God is like a father?" I asked her once, on the rare day she herself brought up the subject of one of her poems.

"No, that Father thinks he's God," she snapped back. Was she impatient that I had not understood her oblique message? Or simply annoyed by the attitudes of her father?

"Our fathers aren't at all alike, are they?" I realized. "I wish mine would care more about my life, and I gather you wish yours would care less."

This insight forgave my misreading of her poem. "You're right, Miranda—much less. My father is OBSESSED with keeping Lavinia and me on the proper moral path and reminding us of our inferiority as women. He would BREATHE for me if he could, since he thinks I don't breathe correctly without his supervision."

"While my father has to be reminded that I need air as much as he does!" I responded.

We laughed in a companionable way, two friends at ease, deploring the arbitrary ways of fathers.

"A few summers ago, before we moved back to The Homestead, I went to call on a friend late one afternoon," Emily related. "It turned to a fine evening, and since Amherst ladies are in no danger on our village lanes, I accepted an invitation for supper. I returned a little after nine—and what a SCENE awaited me!" She grinned, remembering it.

"Father was breathing thunder and lightning, like Jehovah, and Mother and Vinnie were clutching each other in terrified flat-out HYSTERICS. You could hear them on Main Street!"

"Because they were so worried about you, Emily?"

"No—because they thought Father would surely KILL ME, there and then!"

She laughed, but her laughter had a sharpness to it. This story, meant to entertain, chilled me. My responsibility toward Emily, preventing any cause for incurring her father's wrath, was cemented.

When Ethan designed our temple for us in 1857, no one had a clear idea of what we would do with it and in it. As our Amherst life developed, however, the temple seemed to affect most of our family decisions. For instance, the handsome Italian iron braziers heated only half the space, so we had them duplicated in Springfield. These then required a shed to store them in summer. The shed led to a stable and carriage and pair, since my father, at sixty-two, really should not have been walking to the college in bad weather anymore, and we were tired of renting from the livery stable. Then the stable and horses required the hiring of Sam, our splendid red Irishman, to help us in everything. It reminded me of the children's game "The Farmer in the Dell." One thing led round-about to another and another.

Our Shakespeare evenings were established now—an Amherst tradition. The cast of readers sat on the stage, and the audience of guests sat on black-and-gold stenciled Hitchcock benches. My father had them made at the Hitchcock Factory across the river. If you looked carefully, you could see tiny scenes of Amherst Village life painted and stenciled in gold leaf on the backs of the benches. One shows our house, with our family standing under the portico; we are no bigger than acorns.

Christmas 1858 was our second in Amherst. We were using the temple for a momentous event. There were candles everywhere and ribboned wreaths in every window. The braziers and the guests were glowing. All our friends had come to drink champagne and celebrate Kate Sloan's engagement to Ethan Howland.

I was wearing my ice-blue tulle. I stood with Aunt Helen, watching Kate, whose joy lit the great room. She was onstage with Ethan, showing her ring, an opal in a hoop of little diamonds. She wore ultramarine velvet with a wide lace bertha and a wreath of white roses. Aunt Helen and I could see that Kate was adult and elegant and complete. The New Year, 1859, would usher her into her new role as Ethan's wife. She was being swept up into the stream of life; she was leaving us behind.

Of course I told Emily about Kate's engagement party: the candles, the wreaths, the wine, Kate's face as she sang "Drink to Me Only with Thine Eyes" to Ethan. As I related the story, I could hear how being Emily's narrator had improved my speaking style. I made my account short and vivid and chronological; details were summoned only if they enlivened my little narrative. Amusing Emily had become an education in itself.

Kate's wedding was to be in mid-May, but plans and preparations for it took up our entire winter. There had been a few other happenings: an extra blizzard or two, which extended our sledding—and measles at the academy. Then my literature class presented *A Midsummer Night's Dream* on the stage of our temple. I tried out for Puck, but I towered over midget Oberon and miniature Titania—so I became a reluctant Wall, which amused Miss Adelaide.

"What a comedown from playing Miranda and Cordelia!" she teased me. "But I know the audience never saw such a brilliant and eloquent Wall!"

These diversions, however, did not keep us long from our family job: the wedding. Kate and Ethan had decided to live in Springfield, where Kate had cousins and friends, and Ethan could take the cars to the various Connecticut Valley towns where he worked. So Aunt Helen sold her house and gave the young couple half the profits; Father matched this as a wedding present. Thus, Kate and Ethan were able to buy a small Federal house, a doll's version of The Homestead.

"This will be a showcase for my work!" said Ethan happily. "We'll add a wing when we need it and a music room soon. My clients can see their architect using his own designs."

"We'll have to take the front door off its hinges to squeeze the piano through!" Kate laughed. This was the fine instrument that Father bought for the temple but which he gave to Kate—with the promise to continue paying for her voice lessons.

Living closely with someone like Kate enlarged my father's capacity for affection; it had done the same for me. What would we do without her?

Now we had reached late March—usually the season of mud and despond, the price we New Englanders paid for exquisite May. But in 1859, for the Sloans and the Chases, March was a season of anticipation and joy. We had lived in Amherst two winters—one in the plush jungle and one in our own house. I would be sixteen in the fall; Kate would be nineteen. Our family life had developed and evolved in the same way as our property, and the wedding preparations were in full swing.

Father engaged Madame Lauré to come from Boston to make Kate's wedding dress—and mine, as her attendant. It was a Thursday, after school, and it was almost April; Madame Lauré and I were alone in the house, fitting my dress. The delicate spring light washed over us, over my reflection in the pier glass. We had moved it to Aunt Helen's room, which had the best light. Madame Lauré laced me into my first stays. I was overcome at the transformation wrought by two inches removed from my waist and added to my bosom.

Kate was to wear heavy corded silk called "lutestring." I would wear the same fabric, in the fragile green of little May leaves. Madame Lauré dropped the heavy skirt over my head, over my grown-up crinolines; she fastened the little buttons on the basque jacket. I studied myself in the mirror, a fashionable green tulip shape. I was startled by my own reflection. Was it possible that I was beautiful?

Suddenly there was a brisk, efficient knocking at the front door. Madame Lauré and I were taken aback. There was no way I could change quickly and no one else to go to the door—and all callers and messages were important as the wedding approached. So, feeling almost in disguise, I trailed my silks and crinolines down the stairs and across the hall.

I opened the front door.

He was a young man just a few years older than me, tall, with dark hair and arresting silver eyes. He was as startled as I was, but he collected himself and bowed briefly and correctly.

"Miss Chase? I am David Farwell. Professor Chase has very kindly invited me for supper."

I answered as politely as I could, hiding my surprise. "Won't you come in? Father will return soon from the college, I'm sure."

When students came to the house, Father saw them in his library, so I decided to take this one there. We entered the library wing, where the spring sun was gilding jonquils and pussy willows in a pewter jug.

"You did that, didn't you?" His smile carried over into his pleasing voice.

"I did, but Father may want me to move it. He gets very upset when my flowers shed on his papers." How did this young man know I had done the arrangement? Had Father mentioned this skill—a surprise itself—or had David Farwell surmised it by looking at me?

"Then you should use laurel leaves instead! Actually, you make me think of Daphne and the laurel, with that wonderful color you're wearing."

"Then I'd better leave you, before I turn into a laurel tree!" And I departed, swaying and rustling, a convincing young lady—thanks to my stays and crinolines—astonished by my casual reply.

I heard Aunt Helen and Vera, our new Swedish hired girl, returned from their marketing, talking in the kitchen. When I told them our dinner guest was here, Aunt Helen hurried off with sherry. I set the table with Vera, wishing David Farwell would see me in my green silk one more time.

Madame Lauré appeared to remind me that she needed to take the dress with her to make the alterations. Reluctantly I climbed the stairs and came down for dinner in my Sunday dress, a striped mauve silk, but I did not change the transforming underpinnings.

Kate and Aunt Helen noticed my elegant new shape instantly. Kate's hazel eyes widened with a question; Aunt Helen hid a smile and seated us without comment. My father saw nothing and was in tearing good spirits.

"Ladies of my real family, let me present one of my academic family: David Farwell, my academic grandchild!" Father clapped a hand on David's shoulder. Aunt Helen had seated our guest to Father's left, opposite me and Kate.

"David is my favorite student's favorite student," Father continued. "I taught Joel Parsons at Harvard, and now he is head of classics at Exeter, my dear old school. Dr. Joel Parsons has sent me David to finish him off!"

David Farwell smiled, his fine-boned face lit with intelligence and humor. "Sir, with respect, I'm coming to Amherst to be started, not finished off!"

Father appreciated this. "Quite right, my boy! We'll give you an education in classics that will last your lifetime. Now tell me, what translation of *The Aeneid* are they using at Exeter these days?" And they were off in their own world.

While they talked, I studied David. The most striking thing about him was his total ease. He was at once poised and relaxed; he was without tension or effort. He gave my father his entire attention, unaware of his effect on others.

"Tell me, Miss Chase, are you a classicist too?" David looked directly at me, and I met those remarkable eyes. Now I saw they were very light gray, with black rims around the iris. His thick lashes were black too, even darker than his thick hair. I must have been staring; I immediately lowered my gaze.

"I don't have Greek yet," I told him. "But I truly love Latin. It sounds like the sea."

"Indeed it does!" This pleased him. "Or like our Lake Michigan. The Great Lakes are inland seas, you know. We have tremendous storms in winter, and the surf sounds just like Latin."

"Miranda enjoys Ovid only because he tells love stories," Father teased me.

"That's not fair!" I felt a slight flush rise in my cheeks. "I enjoy Ovid, Mr. Farwell, because he tells true feelings. When Daphne tries to run away from Apollo, then I feel her terror too."

"And you ran away just like Daphne this afternoon, didn't you?"

"I had to, before I took root!" After having so many conversations with Emily, I was well rehearsed for this sort of repartee.

David Farwell and I exchanged smiles, pleased with our banter—but Father wanted him back.

"I don't know Illinois," he said. "Do you live in Chicago?"

"We used to, sir, but the stockyards have pretty well taken over the city," David explained, buttering his bread. "Everyone wants to move out of town and build to the north. My family and some of their friends all moved together and started our own town, right on Lake Michigan. We called it Lake Forest."

"Is it a village, like Amherst?" Aunt Helen asked, passing the bowl of peas and carrots to our guest.

David spooned the vegetables onto his plate. "Not really. It's all too new. There was only prairie there until ten years ago. We chose the place for an extraordinary stand of oaks, mile after mile along the lakeshore. We built our houses right there among the oaks. We saved them all."

"Did the Indians never damage the trees? Firewood must have been scarce on the prairies," Father said.

"They say the Indians protected the oaks too. They used to have their rituals and ceremonies there. You feel it, even today. I simply can't describe those oaks to you, Professor Chase, they're...noble."

"There's a sacred grove at Epidaurus," Father recalled. "You sense its deep holiness. Your forest sounds very like Epidaurus."

"My father will give me a year in Greece when I graduate," David announced. "Then I'll see Epidaurus, and Delphi, and Sounion—Sounion most of all! Byron wrote..."

I stopped listening and just watched David Farwell. Van Dyck should have painted him. He was long-boned and elegant, with beautiful wrists and hands. He had a straight, narrow nose, winged eyebrows, those strange silver eyes. Then he glanced at me, and I caught his look and understood my attraction to him. He had a quality best named in Latin: *bene volens*. David Farwell was benevolent. He wished me well.

The talk moved about the table. We spoke easily about winter sports, about Kate's wedding. David spoke of his parents—his father and step-mother, married many years after the death of David's mother—and mentioned his little stepsister, Frances, who loved to hear Father's book at bedtime.

"You return to Exeter tomorrow?" I asked over the custard dessert.

David nodded. "This was a short trip. Merely to introduce myself to the college."

"And the college to you," Father added with a smile.

I found I was disappointed that this brief visit would be my only contact with David Farwell. Perhaps when he returned in the fall as a student, we would meet again.

After supper, he left with a word for each of us.

"Mrs. Sloan, that dinner made me homesick. Professor Chase, I wish I could start Amherst tomorrow! Miss Sloan, you have my very best wishes for your upcoming wedding." Then he took my hand to shake, and his smiling eyes met mine. "Miss Chase, beware of gods prowling in the underbrush!"

I might have told Emily about meeting David Farwell, but when I called at The Homestead next, she was entirely focused and centered on her own urgent concerns.

"At last! Now, Miranda, we must talk seriously. I have some important news. I think I have found my surgeon."

I was shocked. "Emily, how terrible! An operation?"

"Not for me, for my poems!" She laughed at my misunderstanding. "I want you to read this and give me your opinion." She handed me a recent copy of the *Atlantic Monthly*, folded open. She indicated an article by Thomas Wentworth Higginson called "Ought Women to Learn the Alphabet?" This was an ironic but overwritten piece, stating and restating women's intellectual equality with men. It ended with a baroque flourish:

First give woman, if you dare, the alphabet, then summon her to her career; and though men, ignorant and prejudiced, may oppose its beginnings, there is no danger but they will at last fling around her conquering footsteps more lavish praises than ever greeted the opera's idol, — more perfumed flowers than ever wooed, with intoxicating fragrance, the fairest butterfly of the ball-room.

"I call this very overdone," I told Emily. "His style is like Mrs. Austin's parlor, all satin and fringe. Why would you want his opinion of your poems? You write much better than he does."

"But he does believe in a woman's gifts! Somehow he speaks to me. I feel a sympathy, a kinship. So I'm choosing a few suitable poems to send to him. I feel I could bear 'surgery' from Mr. Higginson. He has none of that fatal CONDESCENSION toward women."

"Emily, are you quite sure?" I dissented with care. "His style is so ornate that he might not appreciate your simplicity. He might fault you for not using as much decoration as he does."

"Miranda, I have DECIDED," she stated firmly, taking the magazine from me. She laid it in her lap and gazed down at it as she spoke. "He will give me a fair hearing, a true reading. Just knowing he is influential and available has cheered me ALREADY."

I thought of all the literary lions who strutted and roared at The Evergreens, where the Austin Dickinsons had established an influential salon. There the college faculty mingled with literary luminaries—poets, journalists, essayists of regional, even national, renown. Any one of these, including Emerson himself, would have been glad to advise a Dickinson and smooth her way to publication. But willful Emily turned instead to a stranger. Why? Her shy arrogance made her motives forever inscrutable—at least to me.

I returned home, stepping carefully to avoid the March mud, and discovered a letter waiting for me on the sideboard. I did not recognize the bold hand or the crisp gray stationery. Curious, I examined the postmark. New Hampshire?

I stared at the envelope, feeling a tingling rush of excitement. Wasn't Phillips Exeter Academy in New Hampshire? Surely there was only one person who could have written to me from that state. David Farwell.

Standing in the front hallway, I carefully opened the envelope. I leaned against the sideboard and angled the paper to better catch the fading sunlight through the front windows.

My Dear Miss Chase,

It was a great pleasure meeting you and your gracious family. You all made me feel very welcome. I was sorry when the evening came to an end—I felt we could have talked on for hours.

This may be presumptuous of me, but I would greatly enjoy continuing our conversation through a correspondence. I felt we had a good deal in common. Do you agree? Perhaps, then, if it is agreeable to you, I shall find I have a friend already when I return to Amherst to attend the college.

With best wishes,

David Farwell

"Miranda, what are you doing standing in the hallway?" Aunt Helen stood at the other end of the hall, her arms wrapped around a rolled-up carpet. Kate stood behind her, holding up the other end.

"I—I was just reading my letter," I explained. I held up the paper.

Aunt Helen nodded. "Ah, yes. From young Mr. Farwell. He sent a very nice thank-you letter to me as well." She stared at me for a moment, and I wondered if she was trying to guess the contents of my letter. Then I realized I was standing precisely where she wanted to lay the rug.

"I'm sorry!" I scrambled out of the way, allowing Aunt Helen and Kate to troop past me. I slipped the letter into the pocket of my dress and helped them lower the heavy carpet to the floor.

Aunt Helen stood and placed her hands on her hips, surveying the rug. "Much better," she declared. She brushed a stray silver hair back toward her low bun. "Yes, that David Farwell seems a nice, well-brought-up young man. Your father will enjoy having him as a student."

"Yes," I agreed. "The college is lucky to have him."

I must have written six drafts before I deemed my reply to David Farwell acceptable. I now understood Emily's flurry of paper every time she sat down to write even the simplest note. I wasn't quite sure what to say to my new correspondent. His letter merely expressed an interest—he gave me no real information. Well, I had met the challenge of the uncharted territory Emily Dickinson had presented, I reminded myself; surely I could compose a simple letter.

Still, I paced, fretted, crumpled. Then finally a letter emerged.

Dear Mr. Farwell,

Thank you for your gracious note. I agree; I too felt we had many interests in common. I would be happy to serve as your introduction to Amherst, particularly if you introduce me through your letters to Illinois.

I know what it is like to be a newcomer in this town. We came to Amherst from another world. Has my father ever mentioned our time in Barbados? I imagine the Greek islands must be similar—sky and water meeting each other every morning at an endless blue horizon. In Barbados it was easy to imagine an angry Neptune at work during the hurricane season and a placated Guardian of the Deep during the rest of the year. Winter in Amherst was quite a jolt to the system after island life—though I imagine to one from Illinois our Amherst weather will seem mild.

I would be very interested in hearing about your studies. Father is quite proud of his Exeter education and counts his years there as among his happiest. Do you feel the same?

I must go now; Aunt Helen is calling us to supper. I will be happy to hear from you again.

Best regards,

Miranda Chase

I gave the paper a delicate blot, folded it in half, and placed it into its waiting envelope. If I read it over even once more, I should find fault with either a phrase or the curl of an "a" or the crossing of a "t," and I should never send it at all. Once again I felt sympathy for Emily's endless revisions. I went downstairs and left the letter with the other mail waiting to be collected in the tray by the front door. I tried to put any additional corrections or word changes out of my mind as I set the table.

I heard Kate laughing behind me. "Miranda, what's gotten into you today?" she asked.

Quizzically I glanced at her. She pointed to the table, and I discovered what she found so amusing: I'd reversed the knives and the forks. I hastily corrected the silverware, explaining lightly, "I was just working out some phrases."

Kate placed folded napkins beside each plate. "Phrases to use in, say, letter writing?"

I flushed but couldn't help laughing at my own transparency. "Something like that," I replied. Together we headed into the kitchen, giggling like conspirators.

For one entire week I was distracted and anxious. Was my letter to David Farwell appropriate? Foolish? Too distant? Too familiar? Unless—*until*—I had a reply, I would not know.

At school, Lolly looked surprised when I gave the wrong answer in botany—one of my better subjects. I gave a small shrug. "Just thinking about things…" I trailed off, hoping Lolly would fill in the gap herself with whatever made the most sense to her.

She smiled a knowing smile. "Are you thinking about the weekend picnic?" she asked. "I was so pleased when Caleb Sweetser invited us both! I was so afraid I wouldn't know the other girls. Have you decided what to wear?"

I had forgotten all about the picnic — and was relieved to have something to distract me. Lolly looped her arm through mine and chatted about dresses and hats as we strolled home.

Where I found a letter from David Farwell.

Dear Miranda — may I call you Miranda?
I was greatly cheered to have received your kind response. I would love to hear all about your time in Barbados and would be happy to tell you all I can about the far less exotic Illinois.…

And so, with his reply, I found myself a regular letter writer. After that first note, David Farwell wrote to me every few days, simply when he felt like talking to me — the way the dolphins used to come visiting in Learner's Cove. It was an additional dimension in my life, and now that the anxious uncertain stage was over, I was once again able to concentrate on my studies — and on Kate's wedding.

Emily was as engrossed in the wedding plans as if Kate were her own cousin. One day, as she and I were discussing Kate's future house, she once again delighted me with the social realism beneath her exterior affectations.

"Kate will be given three punch bowls, and she will sit on the FLOOR," Emily predicted. "So I am having four chairs made for her. Mr. Shiltoe is copying our pair of Sheraton side chairs — the ones in the front hall. Ours are often admired."

That was Emily's way: lavish to someone she was too shy to meet! Then she breathed flame on hearing that our Boston florist was uncertain about our wreaths and bouquets.

"Not enough lilies of the valley, INDEED! Tell him I have a whole HILLSIDE of them for Kate and for you. He may have them all. And tell him he must pick them the day before, and HARDEN them in ice water overnight. You can't expect HIM to know that!"

Emily was full of contrasts. Now she was imperious, a Dickinson of Amherst sending orders to the peasants. In another moment, she would switch to the unworldly and vulnerable poet, cowering in her privacy. But the lily news would delight Kate, I knew.

"Emily, you're a true friend," I said.

"Nonsense! Flowers have their rights, and I am their ADVOCATE. I know this is what the lilies would choose for themselves. They will enjoy being the ORNAMENT of Kate's good fortune!"

I was startled. I didn't think Emily had a high opinion of marriage. "Do you consider Ethan good fortune? Kate surely does!"

"I hear he is charming and talented; he sounds like a good match. But I meant fortune beyond Mr. Howland—I meant Kate's voice, her divine gift. She will always have an IDENTITY—she need never be OWNED. How many women can say as much?"

"Won't you be able to feel that same way when you start publishing your poetry?"

Emily became evasive again. "Not yet, Miranda. I am not READY yet. If I published now, I would be put in with all those syrupy MUSINGS that American women typically compose! Mr. Bowles prints them in every issue, and he DEMEANS the female sex in doing so!"

"How, Emily? How can Mr. Bowles insult women by publishing their poetry?" I was truly curious as to what Emily believed.

"Why, he CONDESCENDS, Miranda. He is showing that women are impulsive creatures but that he, Samuel Bowles, is MAGNAN-IMOUS—and those poems are nothing more than silly, bubbling froth. They should never see the light of day. He is encouraging BAD writing by publishing those shameful examples. No, I will never let him lump me in with those AMATEURS!"

Perhaps Emily's feelings about Mr. Bowles's attitudes toward women's writing was the reason his wife, Mrs. Bowles, seemed to have been placated. I understood from Mrs. Austin that the crisis had been averted, the frayed feelings smoothed over. I had also noticed far fewer letters addressed to the *Springfield Republican* editor.

"But you say 'not yet.' Does that mean you will publish later?"

"I will publish when the right time comes. I will KNOW when I am ready."

Emily went to her window to observe her spring birds; this was a sure sign she was about to say something difficult and important.

"Miranda, at present neither my work nor I are strong enough for COMBAT. We could not DEFEND ourselves against ATTACK. My poetry needs to be more COMMANDING—and so do I. It is better to wait until my poetry can sweep all before it like a JUGGERNAUT!"

I could not argue with her. Truly, Emily's efforts were not made to popular specifications; perhaps she was right to wait for a forum that would respect her serious intellectual presence. Again, I marveled at her patient fortitude and at her confident genius. And yet while she labored on in her solitary yet expectant way, I prayed that for her sake the audience she found one day extended beyond the immediate vista of her own appreciative imagination.

For some reason, I continued to put off telling Emily about meeting David Farwell and about our correspondence. Each letter seemed to bring us closer together, each building on the previous exchange. I felt as if we were revealing tiny bits of ourselves, a new facet each time to hold up to the light, so that by the time he arrived in Amherst, we would each have a sense of the whole. I began to feel that I understood myself better through revealing myself to Davy.

I was pleased when he sent Kate a wedding present: a stunning silver bowl, perfectly simple, with a curved lip like a lotus flower. Father said it was a replica of the one made by Paul Revere, the Revolutionary hero. Ethan whistled and accused Kate of a secret romance. To me, in the privacy of our correspondence, Davy wrote that he wished he could have brought the gift in person so that he could be my escort. Again, I found myself in complete agreement with David Farwell's sentiments.

I had worried, as we were planning every meticulous detail of Kate's wedding for weeks beforehand, that such intense anticipation would detract from the simple joy of the event. After the first hour of Kate's wedding day, however, I realized that all our planning and preparation were essential—to give us unflawed memories.

We were awarded a windless blue-and-white May day, with small harmless clouds. This meant our guests could be in the flagstoned north garden, where Aunt Helen's spring bulbs were a radiance. Kate and I planted them last fall. In October, no one had mentioned a spring wedding—but somehow Aunt Helen's tulips and narcissi and hyacinths had all come up white. With half the guests outdoors, there would be plenty of room in the temple — so our family could receive on the stage, as we had hoped.

"We planned the stage for big occasions," said Ethan. "Now Kate and I and our wedding are your first truly large event."

"And Kate's first concert will be our next," Father stated.

We arranged the two dozen little apple trees, which had been huddling on the terrace, flowering hopefully in their burlap bags. Ethan, two of his friends, and our stableman, Sam, moved eight trees to the back of the stage and concealed their roots with laurel. They carried the others to the corners of the temple, to the walls between the windows, and to the gravel beds in the atrium.

Suddenly we were in an enchanted wood — a forest of white blossom, pink buds, and tiny pointed leaves. Ethan, who designed it, called it the "bride's orchard." After the wedding, we planned to plant a dozen of the apple trees by our kitchen garden. The other dozen would go to Kate and Ethan, in the same wagon as Emily's chairs.

Vera and her helpers bustled in and out of the kitchen, fixing platters and cooling wine. Because the bride and groom were scheduled to take the 6:04 to Boston, the wedding was going to be at two — that is, too late for lunch and too early for supper. The caterer brought little lobster biscuits and a lacy cake, but we would not serve a real meal.

I went to check my arrangements, completed yesterday evening; all were thriving. I used apple blossom and white lilac with budding laurel in the parlor and the dining room. Then I made each of the urns at the front door into a white lilac bridal bouquet with satin ribbon streamers. This frivolity was very becoming to our serious Greek facade.

Under the portico, I met a stranger glaring at my arrangements. "Say, who's the competition here?" It was the florist from Boston!

"The bride's cousin did the flowers," I told him, not revealing my identity as his competitor but relishing the professional jealousy. "May I have the wreaths and the bouquets now?"

I saw Lolly coming up the street, wearing her Sunday bonnet, so I knew it was time to start dressing. Lolly and I carried the florist's white boxes upstairs. Kate was in Aunt Helen's room being laced; her wedding dress hung in the window like a beautiful silk ghost.

Lolly did my stays and lifted the yards of green over my head. Then we tied tiny green ribbon bows among the flowers of my wreath. Lolly pronounced the iced lilies "as crisp as a salad." She was a model of subdued helpfulness. I was learning that at a time like this, women of all ages seemed to put aside all pettiness and vanity, and join selflessly in the enterprise. This was never discussed; it simply happened.

Kate was a tall white lily herself. She wore the modish small basque bodice and bell skirt of the time, so becoming to brides—and Kate Chase Sloan must surely have been the loveliest among these. Her dark hair was smooth and shining, pulled back into a severe classic knot. Emily's lilies framed her face in a starry crown fit for Titania.

There were two carriages for the bridal party. Hoops were hard to transport—one heard about fashionable ladies who required a whole carriage—so we practiced yesterday. Aunt Helen, Lolly, and I rode in the first carriage, and Father and the bride in the second. When we came to the First Congregational Church, we saw the carriages of the wedding guests all along Main Street and around the green. The groom and his family were greeting friends. Mr. and Mrs. Howland were from New Bedford; they were shipbuilders and Quakers. They loved Kate already; how could they not?

We climbed out carefully, and Lolly arranged our dresses. As I carried Kate's train up the steps, we saw that all the pews were filled. Kate clutched my hand; I smiled and nodded. She and I had conspired for a bride's surprise.

"Just stay here," I told Father, Aunt Helen, and Lolly. "We'll be right back."

We left behind three astonished faces and climbed the little spiral stair, which I had swept so carefully yesterday. We signaled Mr. Tate, the organist and our coconspirator, from the balcony.

Mr. Tate began the unmistakable grace notes of Bach's "Jesu, Joy of Man's Desiring," and Kate's voice floated over the congregation like a benediction. She sang her wedding present to Ethan.

The glorious sound and gesture brought tears to my eyes, and from my hiding place I could see Father's face twisted as if he were struggling with his own. Ethan's father and mother took each other's hands and smiled. Ethan glowed with joy, as did Kate.

Afterward, we came down carefully, one step at a time, with a sigh of our silk skirts. I arranged Kate's cloud of veil, put the lilies in her shaking hand, and suddenly the wedding gathered momentum. Mr. Tate became imperative, with Ethan's favorite hymn, "Awake, My Soul," as our processional.

I entered first, past a hundred known smiles, including most of the Dickinsons. Emily and her mother were absent, but this was no surprise. I had given up trying to persuade Emily to attend weeks ago.

Behind me came veiled Kate on Father's arm; her lilies trembled. Ethan and his best man stood at the altar, grave and intent, Ethan's parents watching proudly from the first pew. I took Kate's bouquet and lifted her veil.

I realized I had never really listened to the marriage service before. When Mr. Jenkins read it, I felt terror at the mortal final words: "Till death do you part." How could one prepare for or survive such a loss?

I looked at my father and noticed that fine wrinkles had begun to rake his face like a tree, one for every year endured alone. And for the first time in years, my eyes grew moist as I thought of my mother and wondered what Father had felt when she departed.

I heard the vows and the concluding prayers with a full heart, listening to the service in a new way. Then Mr. Tate at the organ summoned up Bach's cheerful little sheep, grazing safely, and I was carried gently back to reality. We were swept down the aisle, with woolly lambs bounding musically all around us.

Before we knew it we were back at Amity Street for the reception, where we joined Ethan's joyful parents. "Was that truly Kate singing?" Mr. Howland was incredulous at what he had heard before the service. "We've never been treated to her brilliant voice!" We assured him that it was indeed Kate Sloan — now Howland.

The bride lacked a handkerchief, so I ran upstairs to get her one. Coming down, I saw the first of our friends entering the house — so I walked ahead of them, through the flowering atrium, and came upon the tableau awaiting our guests.

The temple was flooded and brimming with afternoon sunlight. The figures on the stage were luminous, defined against a blossoming May orchard. It was a view, a moment I would keep forever.

The rest of the day was a spinning pinwheel of flowers and wine, tears and laughter. We wept when Father toasted Uncle Charles Sloan, Kate's dead father. We laughed when Lolly sneezed from the champagne bubbles despite all our warnings! We posed under the portico for the daguerreotypes, and Kate insisted on having my urns moved to be in the picture—so I wept again.

Aunt Helen and Mrs. Howland went upstairs to help Kate change into a gray crepe traveling costume. I stayed behind with the photographer. David Farwell had been asking me for my likeness, and since I had met him wearing this same green dress, it seemed like a good chance. When I went upstairs, Kate handed me her bouquet.

"I don't want to throw this, Miranda. I'd much rather you took it to Miss Dickinson, to thank her." She pinned on a tiny gray straw bonnet. "You may fetch Ethan now."

When he arrived, Kate took her husband's hand and then turned back to give her last kiss to me. Her green eyes met mine steadily. "I'm leaving here, Miranda, but I'm not leaving you. I never will."

I stood at the head of the stairs and watched them depart. My tears blurred the clouds of rice, the waving friends, the carriage pulling away. For the first time, I saw beyond the excitement of our planning, the perfection of the day itself. I realized that Kate, my dearest friend, my spirit's twin, would never be back. From now on, she would be Mrs. Howland, whose life was apart from us, who loved us second.

Kate was my first young friend ever. Her wise good sense, her sweet high-mindedness, enabled me to become Miranda, my particular self. And her unreserved, unquestioning love changed me forever. Now I had to go on and grow up alone, without her support.

It took me until one in the morning to finish my letter to Miss Adelaide, telling her every outward detail, every inward reflection. I felt as if I had written a novel! And although the day following the wedding was Saturday, not Monday, I broke custom and went to Emily to give her Kate's bouquet. People stopped me on the way to praise the wedding; they were delighted to hear about my errand with the bouquet. It was another thread woven into the fabric of our village life. As Emily told me, her well-known solitude made Kate's gesture to her doubly interesting.

At The Homestead, the hall door was locked, so I went past the conservatory and around to the front. I knocked. There was a long wait, so I used the heavy knocker again, a little louder. Perhaps this was a bad idea; Emily was not good with surprises. I turned to go, and just then I heard steps and saw a curtain twitch. I waited.

The big door was opened by an older woman, stooped and gray haired, with the saddest face I had ever seen. Although we had never spoken before, I knew she was Mrs. Dickinson, Emily's mother; I'd seen her at church.

"Lavinia is out," she told me. The Dickinson family certainly abbreviated their greetings!

"Good morning, Mrs. Dickinson. I am Emily's friend, Miranda Chase. I have brought Emily my cousin Kate Sloan's wedding bouquet."

"I see," she remarked. We continued to stand there in the doorway until Emily called from upstairs.

"Mother, please ask my guest to come up!"

So the sad, silent woman stood aside, and I entered The Homestead. I climbed the broad stairs, distressed by the awkward meeting at the front door — but Emily shrugged, unconcerned.

"Mother cannot cope with people. She isn't shy or timid; she just can't COLLECT herself for strangers. Actually, she can't even talk to her own family. We can hardly hear her from the bottom of her WELL."

I thought of my own mother. She too was not connected. This was another facet of life experience Emily and I shared. Then I shook myself back to the present and my errand.

"Emily, Kate wanted you to have her bouquet, to thank you for being so generous with your lilies."

My friend was charmed. "What an exchange! I give you the raw material, and you return the artifact — slightly USED at the altar! Your florist did these little ribbons very nicely. I'm sure I taught him a useful trick about the ice bath overnight. Now, start at the very BEGINNING."

Using Emily's own rules for narrative, I produced an account that pleased us both — quite different from the outpouring to Miss Adelaide and from what I would eventually share with David Farwell when I wrote him next.

"I hear from all sides the wedding was a PERFECTION," Emily stated. "Father said that Kate's singing from the balcony was 'angelic,' which is his strongest language. He PREFERS angels to women!"

Emily cocked her head and looked at me intently. "My eyes are impaired right now, and I want to get a good look at you." She led me to the window. "Ah, it's as I thought. You HAVE been grieving."

I nodded, hoping my fresh tears wouldn't spill. I wasn't sure how Emily would react to anyone's strong emotions but her own. I didn't want her to feel imposed upon.

Emily, unpredictable as always, responded with genuine empathy. "You and Kate are so close—how could you not feel her going? I know if Lavinia were to leave me, I should weep the PACIFIC. I vow you need some fresh experience to distract you, Miranda—while the AMPUTATION heals."

Emily was right; I did feel I had lost a part of myself. Her insight touched me, though I was afraid her sensitivity was bringing me dangerously close to tears.

I believed she even sensed this; she went on talking quite sensibly, calmly. "I have a plan—just listen. My mother is particularly sad just now, and her doctor recommends a voyage and a change of scene. My father is taking her and Lavinia to a spa—in the White Mountains, I believe. She said once that she was happy there, when she was a girl. Now, Miranda, I am going to play doctor and give the same advice."

She gleamed and twinkled; what was she up to? "What do you mean, Emily?"

"I am recommending the same cure for your sadness: a VOYAGE and a change of scene, right here in Amherst! Won't you visit me here in The Homestead, while my family is in the mountains? We could keep each other company. Your house without Kate may give you pangs for a while. And we could do some important WORK in our time here together. Perhaps we could even sort out my poems? You know that all I do by myself is STIR them; you've seen me at it."

This all appealed to me very much, evoking as it did those happy hours at York Stairs helping Father bring his Greek-dramas volume to life. If we could establish some sort of chronology and order in Emily's poetry, then she might be persuaded to show them to an editor for publication. And her intuition about me was unfailingly correct; I had dreaded the first weeks in the house without Kate, and the marks and memories of our friendship wherever I looked. This was a solution to suit us both.

"Do whatever you choose," said Father when I asked permission at supper. "Remember these aristocratic old maids are always one step short of hysteria—but you seem to handle her pretty well."

"You must come home the very first moment you feel uncomfortable," Aunt Helen fretted. "I really wish your father would forbid it."

"Miranda is not a child, Helen. It's her friend and her decision." Just then there came a firm knock at the door, and Father went to answer it.

Over his shoulder, I saw Mr. Edward Dickinson. To have him drop in on us at suppertime was as likely as Queen Victoria calling on Sam in the stable! The two men went to the library, and we heard their voices faintly for about half an hour. Aunt Helen and I finished our supper and picked at our dessert, waiting. What could they be talking about?

Father walked Mr. Dickinson to the door and then returned to the dining room.

"You have just seen something very rare, very impressive," he said as he settled back into his chair. His plate of cold food had been removed, and he ignored the cake in front of him. "You have seen a fanatically proud man demean himself to ask advice. Edward Dickinson ate humble pie for the sake of his daughter—and she'll never know what it cost him."

"Jos, you'd better tell us what you mean," Aunt Helen demanded.

"I mean that Mr. Dickinson is a protective and observant parent. He is deeply troubled about Miss Emily's tendency toward romantic and sentimental friendships. He told me that, time and time again, she exaggerates her emotions and then expects the same degree of feeling in return. Mr. Dickinson considers Miss Emily's dramas inappropriate and . . . *dangerous.*" He looked at me very seriously, very directly. "He wonders about your visit, Miranda. He is afraid she may work herself up into just such an excessive attachment if you come to stay in his house."

"Are you sure that was all he meant, Jos?" Aunt Helen was very disturbed. I knew what worried her. The same worries that had befallen Susan Dickinson as the recipient of Emily's fevered letters. My stomach tightened at the suggestion.

"That was all he said to me tonight. Miranda, have you personally experienced anything like this with Miss Dickinson?"

I was quiet as I replayed every visit I'd had with Emily, searching for any hint of this unwholesome feeling toward me. I wanted to answer completely truthfully, for my own sake as well as Father's. "Not really, Father," I answered honestly. "She tells me all about her melodramatic friendships, of course, and shows me some of the letters she writes. All the romances are imaginary, you know — they're always about people whom she considers her superiors. But she'd never make up a drama about me; I think I'm not important enough." This was a truth that didn't bother me — it was simply a fact. "She just likes having me there to tell me stories and to hear mine."

"Then it seems to me that Squire Dickinson acted honorably and responsibly, coming here to talk to me." Father was quite ready to dismiss the very odd call.

"He's a frightening parent to Emily," I confided, wanting to plead Emily's side and also hoping I might learn something more about the Dickinson patriarch.

"Is he now? I do get the impression that he sees her as foolish and unreliable — as he sees all women. She doesn't belong in his real world of commerce and power."

"She doesn't," I admitted. "But he sees her world and her interests as *trivial.*" My indignation surprised me but was heartfelt. Mr. Dickinson's dismissive attitude was an affront, for much of what Emily valued, I did as well.

"Miranda, Edward Dickinson is totally single-minded. He eats and sleeps and breathes Amherst! It is more than a patrician's interest — it is his duty, his very life. The town calls him 'one of the River Gods.' He believes that the least detail of the village is his responsibility. He runs for every town office — even dogcatcher and frog marshal — and sometimes he gets only one vote: his own!"

We all laughed; this was a new view of the squire. It made him more human and a bit endearing.

"Let me tell you ladies a story," Father continued. "The winter of 1854 — a few years before we moved here — broke all records for cold. The river was frozen for weeks. One night, Mr. Dickinson looked out and saw a remarkable sight: the northern lights. The baron of Amherst saw his duty to his peasants and went down to the church. He personally rang the church bell — the town alarm — for five minutes. No one in Amherst missed seeing the aurora borealis!"

It was clever of Father to tell us that story. From now on, I would remember there was another side to Emily's parent — that of the Amherst "River God." And it was easier to understand where Emily had gotten her sense of superiority: she had inherited it!

I arrived to visit at The Homestead with a deliberately scanty wardrobe, so I would have to go home for fresh clothes every three or four days. Emily showed me to Miss Lavinia's room, which was across the hall from hers. It seemed staid and impersonal compared to mine at Amity Street—but the shelves were packed with gothic novels. Father would not permit these in the house, so until now, I had not known where to find them. Perhaps, I thought with devilish amusement, I will do some extracurricular reading during my visit!

Since there was still a month of academy classes, Emily had kindly arranged a worktable for me and cleared a shelf for my texts. I was soon unpacked and installed, and Emily and I prepared supper together very companionably—a roast chicken and the summer's first peas. We ate in the dining room and made plans for my visit. I was pleased that Emily was deeply serious about organizing her poetry.

"I have hundreds of poems—literally HUNDREDS! I've been adding to my hoard for years, saving anything worth keeping—from a phrase to a complete poem. We must start tomorrow."

"What if we used this table?" I suggested. "You and I could have our meals in the kitchen, I should think."

"Miranda, how clever of you! We can leave all our papers spread out undisturbed until we finish." Then she added gleefully, "Father would be in a FURY!"

Quickly we established our routine: Emily worked by day at her papers and letters until I returned to The Homestead at four after school. She greeted me downstairs—new for us—and we had tea and shared casual news in an alcove off the parlor. I reported that one of my teachers was leaving to marry and move to Kansas. Emily believed a second robin family was housekeeping in the same nest as the first.

I did my homework until it was time for us to prepare an early supper together, talking idly. Usually Emily had baked us a surprise dessert using a French cookbook.

"Father prefers SERIOUS food," she called to me from the kitchen one evening. "Something WORTHY, like Indian pudding, to move us along the road to salvation. I fear this SOUFFLÉ will cost us time in purgatory!"

Then she startled me by running from the kitchen into the dining room, where I was straightening our piles of papers.

"Miranda, do you know we are committing MORTAL SIN?"

My eyes widened with surprise. "No, Emily—how are we sinning?"

"We are TALKING from ROOM to ROOM! For the first time ever, in this house of constraint. Oh, we are a gloomy lot here, we Dickinsons!" And from then on, Emily called to me deliberately, to spite her absent father's rules.

After the dessert, we got down to business. In the large, dark dining room, we lit two lamps, borrowed from the parlor, and labored in Emily's Augean stables of verse. We sifted through piles of boxed pages and separated the finished poems, putting the best version of each into one folder. The alternate versions went in a second folder, and the disconnected, unused lines or phrases in a third. Then Emily sewed the poems we considered finished into little volumes, loosely stitched at the fold. She would not explain how she grouped them. I could see some general categories—Nature, Love, Death—but I saw no chronology or plan, though she assured me both were implicit.

Sometimes Emily asked for my help in choosing between two versions of a poem. I was gratified when she praised my taste. She often related Sue's comments or opinions; despite Emily's disapproval of Mrs. Austin's lavishly social lifestyle, she clearly respected her sister-in-law's literary and editorial talents. Emily had been sending Mrs. Austin most of her poetry for quite some time. I enjoyed being included among those Emily trusted with her most prized possession—her words.

"My greatest influence is Isaac Watts, whose hymns I am sure you know and sing," Emily offered. "He would admire your ear for meter."

I recognized the name; he was a pastor in the early 1700s, and I did indeed know his hymns.

"His verse is TAUT, without padding," Emily continued. "He was a pure radical thinker, stripping away all the trimmings and go-betweens around God. He has no flesh; he writes the BONES. He has a stark view that I share. Listen!" And in a child's clear treble, small and true, she sang, "O God, our help in ages past."

"I know he wrote 'Joy to the World,'" I said. "But what else did Watts write?"

"There's my other favorite," Emily replied. "'Jesus Shall Reign.' His book *Prosody*—that means the arrangement of poetry—is a 'lantern to my footsteps.' Sometimes I wonder why I write at all, when Watts has said everything there is to say in what I just sang to you."

On the days when I went home to launder my clothes, to catch up on news, and to answer Aunt Helen's litany of questions, I found it easy to tell Aunt Helen the pleasant truth about my visits.

"Working with Emily is really splendid! She treats me as her amanuensis, quite like an adult. I don't think she is really aware of the age difference between us—not even of her own age. She simply acts as if we are equals."

"If she asks you, you can tell her she's almost thirty—a very strange thirty. Tell her she's about twice your age. I want you to be very different when you reach thirty, Miranda."

Aunt Helen, with her unselfishness and restraint and discipline, would never understand what I saw in Emily, who had none of those qualities.

This was a happy time, visiting Emily. Our days settled into an easy, productive rhythm, filling the empty space left by Kate's departure. Until one day at the academy, when Lolly proposed that she should come and call on me at The Homestead.

"Lolly, it's not my house," I protested, surprised by the presumptuous request. "You know I can't invite you there."

"Then tell her to invite me. Tell her you miss me." Lolly's dark brown eyes grew coy, while her full lips pouted. "You never join us in any of our outings anymore. So let me join you." Now her eyes flashed with challenge.

I couldn't understand her insistence until I remembered Emily's own assessment of herself as the town mystery. Hadn't she implied my popularity at school was based in part on my proximity to "the myth"?

I shook my head. "Lolly, you can't make me be rude. I won't do it."

Lolly, used to getting her way, glared at me. She seemed uncertain how to handle my surprising rebellion.

Then Alice Fay, one of Lolly's followers, decided to gain Lolly's favor by falling in line behind her.

"My mother says you're Miss Emily's 'familiar,'" Alice sneered. "All her friends say that."

The other girls all gasped in horror over Alice's comment, so this must have been a fearful accusation—but one I didn't understand.

"Alice, be quiet!" Lolly wouldn't allow anyone else to criticize me, which was loyalty of a sort. "Let's go," Lolly then commanded her coterie, and I watched, still pondering the meaning of Alice's insult, as they filed back inside the brick schoolhouse.

How was I to find out? I couldn't ask Emily, certainly. As for Aunt Helen, the word "familiar" suggested those dark matters she had already hinted at—just over the edge of my comprehension. But I had to know—and Mrs. Austin seemed my only hope. Lolly and her set—girls I had thought of as my friends—avoided me all day, but that was a relief. I went directly to The Evergreens from school, and I found Mrs. Austin and her gardener installing a huge reflecting sphere in her rose garden. It suited the showy house.

"The birds love these in Italy," she stated. "Let's hope our proper Puritan birds are allowed to look in the mirror!" Then she invited me in for lemonade and heard the reason for my call.

"I know the slander you fear, Miranda, and you can relax," Mrs. Austin assured me. "A 'familiar' is a witch's cat, her accomplice in spells and magic. That vicious Alice Fay was saying that Emily is a witch, and you are her companion, helping her do ill. The Archie Fays can just stop expecting any more invitations to The Evergreens."

"So this isn't anything that will hurt Emily?"

Mrs. Austin's face softened into a dimpled smile. "What a loyal friend you are, Miranda! No, it's impossible to hurt the Dickinsons in Amherst; they own it. Someday they might hurt *themselves*—but only a Dickinson can damage the Dickinson name."

She leaned toward me and patted my knee, expertly changing the subject.

"Now I want to hear about Emily's manuscripts. How goes your work? Emily says you are a 'ruthless Solomon'!"

"All I do is choose between versions of the same poem, so we can get all the ones together that are ready to publish."

"And then what?" Mrs. Austin looked surprised. Of course, she would know of Emily's resistance to publication even better than I did.

I gave her a rueful smile. "Then comes the hard part—persuading Emily to show them to an editor."

Mrs. Austin smiled back. "How I wish all her friends would help her the way you do. But she always gets so fatally *intense* and scares people away."

"I don't think it will happen with me, Mrs. Austin. I don't really count as a person to Emily. I'm more...an *audience.*"

Mrs. Austin leaned back against the brocaded settee. "You are much wiser than I was at your age." Then she leaned forward and took my hand again. "And you are very much a *person* to me."

I kissed her good-bye gratefully. I liked her shrewd honesty about Dickinson affairs.

One evening, in the second week of my stay at The Homestead, I returned from school to find Emily—tidy, formal Emily—rumpled and trembling and distraught. I could tell she had been weeping for some time. Her round face was even rounder, her eyes slitted. The curtains were closed tight, locking out the midafternoon light.

"Miranda, forgive me. Having Father away has recalled some poignant Homestead ghosts. We lived here my first ten years, you know. Our family was so close in those days, just the four of us! With Father gone—gone rebuilding our name and fortune—only then did we escape his rod and rule. Every morning of my childhood when he was home, the voice he used at the Statehouse was trained steady on us. Every morning was Sunday school at the Dickinson house."

Emily was coiled in her armchair like a baby as she related this; she unwound herself, rising slowly. "But in Father's absence we were at rest and free. Vinnie was mild and innocent then, and Austin could show his devotion to us without Father there to scorn him for unmanly feelings. And Mother needn't fear Father's stormy moods. She used to play along with us."

Her swollen eyes grew distant, as if they were looking inward at her past. "Mother was always laughing then. There never were happier children when he was gone, not in this unhappy world." Her gaze shifted to me. "Oh, Miranda, how could it all change so much?"

I went to her at once. "It sounds as if you were a very happy family, Emily." I handed her a small linen handkerchief, embroidered like the spring outside with tiny blossoms, but she was so shaken and distressed that I persuaded her into bed in broad daylight. I brought her tea, and fresh pillowcases smelling of lavender, and cologne pads for her swollen eyes—just as Aunt Helen had done when I had my mumps. I saw her smile under the cooling cloths.

"What a delight to be COSSETED! It must be like this to have a mother." Her mouth reset into a straight, quivering line. "I never had a

mother. I had only a merry playmate once, and now—a tragic child."
She gave a piteous half sob.

Not knowing what else to do, I held her hand until her deepening
breaths told me she had slipped into sleep.

Careful not to disturb her, I unlaced my fingers and went to my
temporary room, intending to study. But I was too distracted by Emily's revealing images of her childhood. I was moved by her merry little
ghosts, but at the same time I glimpsed some stunning truths. Emily
recalled a carefree time, but I sensed something quite different behind
her memories.

I saw a silly, irresponsible mother; an effeminate son; two possessive little sisters, overattached to their brother and competing for his
favor. I saw an Old Testament father looming over his awed family,
breathing damnation and hellfire unless they followed his Puritan
rules. Whether this last was true or false, it was Emily's own vision of
Mr. Edward Dickinson.

I tiptoed down the stairs, back to our worktable. I picked up and
began to read the verse fragments scattered about, obviously just as
Emily left them this morning until the upset took over. I searched
the papers for the trigger but found none I could recognize. Finally I
pushed the papers away and sat a long time while daylight faded. This
explained so much about this puzzling, unhappy family: the mother,
with her nervous complaints and obscure maladies; poor Vinnie, with
her lingering angers toward the parent she blamed for sending a great
love away; and Austin, the son with everything except a father's respect.
Affection was like bread, I mused. It was unnoticed until we starved,
and then we dreamed of it, sang of it, hungered for it—and never
knew anything else but the longing for it.

And Emily, whose uneasy ambivalence toward her father drove her
work. Unseen, *unknown,* to him, this daughter's ferocious intellect was
the only one in the family's to rival his, yet it was unrecognized and
unregarded. She was neither his namesake nor his heir. How deep her
misery, her anger. When she reproached God, it was her own vision of
Mr. Edward Dickinson that she addressed.

I was saddened and sympathetic, and felt the need to express this.
Who better than to David Farwell? I had always felt defensive on
Emily's behalf at home because I sensed the disapproval and begrudg-
ing acceptance of our friendship; I felt I could not reveal my own

ambivalence about Emily there. Davy would make no judgments and, in my letter, allow me to simply share these thoughts. I wrote for the rest of the afternoon, and by the end of five pages, I felt unburdened and refreshed. Folding the letter neatly, I slipped it into my pocket to be addressed and mailed from home. Then I cooked myself a simple supper; Emily did not stir till morning.

At the end of a fortnight, we received word that the Dickinsons were leaving the New Hampshire resort and returning to Amherst. Lavinia's note implied that Mrs. Dickinson remained uncheered.

"Her sadness is a QUICKSAND," Emily said, handing me a soapy dish.

"At least your mother tries to be part of your life," I told her a little sharply. "Mine never did."

Emily's immediate understanding surprised me. She placed her wet hand on mine. "Yes," she said, nodding. "You and I were equally robbed, weren't we? Most people take the miracle of a MOTHER entirely for granted."

The next day Emily and I packed up my belongings, and I returned home. Our house on Amity Street seemed vivid and welcoming to me after the formal reserve of The Homestead. "It seemed very impersonal," I told Aunt Helen as I hung my dresses in my wardrobe. "There was nothing that said, 'He chose this. She likes that. We are reading these.'"

Father must have heard our conversation, because he came into my room, clearly amused. "So what does The Homestead tell you instead, Miranda?"

"It says, 'Are your feet clean? Then enter on probation. Remember our superior ancestors!'"

Father burst out laughing. "Bravo, Miranda! Your friend is a regular finishing school for style. Between Miss Dickinson's conversation and young Farwell's letters, you'll soon have a degree in advanced English usage."

I didn't think Father had noticed the letters.

I had never read a love letter except in novels, and ours were certainly not like those. Mostly Davy and I wrote about our extreme mutual awareness, our insatiable interest in each other. We wanted to know all there was to tell — about the years before we met.

"I intend to be a part of your life," Davy wrote over and over. "Here is what I am like. I want you to know all about me, just as I want to know you." Answering a letter like this was very demanding. As I wrote to him, I could tell that talking with Emily had made me more selective, more adept with image and metaphor—though a narrative for Emily was much easier than introspection for Davy.

At our only meeting, I had been impressed with his easy, confident manner—his total lack of self consciousness. Therefore, I had been astonished when I read that he was as uncertain as I was about fitting in with his friends at home.

No one in Lake Forest reads—that is, no one my age. We ride and swim and skate—and that's what we talk about. So I hide my books—and the fact that I love school, and always have! Most of the time I feel as if I were going about in disguise, hiding what I'm really like. Have you ever felt this way?

"All the time!" I answered him. "I talked more about important things with you—the evening you came to supper—than I had in all my time with my academy friends. Let's never wear masks with each other."

Father was right: living up to Davy's letters had taught me a lot about good writing. When he wanted to hear my happiest memory (Learner's Cove) or my most fearful experience (almost losing my foot), then I related it clearly and chronologically.

Davy wrote as easily as he spoke. His letters were vivid, witty, and completely original; no one else could think or write as he did. He was back in Illinois now, reading and playing in Lake Michigan—and thinking about me. He planned to teach his little stepsister to swim, and I had written him a sort of primer of steps to follow. Because I loved Ovid, Davy was doing his own translation of *Metamorphoses*. He was going to start reading Browning on my advice, and I planned to try Wordsworth on his. I knew that the summer would pass, autumn would come, and Davy would soon be back in Amherst, attending college less than a mile away.

This was to have been the summer we returned to Barbados. We had made our plans and arranged our passage, but then Dr. Hugh had a sudden and serious return of consumption, his old enemy. We decided not to intrude on Miss Adelaide at such a time. We tried not to feel alarmed, though it was clear that Father realized he might never see his dear friend again.

Then another letter from Miss Adelaide brought the news I had nearly guessed two Junes ago. Lettie's Elijah had married another girl, Susannah, after we left—and Lettie had had a little daughter that same Christmas. She named the baby for me, but she called her "Mira." I imagined Miss Adelaide had waited until she deemed me old enough to accept Lettie's circumstances without needing too much explanation. An unmarried woman having a child with a man who chose another wife would have required a great deal of explanation for the sheltered thirteen-year-old girl I had been. My letters to Miss Adelaide in these intervening years must have provided her with the evidence that I was mature enough for this delicate information. I wished only that Lettie herself had told me the reason for her cold withdrawal two years ago, but I understood everything now.

This year, I won the Latin and geography prizes at the academy at term's end, and Mrs. Austin invited me for an afternoon visit to celebrate. I took her an armful of Aunt Helen's crimson and purple anemones. She had admired my flowers at the wedding and asked if I would do an arrangement for her newly Turkish music room.

My hostess produced the perfect container: a deep-blue enamel bowl with gold stars, exotic and opulent. I could see Mrs. Austin's quick mind following me as I worked, and I sensed that flower arranging would be her newest society talent. This observation would amuse Miss Adelaide when I wrote next.

"Now you must bring me up to date on Emily's poems," she demanded as we sipped our syllabub.

"Have you seen any new ones, Mrs. Austin?" I asked. "Emily hasn't shown me any lately."

"Indeed I have! I don't see Emily herself, but I receive poems from her almost every week. I can tell the organizing with you did wonders for her. Even when we were girls, Emily was always better at starting a new project than completing an old one!"

Kate so close, so easy to reach. Aunt Helen visited often as well, which softened the blow of Kate's departure. Kate had settled into her little house, among her wedding presents and Aunt Helen's furniture.

I helped her paint the kitchen pale yellow; then we dug a vegetable garden together. The tiny apple trees that bloomed for her wedding were promising real fruit by autumn.

"I never knew I could hold so much happiness," Kate told me. "I'm afraid it will spill! I wake up knowing I have a whole lifetime ahead—years and years to love Ethan and be with him."

Kate practiced two hours every morning and often sang for Ethan after dinner. They were planning a musical soiree for September. Kate had been engaged as a soloist in the Presbyterian church and was learning new music for the services. I warmed my hands at her joy.

July vanished, August lumbered along; Amherst was a dusty green sameness, and I longed for the clarity and brilliance of autumn. My Greek studies were not enough to quench my restlessness, nor could books calm my ardor. I imagined I was a lady shut up in a tower until autumn came, when my knight would return from afar and release me from this exquisite torrent of new feeling.

The Austin Dickinsons had seen what the others had not. I had crossed a threshold; I had fallen in love.

Book VI

⁊

AMHERST

1859–1861

September approached, and I grew uneasy about Davy's return. Although we had exchanged many letters, we had met face-to-face only that one evening. Did I imagine our extraordinary harmony? I felt as Emily must, preferring to keep a man at arm's length rather than to confront his male reality. I considered confiding in Kate, even in Lolly, who had more experience with beaux than I, but finally decided to brave Davy's upcoming return on my own. I found myself sleepless some nights, and I wrote drafts of letters to him confessing my fears, none of which survived the next morning's breakfast fire.

Then Davy arrived unannounced a week early — "to buy my books and make friends with the library!" — and when he called, we chattered like old friends reunited. All my nerves had been unwarranted. We had learned so much about each other from our letters that unease was impossible. I was secretly pleased that Father was out when Davy came to call. I didn't want to share this time of becoming reacquainted with Davy with anyone, and I knew Father would entice his new student into his study and regale him with tales of Aristophanes. Aunt Helen, after helping me with a tray of lemonade and ginger biscuits, left us alone in the front parlor.

"I love the color you turn in summer." Davy smiled.

I wondered what color I'd become now as I flushed with pleasure at the compliment. I studied his handsome face, enjoying his open smile, his smooth forehead, his resonant voice. I watched his hand reach for a glass of lemonade, admiring those elegant fingers. He was exactly as I had remembered him; I hoped I was living up to his own memories of me.

"I'll bring my Ovid next time," he suggested. "Is four thirty all right, on weekdays?"

"Four thirty would be fine," I replied. I took a sip of lemonade. "Except Mondays, of course, when I visit Emily."

Davy nodded. "Yes, 'the myth.' Your letters made her sound fascinating."

"Did they?" I wondered what interested Davy, what details had caught his attention. Then I had the unworthy concern that Emily was more fascinating than I. I pushed the anxiety aside to concentrate on my guest.

"Amherst is a lovely town," Davy said, standing. He crossed to the large windows and gazed out. "It will be a pleasure to live here." He turned to face me. "I'm going to find a place on the river where we can swim next spring."

Next spring? I realized then that Davy was not concerned about next week only; he was planning our whole year—and perhaps even beyond that.

Aunt Helen returned to the parlor "to retrieve the tray," but both Davy and I knew it was her subtle way to suggest our visit come to an end. On leaving, Davy took my hand and repeated what he had written at the close of every letter: "I intend to be a part of your life."

The door closed behind him. I spun around and leaned against it, needing the solid wood to hold me up. Crossing my arms over my chest, I took in a deep breath. Life is about to become very different, I realized. I was eager to face those changes.

I spent an afternoon with Emily before the academy opened, and I was flattered to learn that she had given a great deal of thought to my last two years of school.

"You must use this time to the fullest, Miranda," she advised. "It comes only once. My years at the academy were the CREAM of my life and the only mental training I ever had. You must not waste a second!"

"I promise," I vowed solemnly, barely hiding my amusement at her intensity. "I will use my time wisely."

"I'm serious," she protested, but with a smile. "Now—I have decided you must drop geography and botany, which you can pursue on your own. You must take as much Greek and Latin as you can, and history—you should be SATURATED in history. And take every course there is in grammar and USAGE, in order to speak the language of the greatest minds, the greatest men."

I was touched that she was so concerned about my studies. "Emily, I truly value your interest." I tucked my feet under me, curling up on the settee. "Who were your best teachers?" I was curious about what Emily found valuable, now that she had some distance from her school days.

"Professor Hitchcock," she responded without hesitation. "The greatest natural scientist of his day—and a president of the college."

I nodded, recognizing the name.

"I attended his geology classes at the college, with other advanced academy students," Emily continued. "He made me aware of the natural DESIGNS that surround us in life—in a rock or a pine needle. He was a dinosaur expert too, but that didn't APPLY. My other Mentor was Noah Webster, who was also a founder of both the academy and the college. He is my greatest resource. His dictionary and my Congregational hymnal are my only reference books."

I thought over the curriculum Emily had planned out for me and was pleased. "No mother could have advised me as well," I told her.

"That's true." She accepted my gratitude complacently. "This aspect of being a mother would have been very pleasing to me. But, oh, the rest of it." She shuddered dramatically. "I could little tolerate the ways of a small person, always needing, always demanding, always THERE! It's better I get my motherhood in tiny helpings, like today."

As always, the maples blazed up to light my birthday. Emily gave me a romantic folder, printed in lilies of the valley and tied with green ribbons, "for your correspondence." This made me feel guilty. I really must tell her about Davy very soon, I scolded myself.

Davy brought me an anthology of Latin lyrics, with charming engravings of the poets and their artfully undraped ladies, picnicking among columns. He had been invited for my birthday dinner, which made turning sixteen all the more poignant.

The Howlands also came for my birthday dinner, and I was distressed to see that Kate was looking unwell. She gave me a pale, odd smile. Aunt Helen seated her and called me into the kitchen. As I followed her, Davy and Ethan began a discussion of Greek and Roman architecture, and Father joined in the moment he entered the dining room.

"I suppose you've guessed," Aunt Helen said once she shut the kitchen door. "Kate's baby will be born in March."

"But it's too soon!" I protested. I knew I shouldn't have been so surprised. After all, married people do have babies. But my Kate? Now? "She is just starting with her music in Springfield," I said.

"I feel the same way, but we won't tell Kate." Aunt Helen sighed. "I was hoping they'd have a little time together first. Her music will have to wait till it suits the baby, I'm afraid."

I carried in the platter of vegetables, and Aunt Helen brought in the roast. I noticed that Ethan, who had always clearly adored Kate, was even more solicitous toward her. Neither Father nor Davy seemed aware of any change in Kate.

As always, Davy was at ease and charming. I was pleased to see Kate's obvious approval, and Ethan and Father's interest in Davy's ideas and opinions. Although he was younger than both of them, they still treated him as an equal; his intelligence and presence demanded it.

After dinner, we opened the French champagne Davy had brought with his parents' compliments, and there were toasts to my birthday. Ethan was gallant, and Kate and Aunt Helen were simple and genuine. Then it was my father's turn.

"To Miranda, who grew up when I wasn't looking," he toasted me. I heard an edge to this, but I couldn't define it. "In fact, I almost missed the transformation entirely."

I felt heat in my cheeks. I was confused and embarrassed by my father's toast.

Davy pressed my hand under the table. He rose and locked his silver eyes on mine. "To Miranda, the girl I admire with all my heart." It was the perfect reply to Father's flippancy, and as he lifted his glass and drank to me, our eyes never left each other's deep gaze.

Then his cheeks tinged pink. He lowered his glass and glanced around the table. "Many happy returns of the day," he finished, sitting back down. I dropped my eyes to my lap, my lips curling unbidden into a smile. My heart reverberated with the words, the knowledge: Davy loved me.

Aunt Helen stood and began to clear the table, chatting with Kate brightly about Catherine Beecher's latest article on housewifery in *Harper's*. "Jos," she said to Father, "would you help me fetch fresh well water? I'd like to soak the pots."

I was grateful for her graceful distraction.

With a sly grin at Kate, Ethan offered to show Davy the temple and to tell him all about our struggles with its infamous "rock." Davy seemed relieved and followed Ethan eagerly, leaving me alone with Kate.

Kate was breathless with curiosity and questions. "Miranda, what haven't you told me? Did you know what he was going to say?"

"No, I didn't," I admitted. I grinned at her. "But I liked hearing it with all of you here. It was good for Father."

"Well, he'll certainly have to admit you are grown-up now," Kate said. Her green eyes searched mine. "Are you . . . engaged?"

"No," I said. I had not thought that far into the future, relishing the present. "We haven't had time."

Davy came to say good night, and I noticed a small coolness toward him from Father. Father too would need time to get used to my new situation.

"I know I should have waited," Davy said. We stood under the portico, saying good night. "My toast was something I should have said to you alone. But your father made you sound so childish—somehow . . . not ready for this."

"But I am ready, Davy," I assured him. "I'm glad you said it and that you said it in front of my family."

Davy gently tucked a curl behind my ear. "Whenever I say, 'I intend to be a part of your life,' I think of us as being engaged already, but I've never really asked you—have I?"

I ducked my head and bit my lip, anticipating with pleasure what was about to come next. "Not exactly . . ."

"Then it's time I proposed properly, Miranda." He took my hands in his, and I marveled at their strength. "Miranda, will you do me the honor of becoming my wife? I will do all in my power to make our life together happy and filled with adventure."

I felt tears spring to my eyes. "Yes," I whispered. And as Kate said, we were really and truly, although secretly, engaged. We would keep it a secret, both knowing what storms would ensue.

Even so, I was faint with incredulous joy as he swept me into his arms, laughing. Somehow we had skipped all the usual doubts and vacillations of young lovers and had reached the serene acceptance of a pledged couple. Could it be that already, like Kate and Ethan, we had a shared lifetime ahead?

That night I did *not* write to Miss Adelaide. I didn't want to put her in a position of knowing something so important that needed to be kept from the rest of my family. Not even Kate could know—not yet. I had to go on with my life as though nothing had happened. My letters to Miss Adelaide and to Mr. Harnett for the next few weeks were carefully all about my studies. With school starting, I had a good deal to relate.

I had taken Emily's good advice about my curriculum and dropped geography and botany. Instead I was taking ancient history (which involved a lot of geography, I found) and doing two independent study reports. I was the first academy student who had ever been allowed to work on two—and before my senior year. Just to keep me modest, the headmaster reminded me that I was still a year behind in math.

My first report was to be on early childhood education. This subject had been very much on my mind ever since I started attending a proper school. I could not help but notice that my many years with Mr. Harnett gave me not only a solid grounding of knowledge but also a passionate eagerness to learn. I had not seen this quality in my classmates. What did Mr. Harnett and I do together that was different or right?

To research this, I would spend an hour a day helping and observing in the youngest classes in my school. Also, I would take a full day here and there at the primary schools in nearby towns and villages. I would go all over the valley, taking the cars alone. Father thought I was grown-up enough for this, I observed.

My second report, a history of Greek drama, would be the result of my studies with Emily; she was pleased and proud. My ancient-history teacher, Mr. Shouse, taught at both the academy and the college, so I accompanied him to his college lectures on the Greek dramatists. I made myself invisible in class and saved my questions till later, at Mr. Shouse's request.

When my new schedule seemed to mesh with Davy's college classes, Aunt Helen announced rules for our studying together. These appeared full grown, in armor, like Athena stepping from Zeus's forehead.

"Two afternoons a week in the dining room—at opposite ends of the table. And Davy may come to supper Wednesday, and you may work together until nine thirty. If Miranda cannot maintain her grades, then we shall have to reconsider."

This seemed fair; we did not press for more. We smiled secretly when Aunt Helen passed the dining room and looked in. She saw us, heads bowed over our work, each in a semicircle of books and papers—and ten feet of mahogany between us! This was very far from the romantic tryst my classmates imagined.

Lolly and her crowd were critical of my changed life. They disapproved of my relationship with Davy.

"People say you're much too young!" Lolly lectured, repeating, no doubt, the words of her parents. "Besides, why settle with one boy when you should have many beaux? That way you can make a more considered choice when it's time to think about marriage."

Alice Fay and Melinda Carlyle nodded their agreement. Lolly was teaching them "feminine wiles," and they were eager students. I had witnessed Lolly flirting and heard rumors of several smitten swains, while she held herself aloof. It was an interesting game to observe but not one I would want to play. How much more they would disapprove if they knew that Davy and I were already secretly engaged.

But Davy wasn't the only wedge between me and my schoolmates. They resented my new academic status, sniffing disdainfully at my incessant thirst for education, at my — to them — overzealous academic undertakings. So the disguise no longer worked: I was defrocked, seen to be what I had tried to hide. But at least I wouldn't have to keep switching masks.

When I felt I could be discreet with my feelings, I wrote Miss Adelaide, telling her I had a beau and describing all of Davy's wonderful qualities and the manner in which we got to know each other. "All the letters to you," I told her, "relating both the important and the inconsequential details of my life, prepared me for such a correspondence. I had learned already how to be my most true self on paper; this only became more true in writing to Davy."

Miss Adelaide's letters came directly from her generous heart: "You deserve this joy. You must use every moment in harmony and understanding; a true love grows with loving. I am happier than I can ever say for you and for Davy. I want so many good things for you, and they're starting to happen already!"

I had dreaded the inevitable moment when Emily linked her imaginary affair with my real one. But Miss Lavinia Dickinson was in Aunt Helen's sewing group, where the village telegraph circulated all the Amherst news. When I decided to tell Emily about Davy, around Halloween, I learned she had known about him for weeks. Miss Lavinia had discovered Davy's complete biography before he had even unpacked.

"I didn't speak of it till you were ready," Emily stated. "Such matters get bruised and crushed in the telling. I do not discuss my Master with anyone but you — and him, of course."

I appreciated her sensitivity; I had been concerned that she would have seen my reluctance to share the news of Davy with her as disloyal secrecy. I was curious about the status of her "relationship" with this Master; she hadn't mentioned him in some time. "Do you hear from your Master these days?"

The Dickinsons had brought on a hired girl, Nancy, whom Emily trusted to mail her letters now—so I did not know to whom she wrote. This suited us both. Emily didn't have to wait for my Monday visit to send a letter—she could be voluminous with her correspondence when the mood struck her. I, never comfortable with my role as "spy," had less awkward responsibility. But I took my promise to Mrs. Austin seriously, so I paid careful attention to whatever Emily chose to reveal about her latest passions.

"He is my SHEPHERD, my MENTOR; he counsels me," Emily replied without answering my actual question. "It is a raising of the spirit merely to write him. Sometimes I do, just to feel we are in touch—and then I don't mail the letter." She collected some used papers that were strewn about her rug and fed them to her busy little stove.

I felt relieved by this news. The letters were obviously becoming less frequent. Mrs. Austin could be reassured. Perhaps Emily's interest was transforming from ardent lover to ardent student, far more appropriate roles for the recluse and the married minister to play. As a *muse,* the Master was not the threat he could be as a *man.*

Emily was cheerful today, with the maples' October brilliance lighting her white walls. There were some bowls of blooming narcissus on her windowsills; I leaned to breathe the scent.

"Miranda, tell me, do you and your beau exchange many sentimental letters?"

"Not really," I replied. "We see each other so often now that we don't write anymore. Last summer, it seemed more important to really get to know each other. Our letters were more like autobiographies, I think."

"Well, that's not my STYLE of letter!" She was impatient at this. "A letter should convey feeling, not DATA. Here is MY sort of love letter." She handed me what was evidently a draft, for I saw many crossings out on the penciled pages. And I read the salutation and winced.

Master.

If you saw a bullet hit a Bird—and he told you he was'nt shot—you might weep at his courtesy, but you would certainly doubt his word.

One drop more from the gash that stains your Daisy's bosom—then would you believe? *Thomas' faith in Anatomy, was stronger than his faith in faith. God made me—[Sir] Master—I did'nt be—myself. I don't know how it was done. He built the heart in me—Bye and bye it outgrew me—and like the little mother—with the big child—I got tired holding him. I heard of a thing called "Redemption"—which rested men and women. You remember I asked you for it—you gave me something else. I forgot the Redemption [in the Redeemed—I did'nt tell you for a long time, but I knew you had altered me—I] and was tired—no more...*

I couldn't bear not knowing how the letter would end, so I skipped down to the last two lines.

No Rose, yet felt myself a'bloom,
No Bird—yet rode in Ether.

I felt embarrassed by the letter's beginning, but those last two lines perfectly captured my own feelings of being in love with Davy. Here among the clichés and the affectations, I heard a clear voice and crystalline truth. Encouraged, I went back to the middle of the letter:

I want to see you more—Sir—than all I wish for in this world—and the wish—altered a little—will be my only one—for the skies.

Could you come to New England—[this summer—could] would you come to Amherst—Would you like to come—Master?

[Would it do harm—yet we both fear God—] Would Daisy disappoint you—no—she would'nt—Sir—it were comfort forever—just to look in your face, while you looked in mine—then I could play in the woods till Dark—till you take me where Sundown cannot find us—and the true keep coming—till the town is full. [Will you tell me if you will?]

This worried me. She was inviting him to see her. What could I say? "Emily, tell me. What is your purpose in writing this letter?"

"Why, the same purpose that inspires any letter of SENTIMENT. This...individual, this personage, wants to understand me. He is INTERESTED in me, in my thoughts. I want him to KNOW me."

She shaped a demure smile, folded her hands in her lap, and waited. There was no escape.

"Then this letter is a failure," I told her. "This person won't know you from your letter because *it isn't you speaking*. There is none of your precision, your dignity. You wander about and play peekaboo, as if you are younger and sillier than I. You don't do yourself justice!"

I expected a hurricane wilder than that of Barbados in reply, but Emily was merely thoughtful.

"I haven't sent it yet; I know it still needs work. I am used to communicating with *only* MYSELF. Other people are much harder to talk to."

Perhaps it would all end here. Perhaps she would decide she didn't want to see him face-to-face.

"Just one more thing, Miranda—do you think I sound too OLD?"

I assured her that if anything, she sounded not old enough. Then we took our tea as if this were an ordinary day. Emily had made an extra loaf of apricot bread for Davy.

"Tell him it won second prize at the agricultural fair of 1856," Emily recounted. "Then they put me on the committee for 1857, and every other entry was apricot bread. That was the end of my wielding a judge's GAVEL!"

Where had our autumn gone? The clear days twisted and spiraled past us; they had vanished like the maple leaves. Time rushed toward us and sped away, as fleeting as the valley landscape seen from the train.

By now, Davy and I had our traditions together; we had our own secret language. When we separated in front of others, he said only, "I intend..." But when we were alone, he said it properly, looking in my eyes and kissing me: "I intend to be a part of your life."

I said his name as often as I could, finding excuses to bring it into conversations. Gradually, as we piled up the days of joy, we established a private anthology of shared references. The Connecticut River was the "Tiber." A sanctimonious classmate was "Galahad." Davy's closest friend, also from Exeter, was John Miles—but to us, David's best friend must be "Jonathan."

Davy brought me little presents of Daphne's laurel, our own private symbol. One, an antique bronze spray, Father pronounced too valuable for me to accept—so Davy was keeping it for me. We were making an anthology of classical references to laurel, and I was learning calligraphy and illuminating the capitals.

I found I had extended my awareness and insight into others by loving Davy. Now I could interpret Kate's sigh as she dusted her closed piano. Now I felt Mr. Shouse's silent pleasure when a student lingered with questions. Even the little pupils in the elementary schools I visited as part of my independent study awoke a protective tenderness in me that was new and that I attributed to having opened my heart to Davy.

The days continued to accumulate. When Thanksgiving came, Davy visited a classmate in Boston. Since Kate wasn't traveling, Aunt Helen, Father, and I went to Springfield in our carriage. We brought the dinner with us; the turkey was an easy passenger, but Father claimed the tureen of gravy rode all the way on his lap. We found Kate looking very badly—her olive skin greenish and her usually sparkling eyes dull. She kept her small house polished and orderly—but she did not have the energy for her music. I knew nothing about what to expect from Kate's condition, but she was a constant worry to me.

December, and the first snows began to fall. Our family gave an eggnog party in the temple before the college closed; Davy helped us hang the garlands of evergreens. He was amused by the Amherst standards of austerity for Christmas ornaments. He told me Lake Forest was very relaxed Presbyterian, and everything but Lake Michigan got decorated. He teased Aunt Helen into conceding that "a proper Christmas tree" did not mean a slack Trinitarian—so the three of us planned a surprise for Father and the party guests.

Davy had somehow brought back from Boston on the cars, packed in wooden boxes like exotic fruit, handblown glass in jewel colors. prisms and snowflakes, chains of flowers and stars. At Thanksgiving, he had found a firm that imported the Austrian ornaments; he had been planning this treat all along. He and his best friend, Jonathan, carried the boxes to Amity Street and hid them in the barn. Sam, our stableman, cut a stunning blue spruce and installed it on the stage a few days before the party. Father departed to take the cars for an overnight in Northampton. The coast was clear!

Sam brought in the boxes from the barn, and he and Aunt Helen and Davy and I went to work—wearing scarves and mittens and overcoats, breathing steam. By midnight we had created a constellation, a lacy radiance—a child's glittering dream of a Christmas tree. We stood back to marvel, tired and proud, and drank Aunt Helen's hot mulled wine.

"Now look—here is the spirit of Christmas!" Davy climbed the stepladder one more time with a little gold box. He opened it and fastened an exquisite gold angel to the topmost spray of the spruce. He looked down at us, smiling. "Can you see who she is?"

The angel had a windblown silk robe and silver wings. She had golden skin and short gilded curls. She was me! When Davy came down the ladder, I kissed him—right there in front of Aunt Helen and Sam.

Father, who had an unerring eye for a work of art, saw the tree upon his return and added twenty guests to the party. We started the braziers up a day ahead; the temple was warm for our friends. I wore my modish green silk costume from Kate's wedding and a laurel wreath for Davy—a message in our secret language. Father's students circled and bumbled around me like the moths at the lanterns in Barbados; Davy enjoyed seeing me as the center of attention. They teased me about my victor's crown of laurel. "Miss Chase has won the race! She wins first prize!"

I gave Davy a secret smile from within the circle of students and never told what it was that I had won this December night.

Then it was New Year's. It was 1860 now; Davy found it deeply significant that we were starting a new decade together. He held up his champagne glass to me, the amber bubbles rising quickly, excited by possibility.

"The '6os will be our years, Miranda!" he declared. "We met in 1859; we'll be married in '63, when I graduate. Then we'll have that year in Greece for our wedding trip. We'll see Athens and Delphi and

Marathon. Would you like some time in Princeton after that? You could continue your education there as well."

His silver eyes were bright as he gazed into our imagined future. I sipped my champagne, heady with love.

"I'd like to study there with Harper," he continued, mapping it all out. "Then we'll decide whether I'll teach or write, and we'll start our family."

Our future is right here in front of us, I thought. We are living it now. I basked in the certainty of Davy's planning. He drew me close to him.

"Miranda, darling, just think—we've begun our life together, right now in 1860!"

The big exciting storms swept down the valley again this year. When I called on Emily between blizzards, I found her cheerful and busy with the manuscripts we had organized. She sat at her desk, and I settled into my chair near her.

"I never could have done it alone," she told me graciously. "No one should be asked to put a GALAXY in alphabetical order!"

I rubbed my hands together to warm them. "Are your poems easier now?" I asked.

Emily stared into the fire, watching the flames devour her cast-off papers. "I read the other day that it takes an entire TON of mimosa to make an ounce of a certain French perfume, Miranda. Then I thought, That's how I write my poetry!"

"So are those papers that you're burning what's left after you've extracted the poem?"

"Yes, these words are the CHAFF. But they've been used to the full. Sometimes I write a good phrase in a poor letter, and then I cannibalize it. I use it again in a poem or another letter. Sometimes I try out a good line in two or three different places. Nothing GOLD is ever wasted!"

She smiled at me. "My PRACTICE is paying off. After my years of dutiful scales and exercises, I now have some *skills* to show!"

Her mention of skills made me remember a detail about her from one of our first meetings. Since then, a townsperson—I couldn't remember who—had brought up Emily's proficiency in a certain instrument. "Someone told me you used to play the real piano very nicely."

"Someone spoke correctly," she replied smugly. "I had lessons for years, for my Father's APPROVAL. It used to give him great pleasure to hear me. Bach is Father's favorite, which I understand. Bach is all duty. Bach is a REGIMEN—and so is Father."

"Is that why you stopped playing?"

"No, there were other composers for me. But I came to see all music as another face of MALE DOMINANCE. When I played the piano, Mozart or Haydn or Liszt was standing there at my shoulder, telling me what to think, what to do next. So I stopped OBEYING them. I don't TAKE ORDERS anymore."

I compared this bristling independence with her fawning letters to "Master"—but I did so silently, reacting like a weathervane to Emily's changing directions. I didn't want to debate the pleasure music brought me, so I changed course, leading Emily around to a topic we could both agree on. I wanted to like Emily today.

"Emily, I must tell you, I finished *Wuthering Heights*. I read till two this morning. I believe it's the finest novel ever written. Nothing comes even close!"

"Dear Miranda, English Emily is the SUN in the constellation of Brontës. She is the finest writer of the three, and she carried the heaviest burdens. She is my HEROINE." Emily warmed to her drama. "She was always ill, always poor, always dealing with her mad parson father, her drunken brother, her idle sisters. There she was, without friends, isolated in that stark parsonage on the HOWLING MOORS—and the whole family coughing their lungs out, day and night."

"What a picture, Emily." I wondered if the reality was as dramatic as Emily's description of it. But this being a writer's biography, I thought that Emily would adhere closely to the facts. "How could she write?"

"Truly, one marvels at her fortitude. They say she cooked and washed and nursed all day and then wrote all night. No wonder she died young! I do think of her, when I enjoy my leisure and my privacy here in The Homestead. I owe it to Emily Brontë to USE my good fortune."

I was glad to hear my friend acknowledge this debt. Amherst Emily was not given to feeling obligated and not long on gratitude.

Emily walked to her bookshelf and plucked out a slender leather volume tooled in green. "Today I will lend you her poems, Miranda. I wish they made a fatter volume! Would you like to read me some now? I have been able to lose myself in so few books this week, with the sun GLARING on the snow. My eyes are two daggers of pain!" So we passed an hour, with poor, brave Emily Brontë as our company.

When I began the tedious process of buckling and wrapping myself against the cold, Emily became wistful. "Stay one more moment, Miranda; I won't hear your laugh for a week."

I paused, wondering why Emily would want to keep me.

"Will this detain you?" she asked, a little shyly. "I have DISTILLED another ton of mimosa! Do you remember that draft of a letter to Master that you attacked so cruelly? See if you can be a little gentler with the poem it became."

She handed me a paper; she had certainly condensed the letter, from three pages to three verses.

> A Wounded *Deer—leaps highest—*
> *I've heard the Hunter tell—*
> *'Tis but the Ecstasy of death—*
> *And then the Brake is still!*
>
> The Smitten *Rock that gushes!*
> The trampled *Steel that springs!*
> A *Cheek is always redder*
> *Just where the Hectic stings!*
>
> *Mirth is the Mail of Anguish—*
> *In which it Cautious Arm,*
> *Lest anybody spy the blood*
> *And "you're hurt" exclaim!*

"It's stronger than the letter by far," I approved. "This time it sounds like *you!* Your wounded deer has much more dignity than that bleeding bird, I think." I studied the poem again. "But you really should restrain your punctuation, Emily. All those peppered exclamation marks make your poem look somewhat hysterical."

She snatched the poem back with a chilly stare at my presumption. Just because she accepted criticism on one letter once did not give me a poetry editor's privilege. I was not her chosen "surgeon"; I had better step back into my assigned humility.

The snows continued; February glittered and gleamed. Davy and I were given a glorious unbroken fortnight of skating on the Connecticut River, frozen a historic two-feet thick. The weather curtailed my visits to the outlying school districts for my independent study, so we had even more time available to spend together. We skated after school through all the brilliant afternoons, and then by firelight and moonlight at night. Kind Aunt Helen relaxed her rules for this rare event.

Davy and I glided together upstream and down, mile after smooth white mile—our arms entwined, our bodies joined in rhythm, our breath fused in an intimate cloud. Our matching, repeating motions were languorous and thrilling. When we moved beyond the other groups of skaters, I kissed Davy's lips, pressing the cold apart to reach the inner warmth—until I was faint from his sweetness.

Late one afternoon, just as we were heading for the sociable bonfire onshore, there was a sharp sound like a rifle shot and then a long, hollow boom.

"What was that?" I asked, startled.

"The very first crack of the ice breakup—which means our last day on the river. Skating won't be safe after this."

As we unlaced our skates, Jonathan arrived, and Davy warned him about the ice. "You're an hour too late, I'm afraid," Davy advised him. "It's just like the news nowadays. We heard only that one crack—but that's enough. There's real trouble coming."

That night my mind kept turning back to Davy's remark. All through the autumn, I had been so engrossed in my flowering life—my fascinating studies, the wonder of our engagement, the vision of our future—that I barely noticed events in the larger world around us. There had been a military skirmish of sorts in October. I remembered a raid in Virginia and some hangings. I had hardly read the newspaper; it seemed unimportant compared to the unfolding events in my own life.

But Davy's comment forced my view to widen. His eyes were fixed beyond our tiny sphere; mine had to be too. So every afternoon, I read the *Springfield Republican,* where Emily's friend Mr. Samuel Bowles was editor—and I began to see we were indeed skating on thin ice. The Northeast and the South were ready for a war—an American war.

During one of our study sessions, I brought up some of my worries, hoping for reassurance.

"Davy, this won't concern you, will it? Illinois in the Middle West is not part of this, is it?"

"Perhaps you shouldn't have dropped geography, Miranda." Davy gave me a wry smile. "No place in the United States is separate from any other place. We're all connected by arteries of railroads and rivers."

I hauled out Father's atlas, and Davy showed me the rail and shipping routes converging on Chicago. "All the commerce of the continent goes to and from Chicago," he explained, running his fingers along the snaking lines. "The Middle Western states couldn't exist with only the top half of the Mississippi or some chopped-off bits of railroad."

My heart lurched and sank. "I see, I do see."

Once I understood this fatal geography, I read everything—the daily *Republican,* the weekly news in *Harper's,* and the articles in the *Atlantic Monthly.* My former ignorance was bliss indeed, but I'd never get it back.

It was soon the last day of an uneasy March 1860. Josiah Howland was born the previous night, nearly killing his mother as he came. He was a good-size infant, somewhat tardy—and Kate had a narrow frame. Dr. Smedley told us, as the hours dragged on, that the baby was crosswise, and he could not turn him. At any rate, Josey was a day and a night en route, and we thought we would surely lose our Kate.

Aunt Helen had gone to Springfield a week before to help Kate get ready for the birth. But the Howlands' steep stairs became too painful for her arthritis, and she telegraphed for me to come. With Father's help, I arranged for the time away from school and took the cars to join them. I was there for the first happy onset of Kate's labor at Monday noon—and all through the horror of the endless night that followed. By Tuesday noon, Kate was so exhausted that she would fall asleep between pains and then wake to arch and scream again.

Her agony penetrated every inch of the tidy little honeymoon house—so there was no way to shield me, an unmarried girl, from the whole fearful process. I barely recognized my calm Kate in this violent, pitiful creature. I sat with her, sponging her swollen face, sobbing too. Her desperate grip bruised my hands.

Privately Aunt Helen and I were not very good at hiding our fear that we would lose our Kate, but we were brave at her bedside. By evening, Dr. Smedley told us he would try to turn the baby one more time. There came a spurt of bright blood, a final shriek, and finally, late that night, Josiah Chase Howland was born.

Now that he had arrived, Aunt Helen and Ethan were so proud of the little fellow that they were forgetting the mortal ordeal of his birth. I could not; I never would. "I can't forgive him, Kate. He almost took you away from us."

I was sitting by her bed, the third day. She had been sleeping, but she was still paler than the dainty sheets she had embroidered for her hope chest. I had helped her sew those same innocent doves and scrolls. The doves had lied to us then; they were lying now.

"You'd better start forgiving Josey; he may be the only little cousin you get. Dr. Smedley said I shouldn't try having another baby."

"Do you mind, Kate?"

"Right now, I can't even imagine wanting to do this again! But it will be hard for Ethan; he wants a big family."

I could see she was unresigned to Dr. Smedley's advice, which frightened and confused me. But her happiness was so deep, her lovely nature so calm, that this was not a time for argument but for rejoicing.

Maureen arrived, a cheerful young Irish helper for Kate, and Aunt Helen and I returned to Amherst. Davy called at once. He found me shaken and sobered by my close view of childbirth.

"Of course I've never seen it the way you did, but I do fear it," he confided. "My own mother never got her strength back."

I remembered Davy telling me that his mother had died at the age of twenty, when he was only three months old. He would have been too young to have any actual memories of her.

"Do you know anything about her?" I asked.

"They tell me she was generous and loving, and very beautiful. Her name was Claire. I wish I had even one small memory of her."

Since, in a way, I had never really known my own mother, I knew we shared something important. Perhaps we had never really admitted this "hole" in our life's experience, perhaps we would be able to explore its meaning together.

A few days later, when I visited The Homestead, Emily was sweetly pleased over Kate's little son but was even more excited to show me her latest work. She must have forgotten her recent anger when I presumed to judge her poem, the one based on her childish letter to "Master."

I expected there would be real fireworks when she finally submitted her work to a "surgeon." She was abnormally sensitive to any advice, which she always saw as a searing personal attack. I believed that Emily, in her writing, was saying to the world: "Love me, love my poem without question! I have worked to find this word, to build that phrase; how could you be expected to understand it? You are an outsider. I do not write for you."

Having said all this to myself, I was quite ready to be tactfully evasive when she handed me another paper to read. Here was a letter, or the draft of a letter, with lines marked "...not a glorious victory Abiah...but a kind of a helpless victory, where triumph would come of itself, faintest music, weary soldiers...."

"I see some nice images," I told her carefully. "What is it?"

Now she was a gleeful child with a surprise for the grown-ups. "It's a letter I wrote to Abby Root in 1850. It's a ton of mimosa, waiting to be DISTILLED into a poem!"

"These lines, Emily?"

"These very lines! Now read the poem they have become."

I took the page from her and read.

Success is counted sweetest
By those who ne'er succeed.
To comprehend a nectar
Requires sorest need.

Not one of all the purple Host
Who took the Flag today
Can tell the definition
So clear of Victory

As he defeated—dying—
On whose forbidden ear
The distant strains of triumph
Burst agonized and clear!

I was overcome by the authority and compelling force of these twelve lines. I had always sensed an uneven quality in Emily's work until now—but here I found clear direction to a stunning conclusion. This poem was flawless and complete; I could only praise it.

"Emily, it's your very best. You have pulled all your talents together here. It is a *masterpiece.* I am awed, truly awed."

She blushed, but she met my gaze, standing proud and straight—at ease in the presence of her own excellence attained.

"I know, I know! It was a LONG JOURNEY, some of it by night—but I've arrived."

"Now, Emily, it's time to send this to your 'surgeon.'"

"Not yet. I need two or three others I like as much. Mr. Thomas Wentworth Higginson will want to compare them, I imagine." She looked away from my disappointment.

So even with this triumphant poem in her hand, she was defensive again. She dared not risk exposing herself to criticism.

The next Monday, I went cross lots to The Homestead, thinking again of the power of Emily's most recent verse. When I reached Emily's house, the stair door was locked, so I went around the front. Miss Lavinia opened the door before I knocked; she seemed excited and distraite.

"Miranda, you will have to excuse my sister this afternoon. She has an unexpected guest. She will see you next Monday." Then I noticed a carriage from the livery stable, with a driver waiting—and I heard a man's deep voice from the parlor.

"A livery carriage, indeed!" Aunt Helen was intrigued when I told her. "That means someone from out of town. Could it be one of those men she writes so often?"

"Never!" I was emphatic. "They would never be permitted to come to The Homestead in person."

But next Monday, Dick, the Dickinson stableman, brought me a note. Emily was in bed—"felled" was her word—and could not receive me till next week.

It was just as well: my history of Greek drama was almost due. Emily had intended to help me, but I discovered she was hopeless at organizing a mass of *fact.* She preferred to swoop and dart around a topic like a shimmering dragonfly—and she was much too subjective for expository writing. So I learned to arrange my new knowledge, logically and chronologically, in an orderly structure of fact and opinion. This was much harder than reading *Medea* but strangely satisfying. As in flower arranging, I knew instinctively when a section was right—when I had attained my intent.

Davy had a difficult project too, a paper on Thoreau. On Amity Street, we spread our papers over the dining table and worked in total silence. Every now and then he pushed a note down to my end. (*"If I can't be kissing you, I might as well study."*) At the end of the period, we compared our progress, and Aunt Helen brought us cider.

When I called on Monday, I found Emily convalescent, pale and subdued. Her freckles were showing again; this was always her sign of distress. Something had truly shaken her.

"It was a CATACLYSM," she told me. "At my feet, the hall became ABYSS." She repeated this, testing it: "BECAME ABYSS." One day, I knew, she would use this metaphor again.

"Can you tell me what happened, Emily?"

"I was working in the kitchen; I had no WARNING. Vinnie had taken Mother downtown; there was no one to answer the door. Usually I just let a caller go on knocking. Oh, whatever POSSESSED me?" She wrung her hands; she was literally beside herself, outside her tidy little body. Her pain was tremendous and genuine.

"Emily, who was it?"

"It was my MASTER! And I in my old work apron, with flour on my hands—oh, it was terrible, terrible! It was a VIOLATION!"

The Philadelphia minister—here? I was shocked. What impact would this have on the delicate truce erected by so many concerned parties? "Had he written you that he was coming?"

"NEVER. He knew I would refuse to see him! He had some ridiculous church business in Northampton and stopped on a silly WHIM, on his way back to Philadelphia. He hired a carriage at the depot and just—INVADED. After five years, after all we have been to each other—just because he had some time to fill up between trains! How did he DARE—to me, Emily Dickinson!"

I could see her vibrating. Her rage was visible; I wanted to calm her. "Emily, I can't imagine he meant to hurt you. He was being *sociable*—just taking the chance to meet you, after all your fine letters. He was calling on you only as a friend."

"I do not have such FRIENDS. No coarse, insensitive DROPPER-IN is any friend of mine!"

"What . . . what is he like?" She needed sympathy, but I was not sure how to offer it.

"How could I tell? All I could see was an intruder—a strange, unwelcome man with stiff round whiskers like those of an APE. Miranda, it was NOT my Master!"

Clearly she preferred her two-dimensional correspondent to the whiskered reality. This should set Mrs. Austin's mind at ease; there was no danger of Emily's running off and sullying the Dickinson name to be with this man.

"Did you enjoy any part of his visit?"

"How could I? I do not like SOCIAL conversation, when I am afraid of what I might hear my own voice saying. In letters, I am safe. I can plan, I can edit; I can PRESENT myself! Talking is so raw, so random, so DANGEROUS!"

As she spoke, I recognized the accuracy of Mrs. Austin's phrase "Emily's truth." Emily had her own pane of violet glass—and she herself demanded to be seen through the same filter of fantasy.

I had brought daffodils, but their spring beauty had no effect, nor had any of the conversational topics I offered. After a gloomy hour, I left, wondering how long it would take Emily to recover from her assault.

I soon found out. As I walked along Main Street on Saturday, I heard the sentimental birds calling their nesting plans across the delicious April morning. Then, to my surprise, I came on Emily working in her garden. She never went outdoors past nine, as Main Street filled up with chatty passersby like me.

"Good morning, Little Red Riding Hood!" she trilled, waving a trowel. "Where are you taking your basket?"

"These are molasses cookies for a hayride," I told her. Davy and I had planned an excursion up Mount Holyoke with a dozen of our friends. There was a splendid panoramic view there—the oxbow loop of the Connecticut River. All the Pelham Hills will be silver gilt, with tiny leaves uncurling. We would sing and fly kites; we would sketch; then we would lunch at the Mountain House Inn. Davy had grown up arranging such outings along Lake Michigan; he made me see that the planning was as delightful as the event.

"You chose the PARADIGM of spring for your outing!" Emily gushed. "Look in the guest books when you get up there; you will see my signature OFTEN, from years ago."

"I see you've forgiven your uninvited dropper-in," I ventured. The prospect of a glorious day emboldened me.

"Forgiven him? It was nothing, nothing at all—a passing THISTLE-DOWN between us. He is my guide and my guardian, as always. I've forgotten my little PIQUE."

No one could handle Emily but Emily herself. The college clock struck ten, and I turned toward the common, where I would forget Emily as I met the dear true fact of my sweetheart.

For the rest of the spring, Davy and I planned a particular enterprise for each Saturday. After the hayride to Mount Holyoke, our next project was wildflowers. People declared you could not transplant them, but Emily's garden was flourishing disproof of this. Aunt Helen wanted to start growing some beside our brook—and Davy wished to do her a particular favor. So Emily wrote me transplanting directions, and we went to work.

One day while we were planting, we stopped to sun ourselves by the stream in our yard, playing the *Hamlet* game. Davy refused to find sharks and unicorns in the clouds and saw only Amherst College faculty faces. Suddenly he sat up and turned serious.

"Miranda, I'd like to take a look at your friend's poetry."

I thought this over. Emily had never asked me not to show them. Davy had not read as much poetry as I had, but he had good judgment. Whether he liked the poems or not, I wanted to hear his reasons.

"I'll get the box." As I ran into the house, across the hall and up the stairs, I caught a fleeting image of myself in the mirror. I glimpsed a stunning young woman, flushed and confident, flashing by in the bright swift current of her happiness. I could not quite believe the miracle I was feeling. I had known Davy for only a year.

"What an unusual hand she writes!" Davy remarked as I opened my cedar box. "Does it show she is hiding her thoughts, I wonder?" He took the pages from me and began to read. "The poems don't exactly come rushing out to meet you," he said, stretching out and rolling over onto his stomach.

I felt as protective as Emily did about her work. Could a stranger understand this proud, shy spirit? Davy was inscrutable, fixed on his reading. He studied each poem several times and then placed it in one of three piles. Sometimes he went back to reread a sheet and move it to another pile. Sometimes he asked me to decipher a particular word.

I watched the sun on Davy's long, elegant hands. He must still be growing; his wrists extended from his blue cuffs. I wanted to kiss one, warm from the sun. Finally, he rolled back and sat up.

"Well...?" I asked.

"First of all, your friend Emily Dickinson is her own person," he said. "She isn't copying anyone. Her ideas—that is, the ones I can follow—are all hers. So is her style. After all the curlicues of Shelley and Byron—yes, even your Browning!—these short, plain stanzas are very appealing. They almost remind me of hymns."

"Because she loves hymns, of course! She says they're the perfect verse form. Go on, Davy."

"As I see it, her poems fall into three groups. The ones in this pile are impressive, unique. I understand them, even though I sometimes reject their message.

"This second pile is harder to judge, Miranda. They are serious and sincere, but I just can't follow them. She makes these enormous leaps and expects me to stay right there with her.

"Sometimes she talks *to* God and then *about* Him—in the same poem. She seems to address God in a dozen different ways; it makes me uncomfortable."

"I often feel she is speaking a different language," I said.

"She uses *words* I know, but she manages to give them different meanings. Sometimes I feel she's playing hide-and-seek with me!"

"I often tell her that. And the third pile, Ralph Waldo Farwell?"

Davy frowned. "I'm sorry, Miranda, but I have to tell you I think this last group is counterfeit—false, mannered. She's trying for an effect, wearing a disguise. She plays, she poses. I don't believe these poems, and I don't think Miss Dickinson does either. Listen to this:

> *Herein a Blossom lies—*
> *A Sepulchre, between—*
> *Cross it, and overcome the Bee—*
> *Remain—'tis but a Rind.*

"Miranda, I think I've caught your friend teasing us!"

All of this was remarkably like what I had thought myself but never expressed. I felt vindicated and relieved.

"So present your conclusion, please, sir!"

"Professor, I find this poet to be one-third inspired, one-third incomprehensible, and one-third mannered and fake. But Miranda—these manuscripts are a big responsibility. Does she have other copies?"

"I couldn't say. She's far too casual about her drafts and her fair copies. But I promise I'll keep these ones safe. Which poem did you like the best?"

Davy riffled through the first pile and handed me the one that began, "Success is counted sweetest." "This is impressive—a finished work of art. I would be honored if Miss Dickinson would make me a copy."

"Davy, you pass the quiz. I award you a kiss as a grade."

"My other professors never do that!" He smiled, drawing me into his arms.

For all the joy I felt that fine spring, one relationship was changing. Father seemed almost too interested in the personal details of my life and in playing the role of indignant parent bent on protecting his little girl. If I could only restore his former benign detachment!

He and I had lived pleasantly under the same roof for almost seventeen years. Our houses were large, which permitted privacy; he worked elsewhere and had his own separate schedule. Until we came to Amherst, I had no interests or engagements that might have opposed his. We lived neither together nor apart, our lives were parallel. There was never an occasion when I wanted something different from him.

But now that occasion had come. Father and I had been quarreling for days. We rumbled and steamed, muttered and erupted, like two volcanoes. Indeed, to Davy and Kate I quietly began referring to Father as Vesuvius. Davy urged me to remain respectful and moderate. Yet when we were alone, Amity Street was a battlefield, and Father and I seemed like hostile strangers.

Emily delighted in bulletins from the conflict; these confirmed her ongoing war with her own parent.

"But you stole my PRIVATE metaphor! 'VESUVIUS' is what I call MY father—I thought of it first! I'll prove it, Miranda, you BRIGAND!" I was astonished by Emily's childish pique, but I conceded her prior claim to domestic volcanoes as an image when her poem proved it.

> *Volcanoes be in Sicily*
> *And South America*
> *I judge from my Geography—*
> *Volcanos nearer here*
> *A Lava step at any time*
> *Am I inclined to climb—*
> *A Crater I may contemplate*
> *Vesuvius at Home.*

I congratulated Emily on her irony. She liked my praise but was uncertain about the poem.

"Perhaps I went too far in mockery," she mused. "After all, Father is no LAUGHING MATTER."

I understood. No matter how much I could create a humorous story for an audience about my situation, the tensions between Father and me were quite serious.

I had read that when duelists met, they fought by a code, the "Rules of Engagement." I did not know the code for family fights; this was my first. Should I continue to hide the emotions I had always restrained? Should I believe words uttered in anger? Were these words permanent, indelible? Father and I seemed like hostile strangers.

We called a truce for Prize Day at the academy, when I won the award for Special Academic Excellence—so studying with Davy had not hurt my marks. But when I made this point to Father, we resumed our war. The next battle came when Davy paid my father a formal evening call. He brought a prettily phrased letter from his stepmother, inviting me to visit in Lake Forest this summer.

"That is out of the question," Father answered. He was adamant. When pressed for reasons, he told Davy, "Such a visit would suggest an engagement, and none exists. Whatever present understanding there is between you, I do not acknowledge it. Good night, sir."

After Davy left, Father and I both said a good deal more. He repeated that I was an inexperienced child and needed more years to know myself. I accused him of not knowing me either—and of deny-ing me a greater affection than he had ever offered me. He then warned me that Davy was willful and selfish, like me—and that we had both better concentrate on acquiring education and maturity.

I went to Springfield to visit Kate and lick my wounds. Davy joined me there. We were appropriately chaperoned, and had we been asked, we would have told Father and Aunt Helen about the afternoon's plans. But no one asked.

Davy sat beside me on the grass as I held Josey, who had started smiling. I listened to Kate's good sense.

"Miranda, Uncle Jos is *spoiled.* Up until now you've been just too easy! You're pretty and healthy and smart, you've never given him any sort of trouble—and he's even had Mother and Miss Adelaide James to be parents for him. He doesn't expect you to ever want anything for yourself."

"So what should I do?" I asked.

"Negotiate and compromise. Give in a little; let him believe he's won," Kate advised.

"Come to Lake Forest at Christmas instead," Davy agreed. "Let him think he's made his point—but meanwhile, be independent about other things. Show you have a mind of your own. What would you most like to do this summer, if you can't visit me?"

"Learn more Greek, I guess—and buy some clothes that aren't so childish. Oh, and get a new desk; I've outgrown my old one."

"Then do it all!" urged Kate.

"You'll find it gets easier," said Davy sagely. "Parents usually do come around, sooner or later."

When he returned to Illinois at the end of June, I started my Greek tutoring at the college. Father had chosen Mr. Ennis, one of the younger men in the Classics Department. My tutor was short and thick; he sweated and breathed heavily. I learned more Greek, but that was all I learned; there was none of the spirit of Athens—the scholars, the generals, and the athletes mingling—that Mr. Harnett would have in-stilled in me.

Soon it was evident that our lessons were causing Mr. Ennis to breathe even harder. He stood behind me, panting and pointing to a line—and I leaned away. I barely smiled at his labored Greek compli-ments; I ignored the suggestive love lyrics he assigned to me. Finally at my last lesson, he declared himself, weeping on his pudgy knees. I was angry and embarrassed; I couldn't even be vain about such a ludicrous beau. I considered mentioning this to Father, pointing out that he was being inconsistent in allowing me to be alone in the lovelorn company of a porcine young tutor but not to visit a civilized, well-chaperoned household under the care of Davy's parents. But I decided to remember Kate and Davy's advice, and remained respectful and moderate while I strove to achieve my goals for the summer.

First, there was a flurry of fireworks and fiery speeches for the Fourth of July. The ceremonies were held on the village green, as dry as it would ever be. One of the orators was a Judge Otis Lord, a distinguished friend and frequent houseguest of the Dickinson family. Though he was eighteen years her senior, Emily always fluttered over his frequent visits and enjoyed having meals with him and his invalid wife—the thought of which amazed me.

Miss Lavinia related the story of a typical exchange at one of Aunt Helen's sewing circles, and Aunt Helen then retold the story to me as we hung freshly laundered linen on the line. "Judge Lord once arrived at The Homestead and asked for Emily, who sent down word she could not see him."

"That isn't surprising," I said, straightening the wet sheet. "That's Emily's way."

"Well, not to be put off, the judge marched smartly to the stairs and called up this order." Now Aunt Helen affected a commanding masculine voice. "Emily, you wretch! No more of this nonsense. We have traveled a long way to see you. Come down at once!"

She laughed and picked up a wet tea towel. "Can you imagine?"

"No!" I exclaimed. "What did Emily do?"

"Miss Emily Dickinson not only presented herself forthwith, but they subsequently took to referring to each other as 'Wretch' and 'Rascal'!"

I wiped my damp hands on my apron. "Astonishing!"

Perhaps exasperation was the one emotion that could persuade Emily to change her behavior, for Judge Lord seemed to be the only one of her Mentors whom she actually and regularly saw.

Later in July, Father and I took the cars to Boston. After we agreed to postpone my visit to Illinois, we became friendly again. We had errands to do: Father would begin researching a new book, and I had wardrobe shopping to accomplish. I was determined to achieve the goals I had set for myself, and new clothes were high on the list.

We spent a few days with Cousin Ellen Curtis Lyall, a bride when I saw her last, who seemed to have replaced now elderly Cousin Daisy Powell as the official herald and liaison officer of the Latham family. Cousin Ellen lived on Mount Vernon Street, across and down from number 32. Her husband was Dr. Hallett Lyall, a surgeon; she had a little brown-haired son, Ames, a year older than our Josey. She welcomed us with the grace and warmth I remembered from childhood.

"It's time we had another blond beauty in the family," she said with a smile. "Your Cabot grandmother was very tall and fair too. You're quite like her." She showed us our own portrait of Miss Eliza Cabot, wearing a low-cut yellow silk dress and holding a matching parakeet. Cousin Ellen still "borrowed" the portrait from Father, but she reminded us it was ours. "I'm just keeping it till Miranda marries and has her own house."

I had often felt far removed from my mother's family tree; I was grateful that kind Cousin Ellen had found me a perch on one of its branches. We went over the clothes I had brought; Cousin Ellen was very taken with the laurel-green silk costume I wore for Kate's wedding.

"You'd know that for a Madame Lauré anywhere! We must have another in black velvet, the same French cut. With your hair and your complexion, you must do black velvet. I remember you always wore that at the New Year's parties. You were so serious then, watching the other children. But you're not standing on the edges anymore, are you?"

"No, I'm not—not for some time, it seems." I smiled.

"We'll need to find you some dresses for school and daytime engagements too. Do you go out much during the week?"

"Not this summer, Cousin Ellen. I just study."

"I see...," Her expression grew concerned. "That must be quite lonely."

"It's not," I assured her. "Truly it's not!"

I could not explain to her that the daily visits from Davy through his letters were companionship enough for me.

We went to several grand stores, crowded with clothes for modish Bostonians. Cousin Ellen was endlessly helpful, guiding me toward my own style. "You have a classical figure and wonderful coloring; let us *see* them. You must always be simple and uncluttered. You're a goddess, not a shepherdess, Miranda!"

Father admired the results of our shopping. His favorite dress was the indigo printed challis with the velvet piping and yokes. He admired the gray moire too and the mauve velvet.

"I do like to see a handsome woman, well turned out," he told us. "And you're the one to show us how, Ellen!"

"We want only to do the family credit, Jos."

How easily they chat, I observed, as one personage to another! Someday I too will be this sure of my own worth.

The last day, we crossed Mount Vernon Street to choose a desk for me from among the pieces still in number 32. I had dreaded this errand, stepping back into those shadowed years—but the tenants' new colors and possessions had changed the house beyond recognition. Only the black-and-white entrance hall resembled my memory. It was far less difficult than I feared to choose a Sheraton mahogany writing table from an upstairs landing.

"I much prefer this to a desk with drawers," I assured Father. "There's room for my long legs! And it reminds me of the table you used at York Stairs. This can be my seventeenth birthday present." I was practicing getting my way. It did get easier, as Kate and Davy had promised me, and in our constant letters, I described it all.

When we returned to Amherst, we eased into a slow summer pace, with the town quiet and the campus empty of students. I often went to The Homestead to garden at dawn for the pleasure of Emily's company outdoors. She was entirely different when we were away from her room, where the shelved books and the formal furniture set the mood for our time together.

"It pleases me to give my flowers more liberty than I myself enjoy," she confided one day. "That is my LARGESSE. I say to them what no one said to me: 'Just be yourself!'"

"Davy always tells me that," I offered.

Emily nodded distractedly. "Yes, real friends should." But she wasn't interested in my experience of this ideal friendship; her attention was on herself and her perceived loss.

"Susan and I were that to each other, long ago, before her affections wandered from us and turned toward the fashionably affected." She looked away, remembering.

I wanted to hasten to Mrs. Austin's defense, knowing how much she still cared for her difficult sister-in-law, but held my tongue: I could see that Emily was building toward a fiery display of her own. I had no wish to have her fireworks directed at me.

"Seeing us now," Emily went on, developing momentum, "you must find it hard to imagine that we were ever close—but we were, WE WERE. Of course Sue benefited from my PROTECTION THEN."

Emily glanced my way and arched an eyebrow in response to my skeptical expression. "It's true," she insisted. I had begun to notice that her soft voice became almost shrill whenever she had to assume a posture of persuasion. "We were schoolmates and friends, though our backgrounds were so OPPOSITE. Her father was a mere tavern keeper here, and they say he served himself a few times too often. Ah, I see you are astonished at these origins," she added when I could not contain my surprise. "He and Susan's mother both died when Susan was a girl at the academy. An older married sister in upstate New York agreed to take Sue and a younger sister; her country childhood was spartan. There was little about it that was either pastoral or romantic or FASHIONABLE. She was truly brilliant, you know—but I was always aware of a deep cultural VOID from her unfortunate childhood."

I was offended by her snobbery; if Emily believed Mrs. Austin to be brilliant, her origins should not matter. And this narrative explained to me Mrs. Austin's ostentatious displays and increased my admiration for her.

"If that's how you feel, I'm surprised you show her so many of your poems, Emily."

"Susie has natural taste and judgment. Had she been raised differently, she might have been a real SCHOLAR. She is by far my best critic."

I bristled a bit at this. I had imagined myself in that capacity for Emily. She still saw me as a mere sounding board and didn't value my views. Yet how was I expected to develop as a critic when she never allowed me to have an opinion? I pulled up weeds rather angrily, wondering how Mrs. Austin had accomplished this.

"Do you know what Lavinia calls Mr. Cutler, Sue's brother-in-law?"

"No, Emily, I don't." I tugged another weed.

"It's so cruel I shouldn't repeat it. I do so only to show you how WITTY Vinnie can be. She calls him a 'counter-jumper.'" She giggled behind her spade.

This truly shocked me: not Miss Lavinia's malice but Emily's glee in repeating it.

"But Austin welcomes Mr. Cutler into the family and treats him with brotherly love," Emily went on.

"And Mrs. Austin?" I asked. "Does she do the same? Does she agree with Mr. Austin's friendliness?"

At first Emily dug vigorously without answering me.

"As it happens, they agree about very little. They seem to be pulling in different directions these days," she said at last. "Austin said Sue has become intolerably aggressive and opinionated, and of course he was raised with GENTLE WOMEN around him. Nowadays he confides a great deal to me about his marriage. A sister's love, you know, is unwavering, although one cannot always make the same steady claims for a sister-in-law's."

"Surely your taking sides doesn't help his home life, Emily."

"Oh, but he needs a sympathetic ear, Miranda."

But not your envious heart or treacherous tongue, I thought to myself.

Whether Emily realized it or not, she was showing me a good many ways that she herself was endangering her brother's marriage. There was a stinginess about Emily's position concerning Sue that troubled me. Here were two women of formidable intelligence that each had determined to utilize, although each had selected a different means.

If Mrs. Austin welcomed recent guests such as Ralph Waldo Emerson, Frederick Law Olmsted, and Harriet Beecher Stowe, Emily, on the other hand, with narrow-minded petulance, labeled them fiendish social frauds and intellectual impostors. Nor could she credit her sister-in-law for finding her own path to a goal Emily herself endorsed. No — Emily had to criticize, divide, and conquer. She thereby caused mischief in her brother's marriage — and did so from spite.

I went back to Amity Street when the sight of passing neighbors sent Emily indoors. There was usually mail for me from Davy and often from Miss Adelaide too. She was bitterly disappointed the last two summers, when Dr. Hugh's failing health prevented our returning to York Stairs. I could tell that she truly missed me and my company. "Now that you're almost seventeen, and so much has happened to you, you and I will be even better friends," Miss Adelaide wrote. "Do you think we can hope to see you here next year, in the summer of 1861?"

I could not answer this—or even imagine any time beyond Davy's return to Amherst, so all I could say was "We'll see."

Now in the last week of August, the nights were cool, and all the summer greens were faintly gilded. Aunt Helen had decided there was time before classes began for me to visit Kate and Josey, so I took the cars to Springfield while Ethan was out of town.

It was nice to spend the time on my own with Kate, away from the tensions with Father, from the household chores, from my usual life. One afternoon, we had washed our hair and were brushing it dry on the sunny slope of Kate's garden. We lay on the grass like Barbados lizards, with Josey on a blanket between us. He was an amiable, portable five months, suddenly discovering his toes. We smiled at his concentration, and our conversation darted and swooped from one topic to another without either of us missing a beat. It was as if we were in perfect rhythm, as we had been when we still lived in the same house.

"Do you have any news of Lettie and Mira?" Kate asked.

"Miss Adelaide wrote that my namesake is nearly three, and clever and beautiful. I'll always be sorry that Lettie didn't tell me what was making her act so strangely just before we left."

"It won't matter when you see her again. I can't blame her—you really need a husband when you're expecting!"

I gave her a sideways glance. I sat up and hugged my knees to my chest. "Kate..." I began, a little uncertain how to proceed.

She could tell by my tone that the subject was going to become more serious. "Yes?" she asked.

I stared down at my bare toes, feeling the grass blades between them. "What is it like...to be expecting?"

Kate smiled. "It is a trial, and it is uncomfortable, and it is quite, quite glorious. And it's the perfect time to get your way in any disagreement!" Her green eyes sparkled mischievously.

I gave her a grin but grew thoughtful again. "And...and before then." My voice dropped almost to a whisper, and I found it difficult to raise my eyes from my toes. "What is it like? Is it also...*glorious?*"

I understood the mechanics of lovemaking—Aunt Helen had done her duty when I was twelve years old. That knowledge was supplemented one recess last term when Lolly Wheeler smuggled her parents' *Advice to the Newly Married* manual into school. I realized what I was asking couldn't quite be put into words.

Kate reached over and took my hand, peering into my face. "With the right man, and the right marriage, yes, it is even more glorious than you can imagine right now." She stroked my hand. "Miranda, is Davy...?"

I quickly raised my eyes to hers. "No, of course he isn't. He's a perfect gentleman. I—I just find myself wondering..."

"Of course you do," she said. "That's only natural when you're in love. I thought about Ethan all the time." She dropped my hand and leaned back to enjoy the sunshine. "I still do."

I smiled. Kate's words—but more than anything her manner, her happiness—reassured me. "Thank you," I said.

"I want you to feel you can ask me anything," Kate told me.

We brushed away companionably while Josey sang to us. I ran my fingers through my hair. "Look, Kate, it's dry already." I tossed my curls in the warm air. "Wouldn't you like to have yours short too? It's so *easy!*"

"I never could. Ethan—well, he loves to see it down." Kate blushed. "And besides, mine doesn't curl into its own shape the way yours does."

"Davy likes the way mine springs back." And then I blushed too.

Near the end of my visit, Kate and I were once again sunning ourselves in her yard. Josey was practicing his crawling. Kate kept her eye on him while I read a newspaper.

"What does Ethan say about the news these days?" I asked.

"Oh, he's as gloomy as all the other men. He says that if Lincoln is elected, then there will surely be a war."

I folded the paper and laid it aside. So Ethan also felt it inevitable. "Father told me Lincoln made a speech in 1858 to the Illinois state legislature that practically guaranteed a war. It was called 'A House Divided.' "

Kate nodded, then looked perplexed. "Miranda, do you understand why the northern states are so angry? I've been so busy with Josey I barely have a chance to read the newspaper these days."

"Well, of course it's about slavery, but Davy says that they're not so much antislavery as pro-Union. He told me the North believes that if the country splits, then it will split again—and we'll end up all in tiny jigsaw pieces, fighting each other, like in Europe. Besides, most of the commerce of the Middle West goes down the Mississippi River, and it should not have to go through a nation that has become foreign to reach the rest of the world."

"Well said, Miranda!" That was Davy's voice—and there was Davy himself, coming across the grass and smiling at our surprise.

"Davy—oh—it is you, *it is!*" I ran to embrace him. Then I stood back, abashed. "Why have you come early? Is anything wrong?"

"I'm here to see you, Miranda. I came back early so we'd have some time before classes started and to accompany you back to Amherst, once your aunt told me where to find you." He turned to Kate, who was holding Josey. "And look at this mature young man. Is he shaving yet?"

Kate smiled. "Surely you must stay with us," she invited Davy. "To protect us from robbers, with Ethan gone."

"I'd be less than a gentleman if I refused," Davy said, bowing in a courtly manner.

The next day, Davy rented a buggy; we spent a sun-soaked day together on and in the Connecticut River. I liked the slow, opaque green stream, stirring the reeds along the bank and reflecting the shadowing trees dipping to the jade water. It was beautiful in a New England way—very far from the lively translucent sea of Barbados. We took up exactly where we left off, although I sensed a change in Davy, a maturity that I had not seen before. I wondered at the reasons but was too enthralled with the joy of being with him again to give this much thought.

For a few lovely days, we had a summer paradise. On the last day, we settled ourselves on the bank, taking our time with leisurely kisses. Davy in the sun smelled like watercress. After a while he released me gently. Lulled by the scent of jasmine and thyme, I began to doze. Soon he wakened me with a kiss and a bouquet of wildflowers. "Miranda, we have to talk about the future."

"Now?" I was dazed with sun and sleepiness, and wondered why he wanted to discuss wedding plans this minute and why he sounded so serious. Surely that was what he meant by "the future"?

"All summer, I've been listening to my father's friends talking," Davy said. "They're wise men, powerful men—and they all feel that war gets closer every day."

He had thrown a stone of hard reality into the pool of our enchanted afternoon. This conversation wasn't what I thought it would be at all. I felt wide awake now. "But what can you and I do about it, Davy?"

"You know what I want most to do: get married right away." Davy took my hands in his. "My father is entirely willing."

I frowned. "Well, mine won't even allow an engagement. You know that."

Davy released my hands and ran a hand through his thick dark hair. "I surely do. But I hope he may change when war comes."

He said "when" war comes — not "if." The sun spun and darkened; with his words our idyll ended. We would not remain carefree, and as we returned to Amherst and our future, I felt full of private apprehension and regret as I started my last year at the academy.

There was little talk among the students of impending war, just an occasional remark against the southern practice of slavery, prompted by the students' reading of a new book by Miss Stowe — this was sneered at by Emily as "propaganda" but was diligently discussed by our professor of civics.

Emily had welcomed me back very sweetly. She appeared to remember with contrition her ill humor and unkind words at our last meeting. I had learned in three years that her moods were constantly inconstant. Emily never disciplined herself toward modification or concealment; I was expected to take her just as I found her — that hour of that particular day.

Whenever I found myself relaxing in a patch of serenity with Emily, I realized how hard it was to be forever gauging and adjusting to her shifts and zigzags. I was spoiled by Davy, who never expected me to adjust to wildly shifting moods but presented himself clearly and assumed that I would do the same. With Davy — unlike with Emily — there was also an awareness of *my* feelings. He recognized that there were two of us in our friendship; we were not a planet and its moon, as I so often felt with Emily. I was secure in the knowledge that Davy would not change anything about me and asked only the pleasure of my company.

Now Emily was excited about some bulbs she ordered from Holland. They had just arrived, in lumpy brown linen sacks, labeled in odd pointed script. She gave me a learned lecture about the "Tulipomania" of 1637, when kings speculated in tulips and the great merchant banks were beggared in a day, gambling in bulbs. Who but Emily would know all this lore and still be too shy to enter a library!

Emily had written steadily all summer and was becoming confident about her "PROCESS of distilling poetry." She was still adamant that her work was not yet ready to show to Thomas Higginson, her chosen Mentor.

"That will be the CRUCIAL test for me; EVERYTHING will depend on it," she explained. "I have waited so long to achieve DOMINION, that golden thread of influence and power. I don't want to rush in unprepared, when it is a question of ETERNITY." She was half laughing, half deadly serious.

Very early one morning, avoiding neighborly interest, she and I planted her bulbs from Holland. We worked and talked in a soft silver mist, almost invisible to each other. The Dickinson trees were tall gray ghosts around us. Emily was natural and unaffected, not concerned with "presenting" herself. I enjoyed our odd privacy in the fog.

"It's so easy to converse when you can't see your partner waiting to POUNCE!" Emily remarked.

"No one is waiting to pounce on you, Emily!" I assured her. "You just imagine they are."

"They used to, when I was still going about in society and meeting people. Whatever I said, men would reply, 'What? What? REALLY?' At first I thought it was a new fashion—a modish phrase like 'La, sir!' Then I realized they truly didn't believe what I had just said. They thought I was lying—or MAD."

I stopped gardening and studied her. I believed I was hearing a truth from Emily. I had been curious about how she became so reclusive.

"So I stopped seeing people," she continued, "and having to watch my words. It's much easier now, seeing no one.

"When I met you, Miranda, you were the first new face I had seen in MONTHS. But I plain HAD to MEET the brave little girl who preferred Zeus to Mr. Meeker!"

At this we smiled companionably at each other and softly touched our spades together, toasting our friendship.

September was passing, and the Amherst trees caught fire, one by one. The other fires, the cones of raked leaves in every garden, lifted their smoke signals, and the dark fragrance of autumn veiled the valley. The maples had flared and failed all over town, but they seemed less of a festival than in other years.

Davy and I were allowed three study evenings a week this year because of the Special Academic Excellence Prize I won earlier and also because I was now seventeen. I had turned in my Greek drama paper, but I was discouraged about my early childhood education report. I had worked as a classroom aide at several elementary schools last spring and started again this fall, and took dozens of pages of notes—but I could not reconcile what I saw in the valley classrooms with my own learning experience. I told Davy my problem during one of our study evenings.

"Until I came to Amherst, my education with Mr. Harnett was certainly unconventional—but it *worked!* This year I have seen no learning in the valley schools. It's all *memorizing.*"

"What do you think these schools are leaving out, Miranda?"

"Joy, for one thing! And individuality." I shook my head. "No one cares about whatever it is that makes each child unique. The children are taught just the way you fill muffin tins—each one right up to the brim, with exactly the same ingredients!"

Davy smiled at me. "Then say just that, my darling. There's your paper—waiting for you to write it."

So I went to work, but Davy's restlessness remained. One of the many things I had loved in him was his total concentration on one idea, one person, one event. Now he had lost that unique single-mindedness. One Saturday afternoon, we were walking from the college library, our arms piled with books, and we met Jonathan on the path.

"What a gluttonous pair of bookworms!" he teased us. "Those should last you till graduation."

Davy gave a small smile as his only response, and his face was thoughtful. He spoke when Jonathan was out of earshot. "You know, Miranda, I don't really believe I *will* graduate—not from here or anywhere."

My breath caught, and I looked away. I could not answer him. Once again a shadow had fallen on our lives, and I wondered if it would ever lighten.

That night at our dinner table, I asked Father for his opinion on the likelihood of war.

"All of us are hopeful that cool heads will prevail" was all he would answer, but I saw by his expression and Aunt Helen's that they feared the worst. I went to my bed that night with a chill in my heart that the Indian summer warmth could not melt.

Yet the activities of autumn continued, and we acted as though all was normal. We almost pretended that things were like last year, when Davy and I were so confident and carefree. There were one or two hayride parties, followed by singing around glowing bonfires. The sparks ascended to the autumn constellations, moving overhead in the vast indifference of Time. Davy held my shoulders with both hands as we joined in the bittersweet ballads of lovers parting, lovers lost. Our friends made a fire-lit circle, their faces intent and unsmiling even as they sang. We were all shadowed by uncertainty. There was no sunny future anymore. Davy had said to me one night, "When we go to war, I will want to fight beside my friends." This had a fatal historic ring. From Troy, from Agincourt, from Valley Forge, came the voices of all the young warriors. I heard them saying, "I want to fight beside my friends."

The range of our planning had shrunk. He evaded preparing a scene with me for his Shakespeare class party. ("They shouldn't count on me.") Then he postponed renting a sleigh with Jonathan for the winter term. ("Maybe it won't snow this year.") There was a brittle *temporary* mood between us. Even my promised visit to the Farwells at Christmas seemed unlikely.

Thanksgiving repeated last year's. Davy went to Boston, and Father and Aunt Helen and I took the turkey and ourselves to Springfield. Kate and Ethan were fine hosts, and baby Josey seemed to welcome us too. He was a strong child, active and muscular; Kate looked exhausted from hauling him about. I learned she had had no time for her music. Still.

When Davy returned to college, he brought bad news. His stepmother had broken her ankle while skating; my Christmas visit to Lake Forest, which Father had finally permitted, must be put off—until summer, Davy said. I did not really believe I would ever see Illinois.

Christmas in Amherst came and went, darkened with uncertainty and silent apprehension. The war clouds collected. Now it was 1861.

Davy returned to Amherst just after the New Year and appeared after supper on our usual Wednesday evening. Behind his loving manner, I sensed an enormous strain

"My new courses haven't started yet, so I didn't bring any books," he stated. "I just came to see you and go over the draft of your childhood education paper if you'd like."

I gave it to him, highly aware that there was more here than he was revealing. But I said nothing and allowed him to read the draft. He did so, slowly and carefully. I watched him in silence.

"I am truly impressed," he told me, his eyes warm on my face. "Your ideas are organized and original. You express them very well."

"Thank you," I said, pleased with his approval.

"I hope you will go on studying and developing these thoughts, even after this paper. This could be an important interest for you all your life, Miranda."

It was as if he'd read my mind. "That *is* something I've been seriously considering," I admitted, "ever since I began the research on this project." I worked to find the words to express to Davy the pull I felt when surrounded by the children in the classrooms I'd visited. "I look at their faces and I want to share with them what learning has done for me. The way it opened up the world. I would hate for any child to miss out on that experience."

I studied the outline, something still nagging at me. "But what does the paper need *right now,* Davy?" I asked. "It feels unfinished to me."

He held out his arms to me, and I went to him, sliding onto his lap, still gazing down at my papers. "It needs you to convince us to change, darling Miranda. First you tell us what's happening in elementary schools now, and you document it well. Then you relate what you want these same schools to do instead.

"Now you must persuade us to make these changes! You can be very convincing, you know, when you put your mind to it. This paper lacks only persuasion."

"I'll do my best," I promised. I stood as I heard Aunt Helen's footsteps in the hall and sat down opposite him, scribbling notes in the margins of the outline draft.

Putting on his coat to walk back to the college, he became serious again. "I'm glad to see this passion in you for this subject," he said.

I nodded. "It feels right," I declared. "As if I've been preparing for this work since my own childhood."

"Then you must pursue it," Davy said. "And I want you to always remember how much I want to see you doing this work."

Two evenings later, he was back, again without books—very preoccupied, very distraught.

"Please, Mrs. Sloan, just this once— might I take Miranda to your church? The choir is practicing 'Jesu, Joy of Man's Desiring,' and a friend of mine has the solo."

Aunt Helen seemed to sense his distress and gave permission at once. I bundled up in my violet cashmere cloak, my Christmas present from Father; Davy did not notice it. He took my arm and we walked along Amity Street, under the cold, high stars. Our boots squeaked in the new snow.

"Is snow this same ice blue in starlight, in Lake Forest?" I asked, trying to lighten the mood.

"I never noticed without you to point it out."

We sat in the back of the dim, lovely church. Davy reached to hold my hand inside my seal muff. I wondered why his silver eyes looked so strange—and then I realized they were brimming with tears. That was the moment when I knew. Before he spoke, I knew.

"Miranda, there is something I haven't told you, but—all last summer at home, I was drilling with my friends. We formed a company. We drilled and marched and bivouacked, and took some rifle practice along the beach.

"We'll be commissioned next month—as Battery B of the Chicago Light Artillery. I am a gunnery sergeant. This way, my friends and I will all be together. We're ready for when the war starts."

He heard my intake of breath and gripped my hand harder.

"Darling Miranda, I've thought about this for months. As I see it, men my age have always been caught up in history at a certain time and place—like flies in flypaper!

"Right now, I'm a fellow from Illinois in 1861. I'd much rather have been a youth at Concord, fighting the British—or an ephebe at Marathon, turning back the Persians! But I'm stuck in the flypaper of here and now. I have to do what the times and my place require me to do."

Bach's arpeggios soared, piercing my new wound.

"When do you leave?" I struggled to keep my voice steady.

"Tomorrow morning."

I blinked my eyes quickly, trying to absorb the shock.

"When I decided, last month, I didn't sign up for any courses this term. I came back only to say good bye to you."

"You were right not to tell me while you were deciding. I couldn't have helped you, Davy."

"I wanted us to have a little more time together—but you knew, didn't you?"

I nodded, not trusting my voice.

"All this means is—we'll just put things off a bit." How relieved he seemed to be, with everything out in the open at last. My heart swelled with compassion for him, knowing how much it must have cost him to keep this from me. "I'll do my duty, and then we'll get married the very second the war's over. Meanwhile, will you wear my ring?"

I nodded again, and rose. Bach just made it worse. I had to leave.

We walked back to Amity Street in the chilly starlight, not talking. My pain was bearable, no more than life-size—but I knew it was just beginning.

"Will I see you tomorrow, Davy?"

He shook his head very hard—and I remembered this was all new to him. He was used to loving and being loved; he was used to being happy.

"No, I couldn't. I couldn't stand saying good-bye to you twice, Miranda."

He was probably right about this, I decided from a strange distance; I was adrift in a state of numb detachment.

Under the portico, Davy gave me a long kiss. He repeated our ritual, his wet cheek against mine. "Never forget, darling Miranda: I intend to be a part of your life."

Sometime in the night I woke, clearheaded and aware. Something or someone had spoken to me. I had heard words, distinct and final. Then I heard them once more.

"You will never see him again."

Book VII

AMHERST AND NEW YORK

1861–1863

Voltaire wrote that for days after the Lisbon earthquake of 1755, the streets of the city had been full of people shocked and numb, moving aimlessly through the rubble. I understood what he had described. I was living it.

Davy left letters for Father and Aunt Helen, so I did not have to explain to them what had happened. I thought this very courteous to all of us. Aunt Helen cried and told me I should cry too. "You shouldn't bottle up your feelings," she advised me. "It's unnatural. You should let your grief out at a time like this."

I knew she would not believe me if I told her what I really felt: nothing at all.

"It will still be possible to have a life together, if you decide to marry eventually," Father said, doing his best to be comforting. "It will just start later, when you are older. Which I see as a very good thing," he added brusquely. I believed his gruffness was a mask to cover his own feelings, and I did not take offense.

I did everything mechanically: I got up, I dressed, I ate. I went to school and came home, worked on my education paper, and went to bed. My mind, desperately searching for ways to avoid the threatened agony, finally settled on intellectual activity. I was surprised how Davy's advice to speak my mind had freed me to write as myself — as Miranda Chase. I had never taken my own opinions seriously enough to put them in writing before — and once I started, I found I had a great deal to say.

I spent endless hours at work, at study. After some days, I realized what I was doing and why I was doing it. I was a coward. I was like Davy when he said good-bye, when he announced his decision and then could not see me again. I literally could not bear our parting — so I decided, on some level of my heart or mind that I did not control, to avoid feeling pain by feeling nothing at all. I did not choose this, did not plan it — but it happened, and in a small way, I was grateful.

Once, shell gathering at Learner's Cove, Lettie and I found a little gray mollusk that was unfamiliar to us. It was of the pectin family but seemed to have a foot like a clam. It was a live shell — that is, the creature was viable in its tiny fortress. We opened it carefully, trying to identify it — and were appalled to see it lying exposed, writhing and shuddering, a half inch of agony and terror. We closed it instantly and buried it carefully at the water's edge.

"That little fellow," said Lettie sadly, "he is needing that shell!"

For the first five years of my life, I was safe in my own shell; no one could get at me to hurt me. Then I risked opening up a chink in order to receive the gift of learning that Mr. Harnett offered to me. Later I opened wider for Lettie and the James family — then for the Sloans — but I was still protected. Then, loving Davy more and more, I forgot to be careful. I became open and accessible and defenseless. Now, exposed to unbearable injury, I had returned to the safety of my shell again.

Davy wrote often, active and cheerful letters. He was living with Farwell cousins in Chicago and drilling with his friends in different warehouses. They'd planned a beach bivouac, but their officers thought the weather was too cold. They oiled their stiff boots during lectures on gunnery. Their uniforms were expected any day. He had the highest score as a marksman and had been elected second lieutenant. Any day now, there would be a real war to fight.

All this in his lovely baroque handwriting — it was like hearing from a busy stranger on the moon. The only place where I could hear Davy's voice was in the ritual closing: "I intend to be a part of your life."

A little package came from a bank in Chicago, with dangling seals and stamps and official signatures. It was a ring, a heart-shaped amethyst, with a note from Davy in the velvet box.

My mother wore this while she and my father were "unofficially"
engaged. Please wear it for me, till I can give you your true ring.

I put my amethyst heart on the proper finger at once, and both Aunt Helen and Father admired it — without any reservations about suitability. Oddly enough, this ring restored the goodwill of Lolly and her crowd. They had been waiting for my tearful confidences, which never came—and were quite put out at my unfriendly silence. A classmate who refused outings and buried herself in books and papers was standoffish and odd—but an engaged girl with an absent fiancé was permitted these aberrations. So Davy's amethyst revived my shallow Amherst friendships. As before, I appeared to conform.

The first southern state had seceded from the Union in December 1860, within a month and a half of Lincoln's election. There followed a tense armed limbo. By February 1861, there were seven seceders: the Confederate States of America, with Jefferson Davis as their president. Lincoln, our own president, was inaugurated in March. On Amity Street, we discussed every word, every comma in his speech—as if he knew the future, if only we could guess it.

"Doesn't he want peace? He said, 'I am loath to close,'" Aunt Helen fretted.

"I hear only noble fatalism," said Father. "The whole nation is holding its breath, waiting to see who will act first—but something will happen soon."

Only Emily and her crocuses ignored the news. Her bulbs came up in bright constellations. They were invisible except from her bedroom, just as she had planned.

In March 1861, the academy gave me permission to spend three days in Springfield, observing the teaching at an elementary school there. It had been described to me as "a happy place," and I wanted to see why. I also wanted to take the opportunity to visit Kate.

When I reached her house, I found her so deathly ill that she could not conceal her news: another baby in autumn. Instantly I had a terrible fear, remembering the ordeal of Josey's birth. And Josey was only a year old, so heavy that Kate could barely lift him. But I could not share my concerns with Kate; now she needed only aid and comfort.

"It will be lots easier this time," I assured her. "Aunt Helen and I will help you all summer, and we'll both be here when your time comes. I want you to make me a little girl, with green eyes like yours! Just think of her as your present to me."

At the school in Springfield, I was immediately charmed by Miss Polly Randall, the teacher, a quiet, fair woman about Kate's age. I was intrigued when she took the youngest children apart and worked with them in small circles on the floor, without desks or benches. She sat on the floor too. Somehow this positioning put everyone in the roles of friendly equals—rather than a group of little beginners with a teacher who was literally talking down to them.

My mind clicked acceptance: *I will use this!*

I noticed further that she used no memorizing as such, but rather rhythmic musical chants—which the children joined gladly. They reminded me of the songs Lolly and I used for skipping rope at recess. No one ever taught them to us, but somehow we knew dozens of jingles. Why not use this form for happy classroom learning? It was something to ponder as I rode the cars home and something to keep my mind occupied. Back at my desk, I wrote these observations to Mr. Harnett, knowing that in writing I was helping myself retain these impressions and also connecting, if even in a small way, to something larger than myself.

I was barely home and unpacked when events conspired to cause me to recall a long-forgotten dinner-table conversation at York Stairs. There we had been regretting the growing hostility between the northern and southern states, and the fearful possibility of an actual war.

"If there's going to be serious trouble, it'll start in South Carolina!" Dr. Hugh had vowed that night. "There is enough reckless vanity among the Charleston hotheads to fight a dozen wars." And just as he had foretold, the bellicose South Carolinians lit the deadly torch. They were the first to secede in December 1860. They fired the first guns—against Fort Sumter, a Union bastion, on April 12, 1861.

"Could anything have averted this?" Miss Adelaide wrote. "Were all our prayers for reconciliation unheard? Has God been sleeping?"

"This is the greatest disaster in our history," my father mourned. "We will never be the same. We will win the war, make no mistake—that is, the North will conquer the South—but we will lose our innocence, our purity. This is the end of our national youth."

I often forgot Father's passionate patriotism, but now I felt—from a distance—his struggle to maintain his shattered idealism.

Davy, on the other hand, could not suppress his excitement. He wrote:

Battery B enlisted the day after Fort Sumter. We are trained, equipped, and ready—and we've larked about long enough! Now we have left

*Chicago and come to Cairo, at the southernmost tip of Illinois. From
here we'll move west and south, down the Mississippi. We must open
the river and keep it open, at all costs.*

*I wouldn't have known this grand design before, but I've been
elected captain. (If I was ever first lieutenant, it was over so fast
I never noticed.) All our officers are fine fellows and—except for
me—have succeeded at something in life. I only hope they know
more about fighting a war than I do.*

I felt constrained and awkward as I wrote Davy. My days and my
news seemed so trivial, so irrelevant, next to Davy's active authentic
life. Finally, I decided to write about my thoughts rather than my actions, the mental work that was occupying me. This spring of 1861,
my mind was full of elementary education. I found, as I wrote Davy,
I understood my own thinking with greater clarity; just as in our first
letters, I learned about myself by corresponding with him.

*The children are told that learning is their duty, because a stern God
requires it. Then they are given some dreary nonsense to memorize,
to please and placate God. If they fail to do so, then they're punished.
Thus children learn from fear and obligation, rather than from curiosity and joy. To me—whose world was expanded and brightened
by learning—this is nearly criminal and what I most dearly want
to change.*

Emily was shockingly uninvolved in the current news. She treated
it as someone else's war. She mentioned the Amherst boys who had enlisted—college students and villagers—as if they were off to Europe
or graduate school. She foamed with personal outrage, however, when
the *Springfield Republican* printed one of her poems, unsigned. I knew
the editor, Mr. Samuel Bowles, was her particular friend—but she was
consumed with anger nevertheless.

"He had no right, NO RIGHT!" she spit.

"But didn't you send it to him, Emily? That gave him the right, I
think."

"I never gave him permission to PRINT MY WORK. And he even
gave it a title—'The May-Wine.'" Her voice dripped with disgust.
"He knows I NEVER use titles. He had no RIGHT!"

I decided this was a childish tantrum. "Emily, if your friend is an editor, and you send him poems—then you'd just better expect this will happen."

"He's not my friend anymore. Look at the company he chose for me! How's that for BEDFELLOWS?" She threw the paper at my head, quite accurately.

Emily's poem, a mild little lyric about spring fever, was paired with an effusion by Maude W. I skimmed the first few lines of the latter's filigree verses:

> She came to meet me at the tryst,
> The cool, night breeze around her blowing,
> Her sunny hair in tresses flowing,
> Glad laughter on the lips I kissed.
>
> Each heart-throb thrilled with sudden pain,
> As dimpled hands stretched forth to meet me,
> As rosy mouth upturned to greet me—
> I knew we ne'er should meet again.

I saw that this offering appeared on a full page of other poetic treats, all as sugary as the desserts at Mrs. Austin's soirees. I did not tell Emily, but I agreed that Mr. Bowles was insulting all women when he published such nonsense. This "poesy" should never be seen except in frilled, hand-painted autograph albums. But my friend was so fierce in her miniature red-haired dignity that I tried to distract her with her own wit.

"Tell me what you think Mr. Bowles is saying when he prints these silly verses."

My dangling bait worked.

"He's saying, 'Look what my cat just wrote. Why, it's almost human!'"

Also in April, Mr. and Mrs. Alan Harnett were joined by little Julian. I was told Mr. Harnett's wife, Fanny, had an easy confinement and delivery, which gave me hope that Kate's ordeal in September would go as well. I also could not contain a smile, for with the arrival of his child, I was at last replaced as the subject of Mr. Harnett's prodigious pedagogical experiments.

This happy birth was followed in June by another, when Mr. and Mrs. Austin Dickinson rejoiced in the arrival of little Edward, known as Ned. Mrs. Austin also had a short labor and an easy delivery, which gave me further confidence. I was amazed by Emily, who overnight became a typical aunt—proud, parental, involved. She spoke of Ned again and again, planning his life and her place in it.

"Sue has become so WORLDLY, I will have to see to spiritual matters for him," she stated. "The Dickinson name is assured now! I was never certain I would see Austin become a father. He told me Susan is—not DUTIFUL, as a wife."

"Do all brothers and sisters discuss such matters?" I asked. I remembered my awkwardness in discussing such things with my own dear sweet Kate.

"I cannot surmise what others do. Shall we read some more Tudor legends now?" This abrupt change of subject suggested that perhaps Emily realized she had said too much. I was grateful; I didn't want to hear any more such overly personal details.

"I see my own father in Henry IV," Emily mused. "I know just how poor Prince Hal felt about all that UNFLAGGING moral indignation!" She had given me a stunning gold-tooled collection of Shakespeare's *History Plays* for Christmas, and we were working our way through them.

"Perhaps you need a Falstaff, Emily," I teased her but did not suggest myself for the role.

It was summer now, time for my graduation. I had truly loved the academy—all the more by comparison with the inferior schools I had visited for my report. Learning had been joyful for me.

The Howlands arrived from Springfield, and, to my delight, Mr. Harnett, Fanny, and baby Julian came up from New York. My former tutor had always promised to see me graduate—and now he beamed fondly when I won some prizes and then again as he toasted me at our evening reception in the temple. Father and I agreed that 1861 was no year for a ball.

Later, my mentor was more serious. "Miranda, what will you do now to engage that fine mind? You are living right on the eve of a breakthrough in female education." He went on to tell me that in only a few short years, several colleges for women would open their doors. "There are big plans already for a collegiate institution in upstate New York. The money is coming from a retired brewer, a Matthew Vassar, who is interested in making women better teachers. Vassar will be the first of its kind—all female. But you cannot wait for it. We must find another path for you now. I will put my mind to it immediately."

Dear Mr. Harnett knew me well. The Confederacy might be Davy's great opponent; but there was no doubt that waiting idly for his return would be mine.

Meanwhile I had to be available to Kate, so it was arranged that I spend the summer with various Chase cousins in Springfield to be near Kate and help her care for Josey. There were seven married middle-aged Chases—each with a large young family, visiting back and forth between adjoining houses. It was like finding oneself swimming among a school of friendly rollicking whales! Kate's little house was peaceful by comparison, and we talked as easily as ever while Josey slept in the golden summer afternoons. One day in August, we were drowsing in the back garden. The sun and the humming cicadas had almost put us to sleep. We spoke as if we were dreaming.

Like Mr. Harnett, Kate understood exactly about my feeling adrift—without Davy, without the academy, and without her.

"It's lots easier when life hands you your duties, isn't it?" Kate mused. "I was very lucky, I see that now. As soon as I was ready for my real woman's life to begin, then it did! And you, Miranda..." She waggled a finger at me. "Your need is always to be heading somewhere, pointing in a definite direction. You must find a way to best spend this waiting time so it will connect with your years after the war."

"Father actually made me an appointment with Dean Griswold at the college," I told her. Mr. Harnett had suggested it—the plan that he had hoped would evolve for me. "Then the dean read my education paper and decided I could take one course at a time at the college. They've always taken students from the academy—and I had Father's tenure in my favor.

"Anyway, the dean said he'll take me on trial. I must arrive early and sit in back and not wear hoops!" We giggled at the thought of my seductive hoops inflaming the whole student body. Then our drowsy conversation took a different turn. "Kate, how do you really feel about this baby?"

"Of course I'm afraid of the delivery. They told me I wouldn't remember the pains, but I do — every single one. You feel as if you are being split open."

"Did you have to — start this baby?"

"Miranda, there are a hundred answers to that question! How do I explain it?" Her eyes grew distant; I imagined she was searching for the right words for this delicate topic. "You and your husband both want — love, and then the wife thinks ahead and is afraid of a baby, and the husband never does. And sometimes the wife forgets too — and then she's sorry and angry later."

This did not sound like a blissful state to be in. "Do you think there will be more babies after this one, Kate?"

"Unless Ethan changes a whole lot, there certainly will be others!" She frowned and sighed. "God makes a terrible bargain with us, Miranda. He gives us this — joy, this way of showing love, and a license to use it ... and then we pay with regret and pain and danger. We take what ... *precautions* ... we feel we can, but nothing is foolproof." She sighed. "Sometimes I wonder if I'm strong enough."

We basked in the sun till Josey woke from his nap; then I started supper. I thought about everything Kate had said, especially about the joy that married couples had, and about what it would be like to have a child with Davy. And with these thoughts came once again the dread, the empty, hollow knowledge, the welcome numbness. I ate as an automaton would eat, and I did not tell Kate, then or ever, that I didn't think I would see Davy again.

Aunt Helen came to Springfield at the end of August. The doctor promised Kate he would use ether this time, so we were all hoping for a shorter and easier experience than before — but when it came, it still seemed to me the most fearful of ordeals. Kate was utterly helpless, owned and used by pain in relentless waves. I thought of the great impersonal storm rollers in Barbados — cresting and breaking, cresting and breaking — as I held her desperate hands.

Helen Miranda Howland took twelve cruel hours to reach us. Dr. Smedley, as weary as Kate, said, "You must promise me, Mrs. Howland — no more babies. This is the last baby for you."

The leaves had long lost their gold and scarlet by the time I got back to Amherst, exhausted and shaken by Kate's ordeal. I had also turned eighteen. It was the time when a young woman's fancy turned to thoughts of beaux and wedding bells and babies; but while I had a beau, he was absent, and as I took my place again in the lecture hall, the old rhythms of a schoolgirl's day were the ones to which I conformed.

I chose medieval life as my course at the college. I wanted to learn more about the education and training of the highborn children of those centuries. Both girls and boys were taken from their parents' castles and sent to be raised by another noble family—to learn the arts and skills of war and castle keeping from adults who were not their parents. They had teachers, as such, in only Latin and music. This unusual tradition endured for centuries.

Mr. Chester, our instructor, treated me like any other student when he saw I was in his class only to study and not for social activity. I chose "troubadours" as my research topic, and I lost myself in other wars: in the Crusades, Eleanor of Aquitaine, and Bertran de Born. As I walked to class under the autumn trees, smelling the wood smoke, I felt nearer to happiness than at any time since Davy went away. Study would be my salvation.

My new schedule had interrupted my regular Mondays with Emily, but when she was silent for several weeks, I became disturbed, partly because I had not kept my promise to Mrs. Austin this summer. Aunt Helen had no news of her through her sewing circle, so I called on Mrs. Austin. The Evergreens' front door was autumn gold, with an overflowing cornucopia of harvest symbols.

"It's true, I've not seen her in her garden lately," Mrs. Austin told me. "And you know she never comes here! But there's been a steady stream of poems, I assure you. I wonder if their girl has time for her other work."

"Has Emily seen Ned?"

"Yes, I've had him at The Homestead several times. She sends poems about him too—about his immortal soul, that is."

"What should I do, Mrs. Austin?"

"Write her a note this minute, and her girl can take it to The Homestead the next time she delivers a poem. Now, Miranda, what is the news of Davy?"

Sure enough, a return note came from Emily, asking me to call on Monday. I found her unusually animated, with a flush and a sparkle I had not seen before. She was like a girl with a love letter, secretly elated.

"My dear Miranda, I have heard Kate's good news! What a happy relief for your family! But then after that, no one told me you were home again. Or if they did, it went past me.

"I have literally closed my eyes and ears to village doings these last months. I cannot AFFORD the time away from my writing. These years will be the ZENITH of my career, and I dare not waste an hour of them!"

I heard a new, shrill edge of hysteria in her voice. This explained why she had not tried to renew our regular visits—she was too preoccupied even for me.

"Does this mean you have decided to publish, Emily?"

She laughed merrily, flirtatiously. When in these good spirits, her round face, her dimples, her tip-tilted, sherry-colored eyes, were most attractive.

"Don't PUSH me, Miranda! These days I am writing as never before. Sometimes I feel like one of Mr. Mesmer's mediums! Another self seems to take hold of my pen, and I simply go where it leads. I don't fight it; it writes better than I ever did."

"Are you satisfied with these poems?" I was curious about her writing; was it indeed improving or was Emily becoming lost in her miniaturized world?

"Some—not all." She sighed even as she smiled. "I'll rework them later. Right now, I'm being swept toward the sea. I just have to let the SPATE carry me onward. Why, I hardly have time for my FRIENDS!"

"Who mails your letters?"

"You remember Nancy. She seems very closemouthed, and I care less and less about IDLE TALK. If people never see me, then the worst that they can say is 'She stays in her room.' Meanwhile, I write my poems and work for IMMORTALITY. That is my BUSINESS; even Lavinia says so! I will arrange my life so nothing and no one can interfere with my poetry."

"Do you think your father will permit this isolation?" If she was rarely seeing me, it was likely that the few visitors she allowed had dwindled down to nothing.

"You don't understand the arrangement he and I have reached, Miranda dear. We have never spelled it out, but it's clear as ice between us: if I don't create a scandal around the Dickinson name, then he will not force me into society, and we have each kept our word. This may seem like MADNESS to others, but it suits the two of us very well."

She handed me a small poem to keep and then sat at her desk with her back to me. I took that as my cue to leave. I read the poem once I arrived at home.

> *Much Madness is divinest Sense—*
> *To a discerning Eye—*
> *Much Sense—the starkest Madness—*
> *'Tis the Majority*
> *In this, as All, prevail—*
> *Assent—and you are sane—*
> *Demur—you're straightway dangerous—*
> *And handled with a Chain—*

She was right; her poetry was gaining strength. Emily's desire for immortality just might come to pass.

Autumn of 1861 seemed to have more direction, more momentum for me than the summer. The leaf smoke brought the memories of last fall's bittersweet bonfires—being with Davy, walking, studying, singing around the flames—but I could recall them with more equanimity, and even joy, remembering our happiness. Kate was safe with her little daughter; Emily was writing well, steadily and sanely; and being a student had given a shape to my life again. I had the satisfaction of knowing my present was once again attached to my future. If learning was to be the connection between my childhood and my adult years—well, there was plenty to learn.

Davy too was studying his new subject: war. He had had a part in two skirmishes this fall. He wrote:

> *You could not call them battles. I have never yet seen Johnny Reb—though I know he's aiming at me when I hear his bullets whistling past. It still seems very impersonal. "The enemy" is still an abstraction, not an American man my age who wants to kill me.*
>
> *Instead I am more concerned with the practicalities of camp life, and getting better at it every day. After we march, I can drop down and sleep anywhere, even in the open rain—though sleeping out of doors as we do can make a fellow's clothes moldy. But now we have matting on the ground, and my friend Chuck Baird has a small iron bed, and I have three stools to sleep on.*

*When night falls a few of our young officers come to talk awhile.
Each has his own pipe and somebody comes up with a brandy flask,
and the conversation flows briskly about the last Fight, the next
Fight, and whether it is better to change our shirts now or wait until
the end of the month. Of course, when I dream, it's always of you.*

In December, Battery B, Chicago Light Artillery, received a new
general: Ulysses S. Grant, a West Point graduate and an Illinois man.
Davy wrote, "They say he was a star in the Mexican War. Now at least
we will be led by experience. This is no place for amateurs!"

Father and Aunt Helen and I went over to Springfield for a quiet
Christmas with the Howlands; Kate's babies were the only ornaments.
Helen Miranda had now become Elena, which was Greek for "Helen."
She was miraculously like Kate, gentle and beautiful and affectionate.
Kate happily sang carols for us — "as a change from lullabies!"

On New Year's Eve, we toasted "Victory in 1862!" Then I wondered
what that toast might mean. Any victory implied death and suffering
on both sides. We spoke of "victory" as a beacon on a headland, like
the signal fires that told the end of the Trojan War. But what pain,
what loss, had been required before those ancient bonfires blazed their
glorious news!

In February of the New Year, Davy was involved in an authentic battle.
Fort Henry, a Confederate gun emplacement on the Tennessee River,
fell to General Grant and a fleet of Union gunboats. I followed this
on the huge map Father had mounted in our entrance hall, banishing
a Latham portrait to do so. The map explained the Union's urgency
to reach and hold the great central artery of the Mississippi, and thus
divide the Confederacy.

Fort Donelson, in Tennessee, also fell to Grant in February. Thousands of prisoners were captured, along with what Davy called "the
biggest and best guns in the South." During this battle in the bloody
snow, Davy met rebels close-to, alive and dead — but he still imagined
a distance and a detachment from the enemy in combat.

His Battery B was honored for their marksmanship by Grant himself. He chose them to salute the Stars and Stripes with thirteen guns,
as it rose over the captured fort. Davy reported all this with a zest that

made him sound like a schoolboy on holiday: "Everybody was shaking hands with everybody else and embracing one another. Miranda, my own dear sweetheart, this war can't last long. When the birds wing their way back north for the summer, I shall surely be among the flock." Perhaps this lightheartedness was his defense, in the way that feeling nothing was mine.

Then in April 1862 came a great battle—Shiloh—and the war and the men fighting it changed forever. For the past year, the Civil War had still seemed a political gesture, with long encampments punctuated by short thrusts and parries, and significant intervals when diplomacy might yet have been possible. After the holocaust of Shiloh, a single bloodbath that claimed more lives than all of America's previous wars together, both the Union and the Confederate nations were committed to the very last death.

By the Tennessee River, among the freshly plowed fields of spring, a hundred thousand men fought in bloody mud for three rainy days and nights. At tiny Pittsburg Landing, a random cluster of wharves and sheds, twenty thousand casualties waited on the docks for help. Three thousand corpses lay in the fields around the little log chapel named Shiloh. The bodies sprawled so thickly on the ground that those who went to seek out the wounded treaded on the grisly carpet of dead and dying. Hastily organized burial details interred bodies two deep. Davy wrote me: "And all the monument raised to the bravery of these poor souls was a board on which I cut with my pocketknife the words '35 Union' or '110 Rebels'—which I affix to each separate trench."

For a week, the news swung back and forth; then we heard it had been a Union victory. But in that week, the spirit and concept of the war had changed forever. Now I saw it as a terrible entity with a life of its own. It was an implacable monster, a machine grinding up our flesh and treasure, insatiably devouring the future.

I was in Hell for a week. I will be there in dreams and memories of Shiloh all the rest of my life. Hell is a night sky full of screaming shells, falling on boys asleep—what matter the uniform? Hell is a wounded man drowning in a puddle, too weak to raise his head.

I have seen a flowering orchard shot bare with rifle bullets. I have seen two generals bleed to death. I have seen yesterday's battlefield, ghastly by lightning, where hogs root at the bodies. Days later, we ate the hogs.

I worried for him, not just for his physical safety but for the impact this war was having on his interior, on his soul. Would these heart wounds ever heal, and if so, what hidden scars would remain?

Later in April, he wrote again:

It is all settling down in my mind, Miranda. I know there will be many other battles, but Shiloh was my coming-of-age. Now I see that I reached twenty-one amazingly innocent. I had a comfortable, happy childhood; then I met you and loved you. How could I know what the world was really like?

I always thought men were basically good and wished each other well. I thought the human body was noble and beautiful. Now, I know the body is no more than a fragile covering over the unspeakable—and as to the character of man, every sort has been revealed to me. I have known the very best—but, oh, the worst!

Uncle Thomas Bulfinch came to visit after Easter. He had never met Davy, but he knew about our engagement. He was particularly gentle with me. When he asked of Davy's spirits, I showed him the two letters about Shiloh, and he shook his head sadly.

"A young Greek might have written these from the Trojan beaches." He gave me a weak smile. "Except the Greek couldn't write!"

"Do you think he'll ever be the same after this?"

"No, Miranda—but neither will you. We have always taken our best citizens and changed them in our wars. How are you managing?"

"By hiding," I admitted. I smiled, remembering Emily's poem and the mollusk in Barbados. "By wearing the mail of anguish."

"I guess that wearing armor is your way of surviving. You'll come back out someday, when it's safe. Meanwhile you can study. You don't need feelings for that."

His compassion touched me. And Miss Adelaide's insight was moving too:

Your Davy and my three nephews must have tried to kill one another, there at Shiloh. There is death all around us—neither the ivory tower of your lecture hall nor my walls of sweet fragrant stalks protects us from it. But nothing will ever come between us, Miranda—not between you and me, not ever.

Yes, I thought as I put the letter into my desk, there must be Davys on both sides.

Aunt Helen was very disturbed about the ignorance of her women friends, the good wives and mothers of Amherst. After Shiloh, she spoke her concern.

"You should see them, Jos! They're all chasing around in circles like chickens in a thunderstorm. They know what has happened, but they don't know why—so they just flap and cluck! Couldn't we put them to work instead?"

"One of my old students is high up in the Sanitary Commission in Washington," Father informed her, referring to the coordinating agency that oversaw the various women's relief efforts across the Union. "He can tell you how to organize your ladies for the Union. There are a lot of Shilohs ahead of us, I'm afraid. There will be a tremendous need for bandages and dressings, and they'll all have to be folded by hand."

So Father wrote, and Aunt Helen made arrangements and lists—and in a very short time our house was transformed. Our elegant Hitchcock seats were stored in the stable until peacetime. Now there were backless benches and trestle tables in the temple, and bolts of gauze and cheesecloth crowding the stage. Long rows of capped ladies cut and folded and rolled mile after white mile of dressings and bandages. The temple had become a factory.

In our nearly five years here in Amherst, Father's and Aunt Helen's social lives had evolved quite differently. Father traveled around New England for various academic reasons and enjoyed the stylish alumni and the lecturers at Mrs. Austin Dickinson's opulent soirees. He was much in demand in various circles. Aunt Helen was popular with the faculty families and was a Doric column of our First Congregational Church. Father was less devout. Once we were established in the village, he had dropped his Bible class. He attended church only on alternate Sundays. Now, with the war a year old, my father's and my aunt's circles overlapped.

In the temple Aunt Helen was a martinet; she demanded cleanliness and silence. Any lady was welcome any weekday, from two to five—but only to work and listen to a reading. We began every session with one or two newspapers so that each of us was as well informed as possible with the war's course; then I presented a suitably serious novel, the weight of Dickens or Hugo. The ladies preferred having me read every day rather than taking turns among themselves.

"Everyone is very much calmer now that we have something useful to do," Aunt Helen reported at supper. "But these women talk so *foolishly!* They all tell one another rumors, and they don't have any notion what a newspaper story really means."

So once a week Father joined us for an informal talk and to take questions about war news as gleaned from newspaper accounts. Armed with his big map and a blackboard and a pointer, he taught us by speaking simply and directly, and always with a clear progression. He never condescended, and answered our questions with patience and courtesy.

I was proud of him. When I praised him sincerely, he gave me a wry smile. "I've always wished you could know me as a teacher, Miranda. I'm much better as a teacher than as a parent."

It was a poignant moment of soft regret. So we were both learning and adjusting.

At the end of the day, the workers packed and roped the dressings into bales. Every other day, our stableman, Sam, hauled a wagonload to the main rail line in Springfield. The quantity of dressings and bandages produced was staggering, but so was the thought of a million future wounds, pulsing and spilling and soaking our work. Davy might bleed into a dressing folded by our town's hands.

Spring of 1862 was also an emotional time for Emily, only because of her own unique and personal causes. During the past year, I had become increasingly critical of her astounding detachment from the war. Until now, our national cataclysm had not interested her in the slightest—not even the great bloodstain of Shiloh. She continued with her confined miniature life and its tiny challenges—its birds and books and baking. She read; she corresponded; she wrote and rewrote, unaffected by her nation's deadly division.

Now suddenly Emily was distraught, wringing her hands and her adjectives, totally obsessed with the death of a single Amherst boy. This was Frazar Stearns, the promising young son of President Stearns of the college. Frazar was well known to the Dickinsons and much beloved in the village.

Frazar enlisted early, like Davy. He served in the 21st Massachusetts Volunteers under Colonel William S. Clark, his former chemistry teacher at the college. He was killed in New Bern, North Carolina, only a few feet away from his mentor.

This was the first time I witnessed one of Emily's manufactured passions from start to finish. She took what seemed to me an unhealthy interest in the physical facts of Frazar's death: the details of his wound, the shipment of his poor body, the funeral procession through Amherst, and the service in the church, which of course she did not attend. She described all this to her Norcross cousins in a style just as maudlin as that of those lady poets Mr. Bowles encouraged. The Norcrosses were the family that mostly died of consumption when Emily was a very little girl. These two cousins were a bit older than I; they were the survivors of that winter.

I had never understood Emily's connection with the Norcrosses. She wrote them constantly in a very superior fashion, as if they were toddlers and her responsibility. She instructed them in health and weather; she advised them on morals and preserves. She read these letters to me proudly. She seemed to enjoy pretending a maternal role and ordinary friendship. She proudly showed me this latest letter, which I could only skim:

. . . Just as he fell, in his soldier's cap, with his sword at his side, Frazer rode through Amherst. Classmates to the right of him, and classmates to the left of him, to guard his narrow face! He fell by the side of Professor Clark, his superior officer—lived ten minutes in a soldier's arms, asked twice for water—murmured just, "My God!" and passed! Sanderson, his classmate, made a box of boards in the night, put the brave boy in, covered with a blanket, rowed six miles to reach the boat,—so poor Frazer came. They tell that Colonel Clark cried like a little child when he missed his pet, and could hardly resume his post. They loved each other very much. Nobody here could look on Frazer—not even his father. . . .

The bed on which he came was enclosed in a large casket shut entirely, and covered from head to foot with the sweetest flowers. He went to sleep from the village church. Crowds came to tell him goodnight, choirs sang to him, pastors told how brave he was—early-soldier heart. And the family bowed their heads, as the reeds the wind shakes. . . .

It was hard to believe this fulsome sentimentality could come from the very same pen that created the light, delicious image of Emily as the bear *"handled with a Chain."* And I was uncomfortable with Emily's strange possessiveness about the dead, which I had noticed before. Even before a body cooled, it became her property! Her connection with the dead, however slight, turned instantly into an important and exclusive bond. She did not even know Frazar Stearns well enough to spell his name accurately! I had never heard her mention him until now—when his death in battle suddenly established their extreme intimacy. And Emily further exhorted her cousins to believe that Austin's grief over his friend ("I think he may die too!") was as tragic as Frazar's death.

I was deeply offended by all this forced and self-indulgent emotion. After a week of considering the tasteless "soldier heart" letter, I confronted Emily with my feelings on my next visit. I had never before been so openly critical of her attitudes and affectations, but I was driven by the terrible verities of Davy's letters.

The moment we were in her room, I stood to face her squarely. "I have always admired you for not being swept along by the current modes of thought," I told her. "You write your own truths, and they are yours—even if they go against the popular grain. But what you wrote about Frazar was in another voice. You were conforming to fashion, you were imitating popular feeling—which you have never attempted before. Those weren't your own emotions, Emily—and they do you no honor with me."

She gazed up at me, seeming very small, but I detected nothing false or defensive.

"I DESERVE your contempt," she said calmly. "The little cousins won't know the difference, but you do. How can I explain to you what I feel may have happened?" She began to pace a bit. I waited for her to collect her thoughts. Having expressed myself clearly, I could feel my agitation dissipating.

Emily stopped and looked me straight in the eye. "When I was still out and about in the world, I sometimes bought dresses."

I knew that she had her wardrobe made at home now and that since she didn't like being touched, Lavinia served as a fittings model. I wondered where this example would lead. I nodded to indicate that she had my attention and should continue.

"Well, when I used to shop, I'd try on a dress in a store—and it just wouldn't suit! That letter to the little cousins was just Emily trying on and trying out what a woman was MEANT TO FEEL in wartime—and it didn't fit her. You were entirely right to say so."

As always, Emily surprised me. She had allowed me my own opinions, as she did so rarely, and, even more unusual, admitted her own failing.

A few weeks later, Emily and I shared some genuine elation. At long last, after my years of urging, Emily had actually consulted her "surgeon of choice," Mr. Thomas Higginson—the Unitarian minister and liberal thinker whose *Atlantic* article about women's intellectual gifts attracted her back in 1859. I was first incredulous, then full of joyful congratulations.

"I might have waited forever. I know *you* believed I would!" Emily smiled at herself. "Then he wrote another article in the latest *Atlantic*. It is just as fine; he is advising young writers to keep working." She sat up very straight as she quoted, *"A book is the only immortality!'*

"This seemed like a message aimed directly at me. When I read it, I RECOGNIZED the tutor I had awaited. I sent him three poems and a letter; I asked his frank opinion. Here is what I said to him. I kept the draft for you."

Emily was radiant as she handed me her letter to Higginson.

> *Mr Higginson,*
>   *Are you too deeply occupied to say if my Verse is alive?*
>   *The Mind is so near itself—it cannot see, distinctly—and I have none to ask—*
>   *Should you think it breathed—and had you the leisure to tell me, I should feel quick gratitude—*
>   *If I make the mistake—that you dared to tell me—would give me sincerer honor—toward you—*
>   *I enclose my name—asking you, if you please—Sir—to tell me what is true?*
>   *That you will not betray me—it is needless to ask—since Honor is it's own pawn—*

I was very relieved. Remembering Emily's embarrassing "Master" letters, I had feared she would address Mr. Higginson in the same vein. But this note had an appealing sincerity and dignity. Surely a kindly writer and editor would feel obligated to answer this request.

"That's really lovely, Emily—it's just right. And has he written back?"

"Indeed he has—several times. But they are not the sort of letters one SHARES. Shall I tell you what he said to me, more or less?"

"I wish you would."

"Well, Miranda, he was really very INTERESTED, not just in my poems, in my SELF—as a WOMAN. He asked me a lot of PERSONAL questions. He wanted to know all about me; he was very specific. Here is a copy of what I replied." She handed me the paper.

Mr Higginson,

Your kindness claimed earlier gratitude—but I was ill—and write today, from my pillow.

Thank you for the surgery—it was not so painful as I supposed. I bring you others—as you ask—though they might not differ—

While my thought is undressed—I can make the distinction, but when I put them in the Gown—they look alike, and numb.

You asked how old I was? I made no verse—but one or two—until this winter—Sir—

I had a terror—since September—I could tell to none—and so I sing, as the Boy does by the Burying Ground—because I am afraid—You inquire my Books—For Poets—I have Keats—and Mr and Mrs Browning. For Prose—Mr Ruskin—Sir Thomas Browne—and the Revelations. I went to school—but in your manner of the phrase—had no education. When a little Girl, I had a friend, who taught me Immortality—but venturing too near, himself—he never returned—Soon after, my Tutor, died—and for several years, my Lexicon—was my only companion—Then I found one more—but he was not contented I be his scholar—so he left the Land.

You ask of my Companions Hills—Sir—and the Sundown—and a Dog—large as myself, that my Father bought me....I have a Brother and Sister—My Mother does not care for thought—and Father, too busy with his Briefs—to notice what we do—He buys me many Books—but begs me not to read them—because he fears they joggle the Mind....

Two Editors of Journals came to my Father's House, this winter—and asked me for my Mind—and when I asked them "Why," they said I was penurious—and they would use it for the World—

I could not weigh myself—Myself—
My size felt small—to me—I read your Chapters in the
Atlantic—and experienced honor for you—I was sure you would
not reject a confiding question—
Is this—Sir—what you asked me to tell you?
Your friend,

E—Dickinson.

This was exactly the sort of reply I had feared: Emily at her mannered worst, coy and oblique, hinting and evading and name-dropping. It was evident the distinguished, busy man had asked her serious professional questions, and she had replied in playful peekaboo. I could not approve this grotesque letter; it reeked of bad taste and bad manners. I took up the smallest flaw among many, thinking it the most prudent approach. From there I could determine her sensitivity to criticism today.

"Emily, are you actually telling Mr. Higginson that the big wheezing old dog who sleeps in the barn is your 'companion'? I've never even seen him inside the house. Mr. Higginson wanted to know about your *friends!*"

As I spoke, I grew angry and disgusted. If I was not her friend after nearly five years, then who was?

"Carlo was my friend, in his SALAD days, before we moved back to The Homestead. Father gave him to me years ago, for my PROTECTION."

"Protection from what?"

"Protection from tramps and robbers on those country walks I never take!"

"Well, I think Mr. Higginson was asking about your livelier companions—livelier than the mountains and a dog who can't breathe."

The conversation ended there, Emily making an abrupt change of subject. And despite Emily's affected letter, Mr. Higginson wrote again. The editor and the poet maneuvered a little, and I followed their letters back and forth. By June they had a working arrangement. Emily was to continue to send Higginson poems, and he agreed to comment on them. Meanwhile, he asked her "to delay in publishing."

"As if I would want to publish!" she scoffed. "I told him that publishing was as foreign to me *'as Firmament to Fin.'"*

But Mr. Higginson had agreed to be her official "Preceptor," which seemed to rank just below "Master" in her hierarchy. Emily with an actual Mentor by correspondence — Emily with a real author as her tutor — seemed truly wonderful to me. Perhaps her "golden thread" of fame had become a gleaming possibility.

I completed my course in medieval life and was given high marks for my research paper. For my next course, I chose history of the Massachusetts Bay Colony. I wanted to discover why the Puritans, those defenders of spiritual freedom, fought their way to the New World — and then promptly established moral jails as schools for their children. I found a passionate interest growing inside me for all those unknown children — past and future.

With my classes, visits to Kate, occasional afternoons with Emily, and reading to Aunt Helen's snipping and folding ladies, the spring and summer of 1862 passed in an almost cheerful green-and-golden blur.

Davy was not in immediate danger, except from boredom. After Shiloh, his battery besieged and overran Corinth, Mississippi. Then they marched to Memphis, where they seemed to have settled in permanently. Davy was not fighting; he was waiting for the war to join him.

This is our fourth month of drilling and target practice and painting the guns. I have made my tent so elaborate and comfortable it lacks only a portico, like Amity Street! Here in camp we have a glee club, a Shakespeare study group, and a Bible class for every religion, old and new. We eat our own vegetables from our own garden. Every single man in my company is thinking, What in — am I doing here? *but no one speaks the heresy aloud.*

A later letter was more serious:

At least this lull between battles gives me a chance to visit with my old Lake Forest friends in camp. I don't mean to sound pompous, hauling in Achilles and Patroclus, or Alexander and Hephaestion — but it is a strange and wonderful thing that men's friendships are sweeter and keener in wartime, where Death is always on our minds. I would give my life for any one of these dear fellows, because I know he would do as much for me. We all recognize this new bond between us.

And what of us? I wondered. While the war was bringing Davy closer together with his company, I feared it was drawing him farther from me. And for the first time, I held my feelings away from Davy in our letters. I was wearing a mask of sorts with him, something I had vowed never to do. The war was changing us both.

Davy said there were always traders and peddlers hanging around idle armies in camp. He had sent me several portraits taken by wandering photographers. One was of the battery officers, his boyhood friends from Lake Forest, looking like the young knights at Camelot—intent and dedicated. Then there were two of Davy alone: one three-quarters, looking away, and one gazing straight into my eyes. This Union captain was young, handsome, and earnest—and I did not know him. There was no trace of the open heart, the fanciful spirit, the profound sweetness, I had loved.

Even President Lincoln's recent Emancipation Proclamation was treated by Davy with a measure of cynicism:

Yes, my dear Miranda, the president's words were stirring. But don't believe he acts for the most humanitarian of reasons. There is no humanity anymore. No. By setting emancipation as the price the South will pay for continued insurgency (for emancipation applies only to territory outside Union lines), the president ransoms the black man but does the Moral Righteousness of freedom no Honor. And Lincoln threatens to topple the South's entire economy when he confiscates the slave owners' investments in black capital. By a stroke then our president has turned this war to preserve the Union into a War of Conquest. The South will not soon surrender now.

"Perhaps that is who Davy has become," said Kate in response to this hardened stance. "You have had to change too, Miranda."

Davy asked that I send him a recent likeness, since the one he had—from Kate's wedding—was three years old. I could accomplish this best in New York, where I was going to visit Mr. Harnett for an autumn fortnight. My dear tutor often referred to my academy paper on early childhood education. Now he wanted to discuss a project we could work on together based on that paper, and he promised to make me an appointment for a sitting at the studio of a Mr. Mathew Brady, a New York photographer.

I took the cars to New York in October 1862. The city was bigger and louder and newer than Boston, but Mr. Harnett's house, a tiny seventeenth-century Dutch cottage, was none of these things. Like Alan and Fanny—shyly I dropped the formal mode of addressing him as he requested, though I mostly still thought of him as "Mr. Harnett"—their house was full of warmth and ideas. Books and baby abounded.

"Miranda, we have work to do!" Alan announced on my first evening as we warmed ourselves in front of his massive Dutch stove. "Your paper was exemplary. It laid out all the things the elementary schools had been doing wrong in teaching little children. Now you and I have a chance to do it right!

"My school has asked me to design a whole new program for the incoming children," he responded to my startled look. "The five- and six-year-olds. I've been reading a lot of articles by a German—Friedrich Froebel. Do you know him?"

I shook my head. "No."

"You and he already agree on the important things. You both believe that learning should be a process of bringing out what is already there, inside the child."

"He's right!" I exclaimed. "We say '*educo*,' to lead out—and then we cram knowledge from the outside into the child. There's a story that someone brought a block of marble to Michelangelo's studio in Florence, and Michelangelo said, 'There's a statue in there. Now I will work to release it.' That's what I believe education should be. That's what it had been for me," I added with a warm smile. "Thanks to you."

Mr. Harnett smiled back. "We can build on this," he said. "Now what should be released in a child, Miranda, if that child is to learn?"

"Curiosity—it's there in every child, until it is neglected or smothered. Joy and pride in learning. And security too—a sense of being valued as you learn, rather than punished if you don't."

Mr. Harnett nodded. "A child's mind can be a rich and pollinating place when it is nurtured and looked after. In fact, Froebel called his classes 'kindergartens'—gardens of and for children."

I smiled. "I've always thought that children's faces are like flowers opening—this is a wonderful concept!"

The next morning, I nuzzled sweet Julian and reluctantly handed him back to his lovely mother when it was time to see Alan's school, Friends Seminary, just two blocks away. As I expected, I was deeply impressed with its progressive approach to the ways children learn. I stayed the day, observing, and when we returned to Alan's house, we sat and talked for quite some time as Fanny put together an evening meal.

Over a beef and cabbage stew, Alan had more questions. "What drove you to read, Miranda? That was the first thing that drew me to you. A normal child in a normal family wouldn't have needed books as much as you did, up there in your nursery."

I thought back all those years ago. "I must have been looking for color, change, excitement, companions. Everything I otherwise lacked. I thought I would find them in books—and I did."

"Then let's establish a child's very first vocabulary—one that contains all those things you were needing!"

By bedtime we had it: a hundred short, concrete words that a child could learn easily. Mr. Harnett's words related to a child's daily living: "mother," "supper," "tree." My list included a little fantasy: "lion," "wave," "crown."

As we worked, I saw little fables chasing about in my mind, combining our words. *The lion lives by the blue sea. He wears a gold crown. He is king.* I could imagine the faces of children I had observed in the classrooms I visited—learning by rote in their dreary classes—becoming vivid and eager as they met our tale.

Another evening I showed Mr. Harnett a copy of *The New England Primer,* a Puritan relic that was still being used by many Massachusetts schools. He chuckled over the gloom, the despair, the nagging reminders of mortality, that threatened our unlucky Massachusetts children every day.

"I'll never believe this!" he complained. "Here a six-year-old is being warned to prepare for death when he gets up." He read aloud in a melodramatic voice:

> *Awake, arise, behold thou hast,*
> *Thy life a leaf, thy breath a blast,*
> *At night lay down prepar'd to have*
> *Thy sleep, thy death, thy bed, the grave.*

"These primers should be burned," Mr. Harnett said quite seriously. "The authors should be hung like the Salem witches. These books can only cripple souls. There's no education here!"

Several days later Alan accompanied me to Mr. Mathew Brady's photography studio in a forbidding brick building on Fifth Avenue. I was bowed in and posed against a vista of formal gardens and romantic clouds, totally unlike anyplace Davy and I ever shared. When I mentioned this to Mr. Alexander Gardner, Mr. Brady's young assistant, he was severe and unsmiling.

"When a soldier looks at the portrait of his sweetheart, he doesn't want to see real life, Miss Chase. I know this. I will prove it to you."

I followed Mr. Gardner past a curtain and into a high skylit gallery, where men were staring at photographs. Suddenly I was at war, surrounded by war, overcome by war.

I knew there had been a fearful battle near Sharpsburg, Maryland—by Antietam Creek—a little more than two weeks ago. General Lee tried to cross the Potomac and invade the North. He was repulsed, with fearful casualties.

The newspapers called Antietam the bloodiest day of the war. The Confederacy lost more than eleven thousand men; our Union forces, slightly more. And as my Davy, safely in Mississippi, wrote, these were numbers Johnny Reb could ill afford to lose. And now—here—I was at Antietam.

It was a burnt umber world: brown earth, brown flesh, brown blood. There were fields just harvested, now trampled into bloody stubble. There were grotesque upside-down horses, their stiff legs aimed at the brown sky. And everywhere, everywhere, there was another harvest: the bodies that had been young men.

I walked around the gallery, staring intently at each terrible image. It was impossible to discern gray from blue, but one understood instantly that the color of the uniform was irrelevant before this grim, gory holocaust of young life.

Alan came through the curtain. He swept one glance through the gallery and came to hold my hand very hard. He spoke only once, about a photograph of a hundred bodies fallen beside Antietam Creek. Remembering the little river on the Trojan plain, he murmured, "The Scamander."

We thanked Mr. Gardner and left the Brady studio in silence, but "The Dead of Antietam"—twenty-two thousand ghosts—came with us.

Before I returned to Amherst, I took the cars to Springfield for a short visit with Kate, my mind full of the possibilities of Alan's primer project. I was to write a series of small tales, using our child's vocabulary in progressive degrees of difficulty.

When I reached Kate's house, sturdy Josey Howland, two and a half, helped me with this. He settled in my lap, ready with a hundred questions to demonstrate what a young child would want to know.

"A lion lives by the blue sea," I said.

"Wassisname?"

"Leo the lion lives by the blue sea. He wears a gold crown."

"Why?"

"He wears a gold crown because he is king of the jungle."

"Wassajungle?"

"Because he is king of the forest of green trees."

So we learned together, Josey and I. And watching Kate, I decided her life had eased a bit. She arranged her hair in new styles again and sang ballads for her children in the evening. She had Maureen, who was young, with tireless Irish energy, to help her daily. I thought the worst months of the babies' demands were behind her. Ethan's work was steady and profitable. He predicted an enormous building boom when the war ended, when all the profiteers would need palaces.

"They won't want plain houses like ours, Kate; they'll be showing off in mansions like The Evergreens. I'd better learn to speak Italianate!"

The torches of autumn foliage, and earlier my nineteenth birthday, came and went. I continued working with Alan, as well as furthering my studies. I had chosen a yearlong course on Shakespeare. Emily was avid for the details of Professor Kellogg's lectures and our discussions. I sensed a sadness in her and also another emotion—anger?

"Emily, are you cross that I'm taking the Shakespeare course?"

"I'm absolutely FURIOUS—at myself! My heart is beating like a drum, with rage—pure and simple RAGE. I should have had the gumption to DEMAND those courses for myself when I was your age.

"The Dickinsons started Amherst College, and then they saved it and kept it going—and ruined themselves to do it. The president SEARCHES for ways to repay our family!"

"Then why on earth didn't you ask to take courses there, like me?"

"Because I wouldn't give my father the satisfaction of REFUSING me!" She set her little round jaw with the defiance of a thirteen-year-old.

"How can you be sure he would have refused?"

"Because I know him and his cold, CLOSED mind. He is certain that women are a lesser species and that education is WASTED on them. They exist only to serve men and raise their children."

I heard the sadness underlying Emily's bitter statement; I certainly knew of her father's unfortunate condescension toward women. "Thank goodness our wonderful academy taught us more than that, Emily!"

"True—but whatever we learned was by courtesy of a MALE Puritan God, remember?"

Here I could not argue. I too resented the nagging reminders that every stone and every petal was God's design for us.

"And it's not only Father's fault!" Emily was well into her tirade now. "I blame Mother for letting him DEVOUR her! There's nothing left of her now but a pitiful scatter of bones in the snow. Without her help, I was simply too young and too weak to fight him ALONE."

I crossed to her and nearly clasped her hands—until I remembered how she shrank more and more each year from touch. So I sat beside her instead. "Emily, who says it's too late? You and I could still go together. You're cleverer than anyone—you should see some of those oafs struggling with *Hamlet*!"

I found I was elated at the idea of doing something new with Emily—far from the identical white dresses, stiff in her closet; the white doilies centered on her bureau; the smug white curtains tied at her windows. I wanted to get up and out and away from the tight roses on her rag rug on her polished floorboards—from all the prim, superior, insufferable tidiness of Emily's room. And I knew such a plan would help her immensely.

"But, Miranda—that would change our delicate balance, and Father and I have worked so hard to create it." Emily smiled her cat smile. "We don't CONFRONT each other. I don't embarrass him in public, because he doesn't make me BE in public! We understand each other perfectly."

The real obstacle was Emily's need to stay isolated, to shrink from the world. Perhaps she would accept something she could simply observe rather than participate in?

"What about all those brilliant men who come to speak here?" I suggested. "Father is taking me to hear Emerson next week."

"Ah, yes, the lectures. Father used to ask me to go with him when I was younger, but I always refused—simply from SPITE. It was my only weapon against him, except for withholding my piano playing. Would you believe I once missed hearing THOREAU—from purest spite!" She stood and pulled a volume from her shelves. "Why don't we read some Thoreau now? He will lecture to us alone, a command appearance." And so Emily won the round, but what a hollow victory—and at such a personal cost.

Later in the week, as Father and I entered the lecture hall to hear Emerson together, I thought of Emily and her father, two people frozen in rancor, going their proud parallel ways in silence—and I shivered. I doubted Mr. Dickinson even noticed Emily's efforts to hurt him. I recognized in myself the distance I felt from Emily; it was what allowed me to observe her with this clarity.

I smiled at Father and thanked him for bringing me, relishing his vital presence beside me, and felt sad for Emily. As our thousands of dead young men could have told her, life is fragile, precious, and fleeting. We should reach out and touch those we can while they are still here.

At Christmas 1862, we went to the Howlands for a muted holiday. Josey, who was starting to join the carols, was our "star of wonder," and beautiful baby Elena was our "star of light." I made the children a tiny tree, using Davy's golden angel as the only ornament. I turned away for a moment, and my angel fell like Lucifer and ended as gleaming shards. I wept until Josey joined me—and then I had to stop to comfort him.

Upon our return home to Amherst, we received Miss Adelaide's letter informing us of Dr. Hugh's passing. It was not unexpected; his worsening illness had prevented our oft-discussed return to Barbados. Still, it saddened me terribly to think that this vital and charming man, the man who had truly saved my life, would be with us no more. This was one more sad event in that long, sad winter. All I could do was hope the New Year would bring some sort of new joy. But with the war toll ever rising, I feared that I hoped in vain.

Every day of the New Year 1863, I studied Father's war map in the temple. I understood all too well, from the newspapers and Father's briefings, that controlling the Mississippi was the key to Union victory. Davy had finally left Memphis and had engaged in some small skirmishes and a commendable battle at Arkansas Post. His Battery B took hundreds of prisoners, mostly Texans—"the finest body of men I have ever seen under arms."

Now he had reached Vicksburg, the crucial Confederate fortress on the Mississippi. If this city fell, the entire Mississippi River would effectively be under Union control, and the Confederacy would be cut in half. Its eastern part—Georgia, the Carolinas, Florida, and Tennessee—would be unable to obtain supplies of desperately needed grain and cattle from Louisiana, Texas, and Arkansas to the west. It was Davy's opinion that the opening of the Mississippi River would be of more strategic advantage to us than the capture of ten Confederate capitals.

He was to take part in the siege of the city under General Grant. Battery B was dug in east of the river. As the days passed, he became

> ... *bored with the weary repetition of load and fire, load and fire, load and fire. I am thankful I do not have to see the fearful results of our shells falling on the town. We are part of a barrage of two hundred guns, firing day and night—only pausing when our siege guns overheat.*
>
> *The daily life in the shattered city is past imagining. The helpless citizens of Vicksburg are utterly cut off from the world as we surround them with a circle of fire in our effort to overwhelm their Confederate defenders. And I am deeply troubled to have these hapless Vicksburg civilians as our targets. My men and I prefer to fight armies.*

One afternoon, between the February blizzards, Mrs. Austin invited me to The Evergreens for tea. I wondered if it was to be "an Emily conference." Although she and I met often at the dressing factory or at her elegant parties, it had been some time since we talked privately.

We took tea in her increasingly gilded "drawing room." Aunt Helen had heard from the sewing circle that Mrs. Austin had been in New York, attending the opera and dining at Delmonico's. She had stayed with Alice Vanderbilt, her new and stylish friend, who had advised her to eschew the word "parlor" and put away her plain eighteenth-century mahogany furniture, all Dickinson family pieces. I could imagine Lavinia and Emily bristling at the perceived—and perhaps intended—slight.

"Miranda, I'm starting to worry again!" she told me. She wore bottle-green velvet, trimmed with fringe and braid.

"I think Emily is doing well these days, Mrs. Austin," I reassured her. "She is writing steadily and calmly. Why are you concerned?"

"You know about my Springfield grapevine. My friends there tell me she is writing them about some wonderful new Mentor who is going to run her life—again!"

I put down my teacup and smiled at her. "This time it's true. Mr. Thomas Higginson is an editor and a minister; he has agreed to advise her. He has written her several times."

"Why, that must be Thomas Wentworth Higginson—he's getting quite a name in the *Atlantic Monthly*. And does she take his counsel?"

"She fancies she does. At any rate, he's a professional, and he seems interested in Emily."

Still Mrs. Austin appeared troubled, as if there were more to her worry. "She shuts herself away so completely, writing poem after poem. Is this *sane* behavior?"

"If Emily's poetry goes well, so does she. You really needn't be concerned right now, Mrs. Austin. She seems quite rational to me." Confident that I had allayed her fears, I took up my tea again.

My hostess rose with a rustle and went to a small secretary of inlaid pear wood. She removed a slip of paper from the drawer and brought it to me. "Baby gift," she said simply.

I recognized Emily's hand and what appeared to be a few lines, perhaps a draft of a poem:

> *Now I knew I lost her—*
> *Not that she was gone—*
> *But Remoteness travelled*
> *On her Face and Tongue.*

Emily could not be jealous of an infant, I thought. But a child *did* put Sue, who had recently delivered a baby, at one further remove from their girlhood tie. With Sue's passion reserved for—and torn between—family and social ambitions, where was the room for that former fragile intimacy with Emily? *"Now I knew I lost her"* was a valedictory cry of the heart to a friend who had ceased to be who she once was—from someone who wanted to stay frozen in what once had been. I again acknowledged privately how separate I felt from Emily. Though there was much I admired and enjoyed about her, I found little I would choose to emulate.

Mrs. Austin went to the window and gazed at The Homestead, looming ocher against the snow. Again I observed how close the two houses were to each other. A voice would carry easily. It took some contriving for the two Dickinson sisters-in-law to avoid meeting for months at a time.

"Miranda, what do you *really* think of Emily's poetry?"

"May I paraphrase Davy? He said a third is inspired, a third inscrutable, and a third counterfeit."

This delighted her quick intelligence.

"Austin will love that—he can't understand a single word she writes!"

So perhaps the brother and sister were not as close as Emily imagined. Mrs. Austin returned the slip of paper to the secretary, sliding it into a cubby. "I save them all, you know," she admitted with a smile. "You never can tell!"

I walked carefully back to Amity Street, avoiding the ice patches barely visible now in the lengthening shadows. I noticed how the snow, so beautiful and billowy when it fell, had hardened and cracked to white-lava rock. My thoughts turned back to Emily and the tenacity with which she held to small slights and to feelings of disloyalty and discontent, first against her father and then against poor Sue.

Despite Emily's belief that Sue abandoned her, I had seen no evidence of it. Sue had been nothing but a faithful friend and devoted sister, even though she had claimed an independent life for herself among the silks and satins of a modish set. To the contrary, might it not be Emily, judging harshly with an inflexible heart, who had deserted Sue?

In early March, I was kneeling in the atrium in cloak and mittens, encouraging my pot garden. The snowdrops were my pioneers every year, but I expected the crocuses soon. Father saw me from the front hall and came to chat.

"What news from Vicksburg, Miranda?" he asked.

"Battery B is still dug in, still firing," I reported. "The energetic Chicago ladies have organized trains that bring fresh fruits and vegetables straight to the Illinois troops."

"I doubt if Davy and his men need them as much as the rebels do. God knows what those misguided souls are eating—or wearing or shooting, for that matter." Then he got to his true purpose; he must have already known the events of Vicksburg. "But I wanted to ask you something. Didn't you say your friend Miss Dickinson has been corresponding with that minister Thomas Higginson?"

"Yes. She consults him about her poetry." It was a nice change to discuss something so everyday about Emily.

"Does Miss Dickinson know he is one of that reckless Secret Six who planned and financed John Brown's raid at Harper's Ferry?"

"I didn't know that," I told him. "I hadn't connected it. So I doubt if *she* does. Politics do not engage her."

Father chuckled at this. He was tolerant of Emily's quirks by now.

"Tell her she'd better get political, if she wants to be Higginson's friend. He's no parlor abolitionist, you know; he's a true believer, a fanatic about Negro rights. Today I read in the *Republican* that he's recently taken a commission in an all-Negro regiment, the 1st South Carolina Volunteers. His troops are runaway slaves from the plantations along the coast. Your friend should know that Higginson doesn't just talk about freeing the slaves. He fights for his beliefs."

I was moved by the news of this brave gesture and concerned about Colonel Higginson's safety, with such inexperienced soldiers. When I spoke of this to Emily on my next visit, she was typically untroubled by the events in the outside world.

"I read that too; didn't I tell you about it? Of course I have written him—about his Union Army appointment. I told him to be careful and STAY SAFE, for we need him here. Here's the draft of what I said." She handed me the paper.

Dear friend

I did not deem that Planetary forces annulled—but suffered an Exchange of Territory, or World—

I should have liked to see you, before you became improbable. War feels to me an oblique place—Should there be other Summers, would you perhaps come?

I found you were gone, by accident, as I find Systems are, or Seasons of the year, and obtain no cause....

Perhaps Death—gave me awe for friends—striking sharp and early, for I held them since—in a brittle love—of more alarm, than peace. I trust you may pass the limit of War, and though not reared to prayer—when service is had in Church, for Our Arms, I include yourself....

Should you, before this reaches you, experience immortality, who will inform me of the Exchange? Could you, with honor, avoid Death, I entreat you—Sir—It would bereave

Your Gnome—

I was appalled at this insensitive self-obsession, especially at such a time. "Emily, *really!* This is your friend, who has been kind and helpful and generous to you—and he is going into great danger for the sake of his deepest beliefs. Surely you owe him more than an account of how his decision made *you* feel!"

"I don't see that I do." She pouted. "After all, he has PUT ME OUT by making himself so busy and hard to reach. I was counting on him, and he has LET ME DOWN."

There were times when I wanted to pick Emily up and simply shake her out of her selfishness and her affectations. Given the difference in our size, it would have been so easy for me! This image gave me some amusement as I went home, feeling again how distant she and I had become.

The snow melted; mud appeared all over our village. The spring of 1863 began with hope: Vicksburg must fall soon. The desperate besieged citizens were going deaf and mad; they were living in caves in the battered cliffs and surviving on weeds and rats. A shell burst over their heads every two minutes. There could be only one merciful end, and then the Mississippi would essentially belong to the Union.

Once again it was time to visit the Howlands. Kate was interested in hearing about my trip to New York and Mr. Harnett. I told her and Ethan all about the primer project, and Ethan asked to read the stories.

"Your tales are fine, Miranda," he said after he had looked over the material. "But they just lie there on the page. Why not have pictures to bring them to life?"

"Actually, I was thinking about that. Perhaps starting with the alphabet. Where's Josey's alphabet, Kate?"

She brought over a lugubrious brown book that belonged in a monastery. The illustrations were dark engravings, suggesting joyless duty. The "Apple for A" looked sour; the "Zebra for Z" was old and sick. Ethan was offended.

"How could anyone learn from these?" he scoffed. "A child doesn't need distracting details; he senses mood and *tone*. Look at this—" And with a crayon, in two lines and a swoop, Ethan drew a cheerful apple any child would recognize.

"Of course!" I exclaimed. "Oh, Ethan, make us some more!"

"Well, if you think these could enhance your stories, then certainly. Here's Leo the lion." And there he stood, very solemn, with a mane of ringlets and feet like clawed pillows.

"Now show us the sea, Ethan!" I demanded, laughing.

He dashed off two scalloped waves and three smiling fish. Every lively drawing suggested rather than instructed. It let the child inside a joke.

I could hardly believe Ethan's talent and our good fortune; this would be a book I would have wanted as a child. I mailed the sketches to Mr. Harnett and received his gleeful reply.

These skip and dance—they're perfect! Tell your cousin-in-law we want him to do drawings for the whole alphabet, and six for each of the tales. He has just the lighthearted touch we have been needing.

Thus Ethan was conscripted into our enterprise to reform early education. And my life grew ever more engaging and interesting to me.

Then came the unthinkable: the South invaded the North. After his May victory at Chancellorsville, Robert E. Lee—considered the finest gentleman and the ablest general in either army—crossed the Potomac and led his seventy thousand men across Maryland and up into Pennsylvania. He moved too quickly for sieges, but his troops shelled and captured towns as freely as Grant's ever did. The rebels seized animals and stores and promised to repay the frightened citizens in Confederate money just as soon as they won the war. I wondered what Davy was thinking as our northern civilians became victims too—and as Georgia senator Toombs's prophecy that he'd one day call the roll of his slaves from the foot of Bunker Hill Monument became a terrifying possibility.

The climax came on July 1 at Gettysburg, a small market town set at a crossroads among stone-walled fields and orchards. Two nearly equal armies — a hundred and fifty thousand men — fought through the yellow wheat fields for three days of slaughter. This was named the turning point, the most crucial battle of the war: the South at its taut trained peak, pitting its total strength against the awakening giant of the North.

In Amherst, we hung on the news from the battlefield. The churches stayed open, and women slipped out to pray at night. Father joined the crowds of anxious men waiting silently at the telegraph.

"If we lose this one, it will add years to the war," he stated, returning for yet another bulletin.

July 4 brought a Union victory — at least in the sense that Lee retreated back over the Potomac. But there were fifty thousand casualties — one out of every three soldiers who fought at Gettysburg. Soldiers from both armies lay moaning everywhere — ten times the population of the little broken town. Twenty thousand wounded men covered every foot of a village the size of Amherst. The frantic citizens tried to tend soldiers propped on garden fences, soldiers supine on porches and lawns — or soldiers waiting on blood-soaked parlor rugs, with a book for a pillow — never mind the thousands of dead, whose bodies lay in the putrefying summer sun for days. With human suffering on such a scale, who could call Gettysburg a victory?

Strangely, like a voice from another world, came the news of the surrender of Vicksburg — the very same Fourth of July. Later we learned that the Confederate commander, a Pennsylvanian by birth, set the date with an eye to Union vanity, suspecting he could get better terms on that day than on any other. General Grant's men were compassionate to the pitiful townspeople and their skeleton defenders. There was neither cheering nor jeering.

The southern journals stated, "Vicksburg surrendered to famine — not to Grant."

Lincoln said, "The Father of Waters again goes unvexed to the sea."

Davy wrote, "Now we'll surely get leave."

Despite this pair of important victories, there was a spirit of discord abroad in this summer of 1863. Conscription had arrived, and the

Union was far from united about it. All single men between the ages of twenty and forty-five and married men up to thirty-five had been called up for service in the army, but those wealthy enough could buy a substitute for five hundred dollars or so—as Mr. Austin had done. "Born equal" no longer implied an equal chance to stay alive. Our poorer citizens surely smoldered at this mortal inequality.

The first draft was called the week after Gettysburg, and riots and arson raged for days in New York and Boston. In the cities, the Irish immigrants were the most bitter and violent. They came to the United States with high hopes, little education, and no interest whatsoever in freeing anybody's slaves.

In the *Republican,* we read with uneasy distaste about the New York rabble looting Fifth Avenue stores—and about pitched battles between armed Irish mobs and Negro citizens. Uniformed soldiers, still bloody from Gettysburg, camped in the streets and fought the rioters side by side with the city police. What was happening to the world?

Our village of Amherst was so committed, so devoted to the Union, that we were distressed by these deep divisions—and also by the malingerers and the corrupt doctors who sold deferments. None of this affected me as it should, for I had a note mailed from Kate, that shook me badly.

> *I am telling you this way because I could not face your asking me "Why?" when you hear this news. There is going to be another baby in our house in early spring. As to "Why?" even I couldn't answer that right now.*

In March 1864, when the new baby was to come, Elena would be two and a half; Josey, four; and Kate, twenty-four. My worries for Kate were severe, but for Kate and Aunt Helen's sake, I had to keep them to myself and only assure Kate of my help when that time came.

I did not mention Kate's condition to Emily on my next visit. I saw she had decided to try on patriotism again. She showed me her latest attempt to march with the times:

> *When I was small, a Woman died—*
> *Today—her Only Boy*
> *Went up from the Potomac—*
> *His face all Victory*

To look at her—How slowly
The Seasons must have turned
Till Bullets clipt an Angle
And He passed quickly round—

The poem continued for a few more stanzas and then ended with:

I'm confident that Bravoes—
Perpetual break abroad
For Braveries, remote as this
In Scarlet Maryland—

My response to Emily was noncommittal. I did not tell her that her poem was inappropriate in the wake of Shiloh, Antietam, Bull Run, and Gettysburg, with their gigantic losses—24,000, 23,000, 27,000, 51,000—in battles that lasted only a few days. In Emily's willful ignorance, her poem read like a hearty team cheer for an athletic contest—a jolly "Rally 'Round the Flag, Boys." I was pleased, however, that she was at least trying out her own emotions about the war and applying her creativity to them. I encouraged her to read the war news to better inform her art.

After the fall of Vicksburg, Battery B, Chicago Light Artillery, rested and refitted in Memphis. Davy took a short leave in Lake Forest and wrote me from there.

It is only a calendar year and a half since I left this house, with its
dear familiar oaks and its lake setting—but I feel as if a thousand
years of my life have come and gone. I have been forever changed by
learning that death (which I always believed came in bed, after a
long, productive life!) is actually all around us, just out of sight. I
will never again take it for granted that I am alive and whole.

I have had to call at two houses near ours, on the parents of close
friends, and tell them how each son died. I always make the death
quick and clean and painless, and in the company of friends. How
could the truth help anyone?

And yet. Perhaps it is because I have been here at home, think-
ing of all the beauty here that I want to show you. Perhaps it is the
ability to be warm and dry and well fed for a spell (never, ever will

I undervalue the importance of dry socks!). Perhaps it is simply that the birds are caroling outside, and I can hear them. But I woke this morning strangely confident: the Union will stand, and you and I will have our time. However much this war has altered me, my love for you remains a fixed North Star of my present and my future. No one will ever love you as I do, Miranda. One way or another, I intend to be a part of your life.

I was so glad to see a strain of optimism; lately Davy's letters had been melancholy, filled with a sort of fatalism that made me realize how far he had traveled from the merry, confident young man I loved. I had changed just as much. But this letter touched a place in my frozen heart. When all this was over, if we could see and touch and comfort each other as our new selves, we would be all right.

This July and August 1863, I had to take on most of Aunt Helen's duties in our house and at the dressing factory. Her daughter's condition was becoming a grave worry to her. Kate was sick and exhausted week after week, and Aunt Helen stayed on in Springfield to do what she could.

I hired a new Irish girl, Bridget. She and I took care of the housekeeping, Father's meals, and Aunt Helen's garden. Bridget was genial and hardworking, and very sympathetic about Kate's condition. Her enormous family in Ireland was in chronic parturition, forever breeding and losing babies.

"Indeed, Miss Miranda, it's why I'm here. There's not enough land in Ireland to raise the children we have already. From sixteen on, there's naught for a poor woman but the new baby and the baby to come. It kills them off soon enough."

This last was not what I wanted to hear, so I changed the subject to other matters. Bridget must have sensed my discomfort and did not bring the subject up again.

Every afternoon, as the Amherst women gathered in the factory, I was there as well. Making dressings was simple and undemanding, and left the time to chatter—and without Aunt Helen, I lacked the authority to prevent this. The War Department insisted that we work in silence. I imagined this was for hygiene, but it was appropriate too—when one considered where our dressings were going.

Handsome Mrs. Crowell, whose husband taught Latin at the college, saw my problem and offered to distribute the material and enforce

Aunt Helen's rule of silence. Soon I realized my new friend was the Mary Warner of Emily's childhood—one of the "Heavenly Triplets." She informed me that Abiah Root Bliss, the third "Triplet," was now a missionary in Syria.

"I miss Emily, but I have never known her to change her mind once she makes it up," Mrs. Crowell told me. "If she has decided to live secluded, then I know I will never see her again. She was fascinating as a girl—so original and lively!

"Just tell her I think of her often, Miranda. We shared some splendid times. I long for her vitality and wit. I envy you for being welcomed into her special small circle."

"Indeed, Mrs. Crowell, the circle is sometimes encrusted with nettles."

"Admittedly, but would you permit me an analogy? Do you garden?"

I nodded and waited for her to continue.

"Then you know that one must prune one's flowers ruthlessly, to remove the faded ones of yesterday. Such an exercise is necessary. Only by refusing to crowd the bed with every weak plant is the gardener assured of a vigorous growth—so that the garden will bloom like Eden." She smiled. "It is that way with Emily and her poetry. It is a calling, my dear. Remember that, and be kind." She squeezed my arm affectionately. "And tell her I'm glad she has you for a friend!"

On my twentieth birthday, among the bright leaves, I began my next course at the college. I had chosen to learn and read about the lives of the poorest English children—from the vanishing farms and the new industrial towns—who had no education past the age of eight.

In October, new Amherst citizens joined the bandage factory at our house. Lolly Wheeler and her sister-in-law, Charity, arrived one chilly afternoon. Without school throwing us together, Lolly and I had drifted apart, as I had once sworn to Emily we would never do. I hadn't realized that Charity was now living with Lolly's family while her husband, Lolly's older brother, was away at war.

I set them both to work at once, but Lolly gripped my hand as I began to turn away. I looked back to see a careworn face, still pretty but with a new expression in her once sparkling eyes. Apprehension, perhaps; a caged worry, wishing to be let out. In the instant that our gazes met, I knew we now had much in common.

"Mother is worried to distraction," she whispered. "So am I. And Charity cries all night. This"—she gestured around the large room—"was all I could think for us to do. To be useful."

"You are very welcome here," I told her. "I'm glad you came."

Charity stood and stretched and went to speak with Mrs. Crowell. Lolly brought her face close to mine. "She's expecting. That's why she is staying with us. She has no other family, and if William..." Her voice cut off as tears sprang into her eyes.

I stroked her hair. "Just wait and see," I told her. "All you can do is wait and see."

Just after Thanksgiving, I was walking home to Amity Street, carrying my books. It was dusk; the last autumn bonfires still veiled the village in smoky sweetness. I was not happy, but I was at least contented. Davy was newly arrived in Tennessee, which appeared safe on Father's map. Kate was stronger; Josey was out of diapers at last. The Howlands, having missed Thanksgiving with us, were coming to Amherst for a party for the first time in years, and Bridget would help me do the pies tonight. Tomorrow we would get out the damask cloth and set the table for Thursday.

As I turned onto Amity Street, I was startled to see, through the bare branches, that Father's study wing was lit. It was Tuesday evening; he should have been at a meeting at the college. As I went up the walk, I heard Aunt Helen's voice coming from the study. Could she be weeping?

I ran to the library door, clutching my books, my wild heart racing. Somewhere, deeper than I knew, I had been expecting exactly what I saw. It was like arriving late at an ongoing play, with the characters already onstage: Aunt Helen on the sofa, head bowed in her hands—and a tall older man, a stranger, beside her. He rose when I entered and looked at me gravely, from eyes I knew.

"Miss Miranda Chase? I am Cyrus Farwell." He had those black brows too—over the same shocking silver eyes.

"Davy is dead." It was not a question.

"Yes, my dear. He was killed last Tuesday, at the Battle of Lookout Mountain in Tennessee. I came to you at once—as soon as we got the news."

Aunt Helen guided me to Father's chair. For some reason, I would not let go of my books. I stared at Mr. Farwell.

"Do you know what happened?" I heard myself asking.

"Yes, his colonel sent word to us. The enemy was massed on the summit, guns trained on the fields below. After two days of fierce fighting, our boys stormed Lookout Mountain and planted the flag where Confederate guns had blazed just hours before. But Battery B took a direct hit. Two men were killed outright. Chuck Baird, Davy's particular friend, had a leg wound, and at first it appeared that Davy was only nicked in the chest. He was barely bleeding.

"So Davy carried Chuck to the field dressing station, behind the lines. Davy told the doctor he was fine and to fix Chuck first. They all saw him resting under a tree; they thought he was sleeping. There must have been shrapnel in his chest. All the bleeding was inside, you see."

So he had never used one of our dressings after all.

Mr. Farwell crossed the room and knelt beside me. He took my books, put them on the floor, and clasped my hand. I could not bear to look in those familiar eyes. I saw him open his briefcase. I saw Aunt Helen pouring Father's brandy for us. I heard Mr. Farwell speak again.

"My dear, on his last leave with us in July, David told us to be ready for his death. While he was in Lake Forest, he made his own preparations. These will require time. Right now I know David wanted you to have this engagement ring. It belonged to his mother; now I give it to you." He handed me a small silver box that was inscribed: FOR MY BELOVED INTENDED WIFE, MIRANDA ARETHUSA CHASE.

"I know Davy would want you to have this," Mr. Farwell told me. "Will you allow me the honor of putting it on your finger?"

I removed my little amethyst heart and gave it to Aunt Helen. Again we seemed like actors, doing a scene we had already rehearsed. Mr. Cyrus Farwell put the ring on my third finger: a large oval diamond, rose cut, set in heavy plain gold. The great stone covered my knuckle. It had a final look; it was not the beginning of our love but the end of it.

Aunt Helen must have sent Sam to fetch Father. He rushed in—coatless and hatless at the beginning of December. He stared at us all; then he crossed to Mr. Farwell and grasped his hand. Neither spoke.

I rose, turned blindly toward the open door, and stumbled into the night. My next awareness was of my room. I was in the dark, lying across my bed in my outdoor clothes and boots, when Father knocked and entered. He carried a lamp and a pen.

"Miranda, you must sign these papers for Mr. Farwell before he leaves." He had to guide my hand. I was not trembling, but I could not remember my name or how to write it.

Sometime later I saw it was daylight, and I remembered the pies I should have been making for the party: two apple and two mince, since Father had invited some students. I dressed quickly, wondering why I felt so faint, and hurried down to the kitchen. But where was my pastry that Bridget should have prepared last night? I expected it in a bowl, ready to roll out for my pies.

I was slicing apples when Aunt Helen hurried in. She looked very badly too. Had we all been ill?

"Miranda, whatever are you doing?"

"Making the pies. I know I'm late." I sliced away in the loud silence.

"Dear Miranda, dear child — what pies?"

"Two apple and two mince."

She still appeared confused, so I explained to her, "The pies for tomorrow — the ones I promised for the party."

Then her pretty round face withered and crumpled, and she crossed the kitchen to hold me against her bosom.

"Miranda, child, that party was eight days ago. Of course, we didn't have one —" And Aunt Helen caught me as I remembered, and I fell.

Book VIII

AMHERST AND SPRINGFIELD

1864

For several weeks I had appalling blanks, strange voids in time. I sat in my room, staring into space, unaware of how much time might have passed. Dusk would fall and I never noticed that my room had grown dark.

One day a letter from Davy arrived. I knew it was posthumous, yet I ran upstairs to Kate's old room to tell her the news. I sat in her room for an hour, unable to make myself open the letter. I do not remember that I ever read it. Often I woke at night during a winter storm, hearing the torrent of wild wind outside. At those times I thought I was a little girl again, half asleep at York Stairs, listening to the surf beating on the eastern beaches. I could almost feel the breakers, mounting, rearing, and cresting for seconds—before booming into foam. Like flotsam I was caught in the grisly undertow.

On New Year's Day 1864, Father slipped a note under my bedroom door, asking me to see him in his study. I dressed and went downstairs, and found him sitting at his worktable with a big manila folder before him. The pale afternoon sun illuminated his expression, both sorrowful and resolute.

He cleared his throat. "Miranda, dear daughter, we must begin your future today," he declared formally. "The Greeks, who were wiser than we are in spiritual matters, believed in total mourning for a fixed time—and then a ritual and symbolic closing to the period of grief and withdrawal.

"This day that begins the New Year is a fitting day for you to end your first stage of mourning. A traditional way to do this is to acknowledge these messages from other people who loved Davy." He handed me the folder of letters.

There were scores of them. Dear Miss Adelaide, the faithful Harnetts, my own friends and teachers, Emily, of course, and my neighbors and classmates had written—and so had Davy's. I had not realized what a large acquaintance we had between us—but of course Davy was not a person you could overlook or forget.

"I want to be with you while you answer these," Father told me. "You need one sympathetic and harmonious presence; I would like to be that person. Nothing can change the fact that Davy is gone, but these letters will help you begin to move forward."

I saw that he had a table ready for me, laden with boxes of black-bordered writing paper. I sat down to work. I began slowly, cautiously, braced for torrents of feeling, or worse, an increasing despair. I experienced neither. Gradually I found myself engrossed in the task in a way that allowed me to think about Davy without soaring pain.

Seated at his familiar spot behind his desk, Father was an inextricable component of the process. Sometimes I read him a phrase someone had written or he gave me a line from a colleague's translation he was correcting. We drank China tea and shared his apple-wood fire. His presence at this time reminded me of our old York Stairs days, where I was his amanuensis, as he was now mine.

I heard from many of the college faculty, even President Stearns, still suffering from the loss of his son. "Our college will be darker without his bright spirit," he said. I liked that.

The letters from Davy's fellow officers in Battery B were of two kinds: Some of the men knew him from a Lake Forest childhood and recalled a sunny companion, laughing and carefree. The other letters were from wartime friends and described someone sterner: a leader, brave and high-minded. This was a Davy I had only recently met and had just begun to know.

"He was simply better than we were," one wrote me. "He was made of finer stuff."

Emily had sent me a poem; I could not judge it. Perhaps I would in the future.

> *I felt a Funeral, in my Brain,*
> *And Mourners to and fro*
> *Kept treading—treading—till it seemed*
> *That Sense was breaking through—*
>
> *And when they all were seated,*
> *A Service, like a Drum—*
> *Kept beating—beating—till I thought*
> *My Mind was going numb—*

And then I heard them lift a Box
And creak across my Soul
With those same Boots of Lead, again,
Then Space—began to toll,

As all the Heavens were a Bell,
And Being, but an Ear,
And I, and Silence, some strange Race
Wrecked, solitary, here—

And then a Plank in Reason, broke,
And I dropped down, and down—
And hit a World, at every plunge,
And Finished knowing—then—

Was she "trying on" emotion again? Or was this genuine? The final lines ignited a brief spark of recognition in me. I put it aside to read again later and thanked her for her thoughts at this time.

Mr. Harnett wrote: "I grieve for you and with you, and I know that some part of you expected this. Now that it's happened, it will be necessary for you to re-create yourself and redirect your life—albeit a very different life—incorporating and using Davy's love for you. You will find me at your side to help you in any way I can."

And from Miss Adelaide: "Oh, Miranda, I should be with you! I am haunted by the picture of your grieving without me. Perhaps you will take small comfort in knowing that you are not alone in this grief: all over our two tragic countries, you have a generation of sorrowing sisters. We will all need your strength to rebuild."

I did not really understand either of these, but I sensed my friends' true sympathy and support. No *"early-soldier heart... covered... with the sweetest flowers"* for them.

In the peaceful silence of my worktable, as I blotted and folded my responses, I knew Father was right. Answering these mourning people, connecting with their sorrow, was a healing ritual. I was very grateful to the letter writers and their tender memories. I had been selfish—like Emily—wanting to grab all the grief for myself. And Father's steady concern warmed me more than his fire. When I tried to thank him, he shook his head.

"There are times in life when ceremony is the only balm."

As I slowly regained my equilibrium, Aunt Helen hovered less closely and then decided to return to Springfield to be with Kate until the baby came. I resumed the duties of our house with Bridget's help. Our meals these days were often neighbors' gifts—hams and pies and puddings—a steady reminder of the kindly village custom of treating loss with kitchen messages.

"What you see is the mourning gesture of inarticulate people." Father smiled sadly. "Many wrote you, but few can say the words in their hearts directly to your face. So they make you a pumpkin pie instead."

I might have missed this insight without Father. Every day, in large and small ways, he helped me across the darkness.

In mid-January I went back to work in the dressing factory, where Mary Crowell had handled both the production and the ladies very ably. I had been silent for so long that my voice was hoarse and strained when I first tried to read aloud.

Although the ladies welcomed me back warmly, my presence seemed to have a disquieting effect. After an initial "hello," many of the women whose husbands or sons or fiancés were at war could barely meet my glance. Lolly steadfastly sat beside me, even as her sister-in-law stood and crossed to a seat on the other side of the room. I understood; I was a reminder of what might befall them and their absent loved ones. Gradually, the tension in the room thawed, and I was glad to have, once again, this task.

Now my only remaining duty was to Emily. I had been dreading her lavish reactions to the news about Davy. She would sigh and talk about her own sorrows—and the pains of early death and lost love. But when I realized two months had passed, I decided I must overcome my aversion and make an appraisal. In truth, she had been the staunchest of friends, sending me homemade treats and handwritten notes or scraps of verse nearly every day. One poem, which she said was written for me, brought on a shower of tears. It started with "After great pain, a formal feeling comes—" but I found the last four lines to be the most stirring:

> This is the Hour of Lead—
> Remembered, if outlived,
> As Freezing persons, recollect the Snow—
> First—Chill—then Stupor—then the letting go—

The scaring truth of this poem reminded me again that there were two Emilys, each incomparable: the sentimental ingenue and then the shrewd, practical New England woman. Luckily I found the latter awaiting me—with a rare embrace and a mourning shawl of black challis.

"Do not forgive me for not meeting him when I had the chance. I will never forgive myself." That was all she said on the subject. Then she showed me her private view of snowdrops, strewn under her window like pearls on the snow.

"I always think of us together, that morning in the Indian summer mist. Some memories are INDELIBLE." And I knew she referred also to my memories of Davy and that they would always be with me as a source of comfort. We smiled at each other, recognizing the message that had been sent and received obliquely.

"I wrote Mr. Crowell at the college," she informed me as we had our tea.

I wondered why she didn't say "Mary Warner's husband." Had that once close friendship been so severely strained that Emily could not even mention Mary's name?

"I asked him to suggest something you and I might read at this time," she said. "He sent me this. It reads very like Vicksburg, as you described it."

She handed me Euripides's masterpiece, *The Trojan Women*. After tea, we read the play in that single afternoon. We were taken up and out of ourselves, swept along by its timeless majesty. Emily was the only friend who could have consoled me in this particular way.

Walking home in the dusk, filled with gratitude for Emily's imaginative gesture, I found that the door to learning had been reopened for me—if only a crack. None of my emotions were accessible yet, but apparently my intellect was available again. Sharing this literature together had been a gift from Emily; the tragedy of an ancient war so relevant for me today linked me to a community of feeling, if only for a few hours.

Kate's baby was expected in March, but she asked me to come a few days before her delivery date. "We haven't talked seriously since Davy was killed. It broke my heart that I had to leave," she wrote.

So I packed enough for a short visit, planned Father's meals with Bridget, and took the cars to Springfield.

The entire family greeted me with waves and kisses when I arrived. Aunt Helen gripped both my hands firmly. "You look much improved," she declared.

" 'Randa!" Josey crowed cheerfully, but Elena still hid her bronze green eyes, so like Kate's. I saw her fragility mirrored in Kate, whose own beautiful eyes were now shadowed. She kissed my windblown cheek, and I felt her search my face for evidence of my inner state. When she stepped away, her expression told me she understood my heart was healing but was still in retreat.

Aunt Helen made tea, and Ethan, Kate, the children, and I sat in Kate's little parlor, with the dolls and the diapers and the closed piano. The children continually clamored for Kate's attention, so the conversation was mostly between Ethan and me. Aunt Helen participated intermittently between Josey's demands, Elena's silent tugs, and the needs of the evening meal.

"You must see the proofs of our alphabet," Ethan announced. "I went ahead and corrected them, because Harnett said the publishers want them by spring. Other schools are already ordering them!"

I knew I should be elated by this good news, so I smiled. I trusted that eventually my feelings would catch up with me. For now, I could put on the appearance of appropriate response.

The proofs were wonderful, and we all discussed the books and future projects during supper. After the dishes were cleared, Ethan and Aunt Helen took the children upstairs to allow Kate and me a private visit in the parlor.

Kate sat down with a long sigh. She closed her eyes for just a moment, then directed her glance at me.

"Now, Miranda, let's not waste a moment," she said. "Tell me how you are, how you are really." She smiled gently. "I can see that you are returning to life, that you are doing what one must. But what is inside you now?"

"Oh, Kate," I murmured. I searched for the words. "It is . . . hard. In ways I had not expected."

She settled back and listened as I described my unease; how, even at the end of my mourning, my Amherst neighbors could not meet my gaze. They averted their eyes as though I, like Davy, had been pitched out of life and into something else.

"Will it ever be all right?" I asked her quietly. I believed she knew my deeper and unspoken question: will I?

"You will, my cousin, but of course you will never be exactly our same Miranda after this."

She tucked one of my stray curls behind my ear. I could not remember when I had last cut my hair.

"You will have to grow around the wound to survive, like a tree blasted by lightning," she said gently. "Just as you will have to put aside other people's ideas and expectations for how you should do this."

I realized then just how much I had missed her. We chatted on, and I was reassured that my concerns were common enough, vagaries that attached themselves fleetingly to death's aftermath. In my heart, I knew my life would once again find a steady center. Rather, I was more troubled by Kate. She had gained very little weight this time, and her face was pale and narrow. Her expression was clouded and uncertain; her eyes told me she had moved far away.

"What is it, Kate?" I asked. I took her cold hands in mine. "Now tell me what you think about."

She looked away. "I'm not sure; I don't do much real thinking these days. I just *do*—and then there's no time left to think. Every day is just like every other, and then I sleep at the end of it. Or try to."

"Do you feel the same way as you did the other two times you were expecting?"

She picked up a clean diaper from a pile of laundry that had never made it upstairs. She folded the single item over and over.

"No, I don't." Kate was emphatic. "This is *different*. For the first time I'm really afraid—and I never was before."

I watched as she laid the cloth diaper on her lap, opened it, and then folded it again.

"But you had an easier time with Elena than with Josey," I reminded her. "Surely this time should be no trouble...almost."

She shook her head. "I'm not afraid of the delivery. It's the worst pain there is, but I survived twice. It's *afterward*..."

Kate laid the diaper on the settee, stood, and crossed to the piano. She leaned some of her weight onto her hands as she pressed down on the closed lid.

"How in the world will I manage with three babies? How can I do it, day after day, night after night?"

"But you have Maureen to help you, and Ethan will—"

"No, no, you don't understand." Kate began to shake.

Alarmed, I rose and crossed quickly to stand beside her, uncertain of what to do, how to help.

"My day begins before the night has ended," Kate said, the words coming unevenly as she gulped in air. "Elena cries for me until I take her in my arms. Josey calls that he is 'chivering cold.' Before I know it, I am up with both children and it's not yet daylight. And with that I go and go, cooking, washing, tending the children, all day long, cleaning, mending, and straightening up—well after the house is dark and quiet. And then it starts again. That is why I can't think—I'm so tired, Miranda—I'm so truly tired to death."

My strong, brave Kate began to sob helplessly. I reached out to hold her, but I could not get close enough. Her poor swollen body kept us apart.

"Oh, Miranda, tell me—how did this happen to me? What will I do?"

There was nothing to say. Instead I held her hand and carefully laid an arm around her quivering shoulders as she went on sobbing in her exhaustion and her fear.

In the end, Kate was spared; she never had to do it all, and she was able to rest. Ethan Charles Howland required only three early hours to be born, and his mother was smiling and nursing him by noon. Then I took little Ethan for an hour or two so Kate could sleep while Aunt Helen bustled in the kitchen.

I returned him around four. I opened the door, calling, "Wake up, here's someone hungry!" By then Kate was quite cold—the killing blood clot must have struck right after I took the baby. Dr. Smedley vowed she died in painless seconds. He told us such a clot could not had been guessed or prevented; it was a frequent blow from God against new mothers.

Ethan and Aunt Helen were wild with grief, for which they were utterly unprepared. There was nothing I could do for Kate's husband, and Kate's mother, and my own loss. But I could care for Kate's children.

Baby Ethan was quiet and easy, and took a bottle without distress, having only nursed that once. Dark-haired Elena wouldn't leave my side. Just two and a half, having few words but great understanding, she knew something was horribly wrong.

Little Josey was the most confused. "Why is Papa crying? When will Mama wake up?" he kept asking us. "She's there in her room. I saw her in bed. Why is the door closed?"

It was a fearful time in Kate's house for those she left behind.

When Aunt Helen couldn't answer, Ethan asked me to decide if the coffin should be open or closed; I chose closed. Radiant Kate should be remembered as a beauty. The service was in the little parlor, with Kate's voice teacher at the piano. The mourners spread out into the orchard, the little apple trees from Kate's wedding. She was buried in the rain—in the Chase plot, next to her father. I welcomed the rain. It was as if the skies themselves were weeping.

After Kate's funeral, we returned the platters and emptied the vases. Emily had sent freesias and to Aunt Helen had written: "Will Mrs. Sloan accept these Blossoms for the Hand of her Daughter, with the sorrow of Emily and Vinnie Dickinson?" In her note to me she acknowledged this second loss. "Fate can have no more arrows in its quiver for you that can wound like these." I had not thought of life in these terms and wondered now if any more blows would really matter.

One blank day followed another as we lived on in Kate's little house. Aunt Helen returned to Amherst and to Father, to mourn with him. The household activity and children's clatter, added to her cataclysmic bereavement, was too much for her. These two seemed years slower and sadder than before our family tragedies took shape and multiplied. I wondered fleetingly if the same was true of me.

I walked through exhausting days and empty nights, caring for the children. Like Kate, I was always tired and felt little or nothing but fatigue. I tried to forget the past and could not imagine a future, merely functioning in the present. Maureen, Kate's Irish helper, was strong and steadfast; she was my only adult companion. Luckily I had no social life, for I would not have been able to carry on a proper conversation. The mail went unread, the war news unnoticed. My only events were those in the nursery, and one diaper was very like another.

Ethan too was a husk of a person. We seldom met, as I kept children's hours and Maureen gave him his late dinners. Since late 1862 he had been a project architect at the Springfield Armory, which was doubling in size to feed the insatiable war machine. He burrowed like a mole into his work, grateful he could leave the running of his household to me and Maureen. When he was home, he spent much time behind the closed doors of his small study.

One day I decided it was shameful to detach myself from the war, as Emily had done. Even if I was beyond further injury, I owed it to the Union and to Davy's memory to stay informed. I asked Ethan to bring me the *Springfield Republican* in the evenings, and I learned that our forces were attacking in Virginia, Georgia, and Mississippi. General Grant, Davy's old commander, was now commander in chief of the Union Army. He had caused more men to be killed than any general in history.

Just last year, Davy was shelling Vicksburg. I was studying Shakespeare's comedies at the college and reading aloud to the ladies making dressings.

This year, this evening, I was sitting in Kate's parlor, reading the war news in the *Republican*—and suddenly I realized I was encountering geography and names from last spring. Rappahannock, Rapidan, Orange Plank Road, Wilderness Church—I knew them all. The very same hills and creeks and evil-smoking forests were a battlefield again—but in this May of 1864, the battleground was haunted. The living soldiers, in their desperate twilight combat, were trampling the bones and skulls of last year's unburied dead.

There had been attempts to bury some of the ten thousand corpses after "Wilderness" a year ago—but most were too badly mangled or burned to be recognized. They lay in the woods, blue serge and gray homespun uniforms intermingled. Then came the heavy winter rains, washing open the shallow graves—and then the forest animals followed the rains. Only the skeletons and the glinting brass buttons remained. Now, "Second Wilderness" was being waged over a crunching carpet of bones. From every thicket, the silent rows of skulls watched their comrades.

The image was overwhelming. I cried out in unbelieving horror. Ethan, working in Kate's garden, rushed in.

"Miranda, what's wrong?"

Wordlessly, I handed him the paper. I was trembling all over. The war had wrested me back from the dark unfeeling gloom that had been my sanctuary these last long months.

Now that the dam had burst, I was overcome by waves of held-back emotion flooding through me. I struggled to bring myself to order.

Ethan laid the paper on a small side table.

"Miranda," he began in a low voice, "I don't know what to..."

I knew he wished to comfort me; I knew he could not. I didn't even know if I wanted him to. I sank into a chair to settle my churning feelings. My breathing returned to normal; my heart slowed to a natural pace. I could sense Ethan's concern, and when he pulled up a chair, I noticed for the first time that his thick, fair hair was raked with gray.

"I have learned these weeks that grief and guilt are full-time burdens if you let them be," he said. "I have asked God for strength to go on. I still have my family to support, and yet... and yet without her, I have no family." With this, Ethan squeezed his eyes shut to stop the flow of tears.

My raw emotions had opened the door to his own. This was the first true and personal thing he had said to me since Kate's death. "Let yourself cry, Ethan. Nothing relieves like tears," I murmured. I felt stronger from having released my pent-up grief. Cleansed. I thought perhaps now we could help to heal each other.

On impulse, I touched his hand in understanding. Even the longest night must give way when the horizon parts into earth and sky. There were some things I had discovered on my own that I could offer.

"Ethan, perhaps it won't always be like this," I told him gently. "But now, do you think we should try to talk and share our sorrow?"

Saying this, I thought of treetops that sway and bend in close and shiver together when the wind comes. He looked earnestly at me—at my pale face, my dull eyes, my careless clothes, my used apron.

"Yes." Ethan nodded. "You are right. We can begin by having dinner together in the evenings."

And so we began, and this gave a new shape to my days. After I got the children to bed, I bathed and changed, just as I had in Barbados, for a social time. I arranged with Maureen that she leave our dinner for me to serve, allowing her to get some rest. Ethan and I would tidy up.

Our meals were harmonious and pleasant. We both appreciated the companionship of a literate adult. We tried to keep our thoughts on a given subject and forced ourselves to exchange ideas on books, art, and the children. Some nights Ethan brought wine and we read poetry. When Emily wrote and asked me shrewdly, "Do you dare to live yet?" I could answer honestly that I was trying.

I found Ethan intelligent, charming, and responsive. He had a flattering way of remembering everything I said and quoting it days later. He entertained me with tales of his boyhood in New Bedford, a large, bustling seaport built around whalers and whaling. He had dreamed of going to sea, like every New England boy—but he took a bad fall on a schooner off Gloucester and had a stiff knee. This kept him from being a sailor and later from being a Union soldier.

One late May morning I was surprised by another letter from Emily—not from Amherst but from Cambridge. Her eye condition had worsened, and she was having daily treatments from a specialist in Boston. She was not allowed to read and could only write a few minutes a day. I took this with a grain of salt, as Emily's illnesses always worsened in the telling. Emily had brought her Norcross cousins for company. She liked her Cambridge boardinghouse but said, "I have not looked at spring."

I could tell she missed her boundaries—her personal books and private views and excluding door. I felt pangs of sympathy for her, exiled and vulnerable as she was—a little weak exposed creature, without the safety of her shell.

Father came from Amherst every ten days or so, bringing me clean clothes and college library books and Aunt Helen's touching treats for the children. In mid-June we took a long walk together around Springfield.

"You've been here over three months now, Miranda," he said. "When are you coming home?"

"I—I don't know," I answered. It wasn't something I had really thought about in anything other than the vaguest of terms.

"Are you trying to live Kate's life for her?" he asked.

This caught me by surprise, the boldness of the statement. Yet it rang with a kind of truth; I needed to consider it carefully. I wanted to answer the question honestly—for Father and for myself.

We walked along a shaded path silently, the only sound occasional birdsong and the buzzing of bees. There was a stillness in the air, as if all of nature were waiting for me to examine my heart. I felt no pressure from my father for a quick response; I was to take my time.

"No, Father," I replied finally, honestly. "But right now there's nothing else I want to do. This is the only thing I'm sure I *must* do. Josey and Elena and baby Ethan have helped me too, you know. They have kept me from drowning."

He regarded me thoughtfully. "Do you have any plans?"

"Ethan and I have discussed finding an older woman to help Maureen. Once we do, I can leave here."

"And then what?"

"I—I haven't thought that far ahead yet."

"Well, think of this part of your life as being a corridor. We don't know where it may lead—but it should be away from here." He reached down and gave my hand a squeeze.

I smiled up at him. "Father, I agree."

When he departed, I began to seriously consider our conversation. The reasons to leave Springfield, the future I hoped to have. I knew more of what I wanted than I had realized, as if on a subterranean level I had made myself some crucial promises. I intended to have a life of public service and challenge. All of my studies had led me here—to a path of educational reform. I would guide and affect many, many children—not diaper a particular three!

I knew this passion was deeply rooted in my own experience as an isolated and lonely child whose life would have been barren without access to imaginative learning. But could this interest in impacting the nation's children also stem from a resolution never to be an actual, physical mother? In my self-interrogation I discovered that I had a new, total, and permanent horror of childbirth—its rending ordeal, its fatal result. This decision was irrevocable.

Yet that was a resolution that tore me in two. One morning, especially, I rose to a bright, blowing day. My first thought: *We can do the children's laundry!* After a week of rain, the cellar was knee-deep in rancid little clothes. Then after Elena's nap, I took her for one of our walks up the lane, under newly budding leaves. These precious hours together evolved from my desire to tenderly coax her from her cocoon of silence, just as spring aroused Josey's jonquils from their winter slumber. Elena was still a convalescent from Kate's death. Frail and far too quiet, she needed to begin her own healing.

We stopped to pick a bouquet of wildflowers for Maureen and blackberries for the boys, which I counted out slowly while she dropped them into my sunbonnet. Then we walked on to see the Allens' new baby lambs. We stroked their soft pearl fur, and Elena, at last, broke her silence.

"Mama, baby," she said, pointing to them and to me. At first I nodded my head happily, glad to see her responding to them. But then her gold-green eyes fell again on me. "Mama, baby," she repeated, and this time there was no mistaking her meaning. She believed I was her mama. I gave an involuntary shiver.

After our walks, there were baths and supper and stories and good nights—and I was exhausted. Loving Kate's children, I realized there could be days and weeks and years ahead for me exactly like today. Exactly as there would have been for Kate. As Father had suggested, it would be entirely possible for me to step onto Kate's path, experiencing Kate's submersion of herself into her family, swallowed up by suffocating yet rewarding and tantalizing demands.

And therein lay another reason for leaving that I had hardly dared acknowledge.

I was with Ethan too long and too often these days. Even as Kate's beau, he was always vital and attractive—his thick, fair hair, his intent blue eyes, his rosy, rugged New England looks. Now that I saw him more frequently—and now that I saw no one else—I sensed a growing awareness, a physical response between us. Nothing was ever said or done, but I felt our constant new tension. Once, I touched his shoulder—not by mistake—and he jumped as if I had scalded him.

My nights were full of restless dreams, although baby Ethan slept in my room and woke me often. He was a dear little fellow, but he couldn't help getting cold or hungry. Then when I had tucked him back in his cradle, I lay awake for many dark hours, considering my present and my future. If I chose, I could live here forever, caring for Kate's family. If I was married to Ethan, I could experience much more than the caress along his cheek and jawline that I longed to give. I trembled, trying to imagine the secrets yet to be discovered. But would that mysterious "much more," which even joyous Kate would not describe, compensate for a narrow and unrewarding life here? How could married love transform all my ambition? And Ethan, however desirable, was *Kate's husband;* I would never be able to see him as freely mine. I would always feel that I was trespassing.

Beyond that, there was a darker barrier. Ethan's passion had killed Kate. How could I ever forget that?

While I wrestled day and night with these thoughts and sought the best of roads through a wilderness of emotions, I received a message from Emily. Was it a coincidence or could she sense from afar that I was in conflict? Whatever the explanation, the mail brought an unexpected letter from her and a new poem. The letter—which, surprisingly, was encouraging throughout   urged me to look at the whole world around me and pick the journey that felt best to me. I was so struck by its supportive generosity that I eagerly read the poem:

> *Out of sight? What of that?*
> *See the Bird—reach it!*
> *Curve by Curve—Sweep by Sweep—*
> *Round the Steep Air*
> *Danger! What is that to Her?*
> *Better 'tis to fail—there—*
> *Than debate—here—*
>
> *Blue is Blue—the World through—*
> *Amber—Amber—Dew—Dew—*
> *Seek—Friend—and see—*
> *Heaven is shy of Earth—that's all—*
> *Bashful Heaven—thy Lovers small—*
> *Hide—too—from thee—*

This message from the blue, so timely, so perceptive, stirred me so much that I showed both the letter and the soaring poem to Ethan at dinner. He was puzzled.

"What exactly does Miss Dickinson want you to do, Miranda?"

I was surprised that I had to explain Emily's meaning to him. This poem, more than most, seemed crystal clear. "Turn to Heaven," I said. "Don't hide from it. Pray, then make decisions. Yes, and for me that would mean to explore and be forceful and influential, I guess."

"But those are *masculine* goals!" Ethan scoffed. "Surely she doesn't expect you to play a man's part in society, does she?"

"Perhaps she does." I gazed down at my plate. Ethan took this tone because he assumed that those goals were not mine but Emily's for me. He didn't realize he had trodden on my own deeply felt ambitions.

"Then she has picked the wrong person. You, Miranda, are entirely feminine. You were made to be a lovely wife and mother. That role will be your authority and your creation."

This revealed such a profound division between us that it seemed pointless to pursue the conversation. We finished Maureen's pie and then did an hour of "Childe Harold." Ethan did not read aloud very well; his New England reserve did not permit displaying emotion. But his intense gaze never left me—and in spite of our differences, I knew I'd be remembering it tonight, around midnight.

The very next day a letter came from Mr. Harnett, forwarded by Father:

My school, Friends Seminary, wants to hire you this fall to be my assistant in the new Froebel-based "kindergarten." It is time we began working together again. You will be helping me as you help yourself—as you start your professional life. I need you and I am counting on you, Miranda.

Perhaps this was the signal I had been needing. I considered the offer for several days and nights. Then a stranger's casual remark made the decision for me.

It was a July evening of afterglow, scented by Kate's nicotiana. Ethan and Josey and I were sitting outside, taking turns composing a long poem. Baby Ethan and Elena were in bed; Josey was prolonging his own bedtime through this thoroughly entertaining game. It was such a beautiful twilight that Ethan and I pretended not to notice Josey's obvious ploy. Josey made up a line, and Ethan or I supplied the rhyme to match, charmed by our own wit.

There was a knock at the gate, and a messenger arrived with building plans for Ethan. "I could hear you laughing as I came up the street," he told us with a warm smile. "I thought, There's a happy family!"

He went—and I heard the gate shutting, trapping me inside Kate's garden, inside the role he had just assigned me—trapping me forever. Suddenly I knew what I had to do.

"Josey, the game's over. Go to Maureen. It's long past your bedtime. Scoot!"

Josey must have understood I was serious, for he didn't argue but simply toddled away. And then—before he could speak the inevitable, irrevocable words—I turned to Ethan and took his hand.

"You must hire Mrs. Newell tomorrow to be the children's nurse. She's the best of the women we interviewed." Then I took a long breath and told him I would be leaving next week.

He gripped my hand so hard that it hurt. "Will you be coming back?"

I ducked my head, unable to meet those pleading eyes, knowing I had to be firm. And clear. For both of us. "Only to see the children."

"That's all, Miranda? Only for the children?"

He must have been trying to break my hand with his. I felt his intense gaze, his profound disappointment, and the strong attraction between us.

I couldn't allow myself to be dissuaded. This time I faced those eyes directly. "Ethan, I have to go—*now.*"

His hand and face went slack, his shoulders sagged. He was suddenly middle-aged and defeated, a careworn widower.

"My family will always be grateful for your sympathy and assistance in our sorrow," he told me formally. Then he picked up his building plans and went indoors. I waited until I saw him enter the house, then slowly followed. Despite the sadness I felt, I also knew I had done the right thing, and this made me feel instantly lighter. I barely touched the grass as I crossed the lawn.

That was the end to our evenings together and the end of something that never really started—a tableau in which I never genuinely belonged.

The next week, darling Elena stood in the door with Ethan, waving and calling, "Be back!"—as I had taught her to do when I went to market. Her small voice made me falter for a moment. Even more than the others, Elena had become a part of me.

But now I must save the other parts. The parts that added up to myself.

Book IX

AMHERST AND NEW YORK

1864

When I returned to Amherst, I seemed to have been on a journey of many months and many miles. When I left home almost three months after Davy's death and went to Kate in Springfield, I was like one of Lettie's island zombies: a ghost going through the motions of living but heartless and soulless. When Kate died, for weeks more I felt nothing but pain. Eventually I began to sense the shadow shapes of other emotions: pity for Kate and Davy and their unused gifts; devotion to Elena and affection for Josey and little Ethan; attraction toward Ethan; a stronger understanding with Father. That was as far as I *"dared to live."* And then, soul-searching at Ethan's, I began to find a new sense of purpose.

Whether or not I opened my heart again to another man's love, I believed I must find my life in my work. It was my calling. The affectionate regard I felt for Ethan was just that and no more. And although if I chose to I could have lived in his house forever caring for Kate's family, we both deserved better. I knew that Ethan should be free to fall in love again and find a wife for his motherless children, just as I also knew I could never be content filling another woman's shoes, or her bed. So whatever it was to be for Ethan and for me, we had to be allowed to follow our own paths.

I had joined a growing group, one that was scrutinized and judged against rules that had been set by others. Within the context of the larger community, the bereaved bump and stumble as they turn back to the business of living. They yearn to belong again, but to whom? To what? Long before the weekly grim lists of the war dead altered the marital expectations of my generation, I observed how uncharitable the world could be when the one left behind sought to remake a life.

If you went too easily along, stoically and with purpose—no matter how befitting our New England traditions—they called you unfeeling. If grief left you clinging to memories, you were thought morbid. If you married too soon, they'd whisper you were insufficiently devoted to the deceased, and if, like Father, you never married again, they'd question your devotion to God's plan—for wasn't wedlock man's most noble aspiration?

It was a tricky road to navigate. But navigate it I would. My first promise to myself upon my return was to stay engaged in the larger world, to not allow myself to shrink into Emily's reclusive response. I understood its appeal, but I would resist. So I would attend to the business of living again with efficiency. There was Alan Harnett's teaching offer to accept, and Father had some important papers waiting for me. The first was an official history of Battery B, Chicago Light Artillery. These men served with distinction, from the day after Fort Sumter till the Battle of Chattanooga. They took part in five major campaigns and suffered heavy losses. The battery won many citations and decorations; Davy himself was awarded a posthumous Distinguished Service Cross.

The second was a letter from Chuck Baird, with whom Davy had served at Lookout Mountain. He had married Miss Julia Cooke of Lake Forest during an earlier leave, and they were expecting their first child. Now he was writing to inform me that they hoped to name him David Farwell Baird.

The third document was a serious parchment roll, full of "whereas" and "inasmuch." It was written in a copperplate clerk's script and taped and sealed and embossed. It came from a Chicago law firm and looked like an international treaty.

"You will need your own lawyer for this," Father advised. He leaned against the front of his large desk, the curtains behind him filtering the bright afternoon light. "Mr. Austin will arrange for a notary and witnesses. I hope I may be one."

I gazed at the intimidating document in my hands. "But what is it?"

"This is the document concerning your foundation. Cyrus Farwell has explained to me that Davy wanted you to pursue and develop your own ideas about primary education. Davy established funds for you, for study or travel, or for support of individuals and projects in early education. There are no qualifications; you are to use the money as you see fit. It's entirely up to you."

"I still don't understand." I was dazed. "How could Davy do this for me?"

"On his last leave in Chicago, he had the Farwell lawyers set up a trust, using capital he had inherited from his mother. When invested, this money should bring ten thousand a year.

"Davy named this instrument the 'Miranda Arethusa Chase Foundation for Early Childhood Education.' You will have Davy's bank, and Mr. Farwell and the trust lawyers, to advise you. It is a tremendous honor and responsibility, I will be here to help you however I can."

I had a moment's illumination—a vision like a second of pale summer lightning. For the first time in months I could see Davy clearly, young and intense and vulnerable. I saw him spending his last leave in offices with powerful older men, bankers and lawyers. I could see his serious face, his beautiful long hands moving as he spoke. He had foreseen his own death, and he had spent that precious time considering my future, to carry out his intention "to be a part of my life."

I felt his presence so keenly it was hard to speak. After a long silence, I whispered, *"Thank you, Davy."* I cleared my throat and then said to Father, "Perhaps now Mr. Harnett and I can print our alphabet in color."

Father came out from behind his desk and embraced me. "Of course you can, my brave Miranda." I heard his voice break. "There's no end to what you can do! You will touch a thousand lives. I am so proud of you. And of Davy."

I was as moved by Father's embrace as I was by his words. He was not a parent given to easy displays of affection. I allowed myself the pleasure of sinking into the steadying circle of his embrace. I had thought, with Davy and Kate gone, I would have to live without love given or received. Now there would be another source, another direction for my own unused love. I would pour my energies into Davy's inspiration, for the benefit of children we would never have but who would be "ours" all the same. With my father's arms about me, just as Kate had promised, I felt my life and dreams taking root once again. I felt the actual start of my healing.

That night, I sat in my room, gazing down at the heavy gold ring on my finger, the diamond sparkling with reflected moonlight. I took a deep breath and slowly, tenderly, removed the ring. I would keep it always, perhaps wear it on a gold chain along with the amethyst heart Davy had given me, but as an engagement ring, it held me in a frozen moment with my lost love, the marriage never to be. Now was the time for me to move forward and engage in a future. Davy would be with me through my actions—my life itself would be a testimony of our commitment to each other's best selves.

The next day, a note came from Emily: "Monday, once more." As I walked to her house, I felt again that our years of afternoons were long, long ago. Another girl than today's went cross lots that very first time, and yet another in the February snow to our reading of *The Trojan Women*. My eyes took in neighbors' carefully tended gardens; their lovely designs had always been a source of pleasure for me. But today I saw the borders of marigolds and salvia as flickering bronze and scarlet flames, and I heard the screams of burning soldiers and fleeing civilians. Atlanta was now under siege, and in my commitment to stay informed, it was hard not to see signs of war's devastation everywhere.

But Emily was as I had left her, twittering over her miniature dramas and preoccupations. Dick the stableman's child was down with typhoid. This year's robins had eaten their young; how very unnatural! And Emily herself was unsettled from her trip to Boston; she had barely unpacked. Her eyes were "restored." She still felt "strange to all but my books."

"I have not ROOTED myself yet," she stated. "I do not know the village news. Have the wild geese crossed already? Are the apples ripe yet?" She fluttered to her seat and gazed at me. "But you've been away from EVERYTHING too, haven't you?"

I stood awkwardly, not feeling at home but not knowing how to leave. I thanked her for her last poem about the "bird's-eye view."

She shrugged off my words of appreciation. "I merely thought of your days in Springfield, caged in with demanding little children, as being very like my life in Cambridge with the little cousins," Emily confided. "How much I rely on a person's literary CONTENT! I have to be able to refer to Artemis or Prince Hal, or I DISAPPEAR. Living with the unread is HARD WORK!"

"Little children are quite another sort of work," I corrected her. "It's much more strenuous. You lift and wipe and button and brush. You forget your inner self for days."

This did not interest her, and she changed the subject.

"I suppose you have heard our sad news, Miranda?"

I could see she was longing to tell it. She gazed up at me coyly from under her dark lashes.

"I don't know," I said. "What, pray?"

"I thought your father might have told you. I heard it was in the paper, but I never saw it."

She always enjoyed this conversational hide-and-seek. Today I had little patience for it.

"You still haven't told me what it is I don't know, Emily."

"It happened in South Carolina, on one of those coastal islands. There is a Confederate fort there."

"Emily, I'm not going to play anymore." I sat in "my" chair and crossed my arms over my chest. "Just tell me."

"Mr. Higginson was wounded."

This was actual news. I was instantly concerned. "I'm truly sorry. Was he hurt badly?"

"I don't really know. Too gravely to WRITE, at least." Here she pouted a bit.

This was my clue that perhaps the story was not as dire as she had presented it. I leaned back again. "When did this happen?"

"Last summer—the summer of 1863, that is."

I began to understand. Emily was taking her Mentor's misfortune personally. "And where is Colonel Higginson now?"

"He said he has left the Army and is recovering by the sea with his wife. He wrote me from Newport a few weeks ago. He has not been well enough to write me since. Of course I feel his wound DEEPLY myself."

I considered these facts very carefully. As I understood it, Colonel Higginson had been hurt a year ago. He recovered and returned to civilian life. He had only just now informed Emily of all this, and her feelings were hurt.

On the way home, I realized she had never once asked about Kate's children. It was just as well; I could not have borne hearing Emily describe her unassuaged grief over the little motherless Howlands. My own feelings of guilt and separation were too raw.

The village trees had their dusty late summer look. One of these mornings there would be a scarlet limb on a maple, and then another. Father and I had been making plans: I for my life and he for his. We had talked a great deal about what I would do in New York. I would design more children's books with Mr. Harnett, and I would try teaching at Friends Seminary while our material was being tested in the classroom. But I also wanted to learn a great deal more about other teaching systems and methods. I approached Dean Griswold at the college. Since I had graduated from the academy three years ago, he had been my sponsor and my kind friend. He knew Davy as "Amherst's best."

He welcomed me graciously into his library. "Miss Chase, I salute your courage in returning to the 'groves of academe.' When one encounters tragedy, the only weapon against it is hard work."

"Yes, I am learning that."

"I know and respect your interest in primary education. What are your plans now, to further your career?"

I told him about teaching in New York at Friends Seminary and then explained, "I want to find out how and what little children learn in other parts of the world. There must be a thousand philosophies and systems of teaching. How can I learn about them?"

"You should study ethnography. My old friend Seth Whitman is head of the Society of Ethnography in New York. I'll write him and see if he'll arrange it so that you can work there—as an Amherst student."

A few days later a note came to me on Amity Street. "You will find what you need at the American Ethnological Society on Fifth Avenue," the dean wrote. "They will be expecting you there. Please remember me to Dr. Whitman, my old classmate—and come to see me when you return."

Once this was decided, Father announced his own plans. With the tide of war turning in the Union's favor, Father was taking a sabbatical. Now that the notorious commerce raider *Alabama*—which had seized and sunk scores of Union vessels—had been sunk off Cherbourg, the sea lanes were finally clear. Father would visit many spots he first discovered when he was the age I was now—Rome, Athens, Venice—and would stop at Sicily too, a new vista.

"I will go," he exulted to me and Aunt Helen over dinner one evening, "while I can still clamber about the ruins. Every classicist should know Sicily, where Athenian hubris met its nemesis. With Miranda in New York, I shall mark time among the ruins."

I marveled at this casual reference to me as if his plans were dependent on mine rather than simply on his own wishes. Things were changing indeed!

Father would leave in early October, before the first Atlantic storms rendered the seas too rough to cross. Although we did not say it, this was assuredly a valedictory tour. At his age he was not likely to undertake such a long sea voyage again.

I made my good-byes to the ladies at the factory, promising Lolly Wheeler and Mary Warner Crowell that I would write. I then went to

Emily with more of a sense of obligation than pleasure. She must have felt this; she was responsive and entertaining.

"I was not at my best when you called last, Miranda. I must have been recovering from my drunken spree. Yes, I have been INTOXI-CATED for several weeks!"

"That news never reached the town gossips." I smiled.

She gave me an impish grin back. "Wouldn't they have loved it, though! I've read about the signs of intoxication, and they certainly do match my ORGY when I came home from Cambridge and was re-united with my books. You should have seen me! I opened my books all at once—on my bed, all over the floor—to let the precious words out to breathe. We had been STIFLED!"

"Aren't your cousins good company for you?"

Emily laughed tolerantly. I had forgotten that, according to "Emily's truth," the Norcrosses never got any older or any wiser.

"Those pitiful little lambs? All they need is a Bo Peep!"

"Tell me some more about coming back to your books, Emily."

"I remembered the music of 'Welcome Home'! I heard ANTHEMS. I flew to the shelves and DEVOURED the luscious passages. I thought I would tear out the leaves as I turned them. I ate, I drank, I FEASTED. Then I settled to a willingness to let ALL go but Shakespeare. Why do we need ANYTHING ELSE to feed on?" Now she became thoughtful and silent.

"Miranda, you must excuse me. That conceit of books as food—I must try it out NOW."

It was a good way to part. I had heard her true voice, speaking about her books. Behind the disguises, among the variations, there was al-ways the essential, authentic Emily.

Alan Harnett had taken a small suite of rooms for me in a little house not far from Friends Seminary. The Harnetts' tiny cottage was now too crowded with the birth of their most recent child, Henry. When I reached New York, I found Mr. Harnett jubilant. Our alphabet had sold out two printings by a well-known publisher of textbooks.

"It's a fine start for our reputation, Miranda," he stated. "The draw-ings did it!" This might have been a good moment to tell him about

Davy's trust, but I decided to wait until the final papers arrived from the Chicago lawyers.

The next morning I met with Dean Griswold's friend Dr. Whitman at the American Ethnological Society, a Gothic tower on Fifth Avenue.

"Dean Griswold speaks very highly of you, my dear," the gentleman said. "I believe you will find what you need here." He brought me to the library, full of thick volumes and silent readers—not what I had expected, considering the society's daring expeditions! Here he introduced me to one of the librarians, Mr. Chris Butler, who was a graduate student, telling him that I was to have full access to the library.

Mr. Butler and I discussed my interest in comparing educational systems. He steered me away from the African and South American tribal cultures, based entirely on hunting, and toward the Asian and Pacific peoples.

The Chinese and Japanese educational systems appeared admirable, incorporating the arts and sciences—but irrelevant to our country, as the students must all be noble and male! Reading further, I found myself strongly attracted to two particular cultures: the Pacific, or Polynesian—and the Eskimo, or Inuit.

Neither of these had formal schools, and their priests were the only teachers as such. They learned everything else that their society required from their parents, working beside them. Thus education came naturally, with living and maturing—and life itself was education.

I discovered the Polynesian sexual customs were radically different from ours. The first day I sat in the society library reading of the relaxed nature of Polynesian sexual practices, I found myself blushing. I furtively glanced at Mr. Butler, the librarian, imagining he knew precisely the passages I was reading. I told myself that this was professional material and continued on.

In this society, intercourse was cheerfully encouraged after puberty; incest was the only taboo. The ethnographer linked these attitudes to the economic structure. Children inherited from their mothers only, making paternity a less critical issue. Through these cross-cultural studies I was better able to understand that there was a larger context for our own morals and mores. These were simply *ideas,* not necessarily innate or immutable laws. I began to feel rather radical, as I walked back in the evenings to the Harnetts', pondering such bold concepts. Some nights, as I lay contented in my little rooms off Stuyvesant

Square, I wondered how the Polynesian social attitude would have affected Davy and me as lovers.

Later that week, Mr. Harnett brought me round to the seminary. Rather than a single building, the seminary was a cluster of brick houses, Federal style, and I was pleased to discover that Mr. Jewett, the headmaster, was friendly and informal.

"Harnett here has sold me on the Froebel system," he assured me. "Follow your system, but keep detailed records every single day. We'll need them to compare with the progress of our traditional first-year class."

A fortnight later, Mr. Harnett and I started our kindergarten with a big round table, small chairs, a thick carpet for teaching and story circles on the floor—and a wreath of twelve delighted children. Alternating my time between the classroom and the Ethnological Society library, I realized I was happier than I'd been in a year. The unfamiliar street noises kept me from sleeping at first, but I didn't mind—for the first time since Davy's death, I felt my present and my future were connected. Somehow, the isolation I had endured as a small child had led me to this path, and that early unhappiness finally had a purpose.

The autumn passed with study and work—along with the ebb and flow of my worries about Elena. I was not sure what I could do to rectify that situation, so I forced myself to put it aside, which I did by burying myself deeper into work. The war was many miles away yet always near, its horror never far from our minds. Since Atlanta, the crucial railroad center of the South, had fallen at last—and the reduced Confederate armies could no longer be shuttled about from one campaign to another by train—surely, surely the fighting must end soon.

The lawyers in Chicago sent me the final papers for the Miranda Arethusa Chase Foundation, indicating that the trust was fully executed and that our funds were now available. At last I gave them to Mr. Harnett to read. After he had studied them, he looked at me, his face open, his eyes bright.

"Miranda, right here in my hand, I am holding solid, tangible love. Davy's for you, and the children's love and gratitude for all you are going to accomplish."

His joy and wonder were heartwarming.

"Miranda, let me understand." He was suddenly hesitant. "Do you intend that I work with you?"

"Yes, I do," I assured him. "You showed me the way to learning, and I hope that now we may be partners."

"Davy, you, and me." He smiled. "We three will work together. We will be part of one another's lives."

"Both you and Davy said *exactly* that same thing to me."

"It is true for both of us," he said. He stood, excitement forcing him to his feet. "It is the means to our success," he continued. "We can support the best ideas, the best people, the best work. There's no limit to our future!" Then he faced me squarely. "One last thing." His eyes crinkled at the corners with good humor. "Will you never learn to call me Alan?"

I colored a faint pink and said I would try.

Now that the foundation existed, our next undertaking, as I had told Father in the shock of the news, was to add color to our bouncing alphabet. We climbed up to a huge loft full of fierce clanking presses to consult our Polish printer, Mr. Klawalski.

"This will be the very first book a small child sees," Mr. Harnett—Alan—explained.

Mr. Klawalski turned to me. "You want I make happy book?"

"We certainly do!" I replied. "Happy as a child the day he learns to read. We want lively colors for these cheerful letters."

Our printer studied the smug striped "C for Cat" in our alphabet. "I think you need color like child sees. This I do."

The next evening a scrawny blond boy of twelve appeared at our door. He wore a huge ink-stained apron and carried the galley proofs of our alphabet. Charmingly colored: a single irregular blob of red or blue or yellow lightened Ethan's drawings, as if a child were using the brush. The pure primary colors glowed; each page pulsed with energy.

"These are perfect!" I told the boy. "Who did them?"

The boy smiled and bowed. Like Mr. Klawalski, he used the fewest words possible. "You want happy. I do."

Eventually we learned that he was Stefan Klawalski, his father's apprentice; that he hoped to be a painter; that he took free art lessons at the Cooper Union School in the Bowery.

"Stefan, you're our official colorist," I told him. "We'll pay you by the piece. Now will you look at these children's stories? They need your happy colors too!"

I related all that was happening in New York to Aunt Helen, to Miss Adelaide, and, as promised, to Lolly and Mary Crowell, and to

Emily as well. Our kindergarten was off to a splendid start. Each little beginner in our classroom was moving toward literacy unafraid, free, and joyful. They arrived smiling, asking, "What are we going to play today?" My earlier college courses and Chris Butler's guidance in ethnographic studies had given me the comparative knowledge I needed to go forward with this work.

In November, Abraham Lincoln was reelected. General McClellan, the opposing candidate, was a dangerous contender. There was a shocking amount of support for McClellan in New York City, but the army voted solidly for Lincoln. Davy's old commander, General Grant, was relentless, expending troops without mercy, grinding away at the thinning Confederate armies on every front. The country—both countries, reunited—would need his wisdom in the confusion after the war.

At Thanksgiving, Emily sent a note and a poem: "Here are a few thoughts—a draft, if you will—to stuff your turkey." I read her letter aloud in the small foundation office that Alan and I had opened. I had finally managed to feel comfortable addressing him by his first name. Hearing the children call him "Mr. Harnett" on a daily basis helped me to make this transition.

The poem was Emily at her incomparable best.

> He ate and drank the precious Words—
> His Spirit grew robust—
> He knew no more that he was poor,
> Nor that his frame was Dust—
>
> He danced along the dingy Days
> And this Bequest of Wings
> Was but a Book—What Liberty
> A loosened spirit brings—

I finished my recitation and saw Alan's awestruck expression. "Miranda, you never told me your friend is a genius."

My brow crinkled, and I gazed down at the paper in my hands. "I'm not sure she is. All I know is that she's willful and selfish—and that some of her poems are as bad as this one is good."

"Whoever said genius is consistent?" Alan replied. "Or easy to live with? Mark my words, Miranda—your willful, selfish friend will be known and read for generations. You'd better start saving her stuff."

Alan's words shamed me. Perhaps I was too close to Emily. Her letters described her garden or her work. She never asked questions about what I was doing. She had barely congratulated me or wished me success with my new enterprise. Perhaps I let her maddening airs and moods obscure her poems and their true worth. I thought of the homily "Truth is the daughter of Time." A hundred years from now, our descendants, far removed from Emily Dickinson's daily demanding self, would be able to decide whether or not she was a genius.

As I saw the kindergarten children's preparations for Christmas and began to read the Christmas stories, I was haunted by thoughts of Elena. We were approaching a season of merriment, a time when happy memories are created for tomorrow and the sweet melodies of Christmases past joyously ring. Yet I feared that Elena would have none of these and that her early childhood would be frozen in deep midwinter. Ethan had written that Mrs. Newell was managing "as best she can," and yet Elena was so sensitive, so delicately balanced. Deep in the night when I awoke, I could not help but wonder how she was, what she was doing. My leaving her must have been another blow, another death, just when she had begun to love and trust again.

So finally, when the Christmas holiday came, Alan and Fanny agreed that I should return to Amherst, and from there pay a visit to Springfield.

The beauty of my village in December was an amazement: I had forgotten the brilliant snow, the Pelham Hills in their winter mauve. Everything in New York was gray—the buildings, the streets, even the air. I always felt a dozen people had breathed it before it reached me! The biting valley air was a lovely shock to city lungs; I felt a deep sense of homecoming.

Aunt Helen wanted to hear every detail of the Friends School, the foundation office, our newly created Leo Press—but agreed that this could wait until I had gone to Springfield. And so the very next day, I took the cars to Elena.

When I reached the Howland house, I was appalled by the little girl's changed demeanor. She did not know me at first—but when I said her name her face began to brighten, and she cried out, "Manda, Manda!" Then she hugged my knees and held me fiercely.

I was relieved that there was no awkwardness between Ethan and me, and that any tension that had existed before had evaporated with time. Josey was happy to see me but was far more interested in companions of his own age. Baby Ethan didn't know me at all. But Elena...

She clung to me like a burr for the entire day, using both frantic little hands. When I put her to bed, she cried and hung on to me with true desperation. In the middle of the night, she climbed into my bed in a strange unnatural trance, not seeing or hearing but reaching out to hold me again— while I lay awake, grieving and worrying.

I studied Ethan's arrangements and decided he was managing as best he could. Mrs. Newell cooked and washed—but she was sixty and not educated. She had neither the energy nor the resources for three young children. Jack Ross, Ethan's amiable young apprentice at the Springfield Armory, boarded in the house and acted as tutor to the boys. They played outdoors and enjoyed balls and games. Nobody was mistreated, nobody was dirty or hungry, but Elena, in her rough boys' shirts and knickers, her curls tangled, her green eyes vacant—Elena's spirit was being starved to death.

I planned to lead into this very delicately when I talked to Ethan the next day, but he was there already with his own deep concern—and his news. He was to be married.

"Her name is Ann Mackay," Ethan told me tentatively. "She is a widow from New Bedford, with two boys of her own and a husband lost at Bull Run. Annie is a good woman, Miranda. We were children together before—" At this his voice broke. He turned away and said no more. He didn't need to. His awkwardness told me that love, true love, had had little role in guiding his choice.

Now was my time to speak, very carefully. "I have been thinking about Elena..."

I saw anguish on his face. "I have failed with Elena," he confessed. "She barely speaks at all. She misses Kate more every day, without knowing who or what she is lacking. In the spring, when Ann and I are wed, I believe, I hope, she'll do better."

How? I worried. With two brothers and two stepbrothers and perhaps half siblings to come.

Again I was very careful. "I spent last fall reading about children in other cultures, in other parts of the world. I was very struck by an idea from the Polynesians, the South Sea islanders. They believe that every person has a mana, an essential flame of identity that we would call 'the soul.' They say you must be true to your mana or you will simply fade away and disappear. Elena," I went on, "has the mana of a very gentle, dreamy little girl of three—and yet we expect her to behave as if she were a rough, tough, independent five-year-old boy! No wonder she's confused. No wonder she feels her true self slipping away."

Ethan was quiet, examining my opinion. "I just don't know what to do," he said at last. "You are right. She has been like a little ghost in daylight, disappearing right before my eyes." He sighed. "What do you suggest?"

An idea came to me. "Let me talk to Aunt Helen, Ethan. Perhaps...perhaps Elena should come to Amherst for a while. Let us try to repair her for a bit—and then we can talk about the future."

Ethan nodded as he listened. "Yes," he said finally. "I think we should send her to Amity Street, with all of you. If you are willing, dear Miranda..." His voice trailed off, and I saw the pain in his eyes, deep and heavy with grief. I took his hand.

"I will do my best, Ethan. For you, and for Kate, and for Elena."

Wordlessly, his eyes brimming, he nodded. Then he leaned forward and kissed my forehead, and our plan was sealed.

The train did not frighten Elena as long as she held my hand. We reached Amherst at noon. She was calm and cheerful, meeting Bridget and inspecting the house—but never loosened her grip on me. We brought nothing from Springfield, but by nightfall Aunt Helen had borrowed a cot and some little girls' clothes. Elena went to sleep in Kate's room in her first nightgown ever. For the next three nights she crossed the hall, still asleep, and crawled into my bed with me—and after that she stayed all night in her cot.

Within a week, my aunt and I could not remember our house and our life without her. At Christmas, we decorated a little fir tree for Elena with some of Davy's delicate stars. We took her to the children's carol singing on the green. To my delight, as we rolled out shortbread together the next day for mimosa rosettes, she hummed the tunes. We gave her frilly dresses and petticoats, and an enchanting red cape with a ruffled hood. Her presence made up for father's absence at Christmas, which he was enjoying at some ancient site. This was my first Christmas without him and without Kate as well.

Out of nowhere, it seemed, Elena had a name or an observation for everything, as though she were awakening from a long sleep, as I had. We found her a brown velvet bear with a particularly sweet expression; Elena named him Maple Syrup. We taught her to say, "Happy New Year!" We toasted being together and peace for the nation in 1865.

Book X

AMHERST
1865–1867

During my early years in Amherst, when Kate and I lived as sisters, I learned a great deal watching as she immersed herself in music study. Codas, I came to appreciate, were those independent, often elaborate musical passages introduced at the end of the main part of a movement. Beethoven, more than any of the great composers, favored such dramatic excursions away from the home key. When I thought about Kate, I thought of this and how I had intended only to restore and return her troubled little daughter. I never imagined that as I did, she would transform my own life.

Every morning began when Elena scurried across the hall and into my bed. We discussed the day ahead, and our plans and our duties. She dearly loved schedules and fixed events, which, I had learned from my readings in ethnology, added the structure and rhythm necessary to a child's day.

After this Elena and I dressed together in my room. I helped her as little as possible. I wanted her to be independent about her own clothes, for I could remember the tyranny of buttons in the back! At home with us, she wore loose knit jerseys and bright corduroy rompers. She called these her "clown suits." When we went out, she was a proper young lady in a dress and flannel petticoats—and the scarlet cape, her "Little Red Riding Hood."

Every day, after her breakfast, Elena trotted behind Aunt Helen or Bridget for an hour or two. I spent the morning studying and writing. As I worked, I heard her sweet flute voice and sometimes her laughter. Of all the pleasures of her new existence, her favorite was conversation.

We took an early lunch, and then Elena napped— so that we could have a long afternoon together. We shared one event a day, so she and I tried to extract the most from it. My students had taught me never to rush or crowd their learning. When we went to the village, it was for one errand only. If I wanted to order a book, or if Grandma Helen needed stockings or Elena undervests, then these needs took three separate expeditions and choices. Elena learned the shops and their owners, and loved to be greeted by name as we went around town.

Sometimes Lolly, or one of the ladies for whom I still read aloud in the dressing factory, asked us to come for tea. Elena was not so much shy as wary at these times, waiting to see what was expected of her. She watched the other children carefully. Once she had relaxed, she, like her mother, was gentle and sociable.

We walked home in the pale snow-lit dusk, trying for "mouse talk" with our squeaking boots. Elena had her supper in the kitchen and related her day to her grandmother while Bridget and I helped with the adult dinner. Then I told her a benign version of a Greek myth to give Father pleasure when he returned from abroad.

After the mythic story hour, Elena enjoyed an hour or so of "alone time" with a book or the wooden blocks Sam made for her. This interval lasted as long as she was quiet and occupied, and she knew it! Then one of us tucked her in, with one (one only!) good-night kiss. Her door and mine stayed open all night.

One might call this a day when nothing important happened—and yet everything did. Two minds were stimulated; two characters were affirmed; two hungry spirits were fed. Two people went to sleep smiling.

This involvement, this profound contentment, was difficult to explain to Emily, who lived unattached by elaborate choice. One afternoon I drew on all the language she had helped me to use, trying to explain my feelings. If Emily could only see what having Elena in my life meant to me, perhaps she would also understand Sue's devotion to her children—and thus improve their worsening relationship. And perhaps, secretly, I hoped that it would also help Emily understand me.

"You weren't exactly withering away, Miranda," she said disdainfully. "You traveled, you held a position, you were WORLDLY."

I never knew that my aspirations rankled till now. But of course they would. Like with Sue, who had left Emily behind upon her marriage, Emily was hinting now that I abandoned her too by my widening interests, by my leaving. Diplomatically, I decided not to venture down this rutted lane.

"That's true, Emily, but I wasn't using my heart. I had turned that off."

"But there goes your privacy, your time, your IDENTITY! Can you spare these? I am sure I NEVER COULD." She set her jaw, no bigger than the imaginary child's she was rejecting.

"Elena and I both hungered for mother love. Elena longed to receive it, and I longed to give it. We needed each other desperately!" As I spoke, I realized with bell-like clarity that I could not send Elena away now, nor could I leave her.

"Emily, it's a trade," I insisted. "I get a great deal in return."

"For me, raising a child would be a treason against myself," she declared. "A TREASON!"

"Elena's only three. She hasn't crowded me out of myself—and she never will."

Emily shook her head, denying this. "I would be squeezed out of shape. I would DISAPPEAR! If I had to live with a child, I would sign away my years and my GIFT—all for company that was demanding and selfish and narrow." Here she gave me one of her purring little cat smiles. "But I suppose you will say I was all those things already."

I returned her smile with a sly one of my own. "Not all, Emily. No one could ever call you *narrow*."

"TOUCHÉ! That was *'a hit, a very palpable hit!'* Emily was delighted. "Your ÉPÉE has a deft duelist's touch. I think Sue should learn FINESSE from you. Her preferred blade is the SABER. I wrote about that once..." She turned to her bureau, alert, distracted, self-absorbed, enchanted with herself for the way she had taken command of this conversation and steered it back just where she liked it, to herself. All thoughts of Elena banished, Emily found the right poem in no time. Since our fortnight of organizing almost six years ago, she had kept her writings in her own mysterious order.

> She dealt her pretty words like Blades—
> How glittering they shone—
> And every One unbared a Nerve
> Or wantoned with a Bone—
>
> She never deemed—she hurt—
> That—is not Steel's Affair—
> A vulgar grimace in the Flesh
> How ill the Creatures bear—

To Ache is human — not polite —
The Film upon the eye
Mortality's old Custom —
Just locking up — to Die.

This one jarred and shocked me, with its hate masked as irony. I handed it back gingerly, at arm's length, and Emily smiled at my aversion.

"Now you see why all my best poems go unread! This is another one I could not have written without my SOLITARY days and nights."

"And what will become of it now, Emily, if no one reads it?"

"Miranda, how could I know that? That is not my DUTY. My only responsibility is to WRITE it. Someone else will see that it CIRCULATES." She was serenely sure of this outcome, and perhaps she knew best — best about that inexorable end and the personal economies required to arrive there. As I watched Emily return page to packet, and as I glanced about her chamber, for the first time the wisdom of her seclusion impressed me as purposeful rather than merely calculated. Genius, I had read, knew itself, knew the elixir that soothed and inspired, and when to mine the gold. Perhaps Alan was right; I should judge Emily by other standards. And yet…wasn't I to judge friendship on its own terms — whether or not that friend had extraordinary gifts?

Now I needed to leave; it was time for Elena's bath. I was happy to part with Emily, but suddenly, walking down the familiar streets and smiling back at the scattered snowdrops, it struck me that all afternoon, all through our conversation, Emily and I had been using abstractions — unusual for women of our class and time. I realized that that was why I came here — and would continue to. I too liked a change from "doily talk"!

But I had meant what I had said regarding my joy in parenting Elena. Aunt Helen and I discussed my deep wish and decided she should write to Ethan, asking to prolong Elena's visit. I was certain that, preoccupied with his own concerns, he would agree. Then I wrote to Alan Harnett, assuring him that our work together would continue absolutely but that I must delay my return to New York. I would take a leave of absence from my teaching position at Friends Seminary, but I would not abandon our important goals; rather, I would pursue them from another angle from Amity Street, and with an additional, personal goal of rearing Elena.

The decision felt as natural to me as the rhythm of a beating heart. When there is no home, no place of repose for the soul, as Miss Adelaide once said, an emptiness follows that haunts you all your life. As Miss Adelaide had done for me, I would do for Elena. She would grow up feeling a part of the encircling community that was Amherst.

I told Mary Crowell of my plans to stay while we were at a luncheon hosted by Mrs. Austin.

"Yes, I can see this is the right decision for you," she said, smiling at me. "You look positively serene."

"Mr. Harnett and I will continue to work together," I explained. "I'll work on more books, and we hope to open a model school in New York next year."

The woman seated to my right glanced up from her bisque. "You are Miranda Chase?" she asked. "I've been hoping to speak with you."

"Really?" I replied. "Why?"

"Oh, forgive me," Mary said. "Let me introduce you. Miranda, this is Ruth Witherspoon. Her husband also teaches at the college."

"I've heard about your work with children," Ruth said. "Tell me, will you be teaching here in Amherst?"

"I hadn't actually thought about it," I confessed.

"What a splendid idea!" Mary said. "Many of the faculty wives have been discussing the choices for their children."

"I've heard about some of your ideas for teaching," Ruth said. "It's exactly what I'd like to find for my Molly and William."

"I will give this considerable thought," I promised.

I looked around the table and realized many of the women there were married to men who taught at the college. These women, without professions of their own, nevertheless stayed active and involved in the community, and they took their roles as mothers and helpmeets very seriously. Not only would their children benefit from a kindergarten such as ours but I believed the mothers would be inspired by becoming active partners in their children's education.

I smiled. Emily was wrong; I was not subjugating my own will and goals by becoming Elena's mother. Rather, I was expanding my possibilities, growing deeper and in more directions.

*   *   *

Throughout the spring, Alan and I exchanged frequent letters on foundation business. I circulated among the faculty wives at the college, asking questions to determine the needs of the community. Once I knew how many children we would serve in this first year, I could set about finding a location. This work gave an invigorating structure to my days; my life wasn't solely determined by Elena's schedule.

Spring also brought the last desperate battles of the war. Petersburg and then Richmond fell. When I visualized the whole tragic state of Virginia, I saw it as one of our dressings from the temple, soaked in soldiers' blood. Finally, on April 9, General Lee surrendered to General Grant at Appomattox Courthouse, a village beside the final battlefield. Father had said his study of the ancients taught him that victory would go to the side that could replenish its losses. Both sides began the war by exchanging prisoners regularly; when this ceased two years ago, Mr. Edward Dickinson explained to the ladies of our bandage factory, our Union leaders had decided that our side could "accept" two men dead for every one of theirs. And so it had come to this—this war had literally bled our nation to death. The South was defeated simply because there was no one left to do the fighting. At the end of four years of slaughter, the remains of the Confederate armies were outnumbered by nearly a million men. And they had not eaten in three days.

Our ordered and stoic Puritan village went mad, in a mass delirium of speeches and parades and ceremonies. There were twenty-seven boys who would come home now and seven who wouldn't; we celebrated them all.

We were deafened by church bells and marching bands and hoarse, tireless orators—and even some cannons from Springfield! At night we were dazzled by torchlight parades and huge bonfires leaping on the common. We cheered for an extravagance of rockets that my delighted Elena named "sky flowers." Friends, strangers, and enemies met on the streets of Amherst; they embraced and wept.

There were persistent rumors of a small unyielding Confederate force cornered somewhere in the South. Nevertheless our rejoicing continued from Sunday night to the following Saturday morning. Then a wild-eyed boy rushed from the telegraph office, and a terrible silence fell on the village. The citizens stood about the streets, shocked beyond speech. Then the weeping women started to drift home, and the quiet men began to take down the stands and bunting. The musicians put away their instruments. A single bugler attempted taps and failed on the high note. The unimaginable had happened: four years and three days after the first shots were fired at Fort Sumter, our victorious president had been assassinated.

In his first peacetime leisure, he attended the theater. One of the famous Booth family of actors rushed into the presidential box—and fired a bullet into what Father once called "Lincoln's miraculous brain."

Mr. Dickinson came out from The Homestead, stone-faced; he lowered his flag to half-mast. Then every church bell in town began to ring at once—some held to a slow, portentous tolling, and others were loose in frenzy. This cacophony expressed our horror for the next several hours.

Throughout the war's duration, despite the inferno of suffering that consumed both our nation's energy and its young, I believed with all my heart (as did dear Davy) that the Union must be preserved. But now Lincoln's murder made the peace meaningless and the future dangerous.

The new Capitol dome had been completed just a month ago, just in time for Lincoln's second inauguration. That morning of hope was the first ceremony ever held there. Now our dead president lay in state under the new dome, and the silent citizens filed past his bier to pay their respects, all day and all night. *Harper's Weekly* related that the marble columns, wound round and round in black crepe, looked like a circle of ghastly bandaged limbs, and I read in the *Republican* that crowds of Negroes stood outside the White House, waiting in the spring rain to hear what would become of them. I too awaited the unknown, and I missed my father's wise historical prescience. I wondered when the news would reach him in Sicily.

When the funeral bells stopped tolling at last, I tried to change—as the bells had changed—from panic to an orderly and predictable routine. I had Elena and our life together, and I had the foundation, Davy's gift. These two assets would provide a framework for the years ahead.

Just as the apple trees blossomed, Emily summoned me to The Homestead. We had not seen each other since before Mr. Lincoln's death. At the nondenominational memorial mass that Emily's father arranged so the community could remember the slain president together, Miss Lavinia told me Emily had been unwell—"a nasty sniffle," she said. Her eyes grazed the bodice of my black dress, and her smug expression and preening suggested that she disapproved of its simplicity.

Vinnie, on the other hand, had used this solemn occasion for show. She was dressed in heavy midnight crepe and wore an elaborate bonnet wrapped with an immense tulle veil. Unaccountably, she greeted each and every mourner as if she were her father's hostess, as though this service was an "event" he had orchestrated for people's entertainment. Watching her, I noticed that her youth had slipped away and that she wore the defiant air of a woman facing a world that offered her no meaningful place. I expressed my concern over her sister's health and otherwise kept my own counsel. After the funeral, Emily had been away in Boston with her Norcross cousins and her eye doctor. Since our last meeting, there had been such joy at the war's end, followed by such tragedy, that I naturally expected we would spend my visit talking about the times we had survived—but Emily had other plans.

"'Sweet are the uses of adversity,'" she quoted. I wondered to whose adversity she referred—her own or Mr. Lincoln's, although when she took my wrap I noticed that she looked as well as ever.

"Were you allowed to read or write this time, Emily?"

"Very little. The climax of the day was a hansom from Cambridge to Boston and then two drops in each eye! Then we would walk in the Public Garden, a very UNNATURAL park. You never saw such a vulgar SHOW, Miranda. It was full of hideous oversize flowers, laid out in beds shaped like playing cards. I'm sure it would appeal to Susan's crowd. Of course, I am used to walking in MY OWN MEADOW."

"Did your cousins entertain you?"

"As best they could, poor little WAIFS. At least they kept me busy entertaining them!"

"So your writing goes well, then?" I ventured neutrally, sitting down at the tea table.

Emily smiled mysteriously, obviously not telling all she knew. "I am progressing toward my goal. I am not possessed by inspiration these days—but the muse DOES call in on occasion. It took another banishment in SIBERIA for me to appreciate 'this our life, exempt from public haunt.'"

"Did you continue to hear from your correspondents while you were away?" I wondered if her lack of inspiration was due to a lack of contact.

She sighed prettily. "My Mentors do keep shuttling to and fro! Two of them are in San Francisco now; that is too FAR! And my dearest Preceptor is much too CLOSE; he could come from Boston in a day, unless I prevent it."

I had read that Mr. Bowles was visiting in California and knew Dr. Wadsworth had moved there in 1862. I was amused by Emily's insistence on the correct geographic distance that her romances-in-the-air required. These busy and worldly gentlemen would be astonished to learn how much thought Emily gave them every day—since I doubted if they remembered her once a fortnight.

"And what news from Colonel Higginson?"

She lost her calm, evaded my gaze, and became oblique again. "Oh, he is so TRYING as a friend! I never told him I was in Cambridge. It was too close to Newport, and he was still healing there— from his war wounds. What if he had decided to call?"

Suddenly I was incensed by all this causerie. "Emily, for heaven's sake—what about the war's end? What about *history?*"

Emily's eyes widened at my outburst, then she resumed a placid expression. "The fireworks in Cambridge were very fine, Miranda. We stood on the roof of our boardinghouse and saw them reflected in the Charles River. If the wind was right, we could hear the bands playing."

When she saw my disgusted face, she tried again.

"I suppose that the village celebrated too. I heard that some of our boys were still in uniform, so their mothers must be relieved."

I gave her one more chance. "And what about poor Mr. Lincoln?"

Now she eluded me, among her grand cloudy abstractions.

"Mr. Lincoln has crossed over into ETERNITY, Miranda. He is safe now."

I decided this particular visit was over. As I put on my shawl, she performed one of her agile turnabouts and became a normal, concerned friend.

"And what do you plan for the summer, besides good times with your Elena?"

Reeled in, I told her about the discussions Alan and I had been having. "Our scheme is ambitious and will require more of my presence than I'd expected." I confessed I was concerned about how to best accommodate all I wanted to accomplish and still have the time I wanted with Elena.

Quicksilver Emily was at her sensitive, perceptive best. "All the pieces will make a pattern for you soon, my dear friend. You are very close to finding your true center; I can feel it."

We touched cheeks and planned for another Monday. In the moment, it felt right, two friends sharing affection and plans. It wasn't until I was near to home that I envisioned the endless vista of Mondays ahead: the Mondays after Mondays as Emily's marionette.

My father returned from Sicily in mid-May, gossiping about the splendid tyrants of Syracuse; about Hiero I, patron of Aeschylus; about the doomed Athenian fleet and the captured Athenian aristocrats toiling as slaves in the quarries. Relating this to Aunt Helen and me—like the most gifted of historians—he made us feel this all happened just last year. He was interested and complimentary about my work in New York and Amherst, and impressed that the *American Student* would publish the article I wrote with Alan Harnett. "They have a fine reputation," he stated. "You couldn't do better."

When he saw our rosy, confident Elena and heard her story, he heartily approved her inclusion in our Amity Street household.

"It's the best possible solution," he said. "You just have to look at Elena—she's positively in bloom! And so are you, my dear. We need her just as much as she needs us. Is Ethan pleased?"

"He says it's wonderful for her to be here with us just now, Father. When he visits he sees that she won't let go of my hand for a second. She's afraid he'll take her back to Springfield!"

He nodded thoughtfully. "Does this bother Ethan?" he asked. "Seeing her prefer her life here?"

"I believe he is genuinely happy that she is thriving."

"That is the mark of a true father. Ethan instinctively wants what is best for her."

Father quickly became Elena's friend and her surrogate grandfather, even asking Sam to dam our brook into a wide shallow pool, moving a wicker armchair into the shade of the maples, where he read beside her all through the amber afternoons. Elena did not interrupt him; she played in the water and arranged pebbles, humming softly to herself. Sometimes they told each other myths, Father laughing heartily at Elena's variations. There were sixty-six years between these two companions, but their harmony was a joy to behold. I never imagined that losing Kate would give us such a blessing as Elena for our consolation.

Father also approved the blue velvet curtain I had ordered for the stage. With the war over, we were reviving our Shakespeare evenings. The curtain would allow the readers to be hidden and then revealed, like actors.

"Let's plan our next play evening right now," he suggested. "We've never done *Antony and Cleopatra*. I'd love to read Antony. Tell that imperial Susan Dickinson I want her for my Cleopatra!"

"We should ask Miss Lavinia to play the asp, Father. Emily says she has an 'adder tongue,' and I believe her."

I proceeded to tell him how Vinnie had learned from friends in Springfield, Illinois, that a former law partner of Abraham Lincoln's was spreading a story about the president's early, doomed love affair with Ann Rutledge—a story that Vinnie, like a pig scenting truffles, was circulating here. The man, a Mr. Herndon, was claiming that Miss Rutledge was the only woman Mr. Lincoln ever loved and that she died from want of it. Mr. Lincoln "wandered from his throne," according to Vinnie, and when he recovered he'd lost the woman he should have married and settled for one who brought him only misery.

Our conversation moved on: we began to compare our calendars so we could arrange rehearsal time.

"Do you know your fall teaching schedule yet, Father?"

"Two sections of Homer only—and then Edward Crowell, your friend's husband, will become acting chairman. I have decided to cut down, Miranda."

Since his return I had been noticing his color was unhealthy—a new grayish tinge around the mouth and fingertips. Today his breathing was audible and seemed to be an effort.

"Father, may I ask Dr. Bigelow to come and examine you?"

"One of these days I'll go to him myself, but antiquarian holidays can be very tiring, I find. I'll feel better when I start teaching."

Now I was an official adult in Amherst society. My reading and teaching in New York, the news of the foundation, and our Leo Press—all these combined to make me a welcome guest at The Evergreens, at the president's house, and at college functions. Father brought back a length of violet Italian silk for me, and on a brief visit to Boston, I took it to Madame Lauré. She made it up décolleté, with the modish new narrow skirt. *Godey's Lady's Book* had declared crinolines passé. Now the fashionable line was a straight skirt swept to the back and fullness falling in pleats. After an August evening with the Austin Dickinsons, Father and I chatted in his library. Aunt Helen had retired to bed.

"I noticed you and Mrs. Austin were the only ladies with that new draped skirt," he remarked. He poured us both glasses of Spanish sherry. "I suppose the style will be all over Amherst tomorrow."

"I think it's more than a style, Father," I replied, crossing to take the delicate cut-crystal glass from him. "It's a statement, an *attitude*." I sat in the armchair by the window, enjoying the soft summer breeze. "Those crinolines and hoops made women look helpless and frail—and then the war showed we weren't fragile anymore. You saw me heaving bales of bandages!"

Father smiled and lifted his glass to me. "I did indeed." He took a sip of the tawny liquor. "None of us will ever be quite the same, will we?"

"Except Emily," I replied. "She lives just as she always has, on a desert island of solitude."

"And how do you find that detachment, Miranda?"

I placed my glass on the side table. "Right now, I deplore it—but we can't know yet if her writing makes it forgivable. If she becomes famous, then perhaps her selfishness will be justified."

Father studied my face. "You sound as if you've given this some thought."

"Oh, I have! When I first came back from New York and took on Elena—and then the war ended, and the president was murdered, and my mind was buzzing and boiling with everything I'd learned and done—well, Emily *enraged* me! She just went on as if nothing had happened, sitting in her prim closed room and feeding her birds."

"And how do you see her now?"

I thought about this carefully. "Simply as a blank. She does no harm; she is merely *absent*. Miss Lavinia, the asp, slithers about doing the real damage to people's lives."

He smiled. "Your conversation is always such a pleasure to me, my dear. Perhaps we can thank Miss Dickinson for that, anyway." He stretched his legs and placed his feet on the ottoman.

We were quiet and at peace, reluctant to end the evening. Upstairs, Elena was sleeping in Kate's room, her small arm enfolding Maple Syrup. Somewhere along the way, Father and I had become colleagues.

"Should I use my *American Student* article in my talk about Froebel?" I asked Father. Tomorrow I was to address some faculty wives in the temple—friends of Susan Dickinson and Mary Crowell who might want to enroll their children in our kindergarten.

"Certainly," Father said approvingly. "The material is there, and the prestige of the journal will add to your credibility."

I nodded; that had been my feeling too—Father's approval sealed it. "President Stearns has offered a site for a school; should I invite him to hear me speak?"

"Splendid idea," Father said.

There was another matter about which I wanted his advice. I heard this week for the first time from the foundation's Chicago trustees. Now that the war was over, they wanted to hear my plans for the trust and for the income that had collected. Mr. Roger Daniels, the lawyer for the trust, was anxious to discuss the future. He wanted to know when he might come to talk to me in Amherst. Father suggested we invite him for early September.

My violet silk rustled and gleamed as I crossed to draw the curtains. Satisfied and sated, we sat on in the firelight another half hour, in companionable discussion.

Mr. Daniels arrived in Amherst in mid-September. He was to stay with us, in Father's wing. He had an accent like Davy's, but he was taller, with a certain bony elegance of carriage; the French would call him *racé*. His full hair was dark brown; his eyes were an unusual light ocher. In his early thirties, Mr. Daniels had the look of a Titian portrait—a merchant banker, wise and humorous.

Father lent us his library, where we talked foundation business. Mr. Daniels was very encouraging about our finances.

"There is income accrued since Davy's death, and you should be able to undertake two or three projects at once." He looked at me with his warm eyes. "What would you like to do?"

"Mr. Alan Harnett and I are hoping to start two kindergartens. A small one here that I shall watch over. I have a particular friend, Mary Crowell, who will work with me to organize it. You'll meet her tomorrow."

"Have you a location yet?"

"The college will lend us one, I think."

"And the other school?"

"This plan is more ambitious; you may not approve." Stalling, unsure of how he would react to this grand scheme, I poured us each a glass of lemonade. I crossed to him and handed him his glass, then gazed at him directly. "Mr. Harnett thinks we need a 'show window' kindergarten in New York," I declared. "A place where teachers and educators can come and study, and see our Froebel theories in action. He wants the foundation to buy a house and establish a model kindergarten."

I sat, waiting for his verdict. This was the first time that I had expressed these ambitions to a stranger, albeit hiding behind the wishes of Alan Harnett. I recognized the unusual nature of our relationship—as my trustee he would advise me, but I, younger by perhaps nearly a decade, and a woman, would make the decisions as the head of the foundation.

An approving smile crossed his face. "These are excellent plans, and in the spirit of Davy's trust."

Relieved by his response, I almost missed his use of Davy's first name. When this familiarity registered, I asked, "You said 'Davy'—did you know him?"

"Our families were friends, though he was younger. I confess I had never really talked to him until he came to our law firm to set up the foundation in the summer of '63. I was at home on leave. He was so dedicated, so definite about what he wanted for you—none of us have ever forgotten him."

I was aware of his intense, unwavering gaze. He did not stare; his calm eyes simply didn't leave me. What does he see? I wondered. I tried to imagine myself through this interested stranger's eyes and was pleased to acknowledge that I was proud of who I was becoming. Despite the pain I had endured, I felt strong and enlivened by a future that now seemed possible. I sensed Mr. Daniels's approval.

At dinner, Father entertained us with stories of his trip abroad. Then he turned serious and tactfully asked Mr. Daniels about his war experience.

"I was a captain and then a major on General Sherman's staff, at Shiloh and Vicksburg."

"You saw a great many of the most crucial campaigns," Aunt Helen commented.

Mr. Daniels took another mouthful of his stew, then nodded. "Eventually I was transferred to General Burnside's staff, outside Petersburg."

"We hear a great deal about the war," Father said. "But I often wonder about the news that doesn't travel."

"I always felt Davy was protecting me in his letters," I added. "I think I might have been less afraid if I had known more. My imagination created its own horrors."

"Much occurred that would have been unimaginable to you," Mr. Daniels said. "The face of battle is one I want never to look into again. The malignant personal hatreds wearing patriotic masks; the chances for brutish men to grow more brutal and for honorable men to degenerate into madness. This is what I saw, and again at the prison camp at Andersonville, where our men turned against one another to survive. War may be an armed angel with a mission, sir, but she has the personal habits of a slattern." He gave Aunt Helen and me an apologetic smile. "If you will forgive my terms, ladies."

"Of course," Aunt Helen said, her voice husky with emotion.

"When were you captured, sir?" my father asked.

"As we were nearing Atlanta, on our march from Chattanooga. I was captured at Kennesaw Mountain and sent to Andersonville. I suppose you have heard about that place?"

"A little," Father told him sadly. "It sounds far worse than any battle."

"Whatever you've heard, it's not savage enough. It was Hell, man-made and deliberate Hell. I had never known such evil was possible. I still cannot believe that American men could treat one another as I saw them doing in Andersonville, day by day, week by week."

"Do you think of those terrible days often, Mr. Daniels?" I asked him, awed by his passion.

Mr. Daniels looked sad. "Not by choice, but I can't put it behind me. I'm a different man, Miss Chase. The experience of war has changed me forever."

At dawn there was a thunderstorm followed by a drenching rain, then a blazing sun. As though Nature herself had washed away the evening's grim memories, it was a gentle, even relaxed, Roger Daniels who greeted us at the breakfast table. Aunt Helen piled his plate high, as if a hearty breakfast could repair the pain of the past, and Mr. Daniels tucked in with relish, pleasing her to no end.

Elena was delighted with our guest. She introduced my trustee to her bear (formerly Maple Syrup, now Zeus), and Mr. Daniels shook his paw. I saw that he had a natural ease with children; he neither patronized nor pretended an interest that did not exist. As they chattered comfortably, I wondered whether he had children of his own. As he reached for the teapot, I glanced down quickly at his left hand and saw that he wore no wedding band.

After breakfast Elena took Mr. Daniels to the brook to visit her pool. Within the hour, Mary Crowell came, and we worked through the morning, answering Mr. Daniels's questions and showing him the sketches and suggestions made by Ethan Howland, who, with the war over, was once again in private practice. Gradually, emerging from the collage of architectural renderings and printers' passes, I could almost see the expansive shape of the life ahead for me. As Mr. Daniels listened intently to my presentation, again I thought I felt his respect—and my confidence swelled. It was a heady thing to have the money for a dream!

In the afternoon Mr. Daniels and I were to meet with President Stearns; I suggested we leave well before the appointed hour so I could show him something of our community. As we made our way to the village center, we walked by The Evergreens and The Homestead, though the high hedges guarding Emily's house precluded a good view. We went cross lots, three fields away, passing through stands of hemlock and yellow birch to West Cemetery on Triangle Street. There we began to talk about the role Amherst had played in New England's history, and New England in our nation's. Mr. Daniels observed that the headstones marking the remains of our grim Puritan forefathers didn't look nearly as severe in death as he imagined they had in life.

"Yes," I said, "we New Englanders begin to enjoy ourselves only *after* we are dead." We both laughed.

By the time we passed the ivy-covered Johnson Chapel, one of the oldest buildings at the college, the late-day sun was bathing the facades of Morgan Hall and South College, and the Holyoke Mountain Range in the distance wore a rosy corona.

During our meeting with President Stearns, I was a little distracted, once again, by Mr. Daniels's steady regard across the conference table. But soon we were in deep discussion with that venerable educator. I was astonished to find that nearly three hours passed in his company! He had been impressed by my talk in the temple last month, and as I had hoped, he agreed to lend us a large former laboratory for our Amherst kindergarten. Our plans were now truly under way.

In the evening we dined with the Crowells and some would-be kindergarten parents. There was good talk about education, and I was proud of my trustee's intelligence and learning. Our glances kept intersecting as he studied me and as I tried to get a better look at him. I decided his fine eyes were more topaz than ocher.

Mr. Daniels was supposed to take the morning train, but he lingered at breakfast, ill at ease. Finally he asked if he might speak to me privately.

"I have a confession to make, Miss Chase," he told me in the library. "I must tell you I was here under false pretenses."

I was startled by this admission. "You mean you're not my trustee?"

He laughed and held up a hand. "No, I'm surely that."

"Then whatever do you mean?" I settled into a chair by the window, gesturing to Mr. Daniels to take the seat beside me.

"I came to Amherst in person because I'd already met you, and I wanted to know you better."

This explanation only confused me more. "If that is true, I'd remember it. When did we meet?"

"In Lake Forest this June. I was so thin and weak after starving at Andersonville that the Farwells invited me to swim at their beach and get my strength back. When I changed in Davy's room, there was your lovely portrait—very serious and earnest, with a column and some clouds."

"That must be Mr. Gardner's pose."

"I knew your story very well, of course, and we had exchanged letters about the foundation — but seeing your face changed everything. You became a real person, and I found excuses to be in Davy's room. I swam so often that the Farwells must have thought I had grown gills!"

He chuckled at his own foolishness, and I realized the implications of this information. He liked what he had seen in that portrait! I felt a slight blush rise in my cheeks and hoped he didn't notice. I certainly didn't want him to feel he had embarrassed me.

"When I was well again," he continued, "I decided to come here and see if I could help you with the foundation. I could have sent someone else. *That* was how I deceived you, Miss Chase, and *there!*" He slapped his thighs and stood up. "That makes me an honest man again! Now I'll go to New York and talk to Alan Harnett, and see the property he has in mind. May I come back on Friday?"

"You will be very welcome, Mr. Daniels." And so he departed, leaving the house a little bit emptier.

And so I began to set our plans in motion. Since President Stearns had agreed to lend us the space for our kindergarten, I decided it was only appropriate that he name the school. When I called on him with official papers, I asked him to do so. The mild, sad gentleman smiled at me from his tragic scholar's face.

"Your kindness does your father credit, Miss Chase. I would be obliged if you would call your school the 'Frazar Stearns Center.' My son loved all young children; I would like to hear their voices saying his name."

It was a fitting tribute, and one I was happy to make. He signed the papers with a flourish, and preparations could begin in earnest. I looked forward to being able to report this news to my trustee.

On Friday, Mr. Daniels returned to Amity Street full of enthusiastic plans.

"Alan Harnett and I got on like a house afire," he exulted. We sat on the edge of the stage in the temple, eating apples. "He's a splendid fellow; Mr. Jewett thinks the world of him. He found a house on Washington Square that is just what we need — a four-story brownstone, with a big walled garden for the children. It was very reasonable because it needs renovation, but you'll have to remodel it for the school's needs anyway. I think Ethan Howland should go to New York soon and make us some drawings so we can get started. We'll need some big changes."

"Can we really pay for all this, Mr. Daniels?"

"Easily. We'll do our Amherst school out of accrued income and borrow from the trust to buy the house on Washington Square. We're not going to stint ourselves; this 'show window' kindergarten is very important to us."

I noticed his easy use of "we" and "us" but said nothing. I also observed my pleasure in hearing him do so.

"So I'll go back to Chicago and talk to the bank and the other trustees—and draw up the papers. May I come to you again in three weeks, Miss Chase?"

"Please do. Our autumn colors should be at their finest then."

"And one more thing—since we'll be working together from now on, would you call me 'Roger'?"

"With great pleasure—and you must say 'Miranda.'"

When he was ready to leave in the morning, he seemed reluctant. "There is still so much to talk about...so much I want to learn," he said. "I suppose it will have to wait until I come back to Amherst."

"That will be in only three weeks, Roger," I reminded him with a smile. But when I walked him to the door and shut it behind him, three weeks suddenly seemed like a very long time.

With Roger gone and Father resuming his teaching duties, I found a Monday to visit Emily. She was paradoxical toward the Frazar Stearns Center. She relished every detail involving gossip and personalities ("Stay clear of Rebecca Scott. She's a stormy petrel!") and yet was oddly uninterested in the big educational changes we were introducing. ("As long as everyone learns to read, I can't see what all the FUSS is about!") Yet she was sweetly generous about my pleasure in the ongoing work of starting our kindergarten.

"Didn't I tell you your TRUE CENTER was nearing? I just didn't know what it would be!"

We discussed the new First Congregational Church, a stylish Romanesque monster that was rising directly across Main Street from the two Dickinson properties, and of which Emily highly disapproved.

The lovely old church on the green, so Greek and gracious, was to be unfrocked and deporticoed and given to the college to use for offices. She restated her rejection of the new shrine.

"Austin took me out to the fence the other night," she explained, "and I saw all the view I wanted to. What a SWARM of cupolas and minarets and slate EMBROIDERY! Father will dedicate it, of course, but without my presence. I don't think God will be there either. He'll never find his way in!"

"Emily, you should have a Boswell!" I told her.

"Should I, Miranda? Perhaps when I find my 'manager,' he will do that for me too."

I pricked up my ears. "Your manager?"

"Manager, or agent, or whatever he will be called. Someone who won't edit me, of course—just see my poems are printed EXACTLY as I wrote them. And do the arguing and bartering for me so I won't have to HAGGLE."

"Who is he, Emily?"

"Someone worldly, with a thick skin and a firm will. Someone tough! When I meet him, I'll surely recognize him. Meanwhile, I spin my poetry and hope my diligence will turn flax to gold, as it does in any good fairy story."

It was one of the best afternoons with Emily I could remember in recent months. This time, as I walked home, I was pleased to be able to look forward to future visits with "the myth." Perhaps she was capable of engaging in life beyond her tiny circumscribed space after all.

I placed an advertisement in the *Republican* for a teacher "who loves to learn." The first young woman who applied was very familiar. Her heart-shaped face, enlivened by cheerful brown eyes, her slim figure, her light brown hair, were all somehow known to me. How was this possible?

"You're wondering where we met." She smiled. "You came to some of my classes in Springfield, when you were still at the academy. I remember you took notes on everything I did."

"Why—it's Miss Randall!" I exclaimed with delight. "You sit with the children on the floor, and I've done so ever since!" I was overjoyed at this reunion.

"First I saw your merry Leo alphabet and remembered your pretty name," she related. "Then I read your inspiring article in the *American Student.* Now I hope you will consider me for the job in your school, when it opens."

"Miss Randall, I don't have to *consider,*" I assured her. "The position is yours! I remember you as a truly gifted teacher, and it will be a privilege to work with you. I will ask Mr. Austin Dickinson to draw up your contract."

When Roger returned to Amherst, it was mid-October, and the Pelham Hills were aflame. He was entirely professional, with a large number of papers to explain to me.

"Mr. Austin Dickinson expects us in his office tomorrow morning," he informed me. "Your father will be witness. Then the foundation funds for the projects may be released."

That evening Ethan brought his building plans from Springfield, and he and Roger and I worked on them till midnight. I was fascinated by the new process of architectural adaptation. Should we build window seats for classroom storage? Did we really need that door?

It was marvelous to be working alongside these accomplished men, my opinions and ideas respected. I knew that mine was a unique privilege — there were many women as educated as I who would never know such equality. At least, not yet.

After the ceremonial signings at noon, Mrs. Austin entertained us with an elegant luncheon at The Evergreens. I could see she was very taken with my trustee and anxious to oblige him.

"Isn't there some way the Dickinsons can help the foundation, Mr. Daniels? We are Miranda's particular friends in Amherst, you know," she said, draping a paisley shawl loosely around her shoulders. Small diamond drops sparkled smartly from her ears.

"Your family could assist us greatly by spreading news of the foundation around the Connecticut Valley," Roger informed her.

"Then we will do just that," she declared, tapping him lightly on the shoulder. "I see this as a very *local* story: Miranda, an Amherst girl; Davy, a student at the college; and the center for our faculty children named for another Amherst hero. Everyone reads the *Republican,*" Mrs. Austin told Roger. "We will write our friend Sam Bowles and ask for his help."

In the late afternoon, Roger asked me a little shyly to walk with him under the new canopy of maple glories and birch woods. The slanting sun lit the sassafras and teaberry bushes along our path.

"I want to tell you about myself, Miranda—about what has led me here to this beautiful place and to this important day."

"I would enjoy that," I said.

He took my arm and we strolled along a rutted path, crowned by a fiery display of leaves.

"My parents were both from Portland, Maine," Roger said. "My mother's family was in lumber; Father was a lawyer. When I was six, Mother died. Father decided to make a fresh start, and he brought me to Chicago—which was not long before a fort and a prairie then, in 1840, but an expanding area. Chicago and I grew up together!"

I smiled, enjoying the image.

"I went to Harvard College," he continued, "and then to Harvard Law School. I started practice with my father; we have our own firm—Daniels, Jones, and Sellers. Most of our work concerns real estate transactions—deeds and leases, the instruments by which property is conveyed." Roger looked at me, I thought to see if I wished him to continue. I nodded, and he went on.

"Chicago has grown so quickly," he said proudly, as if the city's accomplishment were his own; it was endearing. "It is lucrative work. For instance, the Farwells, who owned a good deal of the downtown lakefront, came to us for their contracts and advice. That was how our families met."

We continued to walk, and now Roger looked straight ahead, his eyes never straying toward me as they had earlier.

"I married Cecilia Blake of Lake Forest in '57, when she was twenty-two and I was twenty-three. We went to Italy on our honeymoon. Among her other talents, Cecilia was a pianist, and while we were there we were able, through letters of introduction, to meet a composer she admired. She had often played his *Tuscan* Concerto, and she was quite thrilled to be able to speak with him and even to play for him."

So that was it. Roger had taken me for a walk to confess that he was married. The size of my disappointment surprised me; I hoped I managed to conceal it. Then I remembered he wore no ring. Surely there was further explanation ahead.

We had reached the rapids near Swift's Bridge, and here Roger stopped speaking, staring fixedly into the water. Then he turned to me, his eyes dark with pain.

"That is a memory I hold very dear, for it was one of the last times I saw Cecilia so happy—a beautiful young woman at the height of her life and talent and fulfillment, and yes, I will say it, her love for me..."

His voice trailed off for a moment, then steadied. He seemed to have needed the time to gather strength to continue. "In Rome, Cecilia contracted brain fever. It was, *is*—for she didn't die—a most terrible illness, and for weeks I thought she would not survive. She, we, endured days of burning fevers, delirium, and convulsions, for which the doctors could do nothing. At times she knew me, at times not, but always she begged me to stay with her, to save her from death. And I did, or the doctors did, although sometimes now I wonder if it was for the best. For eventually the illness affected her mind, reducing her to an infantile state from which she has never recovered. Her personality became that of a four-year-old whose most coherent utterance now is a childish voice asking for ice cream." He drew in a deep breath. "And this from someone who had been the most beautiful, brilliant, and generous woman I ever knew," he finished.

I took his hand. "I am so very sorry," I said, unable to be more articulate. This was truly a tragedy, and my mind, for a few moments, would not react. There was more in common between us than I might have guessed, for, like me, Roger had traversed peaks of pain. My heart went out to him—he was educated and established, a survivor of war, and yet...he was alone. Then I asked him where Cecilia was now.

We started walking again. Roger seemed incapable of staying still as he related this terrible tale. "She stays with her parents and a nurse in Lake Forest. She vaguely remembers her house but nothing else. She recognizes no one. She may live another thirty years, but she will never change." He took my arm to help me over a tracery of exposed roots crisscrossing the path. "When the war came, I enlisted; the Union needed me, and the doctors said there was nothing more I could do for Cecilia. Last spring, after Andersonville, I came back to Lake Forest. I found her in bed—she's too heavy now to stand safely.

"I had brought her a present—a yellow plush chicken. She grabbed it from my hand and hugged it to her enormous bosom, crooning,

'Roger.' For just a moment I thought she knew me; then I understood. She had named the chicken 'Roger.'"

We reached an overlook and saw the village commons lying low in the landscape. The tips of the trees in the hemlock forest were bending to the southeast, away from the prevailing wind. The sun was starting to sink into the Pelham Hills, and we turned to head back.

"Is there any way I can help you?" I asked.

"You have helped me already, my dear Miranda, by allowing me to unburden myself in this way. We have both known irretrievable loss — and we are both trying to go on living, despite our grief."

He had said nothing about the strong attraction between us. This was not conjecture; it was fact. I felt our extreme awareness at this very moment, in the tingling elbow he held so correctly. But I knew we would not discuss this, and I searched for a safe topic. "Please feel that you can always do so," I said, hoping I did not sound too prim.

"Thank you," he said. "You are very kind."

But I did not feel kind. I felt lonelier than he ever could have guessed. I had family, a daughter, good friends through work — but no one who wanted only myself and my company, as Davy had.

"Roger, let us agree to be friends as well as business associates. And I love letters — writing them and receiving them."

I bent to pick up a perfect vermilion maple leaf and handed it to him, smiling. "This is my first message."

He smiled back, and we arrived at my front door.

And so Roger wrote:

October 18, 1865

Sunday evening, with a rising autumn wind. I am sitting in my library, hearing the sounds of the restless lake. Usually I avoid this room — it's very lonely, with only the lake and my Harvard books for company. But tonight I feel your presence, your interest, and your attention. Shall we talk a bit?

First of all, I believe that Alan Harnett — as your future headmaster — should resign from Friends at midyear and work for the foundation full-time. He should be free for important decisions,

*large and small. We can and should pay him a third more than his
present salary. He will be our cornerstone.*

*Your long friendship with Alan is most impressive. I am jealous
of his memories and of the years before I knew you. You told me he
once said that you and he and Davy were three partners. Well, there
are four of us now!*

I was pleased by his letter. I read twice the sentence about "the years
before I knew you," and as I did so I again felt his hand under my elbow,
guiding me as we walked. Remembering, a small warmth began to dif-
fuse my cheeks, moving slowly through my body. I was going to like
corresponding with my adviser.

Mrs. Austin kept her promise. Mr. Samuel Bowles, dining at The Evergreens, heard about the Frazar Stearns Center and my new and radical
theories on primary education. He called at Amity Street to interview
me for the *Springfield Republican*. I found him a handsome and compelling gallant, disturbingly intense. I could see why Emily fancied him
as a beau; I almost did myself.

"Now we must talk about our friend Emily," he announced when
the interview was over. "You mustn't let her offend you."

When I began to protest that she had not, he waved a hand to cut
me off. "Of course she has," he said with a chuckle. "And if she hasn't
yet, she will. She inevitably does."

I laughed and congratulated him on knowing his friend so well.

"Don't let her put you out," he continued. "She needs you. Now that
she's squared off against Sue, she needs every friend she's got—every
one of us! Sue told me Emily lets you read her poetry. Can this be
true?"

"Actually, she insists on it. And once, years ago, I helped her arrange it somewhat systematically."

"Does she allow you to edit her, Miss Chase?"

"Not a single word—not the least *comma!*"

He sighed, shaking his head. "Now there's the real loss—for her
and for us too. You would think we were *cannibals*, nipping off her
infant's toe or editing his little pink ear!"

He smiled, showing his fine teeth and his dimples. What a flirt!

"This truly enrages the editor in me," he confided. "I want to get my hands on a poem and bring it to its potential. I can always see two pieces of writing at one and the same time: the one under my nose and the one that's there and waiting *inside*—the one that needs shaping and turning and editing to be revealed!"

"Mr. Bowles, did you know Michelangelo had the same thought?"

"Why, of course," he replied. "And I'll use it in my piece about you. 'Amherst Educator Sees Inner Value in Her Students!'"

"I would prefer it without the plural. Why not 'Each Child's Unique Value' instead?"

"Miss Chase, you're *right*. Oh, how our poor Emily could profit from you as an editor! I see her as a genuinely tragic figure, out of step with the times. She just doesn't fit in *anywhere*."

"Anywhere, Mr. Bowles?" I didn't disagree with him but had hoped perhaps as an editor he might have a broader perspective.

"Her best writing is—well, simply too big to handle. It asks too much of one! And as for the worst of her stuff—it's merely harmless. It fits in perfectly with those rosebuds and lockets that I have to print every week. I do this as a public service, you know, Miss Chase—to keep up the spirits of the local ladies."

I shook my head disapprovingly at this statement. "Emily's right; you *are* condescending toward women writers."

"But not toward *genius,* Miss Chase! Emily has flooded me with poems for about ten years now. Sometimes there's a phrase or two—or even a whole verse—that stuns me like a *blow.* I am struck in the solar plexus; I cry, 'OOF!'" He collapsed into the sofa, rolling his beautiful black eyes at me.

I smiled at his display and also at the truth of what he described. "I've had that same reaction, often."

He sat back up again. "But then the rest of the poem is so inferior, so *second-rate.* What should I do? I can't publish it as it is, and she won't let me touch it."

"Does her refusal to accept editing hold her back professionally, Mr. Bowles?"

"It effaces her. She is *invisible.* I could make her the leading woman poet of the century, another Elizabeth Barrett—if she would let me. That's why I call her Queen Recluse, for her maddening royal ways!"

Mr. Bowles kissed my hand and swashbuckled away, leaving my parlor a little empty. His charm and intensity had made him a legendary Don Juan all over the valley. I had heard his name linked to Mrs. Austin's, who was said to relish it, and to a young cousin's, Maria Whitney, who denied it. Now he had just made me feel that he would treasure every moment of our talk, that it was more than everyday business to him. But of course that's just what he did to Emily!

Still, when his article "Amherst Educator Sees Each Child's Unique Value" appeared, it was accurate and lucid. From the reactions to this, and the *American Student* piece, and the news of the center, I suddenly acquired a professional correspondence.

Emily never once referred to Mr. Bowles's article, although I was certain she must have read it. But I sent it to Roger Daniels and received an immediate answer.

> *November 10, 1865*
>
> *I am pleased to see that the world is beginning to take a serious interest in our serious foundation. Since this is now the case, we must move forward.*
>
> *I would like to meet you in New York directly after the New Year, as we have work to do there. Among other things we must talk to the builder about the fourth-floor apartment on Washington Square. You and the staff working there should have a small kitchen at the very least, and we need to settle various other arrangements. I feel we can do this better at the location, working in tandem with Alan Harnett.*
>
> *I would also like, with your permission, to arrange tickets for* Figaro *and* Orfeo.

And he closed with a postscript: "How strange — how lovely — to be looking forward to something!"

Mary Crowell and I continued work on transforming the laboratory at Amherst College into an ideal kindergarten space. Ethan drew up plans for this as well. During one of Ethan's visits at the beginning of November, Father requested that I arrange to have a door made, connecting his library with the parlor. "Elena shouldn't have to go out

in the cold when she comes for her myths," he had said in explanation. "And you're doing all that construction anyway." Then he asked
that Sam move his bed downstairs. He slept in the library now, and
Sam spent the night in Father's old room. I knew what these changes
meant: I was witnessing him diminish.

I poured out my feelings to Roger and realized, as with Davy, we
were using this correspondence to learn about each other, both in
what we wrote and then in how each of us responded to the growing
wealth of information between us.

In response to my letter, Roger replied:

*Your lovely long letter about your relationship with your father, and
how it has evolved, was heartwarming to me. I understand that you
are afraid, that he is weakening. Did it help you to write? Often
summing up for a friend can clarify one's feelings. I stand ready to
listen, whenever you need me.*

His insight touched me. He knew that I was fearing the worst, that
which I could not face about my father. And this was disguised by the
fact that it appeared there was no need for this terror, for we seemed
to have come to a plateau where father was neither better nor worse.
Only little things were signaling what was coming: among them his
willingness to allow Dr. Bigelow more visits, and that gentleman's ad-
ministering of digitalis. And then there was Father's resignation, at
midterm, from the college.

"Dr. Bigelow has extracted me from the department banquet and
the farewell speeches in Greek and Latin." He laughed. "We planned
it that way!"

Aunt Helen and I did everything as we always had, surprises for
Elena, special treats to tempt Father's failing appetite. And so we continued until Christmas, and through the holiday, in a calm heightened
by my certain knowledge that Father would not see another.

In January 1866, as Roger had requested, I planned a trip to New York.
As I packed I was surprised by the attention I gave to my clothes:
what dresses I should wear for meetings about our school, what evening gown would be best for the opera. I decided upon the aubergine

taffeta with a ruche neckline and caught myself wondering if this dress showed my coloring to advantage, and then blushed that I had this thought. Roger and I are professional colleagues, I reminded myself. He and I were still new in our friendship, and he was a man with complicated obligations. I was not sure where I should allow my thoughts to take me.

In New York I was once again staying in the Harnetts' tiny cottage. Father and Aunt Helen had thought it best that I be chaperoned, so perhaps the attraction between Roger and me had been detected even if it went unacknowledged.

Alan and Fanny had given up one of their children's rooms for me. The seventeenth-century Dutch colonists must have all been miniature figurines, I thought as I bumped my high, absentminded forehead on the eaves of the house, but nonetheless I felt at home, enjoying the prospect of what we hoped to achieve together.

And there was another prospect I was enjoying. Roger had arrived before me and had taken a suite of rooms at the plaza. He had left a note requesting that Alan and I meet with him and Elliot Peck, a specialist in stained glass windows, at Mr. Peck's offices in Washington Square at our convenience.

"And I would like to call upon you in the evening," he added, "when you feel refreshed from your journey."

I had arrived too late for this to occur on my first night there, and I was disturbed as much by my twinge of disappointment—what could it hurt to wait twelve hours?—as I was by my sense of relief; I felt almost fearful at the prospect of seeing him, of his direct gaze, of looking into those amber-colored eyes. This was a relationship with rules I did not yet know.

The evening passed far less evocatively than it might have if I had spent it with Roger. I had a noisy but uncomplicated time with Alan and Fanny and their babies. Julian's little brother, Henry, was a cherub, and I was thoroughly happy being entertained by those two and later enjoying a delicious small supper at which the three of us discussed our present and future plans.

The next afternoon, there was Roger: elegant, tall, and calm. Did I imagine that there was a bit of suppressed energy about him? Could he also have been feeling the tension that seemed now to be constantly between us? Or was his restrained demeanor merely his usual way?

He, professional as usual, got immediately down to business, asking Elliot Peck if we might have the use of a small table for our papers and explaining that I had been concerned about our dark north-facing classrooms. Between us, we devised panels of glass — small clear panes set in lead, covering entire walls. Now our kindergarten would be bathed in light, even on the darkest day. We worked for hours, adjusting, debating, considering, yet the time flew by.

After the meeting, Alan, Roger, Mr. Peck, and I celebrated at a nearby tavern with ale and oysters. All through the meal, I was aware of a strange contradiction in Roger. I sensed his attention, but it was deflected: he seemed almost to be avoiding those intense gazes we had occasionally shared earlier. He brought the conversation around to the foundation a number of times, as if he were retreating to the safety of our professional relationship, while Alan and Mr. Peck chatted on about any number of personal things. Only when Alan and Mr. Peck discussed the latest performances at the Academy of Music did Roger refer to anything of a more intimate nature.

"Miranda has agreed to join me for both *Orfeo* and *Figaro*," Roger said. It was here that his eyes finally rested on me. I saw warmth and anticipation in those eyes, heightened, perhaps, by the flickering gas light.

"How marvelous!" Alan exclaimed. "The notices for both have been spectacular."

Roger and Mr. Peck accompanied Alan and me back to the Harnetts' little house. I had longed for a few moments alone with Roger, if only to better gauge his mood. Had I been mistaken? I wondered. Is his interest purely that of a lawyer and his client? But as I was lodging with the Harnetts, even a few moments alone were not possible. My questions reverberated more strongly after Mr. Peck — whom I had met only that afternoon — kissed me good night, while Roger merely bowed his head. Perhaps it was the ale and my giddy sense of accomplishment: I shocked myself by taking his hand, rising up on my toes, and bringing my lips to his cheek.

"Till tomorrow night," I told him.

Before I could see his reaction, I spun on my heels and entered the little house, Alan following behind me.

As I prepared for bed, I marveled at my boldness. Perhaps Roger's formality brought about a little rebellion in me. At the same time, my feelings were completely confused. I admired Roger, I was attracted—and yet... What could we have together? What future was there for us?

I drifted off to sleep pondering such thoughts, and of course no answer came.

I didn't see Roger all the next day. Alan and I had a busy time together going over curriculum and talking to plumbers. Not exactly a glamorous way to spend time in such a fashionable city! But Roger was never far from my thoughts. What would our excursion to the opera be like?

He arrived in the evening, resplendent in white tie and tails, and nearly took my breath away. He was so much more than merely handsome; his presence had a weight to it that made me feel I was in the company of someone very important—someone who took up space.

His eyes told me he thoroughly approved of my violet silks and the ribbon I had woven through my curls. He had a carriage waiting outside, and a tingle of electricity shot through me as he helped me into the coach.

"You look quite beautiful," he told me after he had settled into the seat. "All eyes will be upon you tonight."

I smiled, taking great pleasure in his approval. "That will make the soprano quite unhappy, don't you think?"

"Perhaps you could learn to sing," he teased. "Then the show will be able to continue when she storms out in a jealous rage."

"If I sing," I joked back, pleased with our easy banter, "the entire audience will storm out."

We arrived amid clattering carriages, and I tried to remember all the details that both Emily and Sue Dickinson would enjoy hearing. Sue would want to know all the latest trends and be sure she was keeping up, while Emily would relish her imagined superiority over such frivolous doings.

We found our box and sat in the plush velvet seats. "I've never been to an opera before," I confessed.

Roger took my hand and squeezed it. "Then I'm glad I suggested it. It is my pleasure to introduce you to something that brings me great joy."

I discovered that evening, and the evenings that followed, that there were indeed two Rogers. There was my steadfast and correct trustee, who was always ready with an opinion, advice, or an ear but who maintained a professional distance. And then there was my gallant friend, delighting in watching me discover the city and its pleasures for the first time. We were able to build on the closeness we had achieved through our letters, and over our private dinners and excursions we talked about ourselves intimately—as true friends. I heard about his childhood; he heard about mine. I suffered with him when he related more of his war experiences; he consoled me in my several losses. We were never without conversation.

I realized that Roger's circumscribed demeanor was not due to a lack of attraction—rather, it was precisely that attraction that made him distant. He was protecting me and my reputation. He is a married man, I reminded myself each night as I struggled to fall asleep in the Harnetts' close and crowded house. He has an important position with my foundation, which should never appear to be compromised. He was formal out of respect—and it made me like him all the more. I knew I would be sorry when my New York business was completed—all too soon.

When I returned to Amherst, I heard through Mrs. Austin that Emily's aged dog, Carlo, had died. I was visiting at The Evergreens to be introduced to Sue's second child, a little girl named Martha. I was surprised that Emily herself had not sent me a note on her dog's demise. My feelings were mixed: guilty that Emily and I had become so estranged that she did not share this news with me; relieved that I was not called to witness her grief in extremis. Sue and I wickedly entertained each other with possible elegies to the old hound, mimicking Emily's style at her grandest.

"Don't be put out by Emily's silence," Sue said finally. "She has her hands full at the moment."

"Really?" I asked, smiling down at Martha. "How so?" I couldn't imagine what would keep her occupied other than her writing.

"They've lost their hired girl and have been unable to hire one on. All the household duties have now fallen to Emily and Lavinia."

"Is she writing?" I asked, handing Martha back to her fashionable mother. If Emily's new responsibilities interfered with her writing, she would be despondent.

"Less than before," Sue admitted. "But it is hard to tell. It is possible she is simply sending me fewer of her poems. Martha's arrival..."

Here Sue trailed off, and I understood. Emily might be a devoted aunt, but she couldn't keep herself from resenting how much of Sue's attention was fixed on the children. Despite all the years that had passed since Sue had been able to return Emily's undivided devotion, Emily seemed to resent it anew whenever Sue's obligations and interests took her elsewhere. Perhaps this was why I hadn't heard from her lately; perhaps Emily was pouting over my deserting her for New York.

Well, if she wanted to be in touch with me, she would be. I would not allow her to make me feel guilty or force me to apologize for the way in which my world was expanding, even as hers was narrowing.

In March, Ethan and Ann Mackay—very sensible, very kind—celebrated their first wedding anniversary. Their families and their children—four sons and Elena—crowded Kate's little parlor. For Elena, the occasion signified a new apricot velvet dress and a ride on the cars. Since Father seemed stable, I had made the suggestion to Ethan and Ann that I remain in Springfield while they took a brief anniversary trip. I could watch over the household, and it would give Elena a chance to know her brothers again. In part this idea filled me with trepidation—what if she asked to stay on?—but when Ethan accepted my offer with alacrity, I realized how strongly he must have wondered if we had done the right thing by keeping her in Amherst.

And so we stayed, Elena and I, at Ethan's house, I with the terrible fear that my sweet "little daughter" might decide she wanted her old family, still her real family, after all. Not surprisingly, Elena and her brothers took to one another at once, as though she had never been away, and she enjoyed Ann's two children, Caleb and Samuel—her "new big brothers"—immensely. This equanimity was thanks in part to Ethan and Ann's insistence that I maintain firm discipline against any indoor rowdiness, and in part to their natural interest in, and affection for, one another as new siblings. She looked upon this masculine world as if the boys were creatures from another and more fascinating place, but to my secret and almost palpable relief, she asked every evening at bedtime whether we would be returning to Amherst. Yet I was not *quite* sure why this was so fixed in her mind. Finally, one very cold night when we had all finished an interlude of reading in front of the big kitchen fire after supper, I asked her about it as I put her to bed.

"Because," she answered sleepily, "that is where I live now, with you and Grandpa Josiah and Grandmama Helen, and Sam, and…" Her voice trailed off with a yawn, and I smiled at her.

"Oh, my dearest Elena." I bent down to kiss her, and her arms went around my neck. "You may always stay there with us. And you may visit your father and brothers here too, as often as you like. We are *all* your family!"

And when she fell asleep she was smiling, and I smiled too, with relief and for yet another reason. She and I were sleeping in the same room where not so long ago I spent many hours tossing and turning, only this time my nocturnal thoughts had taken a new direction, and my mind was no longer torn as to the course my life should take.

Spring was a busy time for me. Polly Randall and I spent hours developing curriculum and materials for the Stearns Center, and Mary Crowell and I saw to the renovations of the donated space. During all the Amherst preparations, I was also consulting with Alan Harnett in New York on the progress there. It seemed that endless decisions must be made!

I spent evenings reading aloud to Father, as his eyesight was worsening. Dr. Bigelow assured me the problem with Father's eyes was simply the natural progression of age, but I knew it frustrated my father to be unable to do the reading he so enjoyed. This limitation, however, was more than compensated by Elena's entertaining presence. She kept Father completely engaged with stories and drawings and explanations of her world, which seemed in their companionable way to be blending with his.

My friendship with Lolly Wheeler was slowly renewing. To the great relief of his family, her brother had returned from the war, and so had Lolly's secret sweetheart, who was none other than our former sledding companion, Caleb Sweetser. But the war had changed Lolly, as it had changed all of us. Caleb discovered that she was a far more serious girl than he had left behind, with new ambitions of her own, and the tension it caused between them was the subject of our many conversations.

"He just doesn't understand," Lolly complained. She was helping me fold laundry. It astonished me sometimes how much washing a small household required.

"To be a doctor!" Lolly exclaimed. "Why can't he see that those are worthy goals for a woman? Instead, he thinks to study and to care for the sick and the wounded would cause scandal."

I listened as I matched socks, concerned that this disagreement between them reflected a far deeper estrangement. "Does the school in Boston have literature you can show him? It might reassure him if he can see the materials for himself."

Lolly sighed. "I've shown him. It doesn't matter. All that matters to Caleb is that I behave the way he expects a proper woman and wife should. I don't know—" Her voice broke, and she clutched the tea towel she was folding. She cleared her throat. "I don't know if I can marry a man who believes as Caleb believes."

She began to cry, and I put my arms around her. "You are right to question this," I said softly. "A true love would want you to achieve your heart's desires."

She nodded miserably.

"You'll see," I assured her. "You will go to medical school and you will meet a wonderful man who will encourage you and be proud of your accomplishments."

"I—I don't even know if I will be accepted," she said in a shaky voice. "Should I end my engagement for such an uncertain goal?"

"Only you know the answer to that," I said. "But think of this: even if you were not accepted at that school, don't Caleb's objections indicate a significant difference between you?"

Lolly took a deep breath, calming herself. "Yes."

I took the tea towel from her hands and wiped her tear-stained face with it. "I will help you study," I promised her. "You will get into that medical school."

"Thank you." She smiled weakly, then her brow furrowed. "The tea towel!"

I laughed. "Far better to relaunder a tea cloth than have you wiping your face on your sleeves. Now *that* would be unladylike behavior—and far more scandalous than applying to medical school!"

I knew I could not mend her disappointment and broken heart, but I could support her in her decisions. So we did study together while I also continued my correspondence with Miss Adelaide and, of course, with Roger.

The Frazar Stearns Center opened on my twenty-third birthday, September 16, 1866. Father attended the opening day. He heard Dr. Stearns and me speak, and saw Elena beaming from the first class. After the excitement, he rested but could not rise from the sofa later. He complained of a sore throat, but Dr. Bigelow was not concerned—it was only a cold—and determined that rest was all Father needed.

I brought Father some cold beef tea jelly and an egg beaten with brandy, and held his hand until he dozed off. But the cure would not come; he was noticeably weaker. Soon he was spending most of the day in bed, "Behind a drapery, like Jefferson," he said. One late September afternoon, Dr. Bigelow sat back after examining him and sighed.

"Enjoy your family and the season, Josiah. This is your resting time." To us he said privately, "A few weeks—no more."

I wrote and poured out my heart to Roger. The shortness of breath, the rust-colored sputum, the fever and cough that were this condition's calling cards, paralyzed me—it was like my mother's death all over again.

Roger wrote back:

This is different. This is a fine dying, after a fine life. From all that I know, your father has had a singularly full life, filled with books and ideas, and love around him everywhere. You must take credit for your share in it. When we met a year ago, I watched him with you and Elena, and I listened to him talking about his students. I thought then—I think now—This is a happy man!

Father reclined on the library sofa in the afternoons, receiving very few guests. Elena visited to chatter on about school. Surprisingly, Emily sent warm notes and cheery lines of verse calculated to draw his smile. Emily seemed to always respond when Death was near, as if it beckoned her. Her missives for Father, though, were delightfully disingenuous. They were not Emily at her melodramatic worst but Emily the entertaining raconteur.

One day, Father asked for Mr. Austin to come, and when Mr. Austin returned the next day, he brought papers to sign. I hovered at the doorway, which was still open a crack. Perhaps it was unworthy to eavesdrop, but I did not want the truth held from me. I heard only what I had expected: "Here is your amended will," said Mr. Austin. "And the notarized statement for Judge Lord."

I leaned against the wall and shut my eyes. The inevitable day that I was dreading was fast approaching. Father knew it; it would not be right for me to hide from it. Uncle Thomas Bulfinch came from Boston and moved quietly into the guest room. Bill Baker, a young theology student from the college, replaced Sam in Father's old room and cared for him in the night. Father's "cold" had now settled in his chest, into pneumonia. "It won't be long," said Dr. Bigelow, putting his stethoscope back into his bag as I held his overcoat. "There is nothing more to be done."

Aunt Helen and I tried to maintain the household as usual; we kept our tears private and tried to make Father comfortable. Mercifully, when at last he did leave us, on a lovely late October afternoon, it was while he was sleeping and with almost a smile on his calm face.

He was buried with his volume of Horace and a scroll listing every student he ever taught. His pallbearers were every man in his last course at the college. Those who could not carry his coffin—the veterans, crippled and healing—walked beside it, each with a hand on the wood. This was their unconventional wish; I was happy to permit it.

There was a splendid service in the college chapel, where every pew was filled. The student choir sang Handel, and Dr. Stearns spoke, comparing Father's life to the "educated man" of Marcus Aurelius's ideal.

But how would Father have reacted to that other gesture, spontaneous and tender, which compelled me to love her with my whole heart, even as I continued to resist her? Who else but Father could have appreciated as I did the brief, spectral appearance at the church today of the woman seated in the last pew, her face shielded by an elaborate—and borrowed—tulle veil? I knew she owned no such article, for there was no need: she did not mourn in public. Her chapel was her second-floor room, the room she rarely left.

As the minister brought the funeral service to a close, by chance I turned around—otherwise I might have missed her. I saw her rise and hurry out, head bowed, so as to be neither recognized nor detained by the departing crowd, who would surely have stopped to stare and whisper. Yet her silhouette was unmistakable. Emily, unseen in public this way in nearly a decade, had come to be with me.

With Davy and Kate both gone, there was no one with whom to witness this magnificent gesture. Aunt Helen would not understand, and Roger—Roger and I had not discussed my strange and prolonged friendship with Amherst's myth. I was filled with a lonely despair. Father, of course, was the one I most wanted to share the moment with. Aunt Helen and I gave a reception afterward in the temple. We closed the velvet stage curtains and used the most brilliant maple boughs, with black velvet bows, as our only decoration. Father would have enjoyed these metaphors.

He always enjoyed a party too, so we served the best French champagne to his many friends. I was touched to greet Alan Harnett and Cousin Ellen Lyall, who had come a long way. And Roger had come, as my dignified trustee. Roger's friendship, his instinctive kindness in wanting to be near when the end came, touched me profoundly, as I knew it would have Father.

I found Roger standing at the side of the stage, and without a word he folded me into an embrace. I stood still, not wanting him to release me. He felt so strong, and in command, and protective. Finally, I felt his hold lessen, and I stepped back away from him.

"Can you stay?" I asked.

"If you need me, of course I can," he replied.

"Thank you," I said, my voice no more than a whisper.

He lifted my chin with his finger. "You know you have been loved," he said. "That counts for so much. And your father knew how much you loved him. That is what you must remember. That and how proud he was of you."

I couldn't answer; I could only allow him to brush away my tears as I nodded. I knew he was right—as he had said, this was a fine death after a full life.

Aunt Helen was pleased that I had invited Roger to stay for a few days—having a man in the house during this sad time brought her comfort. I understood this—Roger's presence was solid, strong. One felt protected knowing he was near, and grieving makes one feel vulnerable. He made us feel safe; it was enough.

Roger's presence also helped to distract Elena from her sadness, if only temporarily. She was a resilient child, but I knew she would miss Father as it became more clear to her that he was not going to come back.

On the third day, after breakfast, Roger announced he needed to return to business. "But please," he said, "if there is anything you need, if only to talk, I will be back."

"You'll write?" I asked.

He nodded. "The moment I leave," he promised.

In the weeks that followed, I missed Father constantly—his wit, his learning, his flashes of insight and compassion. We had grown ever closer. Since Davy's death, he had become the parent I had needed—and also my colleague and my friend. He had supported my work and my independence as a woman generously and freely, and his ready inclusion and acceptance of Elena transformed my life.

I fell into a profound lassitude and inertia. I went through all the motions of conferring with Polly Randall and Pamela Niles, our second teacher, as the Stearns Center ended its first semester. I passed the occasional Monday with Emily, and uncounted hours with Mr. Austin, executing Father's simple will. Aside from Mother's fortune, which now came to me, Father really owned very little. He left his classical library to Uncle Thomas Bulfinch and his modest estate to Kate's boys, knowing that mine would one day go to Elena. Without telling me, when I turned twenty-one he had put the Amity Street house in my name.

For several chilly winter weeks, I slipped perilously close to feeling nothing again. I barely wrote to Roger and found it difficult to reply when he wrote to me. I went from meeting to meeting, agreeing and signing. Events and duties yanked me about like a puppet and let me flop down will-less when the need was over. I rallied for the few hours I taught my little charges, then, like a deflating balloon, I collapsed into inertia. I walked through my roles for Thanksgiving and Christmas with the Howlands and all their jostling boys.

Roger sent me a brooch—a violet Burmese sapphire, set in a curling wave. "This is a glimpse of your beloved ocean, to make you smile again. Someday, perhaps, we'll see it together, Miranda."

I was at first not certain I should accept so expensive and rare a gift—particularly when I reread Roger's note. And yet, as heartsore as I was, I could not bring myself to return the brooch. Father's death, the last in a series of terrible losses, had made it difficult to lose even the suggestion of a happier future. As I wrote to thank Roger for his gift, the letter seemed to take on a life of its own.

New Year's Day, 1867

Dear Roger,

At our meetings and in our letters, we have moved from friendship to something more intense and emotional. I have felt this change developing between us, and I suppose that change is given form in the beautiful brooch you sent me. I am not certain that I should accept something so costly, but to find a friend who understands me so well is such a balm to my sore heart that I cannot say no. I thank you for it and will treasure it always.

It is difficult for me to collect my thoughts these days; I feel as if I were caught in some deep well of sadness. It is not only my father's death but Davy's, and before that my dear cousin Kate's. You never met her, but Kate was, saving only Davy, my dearest friend. She died giving birth to her third child; I was at the confinement, and it left an indelible mark upon me. I resolved afterward that I would never bear a child. I have Kate's Elena as a daughter; I will not leave her motherless again. I suppose this means that I will never marry, for what man would be willing to have his posterity held ransom to his wife's fear?

This is another reason why I throw myself with such passion into the work of the foundation. I cannot abandon the opportunities for creativity and influence that Davy planned and the foundation offers. These opportunities will be my life's work. Again, what man would permit the comfort of his home to be disrupted by his wife's career?

The last several years of war and loss have left me (as I suppose they have left many people) adrift and bewildered by sorrow. I need to tell you how very much your friendship means to me.

I was not satisfied with the letter; what would Roger make of it? It hardly made sense, but I could not gather my wits to tell my feelings more clearly. I sealed it and posted it. It was done, and I felt somehow relieved.

When I next met with Mr. Austin on my father's business, he expressed concern. "Miranda, your aunt and I are worried about you. These last few years have been a great emotional strain for you. You have lost a fiancé, a dear cousin, and now your father. And you have become Elena's mother! You are overdrawn, spiritually; you must take the time to restore yourself.

"I would like to see you take Elena and go somewhere quiet and beautiful. All your duties here can wait. I will write to Mr. Harnett and the trustees. Perhaps you should go south, to avoid the rest of our harsh Amherst winter and early spring. I see you smiling—do you know of such a place?"

"Yes, I do, Mr. Austin. I know exactly such a place, for Elena and for me. It's in the West Indies, and it's called York Stairs!"

Book XI

BARBADOS

FEBRUARY–MAY 1867

Elena and I reached Barbados on February 3, 1867. Bridgetown had grown bigger and busier in ten years; I had read that sugar prices were booming. The York Stairs carriage was driven by young Seth, Aaron's nephew, for Aaron was now old and ill. As we rode, he talked about Miss Adelaide, lonely since Dr. Hugh's death and saddened, again, by the news about Father.

"Your face will be the best medicine for her, Missy Miranda," Seth told us.

We reached Cedar Avenue at dusk. The Palladian staircase opened its arms to greet us. I saw a single slim figure at the balustrade.

"Miss Adelaide is waiting to meet you," I told Elena as we climbed the familiar curving stairs.

"Darling Miranda," Miss Adelaide greeted me in her silken soft tones. Her beautiful face still seemed ageless. She held me a long time, as Elena hovered behind me, reverting to shyness. The reunion was bittersweet—combining the past and the present, the dead and the living.

She released me and held me at arm's length. "You have grown into yourself," she said. Then she bent down to greet Elena. "And here is a sweet pea."

Lettie came out of the shadows. I crossed to her, and we held each other wordlessly.

"Let us show this new little one to her room," Lettie said after a moment.

Lettie and I took Elena downstairs to her room, opposite mine. She was uneasy about the monster shadows leaping across the curved ceiling, but Lettie told her they were dolphins. I heard their voices as they unpacked.

"Do you know I did this for your Manda, when she was a little girl?"

"She told me. She likes you."

"And who is this handsome bear?"

"This is Zeus."

"Is it now! I know that fellow Zeus. He is in the Greek tales. He is king of all the gods, and a bossy master."

"My Zeus is very quiet and nice."

"Of course he is. He is your friend."

"Lettie, will you teach me to swim?"

"It will be my pleasure—the very first thing tomorrow!"

I could see Lettie had already eased Elena past her bad moment and into York Stairs. I told this to Miss Adelaide when I rejoined her on the gallery. She had festive iced champagne for us.

"We must celebrate your return, dear child, and we must celebrate Elena. I declare, it has been a long time since I have seen such good manners in one so young."

"She is like her mother that way—and of course I am raising her the way you raised me."

"I hear that all over the country families are raising their kin orphaned by the war."

"It's true," I told her. "And there are many, many girls who will be single forever."

"So we must toast our men." Miss Adelaide smiled, and we raised our glasses—"To Davy, Hugh, and your father." Then she drank to my future: "Perhaps it will start here!"

And so, in spite of the empty chairs that had once been Dr. Hugh's and Father's, Miss Adelaide and I dined cheerfully, recalling many plans, and with a sigh of happiness I relaxed, knowing that in many ways our men were with us, and that this was now exactly the right place for me to be.

On my bed table I found that Miss Adelaide had left me a new Victor Hugo novel and a vase of syringa to fill my high white room with sweetness. I went to sleep breathing it and thinking of Roger, and his strong square jaw. He must have read my letter by now.

Morning brought a dappled radiance that amazed Elena. "A whole new sun!" she cried, bounding into my room.

We dressed in our bright chitons, Springfield copies of Madame Lauré's design. After breakfast, Miss Adelaide and I showed Elena around York Stairs, for I wanted her to meet it in the morning light, as I had.

Elena was enchanted, her eyes wide with wonder. "There's no in-doors!"

Lettie then came in with her daughter. Mira was an elegant gazelle of nine, curtsying like a dancer. She and Elena eyed each other curiously with intense interest, and then Lettie and Mira took Elena off for "swimming school." I did not join them until their picnic lunch, for I had decided that my mornings must be spent working at the shameful mass of papers that had collected since Father died and I became so listless. I wrote until noon and then walked out of my bedroom and down the hill, to diamond-glittering Learner's Cove, and into memories.

Elena had learned to duck and blow in the warm green water. She and Mira played like two young angels in a liquid paradise, and I joined them, shedding time and grief. My little girl and I were the same age, here in the sea. She was awed by the profusion of shells, having studied my precious collection on Amity Street.

"Are these Miss Adelaide's shells?" she asked, turning them over on the sandy shore.

"They belong to the sea. It kept them here, waiting for a little girl who loves shells." I watched as she searched for yellow pectins with Mira, humming a little—as she used to when Father kept her company beside the brook. After our naps, Elena begged for the beach again, but I explained that I did not want her to burn and "get too hot," as Lettie called it.

"And," I added, "I have something to show you that you will like."

I led her to the gallery, where Miss Adelaide had rigged us a fine worktable. Dr. Hugh had willed me his entire shell collection, and this was the perfect time to introduce it to Elena. I brought out the boxes, and we began to arrange the beautiful objects on two tall panels of silvery driftwood. After a few minutes Elena announced she would like to make pictures of them, so Miss Adelaide, smiling, found paper and charcoal, and Elena began to draw, outlining the same shape over and over rather than reworking the drawing. She had Ethan's talent; she was training her little muscles to use it.

"Wonderful," Miss Adelaide whispered, and then she left us to our creative tasks. I felt very close to Dr. Hugh as I worked   remembering his kindness to an odd little stranger. He —and Barbados—had freed me from so much, particularly the fearful taint of consumption that had haunted me. I was certain that he would be happy with my teaching Elena all the shell lore he had taught me.

Much later we dressed for dinner, and then we joined Miss Adelaide on the gallery.

"Lettie told me this is when we play the cloud game," Elena said.

"We certainly do. Why don't you begin, Elena?"

"I see a big gold rabbit — right there!"

I smiled at Miss Adelaide, remembering, and all through dinner we enjoyed reminiscing, this time without so much sadness. Elena asked question after question; it was wonderful to see her ever-widening curiosity.

After our dinner and after Elena was in bed, Miss Adelaide and I returned to the twilit gallery, and I admired the handsome wicker furniture, new since my last visit.

"I was very extravagant and ordered it from India when Hugh was dying. He liked to lie out here and watch the sky, and receive the callers. It made him happy; he said he had had a fine life. Very few Charleston men would say that, these days." She moved comfortably in her chair. "We discussed the idea of returning home, despite the war, to be buried there. But Hugh would have none of that. Our life there was over long before, when on my behalf he swore he'd never go back."

I longed to pick up this elliptical reference and open that locked cupboard. The most I could muster, however, was a polite reminder. "I remember your promise that when I was older you would tell me why you came here. And now I think I am old enough."

She gave a low chuckle. "And so I will. But not tonight. Tonight I want to tell you about the things I've done with our sugar money."

"So the war affected the sugar trade?"

"It surely did — it tripled the demand! All those little courts in Europe give balls and ceremonies and coronations for one another, and all the dukes and princes compete for the biggest and sweetest desserts. Our York Stairs sugar went into ten-foot wedding cakes for two of Victoria's daughters. I declare, Dickens would have had some words to say about those cakes!"

"I saw the new fountain," I remarked. "And the new glasshouse."

"But you didn't see the little hospital in Bridgetown and the two native doctors Hugh sent to England to be trained. And you can't see my Moore grand-nephews being educated—although you will see the results, someday. Ravenel will take on York Stairs when he's grown. Sherman wrecked the Moore plantation in '64. There's nothing left of the big house but the stumps of columns that once held up a beautiful portico."

"Who is running York Stairs for you, Miss Adelaide?"

"I have a fine English manager. He married a native girl, so he can't go home. I built them a house near the mill. Then I remodeled Hugh's old office into a regular Charleston *garçonnière* for the Moore boys."

Now I suspected Miss Adelaide of deliberate obfuscation. She had clouded the water so her own story was lost. One day, I knew, Miss Adelaide would decide to tell me her story. Until then, I could wait, for time meant nothing here, only the long slow days, and the sun and the sea—the glorious unshadowed time of York Stairs.

I slept, worked every morning, swam, and napped. In the afternoon I played with Elena on the gallery or at Learner's Cove. Then I bathed and dressed in the evening and dined with Miss Adelaide; we talked endlessly under the stars—and then I slept again. After two or three weeks of this idyll, I could feel myself rebounding in body and spirit. I made headway on the article for the *Atlantic Monthly*, which was to be a history of the Froebel movement, the foundation, and our experiences. I took Elena to different beaches in the governess cart, driving Hercules, the placid pony. The poor thing was older than I was and almost slept as he trotted! I read Melville and Hugo, and Miss Adelaide taught me to play cribbage. Elena and Mira were now fast friends. Elena idolized the older girl, and Mira relished the attention of her small shadow. Mira was as kind and as gentle as Lettie; Elena was in good company.

I thought of Roger often, especially as I fell asleep. He had thick peaked eyebrows, inviting a caress. Once or twice I felt foolish... what was I *thinking*, to write such a bold letter? I wondered what the consequences would be. How I would miss his friendship if my letter had pushed him away with its frankness and its assumptions. But there was nothing I could do here. It had been sent.

One day I drove Elena into Bridgetown to see the fishing fleet and to buy some plain paper for drawing. We wandered around the port and talked to the ship captains. We returned to York Stairs tired and happy, just before the cloud-show hour.

As we climbed the staircase, I heard Miss Adelaide talking to a gentleman. A neighbor, probably. But there was no tethered horse. Then, at the top step, I clutched the balustrade.

"Miranda, here is Mr. Daniels from Chicago, who has come calling," announced Miss Adelaide at her most Charlestonian. "I have asked him to stay at York Stairs while you confer about foundation matters."

I stood, staring at both of them.

"And," Miss Adelaide went on, "he will help me with all the legal doings for Ravenel Moore's inheritance."

None of this was credible. How could this be? It was as if my brain would not take in what I was seeing in front of me. Finally, I forced myself to step forward.

"Roger." I took his hand, my throat tight. "How...when...did you get here?"

"I contacted your aunt Helen, and she wrote where I could find you. Then I took a mail packet from Norfolk—a very pleasant voyage."

"Let me show you to the *garçonnière*," said Miss Adelaide, the paradigm of a southern hostess, taking his arm and sweeping him away before I could speak again.

She had to pass my room to return to the main house. I waited for her on the path.

"Miss Adelaide, how long is he staying?"

"I'm sure I can't say. However long it takes to settle your affairs. But isn't that for you to determine?"

I saw her smiling.

"What has he said to you?" I asked.

She took my hand. Her expression was unfrivolous, adamantine.

"Miranda, he has come a long way. Let us make him welcome."

Before I came here, I had gone to Boston to stay several days with Cousin Ellen Lyall, and Madame Lauré made me a few evening dresses in muslin and linen, Empire style. Tonight I chose the cerulean muslin and added Roger's brooch. If Roger had come to let me down gently, away from Alan and Ethan and our foundation connections, then the least I could do was hold on to my pride and look my best.

Finally I was satisfied with my appearance and arrived at the terrace to find Elena and Roger deep in conversation. He smiled at me, obviously as delighted to see her as she was to see him. Then we all played the cloud game and had a lovely half hour before I excused myself to tuck Elena in. She was flushed and happy, and told me that Uncle Roger was now her "bestest." When I returned, Miss Adelaide was laughing at something Roger had told her, and she smilingly led us inside.

With a man's presence, our dinner was lively. Roger and Miss Adelaide steered carefully around the war. Instead we talked politics, and President Johnson's mistakes, and the history and evolution of the foundation. We were handsome and festive in the candlelight. I enjoyed seeing Roger through Miss Adelaide's admiring eyes.

After dinner, Miss Adelaide excused herself. "I have early morning business in town," she told us, and Roger and I moved to the gallery, where moonlight now slept on the broad expanse of sea beyond. I listened to the measured rush of the Atlantic unfurling its huge skirts upon the beach. Tonight, the sky was awash in stars, its phosphoric light illuminating and altering everything.

"Have you noticed how all the planets here are in new places?" I said at last.

"Yes, well no, no, I had not," Roger answered. "Miranda, that's not why I came here."

Suddenly I sensed he was nervous. This made me even more nervous than I already was.

"I came to talk about your letter." He looked at me, his eyes opaque. "It made me worried for you — such sadness. And I suppose I wanted to tell you how very much *your* friendship means to me. To talk more about that friendship."

This startled me; it was not at all what I had been expecting. "I — I didn't think..." I was stammering. "That — that there was anything else...to say."

"There is a great deal. And I have had to come all the way here, at no small inconvenience to others, to say it in person."

"If you mean to scold me —"

"Not at all, Miranda. You have had enough trouble of late. I want only to let you know that you are not alone, that you need not bear your sadness by yourself." He placed his hands firmly upon my shoulders. I imagined his intention was to calm me, but his touch had quite the opposite effect.

"You must think me very foolish," I murmured.

"Foolish? Good Lord, Miranda, to lose your Davy, Kate, and now your father in such a brief span of time is a blow that could have destroyed someone less resilient," he declared. "You are strong, but that does not mean that you need to shoulder such burdens alone. I may not agree with your conclusions—"

"What conclusions?" I asked. I could barely remember what I had written.

He released my shoulders and raked a hand through his thick hair. "Your belief that a career necessarily unfits you for marriage. There are many men who would cherish a wife who is as strong and ambitious and confident as you are. I have read about the 'New Woman' emerging from her experiences and responsibilities during the war. I have even met a few but none as lovely as you."

My throat tightened so that I could not speak.

But Roger was going on. I began to feel that he was circling around the main topic of his visit, but I was flushed and weak at the same time, and not, therefore, in any hurry.

"After seeing the countrywomen who came to Andersonville, who brought us their starving families' food, and who, against orders, walked through our filth to tend our dying and bury our dead—I knew women were the superior sex. No man could have done what they did," he said.

The breeze from the sea caught at my skirt and lifted my hair while I stared at him, emotions rushing through me.

"And as to your other conclusion, that no man would want—what was the phrase?—that no man would want *to have his posterity held ransom to his wife's fear,* your fear is not unreasonable, Miranda. But I hope you don't think every man will regard you as a brood mare! Not every man..."

He took my arm and walked me to the balustrade. "That sea is like beaten silver tonight. We might as well look at something beautiful while I tell you something ugly."

I waited. I felt my heart beating and gazed out at the sea as he instructed, readying myself.

"While I was at Andersonville, we prisoners were stacked like corn in a crib. Every kind of disease raged through the camp. I contracted adult male mumps, the most serious sort—everywhere a man can get it. When the war ended and I was discharged, I went to the hospital in Chicago to be tested. The doctors there told me that I could never be a father. My point is that not every man can expect or will expect children."

I put my hand on his, grieving for him. Now I understood why he wanted me to watch the water — it would have been too hard for him to face me as he described this most intimate of losses.

"The friendship and respect I have felt for you since our first meeting has ripened into affection of the deepest, most joyous sort. But Miranda, dear Miranda, you must understand. There can never be marriage between us, and any impropriety would risk a great deal — your work, your position, your daughter. The ostracism that would follow... I have thought about this... and little else..."

And then Roger stopped speaking, hesitated a moment — and drew me against him. We rocked back and forth, our arms, our bodies, becoming one. His touch released sensations that cascaded over me like rushing water. Finally, we moved apart, slowly, shakily.

Roger drew a deep breath. "Say nothing now," he said quietly. "We will think for a few days, and we will know what to do." Then he took me by the arm and guided me down the stairs in silence, bidding me a formal "good night" at the bottom. We separated, and he strode away firmly in the moonlight.

Dreamily, I made my way to my room, my mind swirling. Roger's revelations had entirely erased my reasons for ending our connection. Each of us came to our attitudes about women's careers and motherhood separately and painfully — but we had reached the same conclusions, and we were in total agreement. What reason would there be, therefore, to keep us apart?

There was more, of course. On this beautiful, pulsing island, perhaps especially on this island, I was remembering the Polynesian customs I had read about, the handsome young people enjoying each other without shame or deceit. Reading about the Polynesians had given me a clear image of lovemaking, of intercourse as an expression of affection, good spirits, and goodwill. Did Roger want this experience with me? I had the impression that a man's needs were more dominant and demanding than a woman's. Of course I had never discussed this with anyone — whom could I have asked? Even dear Kate and I had only skimmed the surface of these deep waters.

In bed I turned and tossed. My body would not reach its usual peace. It was not Roger alone who sought this experience. My restless aching called out for the man who had traveled all this way to find me.

I am an adult woman, I told myself, who would harm no one. But as I drew one conclusion, its opposite would appear, and my mind would spin again. It was nearly daybreak before I fell asleep.

The next morning at breakfast, Roger was, as always, the courteous guest, asking Miss Adelaide about Barbados and the York Stairs sugar operation. Conversation then turned to the day's itinerary.

"Since my college days I have had a secret passion, Miss Adelaide," Roger confessed. "And that passion is—wave riding! I used to visit a classmate on Cape Cod, and I learned to ride the waves there. I would love to take Miss Chase and teach her how. Where shall I do that?"

Miss Adelaide recommended starting at Horseshoe Beach and Galleon Bay, which I knew, and perhaps going on to Lantana Reach, where the rolling waves were better suited for the stronger swimmers. She also suggested that Elena might accompany her to the weekly flower market, which was to take place that morning in town and which would give her much joy. Elena was truly excited at this prospect, and Roger and I were free to go off in the governess cart, drawn by the torpid Hercules. Roger did not refer to last night, nor did I, but I felt the electricity between us. He talked around it; he was friendly and, for the moment, impersonal. He reminded me of his more reserved trustee self that I had met in New York!

At Horseshoe Beach the waves were distinct and safe; there was no ditch and no undertow, and we could wade out to beyond the breakers. Roger held me by the waist and pointed me to shore. At the right moment, he lifted me forward to join the breaking wave, and I was able to ride it to the beach on a surge of foam and a rush of exhilaration, thrilled to feel myself a part of the strong sea. I hurried back out to do it again. I remembered, suddenly, swimming with Davy in the Connecticut River and teasing him that he was Michelangelo's young *David*. This was different, for now I was with a full-grown man, not a boy, one with a long muscled back and Greek runner's legs. And I was now a woman, not a teenage girl.

I found myself prolonging the intervals of waiting for the right wave, and I asked Roger's help in placing my arms for each ride. By noon, when it was time to return to the plantation for lunch, I was tingling with awareness and eager for Roger's reaction to this intimate morning—but he would talk only about foundation business as we rode back to York Stairs.

In the afternoon I retired for a rest with Elena, delightfully tired and almost as sleepy as my little charge, who was relaxed and happy from her morning's expedition with Miss Adelaide. When once more I appeared upstairs, Roger was nowhere to be seen, and Miss Adelaide told me he had taken one of the horses and ridden to town.

"He had some business to take care of and letters to post," she informed me. And then, with a sideways look, she added, "You will see him tonight."

I blushed. Could she discern my feelings? But she was steadily arranging some bougainvillea in a silver tureen.

Once again I dressed for the evening carefully, wondering if my bronzed skin was to Roger's liking, wondering if my hair was arranged in a way he would find appealing, suddenly laughing out loud when I realized how girlish and silly such thoughts were. "He will have to see me as I am," I said firmly, but I was not sure I believed my own words.

The clouds were a towering bronze citadel, delighting us all.

"Do you see such sunsets from your house in Chicago?" I asked Roger.

"Yes, but there is no comparison with these 'cloud-capp'd towers,'" he replied. "I have only a fine winter view of the lake, where the city has placed miles of rocks to protect the shoreline." He shook his head. "Nothing else could be like this."

This was the civilized way we talked all through dinner—impersonal, polite. After dessert, when I was counting on a gallery tête-à-tête, Roger rose to excuse himself. I forced myself to hide my disappointment.

"Those waves have worn me out," he explained. "I'll go over our notes, Miss Adelaide, and then turn in." He smiled at her and then at me. "Miranda, I suspect you should get a good rest too, for tomorrow's wave riding."

Of course I didn't. The memory of his hands on my body—and the uncertainty of his thoughts or intentions—made sleep out of the question. What was I to think? How were we to be together? Perhaps he *didn't* intend anything, any more than this. When I found that the next two or three days followed the same exasperating pattern, I grew more and more uncertain. And began to feel irritated.

We had progressed to the larger waves at Galleon Bay, where we went each morning. There I floated, waiting in his arms in the lively luminous sea, watching for just the right wave to crest. When Roger lifted me forward, the wave and I became one irresistible headlong force, racing ashore. I did this over and over; I couldn't get enough of Roger holding me, pointing me, launching me—and then the bliss-ful roar and rush to shore.

"I was the same way with sledding," I told him when he suggested we take a break. "I always wanted one more ride."

Roger was careful not to burn in our tropical sun; he oiled himself and then asked me the favor of doing his back and shoulders. I loved the feel of his muscles sliding under my hands and the gleam of his brown skin. I wished I could oil his chest too and his legs that recalled the elegant athletes on the Olympic vases. He wore a sort of short knit overall, but it could not conceal his stunning classical physique. Sometimes I wondered if he requested this daily anointing to remind me of his masculinity.

Then in the evening at dinner and on the gallery afterward, we continued general conversation. On Roger's sixth night, Miss Adelaide excused herself early, and after dinner Roger and I talked about opera, recalling the performances we attended in New York. The cool breeze lifted my curls as I gazed up at the stars, remembering.

"Opera is wonderfully democratic," I commented. "Young and old, rich or poor—opera speaks to everyone."

"That's because it expresses universal feeling—better than words ever could."

"You're right. Often an aria said exactly what I felt about Davy or Kate—only in Italian. It spoke to me, and it spoke for me."

"Opera goes beyond words," Roger agreed. "Some feelings won't fit into words—like this one."

And finally, finally, he kissed me—gently, deeply. It was not a question, not a prelude. It was simply a statement.

Before this visit to Barbados, I had not kissed a man for seven years, and my response amazed me. I leaned to kiss him again—but Roger evaded me. Instead he stepped backward, smiling in the moonlight.

"Please think about that as you go to sleep, Miranda. We will talk tomorrow, in the waves."

And at last I did think, as I slowly and dreamily undressed in my room, that something wonderful was going to happen, that Roger and I would affirm our bond, a bond neither legal fiction nor social morality could pull asunder. Roger might not be free to marry, but he was free in another way—for a great love, and with me. I would wait and see what tomorrow, and the waves, would bring.

In the morning we headed for Lantana Reach. There the surf appeared taller than at Galleon Bay but still manageable—till we dove under the waves and swam out to beyond where they crested and broke. Then I saw the scale of the dark menacing shapes gathering and looming over us—and my breath failed me.

"Roger, you want me to ride the Alps!"

"You can do it. I'll watch for the right one," he promised, holding me in readiness. We let two monster waves sweep past. Then the third lifted us high over the beach, and he pushed my whole body onto the foaming crest.

"Go!" he shouted. And I felt the entire Atlantic under me, behind and around me. The wave owned and used me, tipping me along its crystal curve, booming in my ears, bearing me ashore wildly—then smoothly—then casually. I was laid tenderly on the wet sand, with a caress. All that violence died in a little frill, running sweetly over my extended arms.

I was lying there, weak and proud and incredulous, when Roger glided in on the next wave to stretch beside me.

"Oh, Roger—I never—never in all my life—" I breathed.

"I know." I heard his whisper, and as I rolled over to smile at him, I saw he was leaning over me, his eyes intent. And then, with a great rush, his face was buried in my hair, his hands were stroking my shoulders, my breasts, until we were entwined with each other, our bodies together in such a rush of passion that I felt my heart would stop. But it *was* beating, and before my body surged into another world, I heard myself whispering, "At last, at last..."

Like my decision to leave Springfield and Ethan, my choosing to become Roger's lover was not sudden at all. I had already gone over and over the reasons I might do so—and understood now the prescience in Miss Adelaide's toast the evening of my arrival here. As it did so many years ago, this place, York Stairs, would once more restart my future. And there was a reason more compelling than any of these: I could not do otherwise. I desired all of Roger's body with all of mine.

I bathed and dressed in my favorite evening dress: Madame Lauré's white linen, draped like one of Artemis's tunics. Before the cloud-show hour, I knocked at Miss Adelaide's door.

"Come in, dear child. How that gown does flatter your complexion!" She turned to a vase on her bedside table and handed me an exquisite rose, a deep rosy gold. "You are a 'Lady Caroline Paget' tonight. Don't you just love the English flower names?"

When I failed to answer, she looked at me closely.

"Is Mr. Daniels leaving, Miranda?"

"No, Miss Adelaide. I believe he would like to stay on at York Stairs a little longer."

"Then I will invite him to do so, tonight. He is surely charming company."

"Miss Adelaide, I wanted to thank you."

"There is no need to thank me for anything." She took my arm, smiling. "You are more than a guest here; York Stairs is your home."

At midnight, as Roger and I had previously arranged, I stepped from my bedroom out to the moonlit path, walking between the tall syringa bushes bowed with blossom, stirring in the sweet night wind. Roger came to meet me and led me down the cedar path to the beach, where he had laid a cotton mat by the silver water. He took me in his arms, saying my name over and over—otherwise we did not speak.

He was gentle yet forceful and insistent; his will and experience carried us along without hesitation. He slipped my dressing gown of satin cream from my body and tossed his trousers after it. We were naked in the moonlight. Slowly, he pulled me down onto the mat, where he began to stroke me gently—over and over, on and on, in parts that woke under his touch. I was faint with love, fresh with pleasure. His mouth sighed over mine, and then he moved his lips to my neck, to my breasts, and then I felt my blood throbbing everywhere, and I began to moan. I felt his sudden weight and his hard brown back over me. I caressed its muscled length in a way I had longed to do earlier on the beach. When at last he entered me, I knew again that this union was what I had wanted from the very first moment, on the day that we met.

Finally, we cooled, and Roger cradled my head in his arms while we lay for a time on the moonlit sand, half dreaming, half dozing, joined in body and in spirit. Then Roger spoke, his voice low.

"Darling Miranda, I promise there will be more for you soon. You'll feel just as I do — swept away by love."

"That is how I feel now, Roger," I murmured, but he was getting to his feet and pulling me up.

"You will see." His voice was gentle. "My love, I'm not going to keep you any longer. You will be very tired in the morning."

I kissed him tenderly. "And it will not matter." I sighed. "Something as wonderful as this could never make me tired."

We breakfasted as usual with Miss Adelaide and Elena, entirely at ease; then we rode to Lantana Reach again and dared what Roger called the "professional waves." We caught three or four, delighting in their height, their danger, their urgent power. We rested on the sand in a harmony of silence. There was much to be discussed, but right now we did better without words. He stroked my shoulders and my back, and I felt a deep sweetness stirring, the same as last night. And I had an inspiration.

"Tonight, could we just go down the path to Learner's Cove and swim there? The moon is almost full; I have always wanted to swim in the moonlight."

Roger smiled. "That is a perfect idea."

He came to my door at midnight, and we walked down the cedar path to the glittering water. Roger dropped his robe and went into the sea naked. After a shy moment, I shed my robe and followed him into the silver water, delightfully warmer than the night air as it caressed our bodies.

Though I was eager with desire, Roger was in no hurry. After spreading the straw mat, he uncorked some delicate French wine.

"This is Pouilly-Fuissé," he explained. "I found it in Bridgetown. When we make love, I want us to drink our own particular wine."

After a few sips of the crisp wine, he began to stroke me gently, his strong male hands tender but insistent, and slowly, more and more powerfully. I was faint with love, with pleasure, with longing — and then something happened that I had waited for all my life. There was a feeling of infinite sweetness, a tide, and as I called out, Roger entered me once again, and we rode it together.

"That was a bigger wave than at Lantana Beach," I murmured, and he laughed tenderly.

"Of course it was, my darling Miranda. That was the biggest wave of all."

I lay contentedly, drinking the lovely wine, and my head was on his shoulder as though it had always been meant to be there. Roger stroked my curls until we grew drowsy, and then, sighing with happiness, we turned quietly into each other, where we stayed until the sea and the dawn sky and the wet sand at the water's edge were all the same exquisite pale mauve. Then slowly, sleepily, we returned to our separate beds.

In the quick, fleeting succession of days and nights that followed, Roger and I reveled in a privacy that would have been impossible anywhere else. During the day, we frolicked with Elena, an almost family of three, building elaborate castles in the fine white sand or picking mangoes and coconuts to bring to the cook for the evening's supper. We took Elena for gentle surfing, where the waves provided us with many small contacts, each one a thrilling promise for midnight. And we often rested on the sand; our shortened nights were tiring! After dinner, on the gallery, when Miss Adelaide had retired, we made our plans.

"I go to New York every month on business," Roger reminded me. "I expect you will want to visit your foundation offices there often."

"I suspect I will," I said with a smile. "As often as possible!"

"With the renovations on the school complete, you will be able to stay in the little upstairs apartment. I can use the garden door and visit you there."

His face was very serious in the light from the evening torches. "I intend to do many other things with you in New York, Miranda, besides making love. Our official relationship is well known. It will permit us to appear together whenever we choose — to go to restaurants, theater, the opera, just as we did before we became lovers."

This sounded delicious, and I smiled. "It will be very enticing to have such a secret."

Roger stayed serious. "I am your trustee; I administer your foundation. We will meet openly but correctly and discreetly."

"The discretion will be the hardest part." I was still smiling.

Now Roger grinned. "It is only for when we're in public. In private you can be as indiscreet as... this." And here he pulled me onto his lap, nuzzling my neck.

If we have no choice but to love illicitly, I thought as Roger's mouth sent tingles along my tender skin, so we should, replenishing commitment to each other with every lush encounter we can steal.

The sad morning came when Roger kissed Miss Adelaide and Elena and me, and bade us good-bye. We continued to wave until his carriage disappeared at the far end of Cedar Avenue, and then we went, subdued, to our usual morning routines: Miss Adelaide to her housekeeping and her arrangements, Elena to her swimming and adventures with Mira, and I to my neglected desk. It was a long and lonely day.

Luckily I had much work that would help me to bear the time until I saw Roger again. And I loved this place, I reminded myself, which, with its great beauty, would keep me cheerful as well. So after our naps Elena and I swam and walked and worked with our shells, and in the evening, after the cloud show and dinner, Miss Adelaide and I took our wine and talked on the gallery. I would never know what she and Roger said to each other, but I discovered she was entirely informed about our particular circumstances.

"Until you are able to marry, you and Roger can't have a house or a social life together," she foresaw. "But you will have your love, and your important work, and your prospect of a shared lifetime. That's more than most lovers ever achieve."

And then, as I had always hoped she would, she told me why she and Dr. Hugh came to Barbados more than thirty years ago.

"Our father was a judge in Charleston," she began. "A well-to-do and decent man."

I settled down comfortably and gave her my full attention.

"Although we lived in town like most of the oldest families," she continued, "we had a beach house on one of the sea islands, a wonderful rambling cottage on Edisto. I spent fifteen summers there, swimming and crabbing and fishing, and, with all the other children, soaked in seawater the whole day long.

"During those years, my favorite companion was Louis Butler Peyton, who lived next door. I had other friends, of course, but Louis was three years older, and he was wonderful. He taught me about hooks and nets and boys' things—he taught me to surf, Miranda! We island children were inseparable, all those summers. We had a contentment, a belonging together. But it was Louis I idolized, and when he went north to college and I grew up—or seemed to—we became closer in a different way." She gave a rueful smile. "I recall even now how the young people courted, how our set dined and danced, and how in the summer we went back and forth between the various cottages across the islands—bearing in mind that those cottages were actually quite splendid. We'd be ferried home in the moonlight..." Now Miss Adelaide's voice turned almost wistful, and her features were soft.

"One night, at Louis's little sister's ball, I was wearing my ivory tulle and a camellia wreath. My complexion used to get very flushed from the waltzing...and I could feel Louis watching me; in fact, his eyes never left me. The very next morning he came to call. He told me that he loved me and that he had never loved anyone else. The little tanned tomboy I used to be, and the girl I had become, were his destiny, he said."

I was delighted with this accounting and drew up my knees in my chair, watching the moonlight play on Miss Adelaide's silver hair.

"So." She was still smiling. "In the spring of 1830, when I turned eighteen, I became Louis's wife. I left my family's home in Charleston and went to live on his father's great plantation out in the river country."

So there it was. There *had* been a Mr. Darcy, I thought, this simple fact confirming my childhood speculations. *But Miss Adelaide...married?* My eyes pleaded with hers to continue.

"Oh, Miranda." Miss Adelaide's eyes glowed as she spoke. "Our first months of married life, on the plantation, were wonderful. We were so much in love, we were so very happy. I spent my days in a nirvana, happy to be a wife, content to fill my hours with little pastimes, waiting for the evenings, when we could be alone."

I thought now of my own recent nights with Roger, and I nodded. Go on, go on, I was thinking. And she did.

"Like other young ladies of quality, I was raised to write in a fine hand, to sing and play the piano, to read with intelligence and discernment. But most naturally, to be a mother. When the babies didn't come right away, I felt I must somehow make up for this lack by being

an especially diligent planter's wife, especially since Louis was working long hours, so anxious, as his father's only son, to please that gentleman. Louis wanted to prove that he had the ability to manage the
family's holdings, which would someday be entirely in his charge, and
I was so proud of his efforts. You must understand that my only wish at
that time was to please Louis and his family.

"So I undertook to be instructed by Louis's mother, to learn plantation life and my duties in that society. At first I took to it; after all the
costume balls and the silly diversions of my youth, I had grown restless
and weary of that frivolous existence. But when I started to pay real attention to the household, I quickly discovered that Louis's mother was
a rather idle lady, given to collecting silver, fine furniture, and clothes,
and that her supervision of the household was quite nominal. There
was not a great deal for me to learn, as she had trained her servants
with an iron hand so they would be capable of running everything for
her. So I began to look farther afield."

Now Miss Adelaide's tone saddened. "I began to see things I hadn't
noticed before — and raised in town, as I had been, I had never really
witnessed the slavery of plantations firsthand until I came to Sycamore
Hill. Town versus country — the institutions were really markedly distinct. The plantation was like a small city, where the Peytons were committed to the large-scale production of long-staple cotton, requiring
human capital of more than one thousand oppressed men and women.
Very different, indeed, from the comfortable, well-treated housepeople
I knew in Charleston, so close to their families that they *were* family. I
heard after the war that many of those people chose to *stay* with their
families, as free people. They were then paid, of course."

But now Miss Adelaide's face tightened, and I saw that her hands
were moving in her lap. She drew in her breath.

"Well, Miranda, I was now a part of this plantation, so I took it upon
myself, with Louis's approval — and, I suspect, his guilt — to direct my
energy and sensibility to curating where I could our slaves' physical and
spiritual health: sitting up with the critically ill, sponsoring 'marriages'
between our men and women, making sure the meager provisions we
provided them were fairly distributed. And after a time, I could not help
but grasp the full extravagance of our crimes against these good people.

"I learned that my own maid and at least three other housemaids
were daughters of Louis's father, Reese Peyton, and this information

was related to me by my maid as a matter of pride. I was shocked, but it woke me to slowly noticing other things. Since we ladies—Louis's mother and sister and I—were not encouraged to venture near the farm areas—the barns, sheds, or fields—it was some time before I even met Charles Haile, the overseer, and far longer before I perceived his true character. That was on a day when he came to the 'office,' where I had gone by chance with a message for Louis from his father. I heard Haile tell Louis that he'd just finished flogging three men for feigning illness, and one was unconscious. There was satisfaction in his voice, but worse, I heard no protest from Louis. Later, when I confronted my husband, he told me in a tone I had not heard before that I must not involve myself in 'the affairs of the men,' that his father would not like it. He did have the grace to look away from me as he said this, embracing me and asking me not to worry.

"But I could not help worrying. Since Reese and his wife were frequently absent, looking after Reese's other properties and interests, Louis and the overseer were left in charge, and Mr. Haile was considerably more destitute of principle than the slaves. I cannot say whether or not in Reese's absence production suffered, but the slaves, in their mute misery, surely did. A wily and cruel man, Mr. Haile maintained order and discipline among that group with his long lash while invoking the creed that the lucky Peyton slaves were seldom sold away and that family situations were never broken up . . . for now.

"One of the slaves, Renty—who was the young daughter of Frank, the Peytons' chief driver, and his 'wife,' Betty, a clean and dignified woman who worked in the kitchen of the plantation house—had been given to me as a personal helper and maid. Her skin was markedly light and her features too Caucasian to be an accident, particularly with parents as dark as Betty and Frank. When I asked Louis about this one night, he simply shrugged and turned away. But all the Peyton slaves knew there was more to it—as I told you earlier, Renty eventually explained that Reese was her true father—and so did Louis.

"Renty and I were practically the same age, and I decided to have her help me put in my gardens. During this landscape work, we talked, and I came to respect and admire her, especially when she ever so quietly begged me to teach her to read. I found that I could not say no, even though I knew it was illegal for slaves to read and write. She learned quickly, and as a consequence of my secret interactions with Renty,

Betty and I too became good friends. She would come to me freely, without fear of reprisal and reprimand, and let me know what was really happening down in the quarters. In turn I would go to Louis to ask him for the medicines and blankets and modest comforts that might ameliorate the conditions or harsh authority those people lived under— to arrange for more rest or to intervene against Charles Haile's capricious bursts of aggression. I did this over and over and over again.

"Eventually, though, under his father's influence, if not Charles Haile's, Louis wearied of my supplications. He addressed me quite vigorously and in a tone I'd heard him take only with the servants. He ordered me to bring him no more complaints and to harden my heart to any human considerations I felt toward the family 'property.' My intercourse with them had been noticed, he said, and was thought dangerously suggestive.

"That night I did not close my eyes. As I watched Louis sleep, I wondered why it was that I had more moments of joy and satisfaction with Betty and Renty and Frank and their like than I did with my own husband's family. Perhaps it was because Louis and I had no children and seemed to have less and less to share, but I found more and more excuses to call Renty to my rooms. Our deepening affection accelerated, as did the reading lessons, the illegality of my actions be damned. 'Unrighteous laws were made to be broken,' I told her. That was when Renty made the ultimate gesture of trust. She drew me into her confidence, telling me what even Frank and Betty did not know: she was pledged to a young man on the plantation who was called Thom, and they intended to run off and make their way to freedom in the North.

"For days after, I shivered every time I thought of the risk— but when I met Thom, strong and magnificent and forceful about his intention to die first rather than face manhood as a slave, I was impressed. The reading lessons were, I learned, part of the couple's design to prepare themselves to one day earn their wages, just as the eggs and vegetables Thom bartered for extra clothing and heavy shoes were intended to help them survive the rigors of the flight ahead—one that neither had illusions would be easy.

"Hearing this, and weighing their faith against my loyalty to a system I had come to regard as detestable and monstrous, I offered to help. I went to my jewel box and removed sapphire ear clips and a matching diamond ring and bracelet set, wedding gifts from the Peytons and heirlooms I was someday expected to pass along to the wife of the son I was beginning to feel I would never bear Louis. It seemed entirely right to appropriate these objects, purchased by slavery's filthy lucre, for freedom's purpose. I was merely returning them to their source. Full circle. 'Sew the stones into the hems of your clothing,' I instructed, 'and use them to begin your new life. The system is corrupt, and so are the men who will hunt you down. If you need to, use the settings to negotiate for your lives.'"

I was riveted. I barely dared to breathe, so engrossed was I in this tale.

"On nights when the moonlight was cold and ghostly," Miss Adelaide said, "the only sounds perforating the long silence would be the occasional calls of whip-poor-wills and screech owls. That's how it was the night they returned with Renty. The Negro hunters used bloodhounds to track the fugitive pair through the swamps and forests, catching up with them less than three days after they'd set off. In the darkness and the unfamiliar brush, the two became separated. Or perhaps Renty gave herself up so that Thom could continue on. I never knew, because when they brought her back, they ripped the clothing off her body and lashed her until she passed out. And then they took hot irons to the girl's feet, searing her toes together so that she could never run... anywhere... ever again."

With this, Miss Adelaide's gray eyes closed. I reached for her hand, and as I did I noticed that the silver knot at the nape of her neck had unfastened. She was shaking, much as she must have done almost forty years and a lifetime ago.

"Renty never regained consciousness, and within days, Frank and Betty were sold away—separately—to remind the others that God's grace began and ended at Sycamore Hill. I think Frank was sent somewhere along the Mississippi Delta and Betty to a rice plantation farther down south. I tried to find out later exactly where, but my inquiries yielded no information.

"The little stones Renty carried were easily traced back to me. At first Louis's father believed they'd been stolen, but as I watched him calmly put those blistering irons to the feet of the girl he knew was his own daughter—branding her as one would an animal—my fury gave me away, and he realized what I had done. You see, more than breaking the law by helping Renty and Thom escape, I had committed the ultimate crime against my husband's family. I had given their heirlooms to a *slave*—and had therefore made an inexcusable statement:

that I valued her, mere chattel, over the family's proud name. This was the unforgivable sin, and so they asked me to leave.

"My parents had died by this time; Hugh was the head of the James family now. He was one of the pillars that held up Charleston society, but there was little he could say after Reese sent for him and Hugh listened to Reese's attack and his threats.

"'Don't even think of returning your sister to Charleston,' Reese said, 'or anyplace else where the Peyton name is known. I can have her arrested and jailed in a heartbeat, and don't think I won't do it.'

"So you see, we had to leave, there was no choice...I didn't care where we went, really, though I knew that following my married sister, Amelia Moore, to Richmond could ruin her as well, so that was not a possibility. Renty's death, Frank and Betty's shattered lives—I bore a large measure of blame. I was worn out and consumed with guilt, and I could only hope that Thom had made it and that my service in this regard had been of some use.

"Hugh gave up his medical practice, and everything else, and brought me to Barbados. His consumption, while real, was never our only reason for resettling. And, of course, we've never been back."

"And Louis Peyton?" I asked in a whisper, needing to know the final outcome for the entire cast of characters.

"I believe, I *know*, he spoke strongly to his father. But I had made an impossible situation for him and for our marriage. I could no longer live there. And he could not—I would not have wanted him to—leave. What would we have done? Where would we have gone? We would have been outcasts, pariahs in a society that could never accept us again. And I had hurt Louis beyond repair, giving away his gifts to a slave. No, I destroyed our marriage—and I deserved what I got."

I reached to take her delicate patrician's hand. "You made a better life in the end," I said, thinking of all the island people she had helped through the years at Dr. Hugh's clinic and by her simple humane acts of concern.

There was a long silence, peaceful, contemplative. After a time she spoke again.

"My Moore relatives learned that during the war, Sycamore Hill was heavily damaged and pillaged, the mills and gins and all the cotton burned and its human capital scattered to the wind. Perhaps this was Renty's revenge."

I stood, then sat beside her, putting my arms around her frail shoulders. We stayed like that for a long while, never speaking, the soft night breeze occasionally lifting a tendril of hair, bringing the sound of a barking dog, a scent of jasmine. I was spellbound—a story from the past, so vivid in the present. And yet, I sensed it was as if a load had finally lifted from Miss Adelaide's shoulders. Again, I took her hand in mine.

"It *wasn't* your fault, you know," I said, gazing directly into her eyes. "All you did was try to help in terrible times."

She said nothing, but I could see that at last she was relaxing. The terrible ordeal, the long-held-in story, now had gone, borne away on the softly scented night wind.

She nodded. "I never saw Louis again," she said finally. "I know he never remarried. I heard he rode with Beauregard for two years. Imagine, in his fifties! He was killed at Petersburg. So you see"—she turned to me with a smile—"I couldn't bear to see true love wasted—again. It is a rare thing. Precious. I only hope my efforts work better this time, for you and for Roger."

"They have, and they will," I promised her.

We rose and, arms around each other's waists, walked down the stairs toward our separate, contented dreams. I knew my time in Barbados was vanishing, as the frilled ripples of Learner's Cove sank into the creamy sand. But I was strong and energetic and hopeful; I could not even remember the lethargy that I had felt when I came here. I looked forward to Amherst, where Elena and I would have another spring—and to my work and my love, waiting. When it came time for us to leave this astonishing island, my heart would be full—full of the love and contentment and beauty I had found here and would continue to have as I returned to Amherst.

On the dock at Bridgetown, Elena worried till her shells and my panels were carried aboard, and Lettie kissed us both. Miss Adelaide and I embraced; we needed no words for our parting. I had already told her that I would write every week. Then Elena and I walked onto the ship and stood at the rail till Barbados was a faint violet shadow on the horizon. Two dolphins frolicked in our bow wave for a while; then they slipped back to rejoin their friends.

Book XII

AMHERST AND NEW YORK

1867

I had left Amherst in deep winter, the biting winds stinging my cheeks, my accumulated cares layering frost around my heart. I returned to late spring; Amherst and I had thawed together. Once again Barbados had healed me and ushered me into the next phase of my life.

All those years ago, when, as a child, I had grown strong upon that island, I had discovered a physical and active world, a world in which I was not dying. Once more, Barbados had awakened my body, this time enabling me to embrace my new life as Roger's lover.

Aunt Helen must have heard the horse's hooves as our carriage drove up to the house. She flung open the front door and ran toward us before the driver had even instructed the horses to stop.

"Grandmama Helen!" Elena cried beside me, waving furiously.

We clambered out of the carriage while Bridget and Sam organized the removal of our trunks. Aunt Helen swept us into an embrace; I buried myself in her flour-and-lemon scent, Elena squealing and snuggling with furious intensity.

Aunt Helen gazed at us appraisingly when she released us. "Look at your sun-kissed faces. You're positively aglow."

"My shells!" Elena cried as she spotted Sam carrying her precious cargo. Aunt Helen and I linked arms and chatted our way into the house.

I was arriving home at the end of May, a time of mud and promise in Amherst. Today the contrasts delighted me: the dark fecund earth, the delicate first blooms. Every flower, every dappled shadow edging across the lush grass lawn, seemed infused with renewed energy, made all the more intense in the vivid scarlet sunset. The colors, the scents, resonated in me like a struck gong. Was this how Kate had felt when she and Ethan began their lives together as lovers, their new physical knowledge of each other? Did her body feel suddenly, completely, alive?

By the time Aunt Helen and I had arrived in the house, Elena had already charged up the stairs to dictate the proper handling of her precious collection. Aunt Helen and I chuckled at her bossy little voice, giving orders.

"She certainly knows her own mind," Aunt Helen observed.

"Do you think she gets that from Kate?" I asked.

Aunt Helen smiled. "I think she gets that from all of us. Which makes her quite the formidable personality."

She gave my shoulders a squeeze. "The trip has done you such good," she said. "I can tell it."

"It was exactly what I needed" was all that I said. It was far too soon to mention Roger—too soon for Aunt Helen and too soon for me. Leaving Barbados was like being brought from one world to another without being able to distinguish readily which was real and which the dream.

During my months in Barbados, Aunt Helen had spent much of the time with Ethan in Springfield, visiting her grandchildren. I was happy to hear that Aunt Helen and Ethan's new wife, Ann, got on splendidly during this extended stay. I had wondered if it would be difficult to see her daughter's husband married to another woman. Now I was relieved to see that the delight she took in Kate's boys, and her obvious relief that her grandchildren were well cared for, counteracted any lingering discomfort.

Bridget had kept the house dust-free while we were gone and had collected the mail that arrived in our absence. I was astonished to see the stack that had accumulated. Aunt Helen saw my expression and gave me a rueful smile.

"I have not been able to bear facing it all," she confessed.

"I'm sure there is much that is my responsibility," I assured her, picking up the pile of letters, newspapers, circulars, and journals.

"My subscriptions!" Aunt Helen shook her head. "How will I ever get through them all?"

"Tomorrow," I said. "We'll do it together. But tonight, let us enjoy our reunion."

Aunt Helen smiled and gave me another quick hug. "How I've missed you. We have so much catching up to do!" She bustled off into the kitchen, where I could hear her humming and pots clanking.

Elena appeared at the top of the stairs. "Would you like to come help Bridget in the garden?" I asked her. She dashed down the stairs and took my hand. I grabbed a basket by the back door, and together we went outside to a scarlet sunset. We strolled to the kitchen garden, where Bridget was working, and we three tore loose the spinach and the dandelion greens for dinner. I pressed a clump of soft earth between my fingers. "We should be getting the seedlings planted," I murmured. "The ground is just right."

"Let me!" Elena cried. "I want to do it."

I had not realized I had spoken the words aloud, but the eagerness on Elena's face gave me an idea. "Would you like a garden of your own?"

Elena's eyes widened, and she nodded her head vigorously. "Yes, please!"

Dusk enveloped us as we returned to the house. Dinner was brief that first night; Elena nearly fell asleep before our main meal was finished and missed dessert entirely, and I was ready to do the same. By the time I carried Elena up to bed, Aunt Helen and Bridget had already cleared the table and started the washing up. I said a brief, sleepy good night and at last completed my homecoming by falling asleep in my own dear room.

The next morning, Aunt Helen, Elena, and I went to work creating Elena's private garden. We dug the rows, planted seeds, and transplanted some of the shoots Aunt Helen had started inside to their new home in the earth. Elena was particularly pleased with the small tomato plant we bequeathed her. When I left them to tackle some of my waiting chores, Elena and Aunt Helen were drawing a careful map of the new garden so that Elena could make identifying signs for each plant variety.

I carried the mail into the study and separated it. I placed Aunt Helen's pile on the small table by the armchair near the window, then sat down at the desk. Soon Aunt Helen came in, carrying a tray with a pitcher of fresh lemonade and a plateful of cookies.

"Mmmm," I murmured, biting into the rich shortbread. "Precisely right for facing all this mail." Returning my attention to the pile, I spotted a broad, familiar handwriting. Roger. My heart soared at the sight of my name on the envelope. If my own name, rendered by his hand, could trigger such a flush of sensual memory, could I risk reading the entire letter in Aunt Helen's presence? I glanced at her as she sat in her armchair, a newspaper turned to catch the afternoon light. She seemed quite engrossed. I opened Roger's letter.

Dear Miranda,

You will, by now, have returned to Amherst. I hope that your sojourn in Barbados has left you refreshed for the tasks that we have ahead of us in the next several months. . . .

It was a very proper, businesslike letter, filled with useful and encouraging news of the foundation's progress while I had been away. But there was nothing personal, no mention of our changed relationship. No word of love. From the evidence of Roger's letter, I might have dreamed our nights in Barbados.

"I don't know how I will ever get through all of these subscriptions," Aunt Helen muttered. She lay the newspaper down on the side table. "Well, it is no longer truly news if it was printed back in March, I suppose. Are any of those letters from Mr. Daniels?"

I hid my confusion. "Yes, this one is," I said.

"I thought he might have written you in Barbados," Aunt Helen said. "He was quite keen to learn of your whereabouts."

"Yes," I said absently, my attention returned to the letter.

"Miranda, is something amiss with the foundation?"

I forced myself to look up and smile. "Not at all, Aunt. Why should you think so?"

"You looked—stricken—for a moment, my dear."

"Everything is fine," I assured her, folding the creamy paper and slipping it into my pocket. "In fact, the remodeling of the new building is ahead of schedule, and we have had a large number of inquiries regarding enrollment here in Amherst."

"That is certainly nothing to frown at," she said comfortably. "I had been worried when he contacted me. Matters seemed quite urgent."

"It was a misunderstanding," I said, struggling to give my aunt an answer that would satisfy her without betraying my own confusion. "I had written Mr. Daniels a letter that he felt needed an immediate response, and when he found that I had gone, he was concerned that the matter might not be resolved in a timely fashion."

"So nothing is wrong now?" Aunt Helen looked at me.

I forced another smile. "Not at all. For a moment I think I was as overwhelmed as you by the sheer amount of mail—and the work it represents—that piled up while we were gone."

Aunt Helen put her newspaper aside with a grimace and picked up an issue of *Frank Leslie's Illustrated Newspaper* from her stack. "I can well believe it, my dear. And I'm glad that you and Mr. Daniels sorted out the problem. He is a very interesting man." She smiled and opened the magazine.

I took up another letter, opened it, and stared at it without seeing. What was I to make of Roger's letter? Was he merely being cautious lest my letters be read by someone else? Did he regret what had happened between us? The mere sight of his handwriting had called up memories that made my hands tremble as I opened his letter. Was it possible that our joining had meant less to him? I could not believe it. But we had, both of us, left the enchanted isle and returned to our workaday world. It would take some time for us to find a way to work together and to express our love. I must be patient. I must believe.

I returned my attention to the letter in my hand—an invitation to a lecture now several months past—and put it aside to answer later. The next letter was addressed in Emily's distinctive handwriting. Rifling through the stack, I found several others and pulled them out to read together.

The first letter was an invitation to visit on Monday afternoon. The request had gone unanswered for three months; I could imagine her petulance in hearing no reply. This was another contradiction Emily never recognized in herself. I'd seen her rage against the silence of others—while insisting upon silence for herself. She admonished others for "chatter" and "social insistence" while demanding they respond instantly to her irregular contact.

I was surprised, however, what with her gossiping sister living in her house, that Emily had not known immediately that I had gone to Barbados.

When I opened the second letter, it was clear that Lavinia had performed her duty and informed Emily of my itinerary.

Miranda,

 You have forsaken winter and taken crimson and violet with you. In Amherst the air is hushed—there are no birdcalls now. But though you have gone, I know you will return. I remain, as ever,

            Emily

Emily's acknowledgment of my trip made me all the more curious about the third letter, dated a month ago. She knew I was still away, yet she sent another message.

This one was a poem without a personal note.

> *The Definition of Beauty is*
> *That Definition is none—*
> *Of Heaven, easing Analysis,*
> *Since Heaven and He are one.*

"It is as if it doesn't matter whether I read these or not," I said, perplexed. "She's sending them for the sake of the sending, I think."

Aunt Helen sniffed. "You know my feelings about that woman. She is as strange as...well, I actually cannot think of anything to compare her to!"

I laughed. "You're quite right, Aunt Helen. Emily is incomparable."

Aunt Helen glanced at me. "Two hours is enough time to work on your first full day back," she stated. "Give yourself a chance to rest and recuperate from your journey."

"I think you're right," I told her. "Shall we come back to this later? The weather is too beautiful to stay indoors."

"Quite true." Aunt Helen stood and rubbed her hands together as if to warm them.

"Is your arthritis bothering you?" I asked.

"Nothing to fret about," she assured me.

With her lively manner it was easy to forget that Aunt Helen was growing older. After all, she was only a few years younger than Father. I vowed to help her more with the household duties to ease some of her burden.

I suggested we go for a walk, and we wrapped ourselves in woolen shawls: early spring in Amherst was not always warm, particularly compared to the weather I'd been enjoying in Barbados, but arm in arm, we toured our neighborhood, taking note of new plantings and tiny decorative changes around us.

"I see Adele Summers has repainted her porch trim," Aunt Helen pointed out.

"It goes nicely with the shutters," I agreed. "And I see her cat had another litter."

I took in deep, satisfied breaths. Although Amherst did not provide the exotic floral perfumes mixed with salted spray of Barbados, the scents of the New England spring were invigorating. We passed The Homestead on Main Street, and I automatically glanced at the upstairs window. I certainly am well trained, I thought, and then pushed the unworthy idea aside. "I really must go see Emily soon," I said, though I was oddly reluctant, contemplating the idea.

"If you must," Aunt Helen said. "But surely not today. Let us go back to the house. This cool spring air has made me hungry."

After lunch I peeked in on Elena, who was already fast asleep, surrounded by her shells. I carefully removed each one, worried she'd roll over onto them in her sleep. I placed them in rows on her desk, enjoying their faint, briny smell, their undeniable reality a testimony to our having actually been to the islands.

Then, although it was the middle of the day, I too lay down upon my bed, letting my thoughts drift, my body remember.

I slept through until the next morning. We had been at sea, on trains, in carriages, in many different climates and cultures, all as part of our return home. I knew Aunt Helen was right: it would take time for my body to adjust. Elena, however, seemed entirely reacclimated. When I came into the kitchen to discover that she was tucking into a large Amherst-style breakfast—griddle cakes, fried ham, coddled eggs—I knew she had made the transition and that all was well.

"Then we practiced swimming with the waves," Elena was explaining to Aunt Helen. "Miranda can float very well. But Roger was the best of all."

I clutched the high back of the wooden kitchen chair. The power of my grip made the chair legs scrape a bit on the floor. Elena looked up from her plate at the sound. "Will Roger visit us soon?" she asked. "I want to show him my room."

"Mr. Daniels, dear," Aunt Helen corrected. Her tone was wary. "And when do you expect to see Mr. Daniels again, Miranda?"

"I cannot say for certain. There will undoubtedly be foundation business for me to attend to in New York," I suggested, attempting to regain my composure. "It's only four months until the school opens there, after all."

"His business with you was more urgent than I surmised," Aunt Helen said coolly, "I am surprised that you did not mention his visit."

"I'm sorry," I said simply. "I was more tired than I knew yesterday." I could see that she was unsatisfied and that Roger's visit to the island required further explanation.

"There are some things more easily resolved in person," I continued. "As I said, we had misunderstood each other in our letters. Mr. Daniels was determined that we clear up the misunderstanding so that we could go forward. He was also quite a help to Miss Adelaide — he is now her representative on several matters regarding Dr. Hugh's property."

Reminded of my genteel and proper chaperone, Aunt Helen's frown of concern softened. "I am glad, then, that I helped him to reach you."

I sat down and joined Elena at breakfast, but I knew I would have to be careful of what I revealed about my relationship with Roger. If Aunt Helen were to learn what had actually occurred in Barbados, she almost certainly would not view the situation as I did. In the intoxicating air of Barbados, I had had no difficulty in putting aside thoughts of what might be considered impropriety. Returned to the bracing, Protestant air of Amherst, back to relatives and expectation and concern with appearances and social standing, I saw that I needed to be careful. Aunt Helen was not hidebound, but neither was she unconventional; in an argument about the absurd value placed upon virginity, we would almost certainly be on different sides. Those rules had receded into the background in lush and pliant Barbados; this short conversation had caused them to leap to the fore. But I was also determined to guard against the encroachment of rigid New England mores upon my newfound happiness.

After the first few days at home, I slipped easily into working for an hour or two in the morning while Elena tended to her new obsession, her garden. Afternoons, I made good on my private, personal promise to help Aunt Helen more with the domestic chores, despite my embarrassing lack of natural aptitude. I could tell she enjoyed my companionship and the passing on of womanly arts, and — as I intended — she didn't suspect that my increased interest was an effort to lighten her load.

I also began to organize my work schedule. June was fast approaching, and the New York school would open in early September. The major building renovations were complete, with only cosmetic choices left to be made. We needed to furnish the upstairs apartment, which had gone far beyond simple kitchen facilities in the final design. We would invite important educators and school administrators for conferences, to observe the school. As some of these visitors would be unchaperoned ladies, we must provide safe and respectable lodging.

I put my pencil down and allowed myself a bit of daydreaming, watching the soft cottony clouds drift across a pale blue sky outside the study window. Might those lodgings enable Roger and me to be together? I smiled. Whatever the distance between us now, I was certain that, face-to-face in New York, Roger's feeling for me would match my own for him. Would anyone question ordering a larger bed? I flushed at the thought. Then I admonished myself to concentrate and focused once again on the papers in front of me.

By the end of the week, I had separated my foundation tasks into two columns: New York City and Amherst. I was pleased to discover that this summer my duties in New York would require my presence in the city several times before the opening reception. Roger would also need to be there, and at that thought my blood quickened.

But for now I had Amherst calls to make. First on Sue Dickinson, for suggestions on our all-important guest list for the New York reception when the school opened. I would send her a note today; this was a task that she would enjoy. Mrs. Austin relished her role as intellectual and social matchmaker; it was a position that suited her well. Lolly had invited Elena and me to tea next week. Mary Crowell had sent an announcement of a lecture that she suggested we attend together. And there was Emily's request.

I frowned. Planning a visit with Emily felt more like a duty than a pleasure. I did not think I had felt quite so much this way before I had left for Barbados, but Emily's recent letters put me off in a way I couldn't quite articulate. I had already realized that there was an arrogance in her insistence upon communicating even if no one was there to receive the message. Now it was coming to me slowly that that was what Emily always did, in her notes, in her poetry.

I walked cross lots to The Homestead and rapped on the door, and was greeted by a surprised Vinnie.

"Oh, Miranda!" she gushed, "Emily will be so pleased to see you."

She gripped my hand and tugged me into the house. Startled by her aggressive enthusiasm, I stumbled a bit over the threshold.

"I must tell you," Lavinia confided, "Emily has missed you. She's had no company at all while you were away. Other than me, of course," she added.

I hid a smile. There was nothing unusual in Emily's seclusion, but perhaps in these winter months, without her garden or bird-watching, Emily had relied a bit too heavily on Lavinia for Lavinia's comfort. I suspected Vinnie was the one who was glad to see me back, to distract her demanding sister. I heard Emily's door open upstairs, then saw the slanting light illuminate the upper hallway. "Lavinia, I believe you are detaining my guest," Emily scolded.

I smiled. This was the Emily I knew well, who had been listening at her door since Vinnie brought me into the house.

"I'm welcoming our neighbor home," Vinnie replied. She made a little shooing gesture at me, waving me toward the stairs.

Emily hovered in the doorway, her pristine white dress looking crisp and cool.

"Why, you've gone as bronze as a Greek soldier's shield," she said as a greeting.

I laughed. "I was certainly not off to battle in Barbados."

"Of course you were," Emily countered. "Battling INERTIA. Battling sameness. Battling for your soul."

I was startled at the image. She was right on all counts. I had gone to Barbados as a way to wage a war against ennui. I battled my fears about Roger and then fought with the constraints placed on me by society.

"Then I need some laurel from your garden for my victor's crown," I said, settling into "my" red chair. "For I have surely won."

"But what of your friends?" Emily demanded. "For we were the sorry victims you abandoned to go to war."

I choked back a laugh. This too was an Emily I recognized. I remembered how she had taken the enlistment of her Mentor Thomas Higginson during the Civil War as a personal slight.

Emily sat at her desk and arranged her skirts in a peevish manner. "Now, Miranda, I must scold you. You never told me you were leaving. And to be gone so long! Think of how I felt!"

Her posturing irritated me. "Your brother must have told you the state I was in before I left," I said. "He was the one who suggested a trip away."

"Perhaps he said something to me, but I don't recall. We don't speak regularly, you remember." Then Emily's brows knit together. "And how is your delightful charge? It is ... *Elena?*"

"Splendid and thriving. With quite a personality of her own. She—"

But Emily was not interested. "Are the flowers in Barbados quite exotic? I remember that you learned your admirable flower-arranging skills from your Miss Adelaide on that mysterious island."

I barely knew whether to laugh or to scold: she remembered my flower arrangements but not my daughter's name!

"The flowers are lovely. And yes, you are right. Miss Adelaide taught me a great deal."

"And while she was teaching you domestic arts, did she never teach you to cook?" Emily teased.

When I had stayed as Emily's houseguest several years before, I had confessed my complete inadequacy in the kitchen.

"No." I smiled. "Aunt Helen has been my tutor in that art, but I will never achieve your artistry as a baker."

"It is by necessity that I take on such chores, though I am pleased that my efforts do not go unnoticed."

For all of Emily's rejection of "doily talk," this was our laciest conversation by far.

Emily sighed heavily. "We have had such a time finding the right girl," she complained. "The household falls heavily upon my shoulders."

"There is always so much to do," I agreed. "I don't know how I will ever manage it when I have a household of my own."

Emily stared at me. "You? Running a household?"

Her surprise insulted me. "Of course. Why should I not?"

"You're so young," she protested. "And independent. I can't imagine you married. I always assumed you had come to the same conclusion I have made regarding marriage."

"Why would you think that?" I bristled.

"Why? Because it is sensible. Perhaps even more for you than for me. You have ambition. You travel. You want to see the world, be influential. How could any man accept that?" She thought for a moment. "I, on the other hand, could be a wife, to the right man," she said almost smugly. "I would always be at home. And if he would leave me be, then I could write as much as I wanted to. But there are other reasons I could not marry. Men expect ... children."

I was not sure if that was what she had meant to say, but I did not want to pursue it. Perhaps touching on such a personal matter unsettled Emily, for she quickly changed the subject.

"How did you spend your time on your island paradise?" she asked.

"Enjoying myself," I answered.

"How did you accomplish that?"

I thought. I would not discuss Roger with Emily, certainly. What had I taken pleasure in before his arrival?

"I was able to see the natural world around me," I said. "I could take the time to really pay attention."

"Ahh, then your journey was worthwhile." Emily nodded her approval. "So few people really NOTICE things. But we do. We're alike in that."

This comparison to Emily did not rankle. Her capacity for intense observation was a quality I admired. Having arrived at a more harmonious moment, we settled down to a happy discussion of the books she had read in my absence.

But once I had left her close and suffocating room, I felt unsettled. There was a neediness in Emily that I had not seen before. She always demanded attention—her very manner compelled it—but this was different. She had never wanted *my* attention in particular before. I had always felt like a captive audience in Emily's personal drama rather than a real person. Yet it seemed to be my specific presence she had missed—why else make her laughable attempt to ask after Elena, except to enter into what was important to me, if only for a moment? Perhaps for the first time she had admitted my importance to her. It was how friends were meant to feel about each other. Then why did it bother me so much?

Is she a friend? That had always been the question. I had never been sure what our relationship really was, and if it was not friendship, then what might it actually be?

The next day as I sat at my desk, Aunt Helen came in, bearing a tray holding iced tea and ginger biscuits. "I thought you might be feeling a bit parched by now." She sat down in the side chair beside the desk. I thanked her and took a sip of the cool amber liquid.

"Is there an understanding between you and Mr. Daniels that perhaps I should know about?" she asked, coming straight to the point.

I should not have been surprised, but how could I answer? I would not lie—I would not claim that he was an unmarried man and a suitable prospect. But I could not tell the complete truth—particularly now, when the feelings and intentions that had seemed so plain on Barbados were still muddled and unclear.

"Mr. Daniels is not free to marry," I said. I sipped my tea and avoided looking at my aunt. "He has a wife, and she is an invalid. He does not speak of it because he does not wish to be looked upon with pity, although he is quite deserving of our sympathy. As is his poor wife."

I gave Aunt Helen a brief outline of Roger's situation. "Mr. Daniels has always treated me with respect," I added. "I cannot deny there is a— a sympathy between us, and he told me of his history so that I would have no misunderstanding of our circumstances."

"Oh, my dear!" Aunt Helen cried. "I don't want you pining away for him."

So my attraction and my confusion in the time since I had returned from Barbados had been that obvious. "Do I seem to be the pining sort?" I teased.

She would not be diverted. Aunt Helen laid her hand on mine. "My dear, you have had so much disappointment. First losing Davy, and now, if Mr. Daniels is someone with whom you had hoped..."

"Dear Aunt Helen, I value Mr. Daniels for his enthusiasm and his knowledge; the foundation benefits greatly because he and I work together." It was not an answer, precisely, but it was the truth. My direct honesty must have reassured her—she knew the truth when she heard it.

"I am glad. And much relieved, though it is a shame! Poor Mr. Daniels."

"And his poor wife," I added, meaning it.

Aunt Helen left my room, and I tried to return to my work. I had written to Roger a few days before to explain that I would not be able to make the trip to New York until July, a full two months since we had parted. The delay was unavoidable: there was too much to be attended to in Amherst before I could comfortably leave. And settling in until July would do Elena good; she needed to become reacquainted with her Amherst routine before my leaving disrupted it. I had written, I think, with the hope that his disappointment at the delay would evoke from him a fuller, more passionate expression of feelings than did the two letters I had received from him since my return, both of which had been short and formal. It was too early to expect a response yet, but I was certain that his heart was as hungry as mine for contact.

Then I laughed, thinking back to my afternoon with Emily. I had not told her I meant to leave again so soon, and thus I could not please her with news that I was postponing my departure!

I received Roger's letter a week later.

Dear Miranda,

I entirely understand the necessity of delaying your trip to New York. You have work to do and so do I. My trip to Barbados, undertaken on short notice, left me with a good deal of unfinished business for the foundation and for other concerns. The delay will permit me to neatly tie up these loose ends and devote myself entirely to the business of the school.

I hope Elena and your aunt are well.

I remain, yours

What was I to make of this? Roger expressed neither disappointment nor hope. Only the brief subscription at the end, "I remain, yours," gave any hint of feeling. Was he mine in any sense other than that of the formal letter writer? I sat at my desk, the afternoon light streaming onto the page. The words blurred with unshed tears; I was confused, angry, hurt, afraid. I was unsure which of these feelings was the proper one — mine was not a situation in which a well-bred, well-educated young woman expected to find herself, and to whom could I turn for advice? Was it simply that the magic of our love on the island had been just that — fantasy, dispelled by our return to the real world? Had we really imagined we would be able to carry on this relationship? Roger was married, and I had chosen to become his lover. By Amherst standards, by the standards of the society in which I had been born and raised, this was scandal. It was wrong.

But it did not feel wrong. Wrongness was far removed from my actual experience with Roger and the true nature of our relationship. I had no interest in marriage per se: I would like to share my life with Roger and have my union accepted by the people I loved, but as I had no desire to give birth to a child, I felt no hurry. Elena was all I needed, and I could mother her without a husband. But what would the people I loved—Aunt Helen and Elena, and Ethan and his family—think of my relationship with Roger? I might feel that I should be free to do what I liked with my own body, but the matter was not that simple. If Aunt Helen could hear these ideas, she would likely lock me up and throw away the key! And Ethan! He would remove Elena from my custody before my depravity could damage his daughter's moral growth.

Loving Roger might not feel wrong, but it was dangerous. Perhaps, I thought, this was why his letters were so passionless, so guarded.

But I so needed to confide in someone. At this moment I missed Kate sorely. There was so much we would be able to share now that I had shared Roger's bed—the delicate feelings Roger inspired, the wonder of the union. Kate might have been scandalized by the circumstances of my love for Roger, but I could not believe my cousin would have shut me out entirely.

But there was someone I *could* confide in: Miss Adelaide. So I poured out all my concerns, my radical ideas, my fears, in a lengthy six-page letter. It felt good to express these ideas even though I knew that, by the time I received a reply, my New York trip and its accompanying anxieties would be behind me. I understood a bit about Emily's need to write, even if the recipient would be unable to respond to the immediate concerns of the letter writer. Perhaps I had judged Emily too harshly.

I left for New York on July 6. Roger had informed Alan Harnett that he would be happy to collect me from the train station himself. Roger had taken rooms in a genteel boardinghouse midway between Washington Square and the Harnetts' home on Rutherford Street. The location was convenient for meetings, but I found myself hoping that Roger would be spending his nights with me.

As I reached the end of the train ride, I leaned against the high back of the seat and shut my eyes. I was grateful that I had had a train compartment to myself for the last few station stops, as I wasn't sure I would have been able to carry on the superficial banter of strangers thrown together in such circumstances. I had been anticipating this moment for so long; it was hard to believe it had arrived. I pictured Roger on the platform, tall and dashing, his hands clasped before him, as I'd seen him stand countless times. What was he feeling? Was he as excited as I? As nervous? It was such a startling combination of emotions that I felt nearly breathless.

With a great screeching of brakes, the train came to a stop. I tugged the curls at the nape of my neck and my temples, arranging them in the soft tendrils that Roger had loved to stroke. I stood, smoothed the creases from my blue traveling suit, and adjusted my hat. I took a deep breath and alighted from the train compartment.

The platform was crowded—men and women disembarking, people calling to servants for their luggage, porters darting in and out of the milling travelers. I spoke quickly to the porter, indicating my large leather valise, and he set it beside me.

"Do you need a carriage, Miss?" the porter asked.

I scanned the crowd, wondering where Roger was. "No," I replied, a little uncertainly. "I am to be met."

The man tipped his cap, nodded, and vanished into the crowd.

I turned and stared back along the track. Was Roger waiting at the other end? It would be easy to miss him amid the throng. As people boarded the train and travelers met their parties and left the station, the platform cleared. The train let out a whooping hoot, and then slowly, loudly, in a gush of steam, it pulled out of the station.

My heart sank.

Could Roger have misunderstood the time? Or worse—had he decided that this meeting was a mistake, that our time at York Stairs was a mistake? The cool formality of his letters since Barbados had prepared me to half believe such a thing was possible. With Roger returned to everyday Chicago, had my willingness to enter into an unsanctioned relationship appeared to him in a different light? Had his opinion of me changed?

I shook my head. Whatever I knew of Roger, he was not a coward. Even if he had second thoughts, even if he believed we should forget what we had been to each other and return to a formal, collegial relationship, Roger would not announce it to me by leaving me standing at the train station. I folded my hands and prepared to wait all night if necessary.

"Miss Chase!"

It was Roger's dear voice.

I turned to see him striding toward me. I wanted to run to him and be enfolded in his arms, to smell his scent and learn the lines of his face anew, but something, his expression or the formal way he carried himself, held me back. He extended his hand and shook mine.

"A thousand apologies, Miss Chase. The carriage that lost its wheel and tied up traffic did not realize I had an appointment with a very important visiting dignitary." In one movement he had pulled my arm through his, taken up my portmanteau, and turned me toward the waiting carriage. "Now, let us get you out of here."

Bewildered, I let Roger hand me up into the carriage and give the driver his instructions. Then Roger himself climbed into the carriage and closed the door.

He took the seat across from mine and looked at me for a moment, as if to memorize me.

"You are still lovely. Amherst agrees with you," he said lightly.

How should I respond? I longed to reach across and touch him, to kiss him, to know he felt as much as I did. Instead I smiled tightly, waiting to be guided by his behavior.

"Miranda, sweet Miranda." Roger looked away from me, out the window. "I know we said—in Barbados we said many things, believed many things would be possible. And perhaps in time they will. But for now, for this visit, I think we must be—"

"Colleagues?" I asked. There was a cold, empty space in me.

He looked back at me and smiled. "Always that. But...discreet. Working as closely as we must, surrounded by so many other people, any behavior which might hint that we are, have been, other than just colleagues, would be dangerous."

"Dangerous."

"To the foundation. To our work. Your work. Even our friends would likely misunderstand—" He stopped and cleared his throat. "I meant every word that I said to you, every gesture, every touch we exchanged in Barbados. It was not until I returned to Chicago that I faced up to how our feelings jeopardize the foundation. For your sake, and for Davy's, and for the sake of the many children I hope that our schools will help, I hope you can be patient with me, and believe that, while once we leave this carriage I will assume the manner of a friend and coworker, my feelings are as much engaged as ever."

I pursed my lips to keep tears at bay. "Of course you are right," I said after a moment. Had I not had the same fears myself? But it was such a cold welcome, so different from the warmth I had dreamed of.

Outside the carriage, the streets streamed by in a ribbon of color and activity.

"It will be wonderful to see Alan again," I said at last. "His letters are full of excitement." As I said it I pictured my former tutor's boyish face, beaming with pride.

"He has worked very hard," Roger agreed.

I reached out to take Roger's hand, then thought better of it. "We all have. And there is much more to do."

Roger took my hand in his and twined his fingers with mine. "We shall be very much together in the next few days," he said. He raised my hand to his lips, touched it gently there. For a moment the light in his eyes was all that it had ever been, a bright flame that made my heart flutter. Then he released my hand. "And we are almost there." It was as if a shutter had slid into place, hiding the passion I had briefly seen in him.

The carriage turned onto Washington Square and halted at the front door of the school. For a moment, before Alan stepped forward to hand me down, I took a long glorious look at our new building and felt a flood of joy that crowded out all my other confusion and hurt. We were about to see a dream come true.

"Thank you for meeting the train," Alan was saying to Roger. "So many last-minute details to see to, I fear I would have been late."

"Punctuality seems to have been a problem today," I murmured.

"Well, we are all here now," Roger answered and stepped back so that I could be first into the building.

I was at once struck by the light—warm, sunny, and inviting. In front of me was the central staircase, with a brightly painted railing. To one side was a large classroom. "There are still a few decisions to make about fabrics and paint, as well as some finishing of the woodwork," Alan said. "But most of the structural changes have been completed. Here we took down one of the walls." He pointed. "So we can accommodate more activities in a single room. This classroom will be for the littlest children."

An upright piano stood in one corner; our low tables and chairs were in the center. Brightly painted cubbies and trunks stored the class materials.

"I love the whitewashed floors," I said.

Alan ushered us through the back door. A high wall separated the garden from neighboring plots, and an ornate iron gate opened into the alley.

Roger pulled a set of keys from his pocket, selected one, and opened the iron door. "You see," he said, "it's quite a wide doorway, to make deliveries easier."

"I see," I agreed. For a moment I imagined a scene: the garden silvered in moonlight, Roger at the gate, me in a silken wrapper, waiting. My eyes slid shut; I could feel his touch, his kisses, the humid air sliding across our skin as it had in Barbados.

"...still several small wrought iron benches to be placed around the garden," Alan was saying.

I turned back to him. "How wonderful it is." I smiled and stepped forward to put my arm through Alan's.

We went back through the gardening pantry, as Alan called it, and went up to the second floor to two smaller classrooms for the older children, who would have an easier time climbing the stairs. For that age group, we felt the class size should be even smaller, as they would be beginning to develop their reading skills and would benefit from more individualized attention. There was also a music room with another piano, with space enough to exercise and dance.

The third floor held a reception room for parents and guests, an administrative office, and a more traditionally designed classroom for adults. Here we would train future teachers. And here Elliot Peck's beautiful stained glass windows were perfect in their setting, making full use of the unobstructed sunlight.

Finally we climbed the stairs to the fourth-floor apartment. Stepping over the threshold, I exclaimed with delight. The walls were a pale yellow with white trim, and the curtains and bedding were a deep, rich sea green. A large oak wardrobe stood in one corner, and a vanity with a mirror and covered stool sat in the other. Delicate wrought iron carvings covered the bed, with small tables on either side. Looking up, I discovered to my delight that the tin ceiling had been embossed with shell designs. I smiled at Alan.

"I never forgot your shell collection," he said. "And how much you loved it."

"Elena continues the tradition," I told him. "It is perfect. I feel completely at home."

Roger put my portmanteau beside the vanity table. "We will leave you here so that you can rest and dress for dinner."

"Fanny and I will call for you at seven," Alan said. "We have a reservation at Delmonico's. And before I forget"—he fumbled in his pockets and pulled out a set of keys—"these are for you." He bowed as he handed them to me.

I took them with an equal feeling of ceremony. After a moment I walked the two gallant men back downstairs.

"I'm so glad that you are here," Alan said warmly at the door.

"So am I," I told him. I kissed his cheek, acknowledged Roger's bow, and closed the door on their retreating forms.

Upstairs in my room, I noticed that a bouquet of deep gold roses sat upon the vanity. The note attached said only "Congratulations" in Roger's familiar hand. But they were Lady Caroline Paget roses. No one but Roger and I would know the significance of his choice. I felt oddly warmed and encouraged by the gesture, despite his words in the carriage.

I had been concerned that talk of the foundation would bore Alan's wife, Fanny, but in our excitement we spoke of very little else. However, Fanny clearly felt almost as involved as we were and, far from being bored, entered into the discussion with passion.

"Alan uses me to try his ideas; how could I not form some of my own?" she said. And as a mother of small children, she offered her own opinions about child rearing and education from a very knowledgeable position.

"You should consider training mothers, not just professionals," she suggested, dipping her spoon into the creamy mushroom bisque. "There are many mothers who would welcome guidance. Not a day goes by that I do not worry that I am not providing all that I can and should for my children's development."

Alan laid his hand over hers. "You are a wonderful mother," he protested.

Fanny colored with pleasure at the compliment but shook her head. "Do you see my point, though? If I, a paragon of motherhood," she said while she gave Alan a teasing look, "feel uncertain, think of all the others. Even the best mothers need reassurance. And so many would benefit from guidance and tuition to better prepare them for this important role."

"Fanny is right," I said. "I'm sure there must be some way to include concerned mothers more directly in our program."

The duck arrived, along with the *pommes Anna* and creamed spinach. As the waiters served, Alan sat up straight in his chair and laughed. "Do you know what we have forgotten?" he said, almost incredulously.

"What?" Roger asked.

"We are preparing to open one school and expand another. With all this talk of training mothers, we have forgotten one very important step: training more teachers."

"But that has always been part of the plan," I protested. "We built a classroom for the purpose in Washington Square."

"Yes," Alan conceded. "But that will not get under way for some time. There is still too much to do in establishing the model classroom. If we are as successful as we hope to be, we will need to train the teachers sooner."

"Alan is right," Roger said, buttering a roll. "We must be able to place skilled people the moment there is demand."

Alan nodded over a forkful of duck. "That must be your next task, Miranda. Polly Randall can take over your kindergarten section so that you can concentrate on teacher training. This very fall."

"Do you think so?" I asked. "I would have to work out a curriculum and find pupils in a very short amount of time."

"You can do it," Alan assured me.

I looked across to Roger. He nodded. "I agree. You can do it, and you must."

Fanny smiled at me. "I shall add my vote as well. You may find you need teachers in a year's time. You do not want to turn students away because there is no one to teach them!"

So it was determined, and yet another facet of our foundation would begin to be shaped and polished.

After dinner Roger accompanied us to Washington Square, where he bade me a chaste good night. Fanny and I kissed each other's cheeks, and Alan took my two hands in his own. "Now that you are here, it truly feels that we are under way."

"We are," I promised him.

I unlocked the door, and Alan and I stepped inside. He lit the lamp just inside the entrance and then the lanterns that sat on the front table. "I will see you to the apartment," he insisted.

Together we climbed the four flights, our lanterns casting dancing shadows on the walls. We reached the apartment, and Alan opened the door for me, holding up his lantern to illuminate the room. Here the shadows were soft and velvety, as if the room were cloaked in velvet. I crossed to the vanity and lit the lamp there, and Alan turned on the gas in the wall sconces.

"I will leave you to your rest," he said. "I can show myself out. After all the renovation work I oversaw, I think I could easily find my way out in the dark."

"I am sure you could," I agreed, smiling. "But humor your pupil and use the lantern to go back down those stairs."

"Good night, Miranda," he said.

I heard his footsteps echoing through the dark and quiet building, and then the door closing. I was alone.

The night was hot and humid. New York City did not offer the refreshing breezes of Barbados or the cooler temperatures of Amherst. Siobhan, the hired girl who would help maintain the school, had provided me with a pitcher of water and towels. I dipped the edge of the towel in the water and dabbed at my temples, my forehead, the back of my neck. I felt curiously alert despite the heat, the hour, and the long day of travel.

I had imagined, I had hoped, that at this moment I would be preparing for Roger's arrival. I looked around the beautiful room, imagining Roger there with me, his hands, his lips, the elegant and inviting bed. The thought made my body restless; I ached for him, but Roger was not here. If he had never come to Barbados, if we had not become lovers, what would I be feeling at this moment? Pride at what we had accomplished so far and the need to do more, much more.

I undid my buttons and stays, stepped out of my dress, and slipped on a light cotton wrapper. The apartment was hot and filled with my imaginings of Roger and myself. The garden would be cooler, I thought. Taking up the lantern again, I went back downstairs. As I stepped into the garden, I was enveloped in the delicate scent of roses. There was a breeze almost as soft as in the Barbados nights. I sat on one of the benches and made myself consider how I would go about recruiting teachers. I might have sat for an hour, perhaps more, making lists in my mind, things to tell Alan, questions for Roger. The more I thought, the further I was able to push my disappointment at Roger's subdued greeting. My work was, for this moment at least, truly the most important thing.

At last I went upstairs. The apartment was empty of ghosts, and I slept well.

If I wished for work, the rest of my visit to New York supplied it in plenty. There were so many details and decisions involved in opening a school. Alan and I made sure we had enough copies of our Leo books for the enrolled students. We made final decisions about the decor and went over the curriculum. Roger was in and out of the school, discussing foundation business and funding. Each time I saw him, I felt a momentary shock; if my mind had accepted that, for now, he was only a colleague and a friend, my heart and my body pined for the lover. And there were moments when I thought he felt the same way, but he said nothing. There were documents to sign, letters to write, a future to build for the foundation.

When Roger saw me off at the station, I felt again that flutter of anxiety, an unspoken question: "And now?" Roger did not answer my anxieties directly.

"Have a good trip, Miranda," he said formally and bowed over my hand.

I thanked him and was about to withdraw my hand, but he raised it to his lips in a brief kiss. In that instant I thought I saw naked longing in his expression, and when he looked up, I was sure. But he stepped back quickly and the moment passed. I thanked him for his good wishes and his continued help, and boarded the train. It was just as well that I had the compartment to myself for several stops. We had proved we could act as colleagues for the good of the foundation and our work, but for how long? We would see each other the following month, and again in September for the opening. Who could say what would happen? I refused to think further into the year than that.

The moment I alighted from the carriage in Amherst, Elena proudly showed me the berries she had collected from her very own bush.

"They're for my pies," she declared. "Grandmama Helen and Bridget are showing me how to make them."

"She is a very good student," Aunt Helen said. She gave me a wink. "Not like *all* my charges."

Later on, as we waited for the pies to bake, we went outside to escape the oven's heat. Elena was nearly bursting with anticipation and needed to be distracted to keep her from returning to open the oven door to check on the pastries' progress, so I described the new school building and all the work there was yet to do.

"Was Mr. Daniels there?" Aunt Helen asked.

"Oh, yes," I told her casually. "He heartily approves of all our new proposals. He says that the endowment is thriving, and if enrollments continue at the current pace, the Amherst school will be self-sufficient quite soon. New York will take longer, but it is a far more ambitious project."

I could tell from her manner that Aunt Helen was reassured that there was nothing inappropriate in my relationship with Roger. And for the moment and by her standards, there *was* nothing inappropriate.

Miss Adelaide's reply to the letter I had sent before my trip was waiting for me, filled with her warm common sense.

There is a bond between you and Roger that is palpable. It goes far past mere attraction and is built upon mutual respect. You and I know all too well that the rules society dictates or deems appropriate may not be right at all. In my younger life I tried to abide by my society's code, and you know the tremendous cost. But I believe you have too much sense not to understand that flouting those codes may also have a bitter cost. Somewhere between one extreme and the other, your path lies, and while it will be a hard path to find, I believe it will in the end lead you to great happiness and accomplishment. I agree that you should not burden your dear aunt with information that would make her feel compromised; I am glad that you confided in me. Know that you always may and that I will support the choices you make with your heart with all of my own. They can bring only good.

How I treasured Miss Adelaide. My letter had been written when I hoped for a reunion with Roger that was quite different from what had occurred. But her letter seemed to me to honor his caution and my choice at the same time. Reading it, I felt more hopeful of Roger's feelings. Rereading the letter, I realized that, despite my own mother's absence, I was privileged to have two mother figures in my life. Aunt Helen and Miss Adelaide were different in upbringing and experience, but each provided comfort and guidance. Aunt Helen had had a more conventional life; Miss Adelaide had taken an action that had changed the course of her life in surprising ways. Each followed her conscience. Each was able to see beyond her own experience to another's point of view. Each lived in the world and contributed to it. I hoped I could emulate both.

Then, ironically, someone quite different from either of those fully engaged women demanded my attention.

"Emily sent over two notes," Aunt Helen informed me. "I told the hired man who delivered the first note that you were in New York and would not be back for at least another week. She wrote you a second letter anyway."

I took the two letters from my aunt. The first requested a visit; the second complained that I had gone again so soon. She had referred to me as a bird, and I was not sure if I was being scolded for being "flighty" or superficial with my comings and goings, or if she was suggesting that I was practicing leaving the nest until I would return no more.

The letters troubled me. It was not what was actually said but rather that she was saying so much! The second letter was particularly troubling because she seemed to be becoming more blatantly resentful of my expanding world. But speculating about Emily's intentions and moods was often a useless enterprise. Instead, I sent her a note suggesting we see each other the following Monday. I received a return card simply saying, "Till then."

"Miranda, at last! I thought you had forgotten the way," Emily greeted me when I arrived. We embraced lightly, and although she laughed, I sensed an edge to her teasing complaint.

I untied my sun hat and laid it on the front hall table. I ran my hand through my hair; the day was warm and the humidity was making my curls rather unruly. "It has been a busy time."

"Of course," she said. "You have been ACCOMPLISHING."

I ignored the mild censure in her voice and turned to a subject she would appreciate: herself.

"And you, Emily? How have you been spending your time?"

"As I always do. WRESTLING for dominion."

We had climbed the stairs to her room. I was not sure if she meant literal struggles — perhaps fighting against the demands of the household and her family — or if she meant struggling with her work. But I was glad to hear her strong language; Emily used weaker imagery in conversation only when she herself was suffering.

"I would guess you were the victor," I told her.

"That remains to be seen," she replied.

"How is the work?" I asked. "I have not seen any of your latest poetry."

Here she colored and went silent.

"There is only dross," she said finally. Then she cleared her throat. "Dross and EMBRYOS," she corrected herself, emphasizing the second image, one of potential, as if she could not bear to admit to producing only "dross" to anyone, not even to herself. "I have burned the dross and am now coddling the embryos to see if they will hatch."

We visited for a pleasant hour more, then I excused myself. She seemed somehow more vague, less certain, as if she were adrift. She did not press me to stay, and I hoped that she would find her voice again soon—I knew she dearly missed it. And I believed I might have found the explanation for her increased—and odd—correspondence. But if her fallow period did not come to an end soon, I worried what the result would be.

Perhaps, however, the situation was less serious than I imagined. I needed to speak to Mrs. Austin on foundation business; perhaps she could reassure me that Emily had not stopped writing altogether.

When I called, Mrs. Austin answered the door herself. "Miranda, come in and tell me all your exciting news!" She bustled me into her parlor.

"And how is that charming trustee of yours?" she asked.

I smiled. "Still charming. He sends his regards."

She settled onto a settee and patted the spot beside her. "Now, my dear," she said as I sat down. "Tell me. How can I be of help to you?"

"As you know, we are opening our new school in New York," I began. "We feel this is an ideal opportunity to draw attention to our work."

"Quite right," she said approvingly.

"You know so many influential people," I continued. "Your speaking to Mr. Bowles on our behalf was invaluable for the Amherst school. Whom do you recommend we invite for our opening reception in New York?"

"Start right there! With Mr. Bowles," she suggested. "He will know the appropriate journalists to write about your groundbreaking school." Her eyes narrowed slightly as she considered a plan of action.

"I will send a note to Mrs. Vanderbilt for a list of her friends who have young children, as well as possible patrons for the school."

"That would be perfect," I said. "Thank you very much."

She patted my knee affectionately. "Consider it done."

The cook entered with our tea and sandwiches, and Mrs. Austin and I chatted amiably about her children and Elena's delight in Barbados. Then I felt it was time to broach a more difficult topic.

"Sue," I said cautiously, "how do you think Emily is?"

"I am not sure myself," she admitted. "She sends notes occasionally, but I have not received any of her poetry in some time."

This surprised me. As estranged as the two women had become over the years, I knew that Emily still sent her poems quite regularly. It seemed that my concern was well founded.

"Do you think she has stopped writing?" I asked.

"I hope not," Mrs. Austin said with great feeling. "If she has, that means all her hard-won solitude has no purpose."

"You're right," I said. "If her seclusion has a creative source and reason, then it is justifiable and, by Emily's standards, productive and reasonable." Thinking of an Emily without poetry was troubling indeed. "And her words, her observations, her muse, all keep her company. If she is not writing, then she is simply, devastatingly, alone."

"I am afraid you are right," Mrs. Austin said. "Please let me know if you are able to glean any information."

"I will," I promised. Once again, I found myself in the position of being asked to watch over Emily. I would need to find time for her.

One evening a few nights later, when Lolly was a guest for dinner, we had an impromptu sing-along, bringing back memories of our carol singing when we were still schoolmates. Elena, listening, found it a matter for rounds of giggles that Lolly and I, two grown-up ladies, were singing like children.

That same evening Lolly and I spent a long two hours over chamomile tea, reminiscing and thinking about how far we had come — and how far we each intended to go.

"I am embarrassed that I was such a snob of a girl," Lolly said. "And so bossy!"

"I'm grateful that you befriended me," I told her.

"What a friend!" Lolly laughed. "I am surprised that you still speak to me."

"You were finding your way," I told her. "In a sense, I had always known I was different, so I felt less pressure to fit in."

"That is true," Lolly said. "It was something I always envied in you."

This surprised me.

"I was probably my most vindictive when I was envying you the most," she admitted.

"You were never vindictive," I assured her. "Just occasionally..." I tried to find the right word.

"Spiteful?" Lolly offered.

"I would say 'bratty' and leave it at that."

"And look at the two of us now," Lolly said. "You with your wonderful foundation."

"And you preparing for medical school!" We clinked teacups and sipped to our futures, my immediate one being a search for adult pupils.

I spoke to the administrators of Amherst Academy, as well as of the college, for recommendations. This resulted in three enrollees: Miss Carol Avery, an older, unmarried woman who ought to have been a fine and caring mother but who had had no opportunity; Miss Kelly Porter, young and straight out of Amherst Academy, and not sure if she would teach immediately or go on to higher education; and Miss Emma O'Neil, a recent immigrant from Ireland who had great hopes of securing a teaching position. The latter did not want to go into service as so many of her countrywomen did upon arriving in America and knew that she would need specialized training to overcome the prejudice many people had against the Irish. All three women had the temperament for working with children and the openness and flexibility to learn to teach in a new, freer way.

We expected our inaugural enrollment in New York to be small, so Alan and his colleague Miss Jonstone would be adequate faculty this first year. But as the weeks passed, I became worried that our first class would be comprised of two students: Alan's son Julian and Mabel Weaver, the four-year-old daughter of one of Alan's former colleagues at Friends Seminary.

Luckily, Mrs. Austin was as good as her word. No, that is not praise enough: she was even better! Together she and I mailed twenty-five invitations to the opening reception to her most influential friends and acquaintances, and my concerns about enrollment began to dissipate.

"Many of these couples have grown-up children or no children at all," she cautioned. "But they will want to know the very latest trends in . . . well . . . anything!"

She smiled, and once again I was struck by her attractive self-awareness. Despite Emily's insistence that her sister-in-law was a self-serving, shallow social climber, I had seen none of that in Mrs. Austin. Yes, she enjoyed society and wielding influence. But it seemed to expand her rather than diminish her or make her small and grasping.

Mrs. Austin included a personal note with each invitation, endorsing the work of the foundation. Her warm generosity touched me. Carefully writing each of her perfect notes must have taken an entire afternoon.

"Once word gets around that not only I but the Whitneys and the Vanderbilts and the Beechers are planning to attend your reception, others — who do have children — will surely follow."

"I don't know how to thank you for all your work on our behalf," I told her.

"Make this day a success," Mrs. Austin said. "That will be my reward."

I had been so busy — contrived to be so busy — that I was able to keep from thinking of Roger, sometimes for hours at a time. There was so much work to do in Amherst, and I needed to set time aside to take Elena to Springfield to visit her family. Aunt Helen could have taken the cars with Elena, but once the school year started, we would have less time to share together. With mixed feelings I wrote to Alan, and to Roger, explaining that I would not come to New York until the reception and the opening of the school in September. More confusing still, Roger's reply to my letter, in which he passed over my absence from New York and congratulated me on my progress with the adult curriculum, was upsetting. Could the man not show a little disappointment in his letters to me? I could not help but wonder if our separation was more difficult for me than it was for him, and though I put his letter aside, it was hard to put aside these thoughts.

Emily was beginning to present a larger problem. I had seen her a few times; each meeting was amiable but not inspiring. Yet after the last one, I received letter after letter from her. First there was an apology, which confused me, for try as I might I could find no reason for her to imagine that I had been in any way offended or put out. I told her as much in a return note. But each following letter implied that my reassurance was somehow not complete enough; she still worried that we were becoming estranged. While it was true that we were no longer spending every Monday together as we had when I was a girl, we were certainly seeing each other on as regular a basis as my schedule allowed. She herself had on several occasions chosen not to receive me on a Monday, when she was fervently writing.

These letters seemed to be demanding something, but I could not guess what. Her writing was at its most opaque; the only obvious thing in them was the need that leapt off the page. This was not the Emily Dickinson I had grown up knowing—that Emily was demanding, yes, but never needy.

This neediness had been implied by Samuel Bowles, I reminded myself, when he had suggested that she would one day offend me. Perhaps he had already experienced it in the letters he'd received from her over the years. This was not some new derangement, as Mrs. Austin had once feared would befall Emily. This was simply a side she'd never revealed to me. Perhaps I had finally achieved personhood in her eyes and was therefore worthy of such attention, as her various Mentors and correspondents before me. But it still left me wondering how on earth I should reply.

Instead of puzzling over what words might reach her, I decided to see Emily in person. Walking cross lots to The Homestead, I could feel the beginning of a change in the air; the breeze that ruffled my hair today was the first harbinger of autumn, and I could feel the renewed briskness in my steps as energy surged after the repose of summer. My afternoon naps with Elena were about to come to a close.

I reached The Homestead and knocked on the door. Lavinia answered, and I realized that they had still not found a permanent girl to help with the household. Perhaps some of Emily's current difficulty in writing was that she was now expected to participate more in the housework, a role she detested. Her pride in her baking skill was her one domestic pleasure and was based upon baking by choice rather than on demand.

"Hello, Lavinia," I greeted the surprised woman. "I know Emily isn't expecting me, but I was wondering if I could see her."

Worry creased Lavinia's forehead. "I don't know. She has been in a mood for several days now." She gave me a smile. "Perhaps you can jolly her out of herself; she always enjoys seeing you."

"Has she been ill?" I asked.

"No, she's been..." Lavinia shrugged vaguely, unable or unwilling to describe Emily's condition.

"May I see her?" Usually Lavinia simply sent me upstairs. She had never detained me before.

"I'll just run up and check with her," Lavinia said. "She has been very resentful of interruptions."

I nodded. This reticence about company, even mine, might mean that Emily was back to her work and wanted to stay focused. If so, that would be welcome news indeed.

Lavinia returned quickly. "I am afraid this is not a good time," she told me apologetically.

"I would never intrude while she is writing," I said.

"Writing?" Lavinia's expression was both sad and puzzled. "She is simply staring out the window and does not want to be disturbed."

"Are you certain she is not ill?" I asked again.

"Quite certain. She is quite fit. Just..." And again she shrugged.

"Will you tell Emily that I will be away for a bit and that I will call upon her when I return?"

"Of course," Lavinia said and showed me out.

I walked home, unsettled by this news. I had seen Emily's quicksilver moods in the past. Perhaps she would rouse from this current state and return to her former productivity. I certainly hoped so.

As my train steamed through the hills and valleys of Massachusetts, then Connecticut, and finally New York, I sank into reverie that was at times calm and at others so full of anxiety, passion, and anger that I thought the people in my compartment must have considered me a madwoman. I had thrown myself headlong into work not only because the work needed to be done but because it was easier to avoid dwelling upon the questions of my relationship with Roger. I had received a few more businesslike letters; the last was folded away with other foundation correspondence in my portmanteau. After reiterating the final guest list for the opening reception and mentioning inquiries he had received about regular "tour mornings" for visiting educators, he finished with congratulations.

What your hard and thoughtful work—and Davy's faith in you—have wrought is about to unfurl its brightest blossom. I look forward very much to the reception for the New York Frazar Stearns Center and to celebrating the fruition of our work.

Was it foolish of me to dwell upon that one word, "celebrating," and hope that Roger meant more than simply raising a glass to toast Davy's dear memory and the success of the school?

Alan had arranged to meet me at the station and was there, smiling, when I stepped off the train. Remembering my last trip, Roger's delay, and the joy of seeing him at last, I expected to feel less pleasure at this arrival. But as Alan took my hand, I was filled with excitement at the work ahead of us. Could I have forgotten how much I cared for my first teacher and how very glad I would be to see him? The sudden joy I felt was as uncomplicated as the clear blue September day.

Alan brought me directly to the school. The driver handed down my luggage to Alan as I stood before the building, looking up at its elegant, sturdy lines. From the street I could see splashes of bright color, the blues and reds of the painted furniture in the classrooms. And next to the door there was now a brass plate. I darted up the steps to trace the engraved words with my fingers: THE FRAZAR STEARNS CENTER FOR EARLY CHILDHOOD EDUCATION. It was real. It was happening. And I had brought it about.

I remember very little of what I said to Alan after that. He showed me the improvements and additions that had been made since my visit in July. He brought me up to the little apartment, kissed my cheek—a frosting of gray had begun to settle upon his hair, I saw—and left to give me a chance to rest after my journey.

"Thank you," I managed. "I am so thrilled to be here. We have a very big day tomorrow."

Alan smiled with sympathy, his own excitement speaking to mine. "Indeed we do. It is a dream come true."

* * *

The sky on September 9, 1867, was brilliant, unsullied by New York's usual coal haze. I woke early and went downstairs to walk through the classrooms again before our guests arrived, polishing away imaginary dust, straightening books that were already in neatly regimented rows, thrilling at the sight of each room, carefully designed to make learning pleasurable for our young students. Siobhan, the janitress, watched with amusement and sympathy as I patted and straightened. At last she pointed out the time.

"You'll be wanting to make yourself fine for all the fine folk that's coming, Miss Chase."

I ran up to the apartment again, and when I walked down the stairs an hour later, guests were beginning to arrive. The press was well represented, as were many of society's elite, elegant women bringing along their well-upholstered husbands. I owed Mrs. Austin a debt of gratitude. Her help in bringing in the crème of New York society, as well as of its intellectual circles, had been invaluable. She arrived resplendent in the modish new silhouette, in a startling combination of green silk and gold brocade, beaming proudly and greeting her friends.

"We could never have achieved this without your help," I told her.

She smiled and took my hands. "I am pleased to have been useful. And to think that I first met you as a shy and awkward child." She stepped back to study me and my simple violet dress. "Look at you. How proud your father would be if he could see you, and all of this."

I blinked back the surprising tears that appeared in my eyes and gave her a quick embrace. "Thank you," I whispered.

She patted my shoulder. "Now go and attend to your reception," she instructed warmly. "There is Emily's 'friend.'" She looked amused. "Thomas Higginson."

I turned at once. Emily's Preceptor, Mr. Thomas Higginson, was a handsome aristocrat with elegant muttonchop whiskers. I wondered why Emily kept her "Mentors" as distant as she did; the two I had met were dashing gallants. I had always imagined Colonel Higginson as a literary entrepreneur, constantly introducing and exchanging people and ideas. But he seemed as at home as Mrs. Austin with all these learned and disparate people. She brought him over to meet me, then vanished to inspect the sideboard. Colonel Higginson confided he was considering an article for the *Atlantic Monthly* about the school, and I told him I knew of him through Emily.

"You know her personally?" he asked, surprised. "She vows she sees no one."

"We met when I was still a child."

"Did you? Then you can tell me—does she exaggerate her solitude?"

I shook my head. "That would be impossible. She doesn't see ten people a year, outside of her family. I have never once been in her company with another person."

He looked baffled. "How do you explain this, Miss Chase?"

I thought carefully. Emily's recent behavior had caused me to wonder myself about her interior nature. But I did not want to diminish her in Colonel Higginson's esteem. He was far too important to her, more important, perhaps, than Emily herself knew. I could see she already teetered precipitously on the edge of his opinion. Her talent was her tether, but I sensed the tone of her letters to him was making her position precarious to him as well—and she had no idea she was in danger of pushing her Preceptor away.

"Let me see if this explains it," I said at last. "Emily's character is one of arrogant shyness. Or perhaps it is shy arrogance. She feels unbearable pressure from the physical presence of others. Also, she begrudges wasting her time with people less gifted." I gave him a sly grin. "Which she believes is just about everyone."

Colonel Higginson and I shared a laugh.

"Did you know Miss Dickinson and I correspond?" he asked.

"Indeed I do. She considers you her most valuable friend and Mentor. You came into her life at a time when she needed both."

The colonel looked troubled. "Miss Chase, I swear I will never be less to her—*and I will never be more.* But in her letters I get the sense that she expects... well, she seems to want more than I offer. Perhaps she misunderstood my suggestion that she visit Boston." He shifted his weight several times, fiddling with items in his trouser pocket. It was clear that he felt uncomfortable. Having experienced that same discomfort myself, I felt in an excellent position to counsel him.

"Miss Dickinson—Emily—is a very unusual person. She is remarkably intense in all her relationships. She has no *casual* friends. There is no gray in Emily's palette."

"Her letters are so *personal,*" he said. "She addresses me with a degree of feeling that—disturbs me." The colonel pulled a linen handkerchief from his pocket and mopped his troubled brow. I liked this good-hearted man for his concern.

"Sir, I have listened to Miss Dickinson's fantasies for years and have never seen her act on a single one of them. I believe you would do her grave harm if you ended your correspondence, for her letters are her hobby and her social life. She has a dozen correspondents besides you! You are in good company, Colonel Higginson—and perfectly safe." I could see his relief at hearing this, and inwardly I felt the same way. It was as if by reassuring him, I had reassured myself.

"Then perhaps I will continue to press her to allow me to visit. Her letters and poems have such a strange power, such luminous flashes," he said. "If she would only permit me to edit them, I could bring her all the fame I know she is secretly craving. I could put her in print tomorrow! But she would rather go unpublished than take my advice and draw upon my experience." He shook his head. "She'll come into her own reputation and honor only after she dies. Then she won't be able to refuse editing—or annoy the editors' wives."

As I watched him circulate through the room, I realized how much I liked him and, even more, how much I enjoyed male company and conversation. Since my transforming hours on Barbados, I had a new ease and sincerity with men. As this thought occurred to me, the crowd parted for an instant and I caught a glimpse of Roger. For a moment I saw nothing else, and the wealth of memory that flooded me made me light-headed. I had not seen him since July, nor heard from him since my arrival in New York. He had made no point of seeking me out at the reception. The moment of longing gave way to a hot flare of anger; if he was here for work only, so would I be.

I turned and smiled brilliantly at an elderly gentleman who asked a politely doubting question about the need for early education. "They hadn't none of this when I was a boy, and I learned well enough."

"Did you enjoy it, sir? Did you run to your lessons every day?"

The old man grinned at some memory. "The master had to beat the lessons into me with a hickory stick! Still, I learnt them. Do you really think all this pretty stuff will make children learn?"

I took his arm and guided him to a crowd of parents who were wait-ing to see the school. "The furnishings and projects will help, of course, sir. But the real secret is to have inspired and inspiring teachers. I had one such myself and liked him so well that he will be the director of the school!" I introduced him to Alan Harnett. The old man acknowledged Alan but was not done with me.

"It still sounds like coddling to me," he said. "Still, I imagine if all my teachers had been as pretty as you, young lady, that might have made a better student of me!"

I laughed and handed my doubter to Alan, who included him in the first tour group. As the reception went on, Alan and I took turns in guiding the parents of prospective students about the school. Roger had stationed himself in the third-floor reception room, where he would relate to the press and anyone who wished to hear it the foundation's history and our goals and plans. In the next room Lucy Quinn, the recently hired office administrator, sat behind her desk and took enrollments. Our books were on display, and I could see that she was also taking orders for copies. Alan's wife, Fanny, helped Siobhan refill the punch bowl and replenish the other refreshments. Lucy Quinn's oldest daughter, Mim, a solemn twelve-year-old, watched over the Harnetts' little ones, Henry and Julian, who looked very handsome in their miniature suits.

I greeted Mr. Butler, my friend from the Ethnological Society, who introduced me to his new bride. As I stood serving slices of our gigantic Leo-shaped vanilla cake, I spotted many familiar faces: our stained glass specialist Elliot Peck, who received many compliments on his delicate work, and several of the staff from Friends Seminary. I was most gratified to see that one of the workmen, a burly Italian immigrant, had brought his wife and three children to enjoy the day and to inquire about enrollment.

"But they would not be taught with our children, would they?" a highly decorated young matron asked me anxiously.

Looking at the workman's children, who were clean and in their best clothes and were sitting quietly, overawed by the reception, I said I would have no objection to having them at the school. "It is quite possible that they would be in the same class." I wanted to be clear about this.

"But they are — that is —" the woman faltered.

"They seem very well behaved, and the older one was intrigued by the globe," I said mildly.

"Why should a child of an honest workman not be welcomed in a school such as this?" A woman's voice came over my shoulder. "If it is only because his parents were born in another country — why,

America is a young country. Shake it a bit and you will see that we are all immigrants. Congratulations on your success, Miss Chase." The speaker, a woman a few years older than I, nodded pleasantly, then turned away. The young matron watched her go, murmuring, "Oh, yes, of course."

"Who is that?" I asked Sue Dickinson a few minutes later.

Mrs. Austin looked across the room. "*Oh.*" The word was filled with meaning. "That is Mrs. Victoria Woodhull. She is recently arrived in New York and is one of Mr. Vanderbilt's pets. She is an interesting woman, Miranda, but I would give her a wide berth if I were you; I know nothing *against* her, but a school—particularly a school as new and unusual as this one—must be particular in its supporters."

"But if you know nothing against her—" I began.

"I know nothing *for* her, either. Mrs. Woodhull appears to be the sort of woman who is...talked about. The only thing we wish people to talk about is the school's educational philosophy!"

I sighed. There would be many such shoals to navigate. The school needed the enthusiastic support of the well-to-do in order to thrive and grow, and we would all—myself and Alan and Roger and everyone connected to the school—have to learn to listen sympathetically without swerving from what we all agreed was the true mission of the school.

As the party came to a close, we ushered the remaining guests into the garden. Mim, Julian, and Henry handed out balloons to all the children in attendance. As the adults drank a toast to the success of the new school, the children each released a balloon. These rose with deliberation and dignity, and drifted slowly over the city like stately confetti.

When Alan shut the door behind the last departing guest, the sun was setting. Lucy Quinn came down the stairs, beaming, clutching a ledger to her ample bosom.

"Good thing you had the good sense to hire me," drawled the transplanted Virginian. Mrs. Quinn, like so many women, had been widowed by the war. We never discussed her feelings about the confrontation between North and South; as Miss Adelaide had said, there were worthy men lost on both sides of this terrible conflict. A pleasant, plump woman in her late thirties, she had packed up her children and moved to New York in hope of finding the work that had proved elusive in Virginia.

She held up the ledger. "I enrolled twenty-two students today! And you can be sure I took deposits in cash only, to secure their positions. Not only that, I sold fifteen alphabet books!"

"You are a genius, Mrs. Quinn!" Alan exclaimed. He flung his arms around her in a bearlike embrace. I had never seen my former tutor so exuberant. Fanny and I both laughed at his enthusiasm while Mrs. Quinn made a great show of straightening her hat and gasping for breath.

Alan turned to me, grabbed my hand, and twirled me around. "Twenty-two!" he cried. Finally he gave his wife a kiss and pulled her close. "Do you realize that means we are nearly at capacity?"

"I am so proud of you," Fanny told her husband. She rested her head upon his shoulder.

Alan's warm gaze landed on me. "We did it."

"Yes," I said. I felt tears welling up and blinked them back. "We did it."

Roger had come downstairs a few moments before with a bottle and glasses. "I knew I had been saving this champagne for a good cause. This is certainly it." He poured glasses and handed them around.

"Siobhan, come and join us," Alan said. "You have worked hard too, getting this all ready."

Siobhan colored. Inviting the servants to the party was not a usual practice, but this was not a "usual" school. She wiped her hands on her apron, then took the proffered champagne glass. "Thank you, sir. I've never had French wine before."

"To our shared success," Roger said.

"To Miranda," Alan said.

"And to Davy," I added. Solemnly we raised our glasses together.

Then, as we sipped, we settled into chairs, filled with the happy fatigue that follows hard and satisfying work. Little Henry crawled into his mother's lap while Alan perched on the arm of the chair beside Fanny. Julian sat on the floor at her feet.

"Should we go out for a celebratory dinner?" Alan asked. "I don't believe I managed to eat anything today."

"I am afraid I am too tired to eat," I confessed.

Fanny gave me a grateful look; I knew I had done her a boon by sending her husband home with her.

"Siobhan, why don't you just leave those until tomorrow?" I suggested. "You have had a long day on your feet." She had begun to gather up the glasses.

"Let me take these up to the kitchen, ma'am, and then, if it's truly all right, I'd be that grateful to take a rest," she agreed.

I saw the Harnett family and Roger out the front door and heard Siobhan retiring. I sat down in the classroom for a few minutes, exhausted and exhilarated, so I was there to answer the door when Roger returned.

"I told Alan I had left something behind," he said quietly. "I barely spoke a word to you today."

I waited. I could not tell what he wanted me to say; I was not certain what I wished to say myself. Roger stood, his hat in his hand, looking at me with a longing that spoke to my own.

"I will not stay long. I wish I could—"

"Why can you not?" I asked. "As far as the world knows, you left. Siobhan has gone to her quarters. You could stay and talk—"

Roger shook his head. "Talk?" His tone made the idea absurd. "For all our sakes, I will only stay a few minutes. You will be returning to Amherst tomorrow, I imagine. I wanted only to ask how you are and to let you know that you are never far from my thoughts."

I wanted to weep with frustration. "I am very busy," I said at last. Did he wish me to say that I was pining for love? Or that I was not? "And when I return to Amherst I will, I suppose, be busier."

"You will not find time to come back to New York again for a time," he said.

"Probably not," I agreed. "Will that present a problem for you?"

Roger smiled unhappily. "It is probably better not even to speak of it," he said. "I wanted only to see you, Miranda. And to tell you that someday..."

"I know," I said coldly. "Thank you."

I stepped back, closed the door quietly, and went upstairs to my solitary bed.

Book XIII

AMHERST AND NEW YORK

1867–1869

I returned to Amherst in a fog of misery. The long journey home gave me far too much time to think: Had I done the right thing in sending Roger away? Worse, had he ever loved me, had I imagined feelings he had never shown? I barely thought about the school or the opening. When I reached home and Aunt Helen lovingly demanded every detail of my trip, I had to wrench myself out of my preoccupation to give her the answers she wanted. I described the day, the press of visitors, their comments, and the enrollment list Mrs. Quinn had compiled during the reception.

Aunt Helen clapped her hands with pleasure. "Miranda, I could not be more delighted! After all your hard work, to get the school off to such a promising start!"

I agreed, hollowly, that it had been a wonderful day, an excellent beginning.

"Is something wrong, my dear? You sound—"

"Just tired, Aunt. We worked very hard to prepare, and the reception was exhausting. And then the trip home..."

The tiny frown of concern between Aunt Helen's brows smoothed instantly, and she swept me up to my room, put me to bed, brought me soup and tea, and instructed me to sleep. "Tomorrow you will be right as rain!"

If only it had been so simple. In my memory the days that followed were misty gray. Not the black, lost days of my life after Davy's death but a strained, nightmarish time when the world was drained of its color. Even the crimsons and ochers of an Amherst-leaf fall seemed pallid and sere. I went through the motions at school and at home, wrote thank-you letters to Mrs. Austin, Alan, and Lucy Quinn for their hard work in making the reception a success. I breathed no word of my unhappiness to my friends and family—particularly to Aunt Helen and Elena. The pretense was exhausting, when everything, even Elena's sweet face, reminded me of Roger. When I thought of him,

429

I doubted my memory, his heart, my heart. Was I not pretty enough? Not clever enough? Had I given myself to him too readily, too easily? Had all our talk in Barbados of a rich future been make-believe? Was I really just a great fool?

If Aunt Helen had wanted all the details of the opening, Emily Dickinson, predictably, did not. I visited her a fortnight after I returned, still in my gray mood but pretending to be the normal, sociable Miranda in the hope that that would somehow become true. When I mentioned that I had met Colonel Higginson, she demanded a detailed description of him and of our meeting. I did my best, and at last she sat back with the air of a well-fed kitten.

"Well, Miranda, and did you like my choice of Preceptor?"

"I did, very much indeed. I found the colonel sensitive, intelligent, and gentlemanly."

She nodded, as if taking the compliment for herself. "His letters have already shown me all of that. Now I will be able to imagine his face when he writes to me. We talk as very OLD, CLOSE FRIENDS, you know."

She was claiming her territory, and I allowed it without demur; competing in this fashion did not interest me. Instead, I acknowledged her special rank in the colonel's esteem.

"Colonel Higginson wishes you were his protégé, Emily," I said. "He told me so."

She was dismissive. "Yes, he would like me to be his REFLECTION in the mirror."

She was equally dismissive when I went on to tell her about the opening and the school. All she would say was, "I am sure it went very well, for that SORT of thing."

"*What* sort of thing?" I was tiring of playing this game.

"The SOCIAL sort of thing, of course. Not my sort of triumph at all. My successes are all PRIVATE ones. I suppose you were CHARMING. Weaving WEBS OF INTEREST. Such a great scurrying to support one little school."

Anger pierced the gray in my heart and my mind like a lick of flame.

"That *little* school will educate hundreds of children who will go and make their marks upon the world. I expect this sort of small-minded belittling from old men and timid matrons, not from the forward-thinking Miss Dickinson! Or is it just because the idea came from me? *One little school*—I don't presume to criticize your poetry, Emily, so don't presume to talk about *my little school*." I was so angry I could barely speak.

Emily stood stock-still, her tiny frame rigid, her hands clenched. And then her light brown eyes crinkled up, and she began to laugh.

"Oh, Miranda! You're like a daisy-spotted hill suddenly ERUPT-ING into flame! My dear Miss Vesuvius!" She crowed as if at a tremendous joke. "You—criticize poetry?"

I stared at her.

Emily continued to laugh, but there was a steeliness in her eyes. "I think all your WORK has tired you. You're clearly not yourself. Go home, go home, and visit me when you're in your right MIND!"

I left, the anger churning in me with each step. As I went, an echo of something she had said about Colonel Higginson occurred to me.

What do you want me to be, Emily, if not a reflection of you?

I did not see Emily again for a long while, nor did I wish to see her, yet she managed to insert herself into my life in a curious way. One afternoon, while Elena accompanied Aunt Helen on her shopping expedition, I was planting bulbs at our front walk when I had unexpected callers—two smiling women, one my age and one younger, wearing plain worn country clothes and antique boots. They believed they were expected; they kept saying, "She told us it was all arranged."

Eventually we sorted it out. The ladies were the Misses Norcross, from Monson. Emily's legendary "little cousins." Emily had decided we should meet and sent them to call—without telling me. I was not surprised by Emily's failure in etiquette: she could be quite exacting about social niceties when it served her or forget them entirely when it did not.

I brought the women inside. They gave my house one or two knowledgeable compliments and murmured, "That's my last duchess, there upon the wall," as they met a Latham matriarch, frowning in the parlor. They had a subtle, threadbare dignity.

"Are you in Amherst for a Dickinson matter?" I asked as we took tea.

"Nothing particular, Miss Chase," answered Miss Louise Norcross, the confident elder sister. "Emily sends her carriage for us sometimes."

"When she is feeling maternal!" explained Miss Fanny, who was dainty and ringleted. "She likes to give us a little outing."

"Do forgive me," I said, "but somehow I had the impression, from Emily, that you were both—younger."

"Emily prefers to have us younger and smaller than we actually are." Miss Louise smiled. "Of course she does the same thing to you. She sees you—or at any rate describes you—as a headstrong schoolgirl."

"And about her own height!" Miss Fanny added.

Our laughter was a treaty, a wordless acceptance. We would not deny Emily's fantasies—and we would not call them lies. This reminded me of a poem Emily had given me a few years ago. I brought out the draft to show the Norcross cousins.

> *Tell all the Truth but tell it slant—*
> *Success in Circuit lies*
> *Too bright for our infirm Delight*
> *The Truth's superb surprise*
> *As Lightning to the Children eased*
> *With explanation kind*
> *The Truth must dazzle gradually*
> *Or every man be blind—*

"Why, this is precisely the way Emily thinks," Miss Louise observed.

I nodded. "It's true. She is saying, 'Never use the whole truth. Change it, fix it, tell it *slant*.' "

We passed a delightful afternoon. The Norcrosses were witty and cultured company. My heart went out to them—forced by poverty and war into vicarious lives. Emily's "little cousins" darned their gloves and drank weak tea, waiting to be needed. They went from one house to another, "helping out" in family crises—journeys and illnesses, moves and births and deaths. They were part of a new generation of surplus women: girls and young women whose lives never developed, whose lovers were killed before they had ever met. These tragic figures, prepared only for the homes they would never have, the children they would never bear, affected me deeply. Or the slightly older women, widowed before their time, often with few resources—social, emotional, or, often, financial. Had they and their generation been educated for a profession, they might have been useful now—working to heal the nation. Without Davy's foresight and generosity, without the foundation, I might have been among the "extra women"—a new phrase in society for an unevenly seated dinner party but also a pitiless truth about a new class.

Again, I found myself troubled by Emily's tunnel vision, her inability to care how she diminished the Norcross cousins by keeping them *small*. She could not see their struggles or their worth. And as Miss Louise and Miss Fanny revealed, she did the same thing to me.

Halloween jack-o'-lanterns were carved, shone their orange light into the frosty darkness, and were discarded. Halfway into November, a letter came from Roger on a day when the sky was steel colored, and the trees, stripped of their autumn colors, seemed to huddle together against the cold and wind. I took the fat envelope up to my room and read it in private. It was as well that I did so.

> *Miranda,*
>
> *I have not written, not because my heart was not full but because I could not think of what I could possibly say. I understand your feelings; I wish you could see that this is a hard time for me as well. My feelings are all that they have ever been, but I know, as you do too, if only you will remember it, that everything you and I value — excepting only our love — could be destroyed by discovery. Would parents send their children to be educated at a school organized by a woman known to be in an illicit relationship? You have said Elena's father is a conservative man. How long would he permit Elena to remain with you if our relationship were uncovered? Would your dear aunt Helen be able to accept so unorthodox a union? You have managed, with tact and charm and your formidable intelligence, to carve out a profession in a new field, a field that stands to benefit hundreds, perhaps thousands, of children.*
>
> *I do not think you would wish to risk any of that.*
>
> *It is fully as difficult for me to contain expression of my feelings, on paper or in person. I was hurt when you sent me away in New York, but after much reflection I know that you were right. That was my own longing speaking and not good sense. That same longing drove me to investigate a solution — a difficult and imperfect one but one that was much on my mind. I have studied the law on this point, and I know it would be possible for me to divorce Cecilia —*

I drew a breath and stared at the letter in dismay. Divorce? I had never met a divorced person; I did not think that anyone in my family had ever done so. No one but those experiencing the most desperate cases of depravity, cruelty, or abandonment obtained a divorce. If Roger, upright and honorable as I knew him to be, could suggest such a thing, his feelings were more engaged than I had imagined.

—but what is possible is not necessarily wise. Divorce would expose you and the foundation to scandal and gossip as surely as discovery would. You might lose the school, or lose Elena, and such a loss could not help but burden our life together, until perhaps it broke under the weight. I cannot allow that.

We have each had a great love that came before. Please understand that I do not trivialize your feelings for Davy when I say that your loss was easier: Davy's death may have been brutal, but it was final. Since Cecilia's illness she has been in a kind of twilight state, neither fully alive nor fully dead, and I have shared that state with her. Your love brought me alive again, and it is painful, for reasons I know you too well to believe you will not understand, to know Cecilia still dwells on the shores of the River Styx. Before you think too harshly of me, remember that I am caught between Cecilia, sleeping in the shadows, and you, waiting in the land of sunlight.

I read the letter through twice, then burned it. He loved me—I had not imagined that—but there was no end in sight, no happiness for us. The sweet, piercing joy I felt on reading his words of love turned to ashes. Then to anger. I had struggled, in the months since we last met, to master my feelings and live my life. Roger's letter, tantalizing in its promise, had torn open a wound that had begun to heal without my knowing it.

And Christmas, that time of light and joy in the Amherst year, was approaching.

The decorations went up. The schoolchildren made gifts and planned a pageant, and we needed many rehearsals for our caroling night through the town. Elena, old enough to understand and anticipate the wonder of the holidays, was caught between giddiness and an uncharacteristically angelic manner. I wore a mask of pleasure, hoping Elena would be happy if I could not. My act did not convince me, and

I think Aunt Helen was sometimes troubled by my unhappiness, but she was too tactful to say anything.

Emily, of course, was not.

Just before Christmas I decided to make up our quarrel. Emily-like, she greeted me as if there had never been a cross word between us.

"Welcome, snowbird." She helped me with my shawl and heavy coat. "Warm yourself by my fire."

"It is bone-chilling out there," I admitted with a shiver. "I had not re-alized before I left my house how much the temperature had dropped." I sat beside her stove and held my hands out to its warming haze.

"Have you been cooped up indoors as I have been?" Emily asked. "Once it becomes this cold, I don't even venture into the garden. I spend most of my time here or in the conservatory." She stood by the window and gazed down at her neglected territory. I noticed small transparent line drawings on the pane; she must have been amusing herself by making finger drawings in the condensation.

"How are your flowers thriving?" I asked. "I fear we lost some of Elena's plants to the early frost." I gave her a rueful smile.

She playfully waggled a finger at me. "Not paying attention, I see. The gardener must always be on her toes. You see Nature as benign, but I know better. She can be FIERCE and UNFORGIVING."

Despite her scolding tone and strong words, I knew she was in jest. I held up my hands in a gesture of supplication. "I admit it, it's true. Elena and I missed our moment, and now Nature has taught us that everything has a cost."

Now she turned wistful. "That is all too true." She stared out her window a few moments, and I worried that my lighthearted comment, completely in keeping with her own, had triggered the melancholia that I had detected in her on previous occasions. But then she turned and gave me an appraising look. "I wonder what cost you are bearing now?"

"What do you mean?"

"There is something sad in you, something that all your worldly TRIUMPH does not touch. You have had challenging times and now you reap your bounty, but it does not wholly . . . touch you."

"I am only a little tired," I told her. "We take the cars in a few days to visit Elena's family in Springfield. There is so much to do."

"No. It is something more." Emily tilted her head to one side, bird-like, and regarded me with fierce inquisitiveness. "If you are not happy with your schools and your little girl"—as she had before, she made them sound trivial, as if they were a child's playthings—"there is something more." Emily looked out the window, silvered with condensation and frost. "Do not tell me you think you are in love, Miranda. I thought you had more IMPORTANT concerns."

I stared at her. I had no intention of telling her about Roger, but I knew Emily would not be put off easily.

"Who is it? Do you intend to marry him?" Her mouth drew into a tight straight line, and she crossed her arms over her chest.

"I do not intend to marry anyone at this time," I said crisply. It was hard to know whether to be appalled or amused.

"Good." Emily smiled. "I have given the matter some thought, and I have decided you should NEVER marry."

"*You* have decided? Don't you think that perhaps that is a decision for me to make for myself?"

Emily gave no sign that she had heard me. "You could never obey a man's WHIM. You could never be his PROPERTY."

"You are right," I said. "And I would never marry a man who would treat me in such a fashion." I did not say that I had known two men—Davy and Roger—who would not harbor such an attitude.

Emily's eyes narrowed, and an odd glint came into them. "You misunderstand me. You are someone who should never...SUBMIT. You do not have the temperament."

I realized with a pang of shock that she was talking about intercourse.

"Emily, how can you possibly know that?"

"I know more than you think," Emily told me enigmatically. She pulled her red shawl tighter across her shoulders, although the little stove kept the room very warm. "I know you believe I am a naive recluse, but before you met me I lived in the wider Amherst world. I am not as IGNORANT as you imagine."

"If you intend to advise me, you had better talk plainly." I was curious as to what she would say.

"I will try. You must listen carefully, for I could not possibly say this twice. I want to PROTECT you."

What in the world—her strange, fanciful world—was coming now?

"My father bought The Homestead back for our family in 1855. Before we moved back in, when there were workmen making repairs here, I came up to the barn very early one morning and went in to get a hoe. Probably he thought the place would be empty at that hour."

"Who thought, Emily?" I could not imagine where this story was heading.

"Whoever it was—that ANIMAL. He was there, up in the hay-loft, with his—mate. They were like a boar and a sow, COUPLING. Squealing and gasping and tearing at each other. You cannot possibly conceive what I heard and saw."

I was speechless.

"I learned all I needed to know about so-called love that morning. Love is not sympathy and tender attentions. Love is bestial violence. Love is RED MEAT."

Her eyes glittered. I was repulsed to see how much she relished describing this incident to me so that I would be persuaded to choose as she had.

"I consider myself very fortunate to have been forewarned," she declared. "Think of the women who must go into marriage UNPRE-PARED." She gave a fastidious shudder. "But I was always conscious of the DARKNESS in men, and I want you to become so too, Mi-randa. It was my duty to warn you." The avidness left her face, and her demeanor returned to that of a prim spinster. I think it was this, as much as anything else, that outraged me.

"But that is not what real love is—coupling in a barn. Emily, you have allowed this one dreadful incident to confirm everything you be-lieve, and now you want me to believe it too! Physical love need not be bestial, any more than an individual need be bestial in any other part of his life. Love and physical love, together, are—" I stopped, caught in a memory of Roger's hands and lips, stirring my heart and body at once. My skin went hot all over, and I bit my lip, recalling ecstasy.

Then I saw Emily's face. Her eyes were narrowed again.

"I am too late, I see," she said with deadly quiet.

"No, Emily—" I reached a hand out to her, but she did not see it. She was watching my face. "It is not—"

"Who was it? Did he persuade you it was LOVE? Oh, yes." She turned back to the window. Her voice, when she continued, was low and sympathetic, but her eyes were avid. "You are still almost a child, despite your accomplishments. When did it happen? Where? How did this man take advantage of you?"

"He didn't." My voice was as quiet as her own, but Emily had touched the nerve laid bare by Roger's letter and my fears about the future.

"How did it happen?"

Haltingly, I began to tell her. I had wanted so badly to confide in someone, and once I began I could not stop. Without my being aware of it, she guided me to my red armchair and sat me there, and put a cup of tea in my hand. The tea cooled as I talked, trying to give Emily, who so loved the small details of life, a sense of the golden warmth of Barbados, where everything, including love, had seemed right and possible.

Emily listened intently.

"But now you have returned from EDEN," she said when I finished my tale. "You do not mean to continue?"

"I do not know what I mean. Roger is right that many people—most people—would condemn what happened between us in Barbados—"

"It has not happened since?" Emily looked at me sharply.

I shook my head. "Time, place, and the world have worked against us."

"Miranda, you know that I do not place much stock in the CONVENTIONS of the world, but I think you have been FORTUNATE. You might have been DISCOVERED and all your plans brought to ruin. You might have MARRIED and lost everything in submission to a man's WHIM. The physical submission is only part of it, Miranda, a sign of the larger submission of your dream and your WORK to his. The WORK is the important thing. At least, to people such as you and I."

I remembered the Emily who had stolen into the church for my father's memorial; it seemed that this was the friend who sat with me now, not the increasingly moody and self-involved woman of the last few months.

"Take comfort in your WORK, Miranda. And in TRUE FRIENDS. In time you will see more clearly and know that this excursion into the—physical world—was an aberration. Men are—well, we need not discuss it further."

My tea was cold. Emily took it and poured more. She passed a plate of her exquisite cakes to me. I sipped my tea and nibbled at a cake, exhausted. It had taken more strength than I had imagined to keep my secret. And telling it had not changed Emily's mind; my experience of physical joy was so different from what she had seen, and her revulsion and terror had not been touched by my story. Emily was what she was. I was too tired and too grateful for her sympathy to be troubled by how desperately Emily wanted me to be what she was.

Eased of a burden of secrecy I had not realized was weighing upon me, I floated through Christmas. To Springfield and back we went, and on New Year's Day Aunt Helen, Elena, and I made our rounds of Amherst's various festivities. This year Aunt Helen surprised me by consenting to stop by The Evergreens for Mrs. Austin's annual open house. "As Mrs. Austin has been so helpful to the foundation, it is only mannerly that we call," she said firmly. As we passed The Homestead that afternoon, I glanced up and saw Emily in her familiar place at her window. On impulse I stopped.

"Would you mind taking Elena ahead?" I asked Aunt Helen. "I would like to wish Emily a happy New Year."

"Can I come with you?" Elena asked, her sweet face red from the cold. "To meet your friend?"

I gazed down at her, wondering how I could make her understand that, due to Emily's nature, Elena would not be welcome. "I'm afraid not," I said. "Miss Dickinson hardly sees anyone. She's very private."

Elena's brow furrowed as she puzzled this out. "Is she all alone?"

I squeezed her mittened hand, touched by her obvious concern. "No, she has her sister and her mother and father with her too."

Elena nodded, satisfied that my mysterious friend was not lonely.

Aunt Helen held out her hand to Elena. "I'm sure Mrs. Austin has all sorts of surprises in store." She gave me a sly smile, and I knew she was registering her disapproval of Sue Dickinson's excesses while taking care not to spoil Elena's pleasure at the outing.

Emily still stood at her window, so I waved. Oddly, she didn't wave back. I hurried up the walk to the door, and as I reached for the door pull Lavinia bustled out, wrapped in several woolen layers. She started, then said, "Why, Miranda, Emily never mentioned you would be visiting."

"I was passing by," I explained. "You are going to the Austins'?"

She nodded. "But of course Emily refused to join me. This year she didn't even bother to make gingerbread for the little ones, so I've had to find an alternative." Lavinia held up a large glass jar bedecked with ribbons. Inside I could see candies as colorful as rubies, emeralds, and topazes. She gave me a conspiratorial smile and lowered her voice. "I must confess, I did enjoy making the selection!"

I smiled back as she gestured me inside. "Emily?" I called up the stairs, surprised that she wasn't hovering in her doorway; she must have heard me talking to Lavinia. Hearing no reply, I went up and knocked at the closed door. "Emily?" I repeated.

"Come in, if you like" came the indifferent reply.

I stepped into her overheated room. She sat at her desk, her back to me.

"I wanted to wish you a happy New Year," I said.

"I saw you," she replied without turning around. "Hurrying, scurrying, establishing your social network in a PUBLIC display of meeting and greeting."

Her hostility was evident, and her interpretation of our leisurely and pleasant tour of the neighborhood was so far from the mark that for a moment I was speechless. The only sound in the room was the hissing of the stove and the scratching of Emily's pen on her paper. Had I interrupted her writing? Is that what made her so unpleasant? Even so, that was no excuse for her tone and her judgment.

I crossed to her desk so that I could face her. "Emily, I came here to share the joy of the season with you."

Emily sniffed and continued to move her pen across the paper.

"Have you nothing to say to me?" Not moments before, my generous-hearted Elena had been worried that this rude and selfish woman was lonely.

"I have nothing to say," Emily replied. "Nothing at all."

Her voice seemed to come from a far distance, hollow sounding, and I knew she was addressing not just me but herself, and perhaps whatever demons were currently haunting her. I didn't know how to respond, so I glanced down at her sheet of paper. My eyes widened. There were no words, just rows and rows of inky lines and hash marks. Judging from the piles of papers crumpled around her, and the heat coming from the stove, Emily had sat here and made meaning-less lines on reams of paper. Perhaps for hours.

I cleared my throat. "Emily, this is a day of beginnings." I was not certain where my words would take me. "New chances to leave old woes behind in the passing year and embrace opportunities that arise in the new. I wish this for you, and for myself as well."

Emily's pen paused, and her eyes flicked to my face, then back down to her paper again. "New. A new approach. A new technique. Perhaps that is what is called for." She leaned back against the slats of her chair and laid down her pen. "Yes," she murmured. "I'll consider that." She looked up at me with her now-placid brown eyes. "I suppose you will be going to the Borgias' palace for the festivities?"

"Yes," I told her. Would this anger her? "Aunt Helen and Elena are waiting for me."

She nodded. "Kiss all the babies for me. Children are what the New Year is truly about" was all she said, but I knew I had been dis-missed.

I pondered Emily's dilemma as I went down the stairs, and the di-lemma she posed me. She was obviously not writing as she had been, and it was affecting her moods and behavior. Yet it was so unpleasant to be around her at this time that I was torn between pity and anger. Anger won out as I continued to walk, until I reached Mrs. Austin's front hall and Elena flung herself around my knees, thrilled that I had arrived in time for the magic lantern show. I knew that if Emily was truly disturbed, Mrs. Austin would find a way to tell me, and as a con-sequence I could, for the moment, push that problem to the back of my mind. This would be relatively easy, as I was finding my increasing correspondence and my work at the Amherst school quite demand-ing, and the winter kept us busy as well with its chores and tasks.

I tried to use that busyness as a drug, to dull the ache in my heart. I felt other pangs as well: I was young, and my body had been thor-oughly and skillfully awakened. Whatever my feelings for Roger were, my body's longings were uncomplicated. In bed each night, no matter that I had worked myself to exhaustion, I lay awake, haunted by the memory of Roger's hands on me, of the taste of his mouth and his scent. When I slept, I dreamed of Barbados, the flower-scented breezes and languorous air—and Roger. I did not sleep well, and when Aunt

Helen fretted that I looked tired, my answer was to work more, in hope that I would sleep more readily.

One afternoon Aunt Helen suggested that I visit Emily. I realized it had been nearly three months since my New Year's visit. Of course, I had not heard from her, but that was not unusual, as she often alternated between silence and effusion.

I sent a note suggesting a visit, and when I received a return invitation, I walked up Main Street through sunlight that had the look of early spring. A verse from one of my favorite of Emily's poems came to me:

> *Consulting summer's clock,*
> *But half the hours remain.*
> *I ascertain it with a shock —*
> *I shall not look again.*

I admired again the clear ring of authenticity, like the striking of a crystal goblet. This perfection had to be genius. I had met and recognized it in a score of Emily's poems — and each time I did, I told myself she should be exempt from the usual social laws. Forget her lies, forget her fantasies, her selfishness: genius lived by its own rules.

Emily must have seen me coming up the street. This time she stood in the door to her room — as she did for that awkward little girl who climbed the stairs so many years ago. How much I had needed a friend that day!

"You are the surest sign of the coming spring," she greeted me. "All of God's creatures are finally ROUSING themselves."

I detected no hidden resentment in this statement — she was not accusing me of a lack of attention, as she had in the past; rather, she seemed simply pleased by my arrival.

"I do feel a bit as though I were coming out of hibernation," I confessed.

"Then let us take full advantage of today's sun and wake up my garden," she suggested.

It was just the right way to spend the afternoon. It was brisk in the garden; spring was still merely a hint, not a complete thought, but our steady work warmed us. Emily seemed in much better spirits than when I'd last seen her. Perhaps all was well with her again, and

I could reassure Sue, and myself, that her course—as individual and unique as it was—was steady once more. When I left her at dusk, a bit stiff from kneeling, I felt a guilty pang for not seeing her more often. My world had expanded greatly since she and I first met, and so much in it now demanded my attention—attention I gave gladly and wholeheartedly. And yet I realized that, preoccupied as I had been with Roger, I had missed the excitement I had felt in those first years of my friendship with Emily, when her quicksilver mind challenged and delighted me, her observations stunned me, and her conversation educated me.

As March mud gave way to the vivid green of April, my life settled into a routine of work and home that was deeply satisfying. The restless hunger of my body continued unabated, but my daylight thoughts of Roger were becoming sweeter and without so much regret. I often looked forward to things in the future without imagining Roger in those plans. Meanwhile, the world around me was bursting into bloom, and the school year would soon be ending. As a teacher and as an avid student, I celebrated this demarcation. Perhaps this was the most appropriate timing of all, for had our goal not been to prepare our students—child and adult—to go forth into the world abloom themselves, to flourish and pick their bounty?

Mulling on this one afternoon, I returned to the house to find several envelopes awaiting in the mail. I recognized Alan Harnett's writing on one and opened it eagerly.

Dear Miranda,

I have received a very disturbing letter and am told that the same letter, or one materially the same, has been received by at least three members of the board of our school. Accusations are leveled in it, at you and at Roger, of a very distasteful nature, claiming that Roger has an "unconventional influence" (whatever that may be—although the writer's intent is clear enough) on you. I need not say that this casts as unwholesome a light on the school and our mission as it does upon you. What is strange is that the letter was emphatic in its praise of our methods and was sent anonymously by someone who signed himself "A Friend of Education."

I have known you almost all your life, Miranda, and my faith in your good sense and integrity is absolute. Although I have not known Roger as long, my certainty extends to him as well. But the board—Mr. Vanderbilt, Mr. Beecher, and Mrs. Whitney, who have received the letters—is very troubled. If they withdraw their support, the mission of the school may be so compromised that it will be difficult to recover. I urge you to come to New York as soon as possible. I regret to be the bearer of such bad news, but I hope very much that by meeting with the board, we will be able to put to rest these unsavory rumors and go back to the important work to which we have devoted ourselves.

I sat for some time, with the letter balled so tightly in my hand that it marked the flesh of my palm. It seemed to me that the pain was all that kept me from fainting. This was what Roger had feared. This was why he had refused to continue in America what we had begun in Barbados. I had thought he was foolish to worry, but I had been wrong, and now everything was in jeopardy. For I knew with cold certainty that if the backers of our New York school withdrew and the school failed, the Amherst school would follow; even Leo Press and our beautiful books might be discredited.

After a time I looked at the other letters. Two of them were from backers of the New York school, essentially saying the same thing that Alan's letter had but without Alan's generous and good-hearted faith in me. It was clear that I must go to New York and defend myself and my school.

I sat down to write a telegram to Alan, promising to be in New York as soon as possible. I suggested that he contact Roger, if he had not already done so. Then I flew downstairs to tell Aunt Helen that I must go.

"Who would say such things?" She was horrified. "I can certainly tell them that you have not set eyes on Mr. Daniels except under strictly chaperoned circumstances! *Unconventional influence* indeed!" My dear aunt began to bustle about the room as if her outrage needed some physical outlet. "What this could do to your work—and to you! Once such rumors get about, it is almost impossible to put paid to them, even when they are entirely untrue!"

As I packed I reflected on Aunt Helen's outrage, and Alan's, with some discomfort. I could certainly say that Roger Daniels had no "unconventional influence" over my work at the foundation or at the schools: my passion for early childhood education had begun long before I met Roger, and if anything I had influenced him! But what these letters implied—that Roger and I were lovers—was true. And as much as I disliked it, I would almost certainly have to lie in defense of myself, the schools, and the foundation.

I spent the evening playing with Elena and talking quietly with Aunt Helen, pretending that everything was just as it always was. My train did not leave until the next day, and although I dreaded meeting with the board, I was so anxious to do something that I could not sleep. Instead, after Elena and Aunt Helen had gone to bed, I found myself writing to Miss Adelaide. I poured out, in page after page, all my confusion, anger, and hurt, my fear, to the one person I knew would not judge me by society's standards but by the standards of her own wise and loving heart. When my letter was done, the sky in the east was lightening, and I was finally able to sleep.

I woke later than I had intended; I would have to hurry to be ready to meet my train. I dressed and went downstairs, where Aunt Helen met me almost immediately with a telegram.

"It was delivered this morning, but you were so deeply asleep. I hope it is not more bad news!"

Anxious, I fumbled with the envelope, ripped it open, and prized out the telegram. It was from Alan and simply said, "New developments. Urge you delay trip; more information to follow." Alan must have known how anxious I was, for it ended with "Don't worry. Alan."

"New developments?" Aunt Helen asked. "Well, Miranda, if you are not going to New York today, you should at least have some breakfast. It will not help to starve yourself, and there are fresh muffins. Mr. Harnett will tell you soon enough what has happened."

It was hard to wait. For the next two days the hours dragged, and every clock in the house ticked too loudly. Even the sound of Elena's laughter as she capered in the garden, rolling her hoop, did not soothe my nerves. Aunt Helen was a quiet, sympathetic presence; I would come out of a reverie to find a cup of tea had appeared at my elbow or a letter had been taken away to post.

And then, when I was awaiting the arrival of the mail, Alan Harnett himself appeared at our door.

"I had to come and tell you everything that has happened," he said after we had greeted each other. "You can imagine that very little of my usual work has been getting done in the last few days."

We sat in the parlor, and Alan began.

"Roger sent a telegram to me, with letters to follow to every backer of the school—the members of the foundation's board and others. Of course, he denied the slanderous accusations in that letter—but in order to spare the board, the schools, and you further embarrassment, he is passing all foundation business to a friend and colleague in Chicago while he is gone," Alan finished.

"Gone?" I repeated. "I'm sorry, Alan. My mind wandered. This is so much to take in. Where is Roger going?"

Alan looked at me with great kindness. "He is going to England, Miranda."

I looked at him numbly. If Roger was no longer to be the foundation's adviser, the last thin cord between us would be cut. I felt as if I were bleeding.

"Apparently an opportunity had arisen that he had expected to decline, but this situation has made it appropriate for him to distance himself from the foundation and from you. It is an excellent solution but one which will be hard on all of us. Roger was one of the foundation's greatest adherents. He assures me that Mr. Martindale will be as enthusiastic—and Roger promises to be available to advise us by mail, should the need arise."

I nodded. "You still have no idea who wrote the letters?" I asked. "Did you bring your copy?"

"I left in such a hurry—I will send it to you, if you wish, but do you really want to see it?"

Again I nodded.

"I will send mine on to you. But as I said, they were not signed. We may never know. The board met when Roger's plans became clear and agreed that this was nothing more than a malicious attempt to discredit the school, by one of our detractors."

"But what can anyone possibly say against the school?"

Alan smiled. "The fact that this person had to resort to personal attacks suggests that he could not think of any real objections. You are too good-natured to see that there are people who are deeply troubled by change. Some dislike the challenge to established order and feel the old ways are best. Some believe that a desire for change is a criticism of the way they themselves were taught—"

"As I suppose it is," I agreed.

"And perhaps it has nothing to do with the school at all. It could be that Roger has an enemy who felt that his involvement with the school was his most vulnerable point."

"Perhaps *I* have made an enemy," I said.

Alan shook his head. "I hardly think so. You are too young to have made an enemy of this caliber, Miranda."

"Do you think I should come to New York to meet with the board?" I asked after a few minutes.

"Not now. I would suggest that you write a letter in which you repudiate the charges, then continue as you have done. Your own good work will remind them of why they backed the school in the first place. And with Roger across the Atlantic..."

Alan stayed the night and returned to New York on the morning's train. That night I wrote my letters to the board, finding a way to deny Roger's and my involvement without telling a direct lie. We were fortunate, Alan reminded me, that none of the backers had given a copy of the letter to anyone in the press—and that the writer had not thought to do so. As Aunt Helen had told me, once a rumor of this sort became public, it never entirely died.

Roger's letter to me arrived on the first of May, just a few days after Alan's departure.

We shall weather this. But to do so, for the good of the foundation and the schools, and to save you and all the good people who are involved in them from embarrassment, I must go away.

Fortunately, I had just been contacted by Mr. John Parker, a friend of my father's and the president of the Great Western Insurance Company. Great Western has been involved in the settlement of the Alabama claims. I do not know if you remember, but the CSS Alabama *was a cruiser built in an English shipyard, which sank fifty-eight Union ships before she herself was sunk by the Union in 1864. It is the United States' position that England violated the International Statutes of Neutrality by looking the other way when the* Alabama *sailed out of the Mersey Estuary to spend months waging war. England refuses to pay the claims of America's private*

*insurers—including Great Western Insurance—and our govern-
ment has become involved. My father—and, through him, Mr.
Parker—has asked me to go to England to represent Great Western
in the case.*

*I had intended to refuse, but it appears that for many rea-
sons—not least the scurrilous accusations in the letters Alan and
the board members have received—it is providential. I have left
my wife well cared for, although I know, with great sadness, that
my presence makes no difference to Cecilia in her unhappy state. A
junior partner at my firm, Will Martindale, will take over foundation business. He is a good man and knows how close to my heart the
foundation is. He will do his best for you and can always reach me
for advice.*

*I shall miss our correspondence, which has meant a great deal to
me. Perhaps someday we shall meet again. Until that time, I wish
you, and the foundation, all good things.*

The letter was cordial and distant, as if he feared someone else
might read it. And perhaps, I thought, he did fear that. But folded
inside the letter was a smaller slip of paper, with a few words.

I have you always in my heart.

R

Those few words undid me. Once again my longing for Roger,
which I had thought was well controlled, welled up. I wanted, now
especially, to feel his arms around me, to be safe and protected. And
loved! The yearning for him was so powerful I felt it like heat on my
skin. I stared at his handwriting and realized those few sweet words
might be my last from him. I might never see Roger again. I might
never hear another word from him. I closed the door to my room and
sat there for a long time, too sad even to cry, running my fingers across
the surface of that note as if it had been Roger's skin.

Through the days and nights that followed, I carried this private
sorrow, unable to confide to anyone but Miss Adelaide. And yet I
could not bring myself to write to her too candidly about what had
happened, for fear that my letter might go astray. I felt sometimes as
though I were being watched, my actions and words judged. Someone

had known, or guessed, or suspected, that Roger and I were more than colleagues.

I threw myself into work, and work, as it always had done, soothed my hurts and distracted me from the great emptiness where Roger had been in my life. And life insisted upon continuing. Trees leafed and blossomed, and each morning the summer sunshine attempted to burn away my sadness. Alan wrote to me of the end of the first year's classes at the New York school, hoping I would visit before the summer break to see the bounty our work had reaped: "Two dozen bright, happy children, busily learning everything and anything we can teach them!"

One morning's post brought a message from Emily. She had written to me several times since our gardening day, just before the turmoil at the foundation, but I had been too distracted to make time for her. Perhaps the tone of those notes—cloying, worrying that she had offended me in some way—had made me want to avoid her. Still, this was not a note but a poem:

> *We learn in the Retreating*
> *How vast an one*
> *Was recently among us—*
> *A Perished Sun*
>
> *Endear in the departure*
> *How doubly more*
> *Than all the Golden presence*
> *It was—before—*

I imagined Emily was acknowledging that we had not seen each other recently. But I did not care for the exalted position she placed me in, in her private galaxy. I sent her a note thanking her for the poem, relieved at least to see that she was writing again.

Over the next weeks more poems arrived, and I grew uneasy. There was something insistent about the steady stream of verse, and I was unable to understand what Emily's meaning was in sending them.

> *'Twas awkward, but it fitted me—*
> *An Ancient fashioned Heart—*

> *Its only lore — its Steadfastness —*
> *In Change — unerudite —*

And another several days later:

> *I showed her Heights she never saw —*
> *"Would'st Climb," I said?*
> *She said — "Not so" —*
> *"With me —" I said — With me?*
> *I showed her Secrets — Morning's Nest —*
> *The Rope the Nights were put across —*
> *And now — "Would'st have me for a Guest?"*
> *She could not find her Yes —*
> *And then, I brake my life — And Lo,*
> *A Light, for her, did solemn glow,*
> *The larger, as her face withdrew —*
> *And could she, further, "No"?*

I could not imagine her purpose in sending me these. They seemed very much to be messages intended for me, but I could not — or perhaps would not — discern their meaning.

I had, after all, a good deal else to think about. There were the curricula for both the New York and Amherst schools to be planned. More trained teachers would be needed soon, and Alan was looking for candidates in New York. Late in June he sent me a list of several candidates, with his detailed notes on each. Almost as an afterthought he enclosed the letter he had received from the anonymous "Friend of Education," with his apologies for having forgotten to send it on before now.

I unfolded it and then could not read it. Not at once, when the shock of its authorship was with me. It was written in imitation of pompous business letters by someone to whom the style did not come naturally, but the style did not disguise it. I knew that hand, the delicate, slantwise arches.

Dear Mr. Harnett,
I have learned of the success of the Frazer Stearns School with great pleasure, for it is on the education of children that America's

future rests. Because this sacred mission is of such importance, I feel I must warn you of an unwholesome relationship between two central figures in the school. Mr. Roger Daniels, the administrator of your foundation's trust, has what can justly be described as an unconventional influence upon Miss Miranda Chase. I believe Miss Chase is too young and inexperienced to understand the consequences of this association. This regrettable influence can only serve, in the end, to cloud the mission of the school and its generous backers. Even the appearance of unhealthy interest might jeopardize a school whose work, I think, is of the greatest importance.

A Friend of Education

The handwriting was Emily Dickinson's.

I felt dizzy and, for a moment, unaware of my surroundings. Then, as the shock wore away, I was left with cold outrage. I folded the letter, took up my hat, and left the house for The Homestead.

Lavinia met me at the door.

"Miranda! Emily had not told me she was expecting you!"

"She isn't, Lavinia. I need only a moment of her time." It was hard not to let my anger spill over to poor Vinnie. "May I go up?"

She stood aside to let me pass, but her face was avid with curiosity. I thanked her and went up the stairs to knock at Emily's door.

"Emily, it is Miranda Chase."

Her flutelike voice bid me enter. "So formal today! So you finally DEIGN to visit? I see that the claims of old friends are less than—"

I extended the letter to her. She squinted slightly, as if the sunlight on the page made it difficult to recognize. "Oh. Yes, that would bring you here if NOTHING else did," she said.

"Why, Emily?"

She tilted her head as if hearing another voice than mine speaking to her.

"I did it for you and for the school. You're very young, Miranda. Little more than a child! You have no conception of how dangerous your LIAISON with that man was to you — how likely it was to separate you from everything important in your life."

"Likely! Emily, your letter was more destructive to the schools and the foundation than anything Roger and I did! What were you thinking? What could you hope to accomplish by—"

"I told the TRUTH." Emily turned back to her desk.

"You told the truth *slant*, Emily. You told enough of it to suit your own purposes and might have destroyed the schools, and me, and a very good man."

"You do not need HIM," Emily said crisply. "Women like ourselves must do without men—to WORK we cannot afford distractions. Women like ourselves—" She appeared to have lost her train of thought. "Do you think I could BEAR to see you dwindle into a SATELLITE of this man? That I could stand that PAIN? I acted to save you, Miranda."

"You acted to save yourself," I said furiously. "You acted to keep me as your pet. It was all very well when I was *your* satellite! But you could not bear that there was another person in my life who was as important as you. More important! You could not bear that there was some experience in my life that you could not share!"

"What of what I have SHARED with you? You forget that there are very few people I admit to my circle. Perhaps there are others who would better appreciate that HONOR."

"An honor is not a friendship! And what you have done is not honorable! It is selfish and cruel. It is all posturing and false drama, without an iota of real feeling."

For a moment this accusation seemed to affect Emily. "I was trying to SAVE our friendship. And I was afraid for YOU. Miranda, that is hardly—"

I could not listen to any more. "What you did was not the act of a friend, Emily. It was the coldest, most calculating self-service." I folded the letter and put it in my pocket. "Do not ever attempt to hurt me or the foundation again."

"Miranda, do not LEAVE this way!" Emily's burnt sienna eyes were cold, but her anger felt like playacting.

"Good-bye, Emily." I was as cold as she.

"You will not be able to REPAIR this," she warned. Then abruptly her anger was gone, and she reached out her hand to me. "Miranda, please! Miranda, this is CRUEL!"

I said nothing more, just turned and left the room.

As I went down the stairs, I heard Emily call my name again, but I did not stop. As I turned toward the back door, Lavinia Dickinson appeared at the kitchen door and watched without comment as I left the house.

I walked unseeing through the town. Confronting Emily had not made me less angry, only deeply tired. When I reached home I wrote to Alan, telling him that I had discovered who the mysterious author of the letter was and assuring him that there would be no further problem.

Then I slept. When I awoke, I felt sad but oddly free. I even felt some pity for Emily, so alone in that great house, keeping half the world at arm's length and driving the rest away. But sadness did not excuse what she had done. I would not see her again.

Mercifully, that summer, with Emily gone and Roger lost to me, I was busier than I had ever been. I taught, I wrote, I traveled to New York to meet with Alan, to help select new teachers. I was invited to lecture on early childhood education and to write essays for newspapers. There was Elena to watch over and nurture, and Lolly to visit in Boston. When I thought of Roger, it was with longing but not despair; my life was now becoming meaningful and full again. And so, summer rolled into autumn.

From time to time as the months passed, I received notes or poems from Emily. None of them referred to our last meeting, and all of them were disturbing. I was still angry with her, and each time I saw that familiar hand on an envelope, I felt a shudder of exasperation, but I was curious despite my anger, and sometimes I did read them. The poems, in particular, suggested a depth of feeling I could not believe—more of Emily's melodrama. One poem I recognized from the time years ago when we had collected her poems into fascicles: Emily was sending earlier work.

> *Come slowly—Eden!*
> *Lips unused to Thee—*
> *Bashful—sip thy Jessamines—*
> *As the fainting Bee—*

Then another arrived, and I knew I needed to do something.

> *Wild Nights—Wild Nights!*
> *Were I with thee*

Wild Nights should be
Our luxury!

Futile — the Winds —
To a Heart in port —
Done with the Compass —
Done with the Chart!

Rowing in Eden —
Ah, the Sea!
Might I but moor — Tonight —
In Thee!

This was a blatant love poem. And not simply a romantic love but one suffused with a deep and erotic desire. I could not imagine Emily expressing that to me, but why else would she send it? Did she imagine such an avowal would move me to take up our friendship again? That as she had forced Roger away, she might offer herself to me as an alternative? I had no intention of seeing Emily again. I wanted the poems to stop.

Sue Dickinson had told me once that she had received similar letters from Emily. And despite the barriers Emily put up against her sister-in-law, they remained friends. Sue was the person to speak to; I would have to explain that there had been a break between Emily and me, but I trusted Sue's tactful sympathy and did not think she would ask the cause. She had requested that I look out for signs of mental disturbance in Emily, and these poems hinted at something I had neither the experience nor the will to handle myself. Let Sue decide what to do. Let her absolve me of any responsibility for Emily.

After we settled on the sofa in Sue's highly decorated parlor, she gave me a shrewd look. "Now, my dear, tell me what is troubling you — for I can see that something is."

I withdrew the poems from my folder and handed them to her. "Emily and I had a falling out," I began. "Several months ago. But she has continued to send me poetry. I don't like to worry you, but — I do not know what to make of these or what to do."

Sue read the poems, nodding her head a few times as she shuffled through them. "I can understand why these would disturb you."

"I don't know what to think. I cannot be Emily's friend. These poems—"

Sue folded the poems, smoothing the paper carefully. "What do you think she is saying with these letters?"

"They appear to be—from anyone else, I would say they were love letters."

"I agree. You must know by now that she does not mean them to be taken literally; I think she would be horrified and offended if you did so. I think this is her way of telling you that you are important to her. An imagined passion is as good as—or likely better than—a real one to Emily."

This I could readily believe. But I no longer wanted to be important to Emily Dickinson. Something of that must have shown on my face.

"I will not ask the cause of your falling out, but I imagine that it has affected Emily deeply. She does not admit many people to her circle, Miranda."

"Yes, that is a troubling part of this," I said.

"What worries me..." Sue began thoughtfully. Then she rose and left the room. A moment later she returned with the collection of letters she had shown me before. She riffled through them, then pulled out a creased and worn page. "Yes, I thought so."

It was a copy of the poem that began "I showed her Heights," which Emily had sent to me shortly before our quarrel.

"She sent this to me years ago. If she sent it to you as well, rather than composing a new poem, it may mean Emily is not writing. If she is not, that explains why she is so... needy."

"Whatever she needs, I will not—I *cannot*—supply to her," I said.

Mrs. Austin shook her head. "I would not ask it. It is enough that you have let me know about this, Miranda. I do thank you."

Gradually the flow of poems I received from Emily slowed, and their feverish tone quieted. Emily did not seem to expect any response from me, and I gave none.

The vibrant autumn landscape faded to brown and gray, and then to the soft snow-edged monochrome of December. And then, in the first week of that month, I received a letter from Roger.

My dearest Miranda,
    It is surprisingly difficult for me to write these words. I have just

received word that Cecilia died in her sleep. I had given up hope years ago for her recovery and had resigned myself to the knowledge that death would be a release for her, but I am still deeply grieved, as much for the beautiful life that was taken from her as for the years in which she has been only a shell. It is a shock, as well, after enduring these long years without hope, to find that the end has come at last for her.

I am returning to the United States. There is much sad business to attend to: Cecilia's estate and the family. I sail in January from Southampton; whatever the hazards of a winter crossing, I hope to make the fastest journey possible.

Even at this sad time I cannot ignore the fact that this changes everything between us. My feelings for you are what they have always been, and I hope to make that clear to you. There must be what society calls a "decent interval," but I hope that at the end of that time, you will let me hold you in my arms and offer to you my heart, my hand, and the rest of my life. I love you.

For a long moment my head whirled and my mind went numb. I stood rooted to the floor as a strange and negative state pervaded my being. It was an odd blankness in which my mind and my heart and my body seemed unwilling to react. Strangely, I wanted this blankness to continue.

"I cannot go back," I said aloud. Roger would have to stay in England. Everything needed to stay exactly where it was. I looked down and saw my hands, holding Roger's letter, shaking so hard I thought I might drop it.

Then I shook my head and began to move, slowly, carefully, not knowing until later that I must have emitted a low, choked moan. But Aunt Helen heard and came running. "Miranda...?" She stopped. "Oh, my darling. What is it?"

I could not answer. Aunt Helen led me to the kitchen and guided me gently into a chair. Bridget, also in the kitchen, immediately brought a cup of tea. Aunt Helen sat down beside me, alternately stroking my arm and patting my shoulder. "Oh, my dear girl, my dear girl," she kept repeating. "You have received bad news. We will rest here quietly together until you regain yourself."

Finally I said, "What will I do?" And again, "What will I do?" I tried to shrug off this strange, empty feeling, but I seemed not able to move or even think.

"Tell me what has happened," Aunt Helen said. "And we will approach the matter together. May I see the letter you are holding?"

Wordlessly I handed it to her, and while she read it, I said again, "What will I do?" It was as though I had lost my ability to think, to plan.

My aunt put the letter down and took both my hands in hers. "At this moment you need do nothing," she said. "Roger will not leave London until January, and the voyage to America, even by packet boat, takes two weeks at least. You need not write to him—he will be gone before a letter reaches him. We will go forward with our lives as usual, and you will soon be able to think clearly. Things will sort themselves out."

Dear Aunt Helen, with her wonderful, commonsense approach to life.

"Thank you." I looked up at her. "I am sure that you are right."

We were interrupted by the arrival of Elena, bursting with the news that she had been chosen to be the Virgin Mary in the school's Christmas play. There was no escaping reality, not even in this warm and cozy kitchen, and I took some comfort in that. My world might have exploded, but everything else seemed to be proceeding at its normal pace. I simply did not want to proceed with it.

"That will change," Aunt Helen said to me when I expressed this thought. "You have received a great shock, and you need time to recover and adjust your thinking. But you will recover."

Again her words gave me solace, and as the next several days passed, I could see that I really had no choice. Christmas was bearing down upon us, and Elena's excitement was not to be ignored. If only for her sake, I must involve myself in all the usual activities. To myself I acknowledged that I had built walls around my heart, comfortable walls, and I did not want them lowered. But in spite of myself—surrounded by the familiar and safe routines of caring for Elena, keeping up with my correspondence and my work, and assisting Aunt Helen with our holiday preparations—thought and feeling returned and, with them, the knowledge that I must somehow find a way to come to terms with the facts: Roger was returning, and he wanted me to marry him.

But not yet, I said to myself, not yet. My feelings were so contradictory; they changed from moment to moment. I was sad, grieved for Roger's loss. I felt a shadowy guilt that any possibility of future happiness with Roger might have been bought at the cost of Cecilia's death. And, most important, I wondered whether, now that there was no impediment to that happiness, marriage to Roger was truly what I wanted.

For more than a year I had assumed so, had believed, with all the ardent longing of my heart, that love was paramount. And yet, in that time, the New York school had opened and begun to thrive. The Amherst school, firmly established, had more applications for the fall term than we could accept. I had lectured on early childhood education in Boston, with Ralph Waldo Emerson and onetime Concord School superintendent Bronson Alcott in the audience! I was becoming *someone,* an independent woman of accomplishment. Could that continue if I were Roger's wife? I knew, after this year, that I could live without Roger; now I would have to decide if I would live *with* him.

This was the crucial question, as my body and my hands moved through the days. My mind embraced and discarded many answers. We attended Elena's pageant rehearsals, we spent many hours baking Christmas cakes and cookies, we decorated the house. It occurred to me that Aunt Helen had not once referred to the emotion in Roger's letter. What could she be thinking now that she had seen with her own eyes his passionate declarations? Did she approve? Disapprove? As far as I could tell, she had had no idea that our relationship had been anything more than a strong and respectful friendship. I thought of asking but decided against it. Aunt Helen was, after all, a grown woman, and surely she was aware of Roger's charms. If she had guessed some time ago that there were the seeds of something more between us, she had certainly kept her thoughts to herself. And had she disapproved of the possibility, I was sure she would have expressed her views.

No, I would not stir that pot. Her behavior with me now was that of the wonderful, kind aunt I had always known, and I would do as she proposed: think carefully and move forward.

And so we bought or made and wrapped our presents, watched Elena—self-conscious and proud together—in her Christmas pageant, and a few days later took the cars to Springfield to spend a calm holiday with Ethan and his family. It was a lovely time, one I did not want to end, where warmth and family joy seemed especially poignant. Elena and her brothers were wonderfully close, and Ethan and Ann's fine intelligence and warm hearts were more in evidence than ever. I hated to leave this island of calm; my eyes filled with tears when the moment came.

The journey back to Amherst passed as a blur, my mind whirling again through every clacking mile. As many times as I had imagined Roger's return, I had never imagined I would question my own heart so sternly. I *thought* I loved him; he believed he loved me. But it had been a long time since we had seen each other. If my stomach fluttered and my skin tingled at the thought of Roger's body, did that mean we were meant to be together? What would be the price, to satisfy the yearnings of my heart and my body?

Emily Dickinson had told me that if I married, I would be forced to submit my dreams to those of my husband. I did not believe Roger would ask such a thing of me, but might it happen anyway, in the course of things? Could a woman have both love and accomplishment in her life?

At home I settled in uneasily, waiting for what I knew was close at hand: a talk with Aunt Helen. A cable—a new and expensive way of communicating—had arrived from London, telling us that Roger's packet ship would arrive in Boston Harbor on January 20.

"You must be there to meet him," Aunt Helen pronounced. "Whatever you decide, you owe him that courtesy. He is a fine gentleman, and he has lost his wife. You must at the very least extend your deepest sympathy." She looked at me. "You know he would do the same for you, if the circumstances were reversed."

She was right, of course. Extending my sympathy would not require a decision, and it was exactly what I should do. I nodded. "Will you travel to Boston with me?"

"Of course," she said. "It would not be proper for you to meet him there alone."

On a bitterly cold morning, Aunt Helen and I boarded the train to Boston. Elena had been invited to stay with a school friend, although when she learned why we were going to Boston, she began to issue commands that we bring "her friend Roger" back to Amherst for her.

Sitting in the chilly carriage, Aunt Helen and I rode in silence for some time. I sat next to the window, watching the wintry gray landscape hurtle by. I had thought that Aunt Helen had dozed over her knitting, until I felt her hand enclose one of mine.

"Miranda?"

"Yes, Aunt?" I kept my gaze out the window.

"You have known me only as a widowed aunt, your father's sister. Can you believe that I was once as young as my dear Kate and as much in love with her father as she was with Ethan? That is why I rejoiced so in her marriage; I know how joyful a good marriage can be."

"But Kate's marriage—she died so young. If she hadn't—if Ethan had not *insisted*—"

"We cannot know that Ethan insisted on anything, Miranda. And in any case, it might as easily have been Ethan who died as my own dear husband did, leaving Kate alone. Life is short, my dear Miranda. Which is why love is so precious."

I turned to her now. "What do you think I should do?" I asked plaintively.

She smiled. "What is in your heart. Mr. Daniels has left you in no doubt, surely, about his feelings. I do not know all of what has passed between you—" She held up a hand as if to stop me from telling her. "Nor do I want to know. You must follow your heart, but if you decide not to accept Mr. Daniels, you must be very clear about it. It is no kindness to him to give him hope if there is none. And I do think, Miranda," she added, with an oddly knowing humor, "that marriage is good for a woman. For *many* reasons."

She returned to her knitting, and I, bemused, to the many things she had given me to think about.

I settled Aunt Helen at the hotel and hired a carriage to take me to the docks. I stood in bitter cold amid a throng of waiting people, stamping my feet to keep my toes from freezing in their boots. There was a dusting of snowflakes; I had worried about the dangers of a winter crossing, but there in the distance was Roger's ship, its great smokestack pluming gray smoke against the silvery sky, and that worry, at least, was no longer important. But the closer the packet came to the dock, the more my thoughts churned. We will always be colleagues, I told myself. And friends. We had shared too much to lose each other entirely. For the rest, time would tell. Aunt Helen had told me to follow my heart, but I still could not be sure where that wayward organ was leading.

I watched as men tossed ropes back and forth and looped them with bewildering speed and agility to moor the ship. Then I looked up to the deck.

There, among the crowd of men and women who lined the rails, I saw Roger's dear face. In that instant my rationalization was undone. I felt a welling of joy, as if I had suddenly recalled every part of him that was dear to me, as though the last year, with its heartbreak and frustration, had never happened, as if we were both freshly returned from Barbados, with the memory of every kiss and every touch etched in our minds. More than that, I recalled Roger the man, who had nurtured my dreams as his own, who had helped me realize the foundation. I would not lose myself in him; I would become more, do more.

I called Roger's name over and over, heedless of the clamor and of the men and women beside me on the dock. And in a moment he saw me, his smile as bright as the sun, as welcome as home. I watched as he pushed through the crowd on the deck and was aware that I was pushing too, trying to reach the gangway to be there when he stepped onto land. I lost sight of him, saw him again, mumbled apologies to the people upon whose boots I trod. The cold was forgotten, the snowfall unimportant. I looked up to see him at the top of the gangway, pushed through the throng, and reached the foot of the gangway as Roger threaded his way past a portly gentleman — my handsome, long-limbed, somber attorney looking for all the world like a schoolboy, his hair tousled by the sea air and frosted with flecks of melting snow.

And then he caught me up, literally swept me off my feet, and kissed me. The longing of more than a year was concentrated in that kiss; I felt dizzy even as I returned it. His warm, masculine smell, the slight raspiness of his shaved cheek, the taste of his mouth — it was as if it were I who had come home.

There was a muted protest from someone at my elbow — the portly man on the gangway, horrified by our public passion.

"Roger, people —" I murmured into his neck.

"Damn people!" He was laughing. "We have the rest of our lives for people!" His arms tightened around me until I gasped, and there, where all the world could see, he kissed me again.

Epilogue

AMHERST
MAY 20, 1886

Roger and I were married in Amherst, in the house my father had so loved. I was surrounded that day by almost everyone important to me: Miss Adelaide was unable to make the voyage from Barbados, but Lolly was my maid of honor, and Elena, beaming with importance, was our flower girl. It was a late-summer wedding, as beautiful as anything I had ever imagined.

We did wait a "decent interval"—not the twelve months prescribed by custom but eight, during six of which only our closest friends knew of our attachment. At the end of that time, we wrote a letter to the school's board, stating simply that we planned to marry, to allay any fears of scandal based on Emily's earlier allegations. Slightly "slanting" the circumstances, Roger explained that it seemed fitting for the chairman of the board to be married, and therefore (his reasoning went), as he was now a widower, who better to take as his bride than the founder of the school, Miss Miranda Chase? In the week before our wedding, dozens of cards and letters arrived for us from the parents of children at the Amherst and New York schools; from some of the children themselves; and from old friends and well-wishers. Davy's father and stepmother sent a beautiful letter wishing me love and happiness for their son's sake, and several of his comrades from the army did so as well. On the morning of the wedding itself, when I had retired to my room to dress, Elena delivered an envelope.

"A man brought it for you."

I turned the envelope over and saw the familiar arched and swooping hand. I was tempted—what would she think to send me on my wedding day?—but in the end I did not want this day tainted by Emily's mysteries and melodrama. I took up a pencil and wrote, "Please return to Miss E. Dickinson," on the envelope, then gave it back to Elena. "Put that on the tray with the outgoing mail, please?" I gave Elena a kiss. "Then run to your own room. My flower girl must be dressed!"

I did not think of Emily again for a long time.

After the wedding Roger and I returned to Chicago, although we came east several times a year—both to do foundation business and to let Elena see her father and brothers and Aunt Helen, who had moved to Springfield to be with Ethan and her grandsons. Ethan's extraordinary generosity in letting me take Elena to Chicago did not fail to touch me, and I made it a point that my daughter—for so I felt her to be—knew her brothers and father well. She is married now, with two beautiful small sons of her own.

I could not bring myself to sell the Amherst house my father had been so proud of, but neither could I let it sit empty. In the end President Stearns at the college found a tenant for me: a department chairman who needed a house that would permit him to entertain students and faculty; until his retirement last year, that gentleman and his wife held court there. For me, the sense of my father's presence, and of Davy's, Kate's, Aunt Helen's, and my own, is still very strong, and now as the new home of the Frazar Stearns Center for Early Childhood Education, this house will always be filled with joyful children's voices as well.

I have spent the entire night in the past, remembering and listening to the echoes of our lives in this place. Now I hear the birds of a new morning, heralding the day ahead. It is time to be busy again: to dress for the trip.

But first I must finish packing. Before I close my last valise, I hesitate over the official brown envelope, with its stamps and seals, that Mr. Farwell had brought with him when he came to tell me Davy was dead. Addressed in Davy's hand, it had contained the first papers about the foundation and the Farwell diamond, in its small silver box. I had always kept it as one of my landmarks, and now I look to see if there are any other papers from that tragic time.

Then I notice it—a small, unexpected envelope I swear I have never seen before, labeled in my father's strong script, "From Miss E. Dickinson to Miranda, December 3, 1863."

That was two days after the news about Davy. The envelope was sealed. Perhaps Father had put it with the Farwell papers in the confusion of that week of which I remember nothing, nothing at all. Perhaps he gave it to me and I had forgotten. At any rate, this letter had come for me, and I had never read it.

I open the envelope. I am shocked to see Emily's younger hand-writing again, like a delicate budded vine. Twenty-three years ago, she had written me:

I will pray you can know, Miranda, my dear sorrowing child, that our friendship, however tempestuous, will endure always. I hope this poem will be of some comfort to you at this awful time, that you will sense how I value your friendship, even as we both "feel the Dark."

For a minute I cannot help but remember how Emily took every occasion, in this case my own grief, to bring the moment back to herself. But then I see the poem, breathtaking in its clarity and simplicity:

We met as Sparks—Diverging Flints
Sent various—scattered ways—
We parted as the Central Flint
Were cloven with an Adze—
Subsisting on the Light We bore
Before We felt the Dark—
A Flint unto this Day—perhaps—
But for that single Spark.

And I am propelled into wonder. Finding this now, so unexpectedly, is like hearing Emily's true voice again. This poem has a freshness, a poignancy, that reaches straight into my heart. And somehow I know that this chance encounter is not chance at all. For on this, her last day, Emily is reminding me of her immortality. I am sure that this poem, and others equally thrilling, will live forever.

I look up, feeling great joy and an unexpected kind of peace. For even more important to me, Emily's last communication is a powerful affirmation of our friendship. The question I had always pondered—were we truly friends?—is finally settled. I am holding the proof in my hand.

I rise, sealing the package, and place it in my valise. I will take it with me and keep it always, knowing from this day forward that Emily Dickinson's sparks of light, and my own life of unexpected triumphs, will remain securely entwined together.

A Note About Afternoons with Emily

BY ADELAIDE MACMURRAY AITKEN

OCTOBER 2006

The story of the creation of this book is a saga in itself. Wherever she is, my mother must be filled with delight. And for the rest of her family, this is the joyful result not only of her individual inspiration but of a collective effort, over more than nine years, on the part of her husband and children, a number of friends, and most recently skilled and sensitive professionals.

For most of her life, Rose MacMurray never dreamed of writing a novel, but from the beginning she was a voracious consumer of words. She taught herself to read at the age of four, and from that moment, she knew that "*There is no Frigate like a Book.*" Words gave her comfort, entertainment, and escape throughout a rather lonely childhood in Lake Forest, Illinois; Paris; and finally Washington, DC.

At Westover School in Middlebury, Connecticut, she spent three happy years immersed in anything related to language and fleeing from anything the least bit quantitative. She was a brilliant student, winning many academic prizes, and she made deep and lasting friendships. Her writing in the literary magazine, primarily poetry, is remarkably sophisticated and skillful. Pictures of her at the time show a large-boned, beautiful blonde with a somewhat sad look. In the social circles of Washington, she discovered that all those years of reading gave her a broad frame of reference that, combined with her quick wit, made her a very appealing companion.

After a year at Bennington, she married Frank MacMurray and settled down in suburban Virginia as a mother and doctor's wife. They met at a dance, discovered a mutual love of Yeats, and continued to delight each other intellectually for the rest of their lives. The rounds of car pools and raising children were sometimes stifling, but she always found solace and renewal in writing poetry. The topics were often taken from her daily life (children applying to schools; hanging out laundry with a friend; reading the quotations on tourists' T-shirts), but her keen observation and humorously economical presentation made many of her poems memorable.

She found her true calling after her children were grown, when she volunteered to teach an elective poetry class in the Fairfax public schools. Fifth graders were her favorite ("before the hormones start to churn"), and she not only introduced them to all the various forms of poetry (sonnets, haiku, villanelles, ballads, etc.) but soon had them writing in those forms as well. Her class was such a favorite that after the school year ended, the students sometimes persuaded her to keep meeting them during the summer. I can remember her beside the pool, surrounded by a dozen or so intent small bodies, heads bent with the concentration of creation. She was nicknamed "The Poetry Lady" and kept in touch with many of her young poets, both boys and girls, long after fifth grade.

As her own family grew, Rose shared this same inspiration and love of poetry with her four grandchildren, filling their shelves with books and their visits with collaborative poetry writing. She infused their lives with images and stories, all while encouraging their own creative spark.

In my memories of growing up, no one could play with words, toss off a pun or quip, produce a fitting quotation, or invent a fairy tale as dazzlingly as Rose. She was affectionate, emotional, and sometimes unpredictable but always hugely entertaining. We would sometimes play our own version of Scrabble, where any made-up word would be allowed if the explanation of it was both plausible and funny.

When my father retired, the two of them finally had the time to travel, and the intellectual curiosity they both shared took them to many beautiful places. On a trip to France, my mother fell and fractured a vertebra, which required a long immobilization in bed. Her sister, Adelaide, gave her a word processor that she could balance on her lap. From that moment, as my mother described it later, some new force like electricity came down her arms and out her fingers, and she found herself writing a novel about Emily Dickinson, her favorite poet.

Her sense of connection with Emily Dickinson is not surprising. Both of them were intoxicated with words and were immensely intelligent and well read, looked beneath the surfaces of things, and shared a rather dark approach to life. Like Emily, Rose MacMurray would have said her first love was poetry, not novels. Therefore, the arrival of *Afternoons with Emily* into her life was a surprise and a challenge that happily consumed her final four years. The night before she went into the hospital for what was expected to be a routine operation, she told me with glee that she had finished her manuscript. A few nights later, after an eerily purposeful round of phone calls to her children and a visit with Frank, she suddenly died.

After her death, my father and I took on the major responsibility of bringing her work to light. He and I had both been an integral part of the writing process: we read and commented on chapters as they emerged and fact-checked some of the historical detail. A family friend, Pat Hass, helped with sage and expert guidance, and saw that it reached the hands of our agent, Donald Maass. My two brothers were concerned and generous with their advice. But as time passed, other priorities intervened, and the prospect of publication seemed increasingly remote. My father's health began to fail, and I began to think that we must be content with simply knowing that our mother had produced something remarkable. But Pat and Don never lost faith. And the call from Little, Brown seemed like a miraculous affirmation of Rose's originality and talent.

A number of people have contributed to this work, and to them we are truly grateful. Emily Dickinson herself was its ever-present inspiration. Though I believe my mother truly captured Emily's voice and spirit, I hope that scholars reading this novel will remember that Rose was primarily a fellow poet. A number of people have contributed to the work since its initial writing: Don Maass is the kind of agent authors dream about, and Helen Atsma has been a patient and sensitive editor, qualities particularly appreciated by the previously uninitiated. Carla Jablonski, Susan Leon, and Madeleine Robins offered valuable contributions. Finally, I can clearly remember my mother telling me how she would like to dedicate her book. The phrasing is mine, since I didn't have the sense to write down her exact words. But the feelings are her own:

This book is dedicated to
Pat Hass, without whose tireless friendship *Afternoons with Emily*
would never have appeared.

And above all to Frank,
with deepest love and gratitude for everything.